THE ADVENTURES OF

TANK AND PUDGE

BOOK 1
THE
CARNIVAL

HAROLD (HP) PHIPPS

Cover art by Stephen Shoemaker of West Jefferson, NC.

ISBN: 978-0-9908136-2-0

Edited by: Amy Ashby

Warren publishing

Published by Warren Publishing
Charlotte, NC
www.warrenpublishing.net
Printed in the United States

*I dedicate this book to the New River and to those,
young and old, who have swum in its waters,
who have fished from its banks, who have ridden
its currents downstream, and who have
admired its beauty through changing seasons.*

CONTENTS

"Life is just a never-ending carnival ride—ups, downs, twists, and turns—so buckle your seatbelt."

—Author Unknown

CHAPTER 1

I glanced at Tank, Pudge, and Gene as we trudged silently up the steep Seagraves Hill toward the captivating carnival lights—shimmering with color and twinkling like earthbound stars—sweet, glistening desserts for our eager teenage eyes. We were drawn to the hilltop like white-winged moths, rising from the banks of the New River, dazzled by the beams of a radiant, one-hundred-watt porch light left on overnight by some sleepy or forgetful farmer. The Stephens Brothers Carnival was back in town, and the shining fairgrounds, the traveling carnival's short-term home, glowed with the promise of entertainment, adventure, and thrills.

Tiny drops of perspiration speckled my friends' youthful brows as we climbed. Plodding uphill, Pudge and Tank were a few steps ahead of me and Gene. The bright, merry lights lured my companions and me upward until we could hear the carnival's siren songs. A mixture of music and sounds drifted downward from the hill above us. Throbbing rock 'n roll, soft merry-go-round melodies, twanging country, the excited chatter of the crowd around us, the brash shouts of the carnival barkers, and the aggressive, high-pitched calls of the other hawkers and hucksters blended to make a concoction of beautiful noise. "Remember, guys, we'll be riding home in Grandpa Charlie's pickup," I said, breaking our five minutes of silence. "He'll meet us up on the carnival grounds. I hope we don't lose him in this crowd. The carnival crowd gets bigger every year."

"It'll be easy to spot Grandpa Charlie. That ole geezer stands out in any crowd. I ain't worried about findin' him," said Gene. "I just hope they got some new rides this year. I'm plumb tired of crappy carnival rides. Last year the best ride was the Ferris wheel, but I had to juice it up a little by shakin' our seats back and forth. Pudge thought we was gonna tip over! Haw! And I couldn't believe that little rusty, rundown roller coaster cost twenty-five cents to ride. It must've been the slowest roller coaster in North Carolina. This year I'm hungry for speed, danger, and thrills."

"I'm just plain hungry," laughed Tank, massaging his massive midsection. "I haven't eaten anything in well over an hour. My energy level is dwindling; I'm losing power with every step; I need a candy apple or two to perk me up. Besides, I'm a growing boy."

"Yep, you're a growin' boy, all right," said Gene. "If you grow anymore, they'll stop lettin' you into the carnival for fear of the damage you might cause to the rides. I wouldn't blame 'em, not one bit. Remember ridin' the bumper cars last year?"

"I was a trifle heavier last year," said Tank, smiling. Tank's real name was Douglas Trent Banner, but only a few people called him Douglas. Everybody, except for a few teachers, called the big boy, 'Tank.'

"Well, when you plopped your big rear end down in your bumper car, it wouldn't even budge, not one inch. Ever'body could bump you, but you couldn't bump nobody. Your lard butt kept your bumper car stuck in one place."

"I'm considering a diet," laughed Tank, drawing in his belly slightly. "Maybe I'll begin next week or possibly the week after."

"Don't think I ain't heard that before," grumbled Gene, examining a tiny hole in the crown of his dark cowboy hat.

Last year Tank had eaten more than his share of carnival fare—crispy candied apples, sizzling hotdogs, hot buttered popcorn, fluffy cotton candy, chilled soft drinks, and silky-smooth ice cream. Gene fancied the candied apples; Pudge preferred the buttered popcorn; I favored the cotton candy. Since first grade, Tank had always enjoyed the full cornucopia of carnival treats. His current mushrooming waistline reflected his perpetual hearty appetite.

"The carnival signs around town said there would be new rides, but I was more than satisfied with last year's rides," said Pudge. "Just because a ride is new, doesn't mean it's going to be any better than the old ones. Maybe we should just stick with the old rides, the tilt-a-whirl, the swings, and the Ferris wheel."

"You make my rear end want a chew of tobacker," snorted Gene. "You're gettin' to be a dadgum stick in the mud, a fearful ole fuddy duddy, or a slinkin' scaredy cat. You gotta think positive about these new rides, like I do. I look at a new ride as a brand-new adventure. A scary ride tests my courage, and unlike you, Pudge, my nerve ain't never been found lackin'."

"Lay off the redheaded boy," said Tank.

"Yeah, leave Pudge alone," I added. Gene turned and faced me. His eyes narrowed; his pale features constricted.

"Hal Grayson, ever'body knows the main reason you're goin' to this here carnival, and it ain't the rides, nor the games, nor the cotton candy—it's to see Sophia Bishop, your honey-bunny."

"Shut up, Gene! Just shut up!" I said. I gave him a shove, causing him to stumble forward.

"Zip it, cowboy," said Tank, pushing Gene's dark western hat forward until it covered his face.

"Put a cork in it," advised Pudge. "Otherwise, you're cruisin' for a bruisin'!"

Gene straightened his hat and started to say something, then abruptly changed his mind. He turned and took a few long-legged steps forward, kicking up dust with his boots. Along with a growing crowd of carnival goers, the four of us continued our trek upward.

The week before the carnival arrived, the town of West Jefferson had been inundated with eye-catching red and white signs that read, "The Stephens Brothers Carnival will be in your town this weekend—Friday through Sunday night. New rides! New games! New thrills! Family fun for everyone! Music! Exotic dancers! Fortune-telling!"

Sticky-fingered Gene, master of the five-finger discount, had lifted four of the carnival signs from the windows of local businesses, had kept one, and had given the remaining three to me, Tank, and Pudge. I had thumbtacked my sign up on a wall in my bedroom. I think other guys did the same.

In a few weeks, the four of us would be entering Central Ashe High School as ninth graders. The high school was almost brand-new since it had opened only two years earlier in 1957. My three soon-to-be freshmen friends breathed deeply as their faces flushed from the exertion of the climb. I panted and gasped, myself. Gene, the only habitual cigarette smoker in our quartet, emitted a hacking cough from time to time. A white-haired gentleman who had to be in his mid-fifties passed us, walking briskly with his wife, who must have been in her late forties. The middle-aged couple, with their shoulders held back in virtually perfect postures, passed us as if we were tortoises and they were hares. They weren't even breathing hard.

A quarter of the way up, we paused to catch our breaths. We were drained, nearing exhaustion. The rainy summer had forced us to spend too much time in front of television sets; too much time inside our houses reading comic books; too many hours playing mindless card games, monotonous checkers, or, less likely, mind-stimulating games like chess. We were out of shape. Our hearts and lungs were working overtime and our legs were already getting tired from the climb.

Ordinarily we would've spent much of summertime outdoors in the North Carolina mountain sunshine, doing chores, playing baseball or softball, and hiking beside, swimming in, or skipping flat river rocks across the New River. That was not the case this summer due to the humidity and rainfall. It had rained almost every day. On some days there would be just a few sprinkles, not enough rain to disturb a cow-pasture baseball game. On other days, the rain was a steady, relentless downpour that turned the clear waters of the New River a muddy brown and sent the dark river water flooding over the low-water bridges, disrupting rural traffic. Standing water submerged low-lying pastures, causing grazing livestock to seek higher ground. Sections of gravel roads turned to mud. If heavy rains continued for more than a couple of days, old-timers enjoyed telling young folks stories of the devastating nineteen forty flood that had wreaked havoc in the North Carolina mountains.

"Durin' the 'forty flood," Grandpa Charlie had said as he and I fished from the New River's bank during a soft misty rain, "I seen a house come floatin' down this river, and through the house's winders I could see, plain as day, a coal oil lamp settin' on the kitchen table still burnin' and throwin' out light. The empty house drifted on down the river, just as level as if it was restin' on its foundation. When it hit the big river bridge, just above Riverbend Store, the house busted into a hunderd pieces. Ole man Alonzo Pruitt and his fam'ly lost their home to the flood, but none of them Pruitts was drownded, thank the Lord."

More often than not, pleasant, soaking rains fell across the high country, rains that were good for the crops and gardens growing in the rich soil along the New River and its tributaries. Still, an agreeable soaking rain was enough to keep kids indoors. The summer had been soggy with too much rain and too little sun— and, for me, too little exercise.

However, the weather had been dry for the past two and a half weeks with plenty of hot sunshine and not a cloud in the sky. Puddles had dried up and muddy paths had become dusty trails. The burning sun left thirsty roadside weeds looking parched and withered. Last week, for the first time all summer, I had ridden my bicycle shirtless, and gotten sunburned on my back, shoulders, and chest.

As we walked upward toward the carnival, I reached up with my right hand and touched my left shoulder. There was no pain. My skin was already beginning to peel beneath my T-shirt. I got sunburned almost every summer, and I enjoyed pulling off the swathes of dried dead skin. The newly unwrapped skin underneath was smooth and slightly tanned.

Once when I was nine or ten years old, I saw a blacksnake that would've measured at least five feet, peel off all of his old, dusky skin by rubbing his nose and body against an old rotting tree trunk. The snake sloughed off his old skin by his determined scraping against the rough wood. The reptile's scaly skin removal reminded me of my Grandpa Grayson pulling off his over-the-calf dress socks. In the afternoon sun, the serpent's new skin color was a brilliant, glittering black.

I had waited for the shining blacksnake to leave the area and then went over and picked up the newly-shed snakeskin. I took the membrane home and put it up on the windowsill in my room next to a groundhog's sun-bleached skull that I had found on a creek bank. I placed a few baseball cards—one was a Willie Mays card—upon the windowsill. Then I put a small glass jar filled with pennies and cat's-eye marbles on top of the snakeskin to hold it in place. I stood back to admire my creative project. I adjusted the spacing of the baseball cards and my room's newly decorated window was complete. My handiwork was perfect! Silently, I congratulated myself on my artistic endeavor. At the age of ten, I was not the consummate interior decorator. My sense of design was suspect, but I knew what I liked.

The snakeskin incident happened way back when I was in the fourth grade. After a few weeks in the windowsill, the snakeskin mysteriously disappeared. I think my grandmother threw it out my bedroom window—if she could bring herself to touch the scaly reptile covering, or perhaps our cat ate it. That ginger cat would eat most anything.

Our male cat, named Tangerine Snow because of his color, (mainly orange with a white face and little white socks), often left mice, voles, and even small snakes on our kitchen's doorstep. I took these animal carcasses as Tangerine's tokens of gratitude for our giving him a home with food, water, affection, fluffy pillows, and a small pad next to a warm kitchen stove for naps. Grandma Grayson didn't appreciate Tangerine's gifts of dead snakes. She had a dread of snakes alive or dead. Grandma wouldn't even look at a picture of a snake.

"Halbert Joseph Grayson! Come here quick and get rid of that snake carcass on the kitchen steps," Grandma Grayson had shouted while fixing supper on a hot July afternoon. I ran into the kitchen. "That ole cat has left three dead snakes on the steps this summer. I can't work here in this kitchen with that dead snake starin' up at me through the screen door. Them cold dead eyes gives me the nervous shakes. I can't stand it. Throw the carcass in the river and be quick about it."

My sixth-grade teacher, Mrs. Victoria Bender, would've called Grandma's extreme fear 'ophidiophobia,' the abnormal fear of snakes. I learned a lot about phobias in the sixth grade. I could've learned a lot more about the entire sixth-grade curriculum if Gene hadn't been constantly disturbing the class. Gene got along with most of his teachers, but not Mrs. Bender. In contrast, Tank enjoyed Mrs. Bender's lessons, but the big boy got along with practically everyone.

On the day after I had watched the dark reptile shed its scaly skin, I told my fourth-grade classmate Gene about it while we were in the school library. Fourth-grader Eugene Clifton Clodfelter proclaimed, "There ain't no harm in havin' a blacksnake around. A blacksnake ain't no poison snake. My daddy won't kill nary a blacksnake on our farm. Daddy says that blacksnakes is as good as any cat to keep the rat and mouse poppalation down. Besides, I'd ruther be bit by a blacksnake's little bitty teeth than by a big ole long-toothed rat!"

On that late summer afternoon at the carnival, a caravan of eager people paraded up the Seagraves Hill toward the sparkling fairgrounds perched above. A lesser crowd marched down the hill, leaving the carnival. The Stephens Brothers Carnival was as close as Ashe County citizenry could get to the jovial pageant that folks way down in New Orleans called Mardi Gras. There was a feeling of cheerful celebration permeating the humid mountain air.

There was no formal forecast of rain, but around noon, the humidity, after a rather lengthy absence, had returned to the high country with a muggy vengeance. Distant thunder echoing through the mountains signaled the return of rainfall, probably as early as tomorrow.

Below us, we could see the three stoplights of the town of West Jefferson change simultaneously from red to green. The temporarily stalled line of automobile traffic proceeded at a snail's pace, bringing more Ashe County citizens into town and then on up to the fairgrounds where the carnival was situated. Parking was scarce on the fairgrounds hill, and most of the parking places had already been taken. Instead of "the fairgrounds hill," most folks called the mini-mountain "Seagraves Hill," named after a family who once owned much of the land around West Jefferson. Ashe County carnival patrons had to park on the small town's streets, and then make their way up the steep, winding trail.

Tank's father had dropped me and him off at one of the red lights downtown. Tank and I had met Pudge and Gene in front of Blackburn's Department Store. We were all going to catch a ride home from the carnival with my grandfather on my mother's side, Charles Franklin, better known by almost everyone in the county as Grandpa Charlie. Riding in the back of his pickup around the winding mountain roads was almost as much fun as any carnival ride.

As we climbed upward, Tank pulled a white handkerchief from his jeans and wiped perspiration from his broad forehead. Two dark half-moons of sweat materialized under my T-shirt's armpits. A drop of perspiration plunged from Pudge's nose to the dusty ground, followed by another droplet. Two tiny, wet craters formed in the dust at his feet. Gene removed his cowboy hat and regarded the hat's damp sweatband. He wiped the sweat away with his long shirttail, then ran his fingers through his thin, wispy hair. Gene replaced the hat that made him look even taller than he really was.

We were surprised to see three Negroes in the descending crowd, leaving the carnival. The older, gray-haired Negro wore a navy-blue suit with a white shirt and a light blue tie secured with a neat Windsor knot. The younger boys were dressed in typical teenage attire, T-shirts, blue jeans, and sneakers. Blacks made up a small portion of the county's population. Grandpa Charlie said that way back in the days of President Abraham Lincoln and the Civil War, most mountain people didn't believe in slavery and the few who did believe in the bondage of Negroes were too poor to own a slave anyhow. Black folks were seldom seen at carnivals, in movie theaters, at high school basketball games, or at Fourth of July parades in West Jefferson. Colored people kept mostly to themselves; they had their own schools and churches.

"That cracker deputy had no reason to turn us away," said the lighter-skinned Negro boy.

The smaller, darker teenager muttered, "We got just as much right to go to the carnival as anybody else, Mr. Cox. You said so yourself. That county deputy was downright mean to us!"

The old gray-headed, dark-skinned gentleman said, "All white folks aren't like that deputy. Some have been mighty kind to me and to you boys, too. A change in those folks like that deputy will come someday. Their hearts will change. We must have patience."

"I'm about out of patience, Mr. Cox," said the lighter skinned Negro boy. "A man like that deputy just grates on my soul."

"I'll tell you what, Arthur," said the older man. "When we get to my home, I'll teach you boys how to play chess. I believe Elizabeth was baking a pie when we left. We can have a late dessert with ice cream, of course. How does that sound?" The two boys nodded and smiled. The three outcasts continued their slow descent toward the town of West Jefferson.

Tank paused and watched the dark-skinned trio go down the hill. He frowned and shook his head.

"Those fellows have every right to go to the carnival," he said. "Something should be done. Somebody should say something."

"Well, there's nothing we can do about it. Nobody will listen to us until we're older," said Pudge. "Just leave well enough alone for now."

"But it's not well enough; it's wrong," said Tank. "How would you like to be treated as they were?"

Gene said, "Fellers, if a lawman was involved in sendin' them colored boys back down the hill to town, we'd best not get caught up in the trouble. My daddy says, 'Trouble begets trouble.' I ain't hankerin' to talk to no sheriff nor deputy tonight. I'm here for the carnival rides, candied apples, buttered popcorn, and nothin' else. Don't say nothin' about them black fellers' complaints to nobody, and don't go near no lawman. Like them colored gents, we might get sent back down the hill if we speak up about this situation. What do you think, Hal?"

"I agree with all three of you," I said. I was considering a future run for freshman class president at Central Ashe High School. I thought my response to the question politically appropriate.

Tank shot me a look of disapproval, but I shrugged my shoulders and continued my ascent. I stumbled over a medium-sized, oddly-shaped rock in the pathway, but I didn't lose my balance. Tank reached out and caught my elbow as I steadied myself. Gene and Pudge laughed at my awkwardness.

After more climbing, the path widened a bit, and we encountered a town policeman helping a drunken man descend the hill. The lawman might've been a county deputy. I get the town police and county deputy uniforms mixed up. The tipsy gentleman stumbled many times, but stayed on his feet thanks to the help of the policeman who held him by his shirt collar and his elbow. The pungent odor of cow manure that surrounded the pair could be traced to the dark stains on the intoxicated captive's shirt.

"Let me go, dammit! I don't need no help fum no County Mountie. Hellfire, I'm strong as a hawse an' meaner'n ary mule!" shouted the drunken fellow. "I eat a bowl of timber rattlers and copperheads for breakfast this mornin'. For better taste, I sprinkled on a few tablespoons of black widder spiders. Them nourishin' foods is why I'm so dadgum stout. My arms and legs is like steel springs. My teeth, them I got left, is so hard I can bite a snappin' turtle's head clean off! Why, I could climb that mountain over yonder and never even breathe hard."

The drunken man waved his unsteady right arm in the general direction of Mount Jefferson, which was enveloped in the darkening shadows of an approaching sunset.

"Sure you could," said the policeman. He tightened his grip on the blustering man's shirt collar. "Now if you can just manage to stand up, I'll get you home safe and sound."

"I'll tell you a secret, Local Yokel. Shhh! You might as well know that I'm fixin' to beat yore law-dog ass when we get down to the foot of this here hill. I've whupped many a man bigger'n you. Don't say I didn't warn you, Ozzifer. You might beat me in a fair fight, but I don't fight fair! Hee! Hee!"

"Just keep walkin'; I'm takin' you home, Mr. Sheets. I'm doin' you a favor. I could arrest you for public drunkenness," said the officer.

"That's mighty kind and neighborly of you, deputy," hiccuped the drunk. "Call me Zeke. They ain't no reason we can't be frenz—ole pal, ole buddy, ole chum. We can have a drink when we get to my trailer—right after I give you the aforementioned ass whuppin'."

The lawman helped the drunken, faltering man down the broad path until Zeke Sheets stopped and refused to budge.

"Get your damned hands off me, you good-for-nothin', low-down law dog!" bellowed the old man. "You're livin' proof that a pile of mule droppin's can swell up, grow legs, and walk around like a human bean."

Abruptly, the intoxicated fellow became more abusive and began hurling burning insults, stinging epithets, and chilling profanities directed at the officer's occupation and at the lawman's immediate family with special emphasis on his family tree which included several lawmen.

"Lord, that ole man can cuss, can't he?" said Gene admiringly. "Hold up, fellers. I want to listen. I might learn somethin' new about cussin'. Come on, we'll foller 'em a little ways down the trail. Don't get too close, just close enough to hear."

When it came to cussing Zeke Sheets had few equals. His reputation was countywide, and I had heard several stories about him. Once, Gene's uncle, Shade Barlow, had tried to out cuss Zeke in the Country Clipper Barbershop in Jefferson, the county seat. Gene witnessed the cussing and told me all about it. It so happened that both men were getting haircuts at the time. Everyone in the shop said that Zeke won the cuss contest hands down.

Zeke Sheets' coup de gras came when he called Mr. Barlow "A damn flop-eared, mule-kissin', communist-lovin', fart sniffin', son of a cross-eyed bitch."

His opponent's losing comeback was, "You're a damn skirt-chasin', cattle rustlin', booger eatin', son of a Tennessee bastard."

After some derisive barbershop laughter was directed at both contestants, Zeke Sheets was declared the winner by a vote of the customers awaiting their haircuts. Shade Barlow, the county's most successful moonshiner, claimed the reason he'd lost the profanity challenge to Zeke was that he hadn't drunk any moonshine in two or three days.

"I cuss my best when I am about half drunk. Likker loosens me up. I ain't no good at cussin' when I'm sober," Mr. Barlow said. "But Zeke won fair and square. I reckon I'll have to pay for his damn haircut."

"I'll drink to that!" Zeke called out from the rear of the barbershop. He had been busily pouring some clear liquid from a Mason jar into several 7-Up bottles.

"I knowed your grampaw, Cleve Farmer," said Zeke to the young deputy who was escorting him down the fairgrounds trail. "He was a damn law dog just like you and the worst sumbitch ever to walk these hills! The low-down skunk caught me one time, holdin' the front end of a long rope with a stole cow tied to the other end. I told him I had just found the rope and was takin' it home to Daddy. I told him I didn't know what was on the other end of the cord. I didn't get nowheres with that story. The ole bastard of a deputy took me straight off to jail and caused me no end of trouble. I was just a boy, no more than seventeen years of age, but Cleve Farmer didn't show me no mercy. To get me out of the mess, Daddy had to hire a high-priced town lawyer and buy the cow to boot."

"Sounds like you was stealin' another man's cow," said the deputy. "Come along now, Mr. Sheets. We ain't far from your home."

The drunken man complied and staggered forward a few steps and then fell down.

"Oopsy daisy!" he laughed. The deputy helped Zeke to his feet, and they continued on their way until Zeke Sheets paused again. "Wait a minute. One of my damn suspenders has come loose. Gimme a minute to fix it. I don't want to lose my britches."

"Come on!" said the deputy, looking at his watch. "I have to get you home and get back up to the carnival. I'm on duty."

"We named her Betsy," said the drunk with a grin as he fumbled with his suspenders.

"What?" asked the deputy.

"That little heifer I was wrongly accused of stealin'. We named her Betsy. She growed up to be a purty good milk cow, but was awful bad to kick at milkin' time. Broke Daddy's wrist one time whilst he was milkin' her. Daddy cussed Betsy 'til he was blue in the face. He called that little Guernsey cow a son of a bitch and a dirty bastard. Betsy just laid down and commenced chewin' her cud like she didn't have a care in this world. That made Daddy madder than a Baptist preacher with a bone-dry collection plate right after Sunday preachin'. Daddy fumed, swore, and fretted. He tried to kick the milk bucket, missed, and fell flat of his back. It was right funny, come to think of it."

As the two men continued down the steep path, Mr. Sheets would, from time to time, break into a fit of giggles. Once he snickered until he became red-faced and breathless.

"Come on, Mr. Sheets. Let's move a little faster," said the deputy. The officer's expression remained stoic during the laughter and the verbal abuse. The deputy forced Zeke Sheets to walk faster. Soon they were out of earshot. The two men descended the trail until they disappeared.

"Well, they're gone. Did you learn any new cuss words, Gene?" asked Pudge. "Did Zeke Sheets teach you anything?"

"Nope, I didn't learn nothin' about cussin' that I didn't already know. Let's turn around and get on up the trail. I'm cravin' some carnival popcorn."

"I'm in the mood for a few hot dogs," said Tank.

A soft wind swirled down from Mount Jefferson and brought with it a smidgen of coolness and relief. The humidity was pushed aside for a moment or two. The four of us stopped our ascent and breathed in drafts of fresh Mount Jefferson air. Within a minute, we renewed our climb toward the carnival grounds.

Looming over the small towns of West Jefferson and neighboring Jefferson, the dark mountain was, according to some of the older county citizens, part of Harriet Tubman's Underground Railroad during the days of slavery. Runaway slaves supposedly hid out on the mountain while humanitarians and abolitionists brought them food and supplies for their journey northward. The mountain itself had gone through several name changes. Some of the old names given to the dusky mountain were offensive to the black race, so the name Mount Jefferson eventually became the official designation of the lofty peak.

"I'm glad we're not climbing Mount Jefferson to get to the carnival," puffed Tank. Raising his left hand, he pointed to the shadowy mountain in the distance. He lowered his hand, then leaning over, put his hands on his knees and breathed in deeply, exhaling gradually. "This Seagraves Hill is tough enough for me. *Whew!*"

The Tank's perpetual smile and ruddy face were framed nicely by his flattop and the contrasting longer hair that swept back from each temple, just above his ears, to form a neat ducktail in the back. Tank called his hairdo, a blend of short crewcut hair on top with long hair on the sides, "the combo." Gene called the Tank's hairstyle a "flattop with fenders." Tank's thick topmost hair, butch waxed to perfection, gleamed like polished bronze in the fading sunlight.

Tank's hazel eyes darted about and then focused on the glow of the carnival lights still far above us. He wore a navy blue extra-extra-large T-shirt and jumbo-sized blue jeans. Regardless of his size, his clothes always fit him well. His mother, who was a skillful seamstress, saw to that. Tank's Keds sneakers were unblemished, new, and white. His bulky arms and legs showed a hint of sturdy muscle beneath the excess flesh and the fingers on his hands were broad and powerful. Tank ambled forward in a purposeful, elephantine gait.

Last year, at the Stephens Brothers Carnival, Tank, Gene, Pudge, and I had been wandering around the carnival grounds, sampling food and soft drinks from the concession stands, and participating in some of the carnival games. We had noticed a small crowd around a game called the High Striker, a contest that purportedly measured physical strength. The apparatus consisted of a long, yellow vertical tower, almost twenty feet high, with a silver metallic bell on top. At the tower's base rested a puck that rose to various levels, depending on how hard the padded arm at the other end of a spring lever was struck. The rubber padded base was walloped with a huge wooden mallet that resembled a sledgehammer. The levels of strength ranged from Scrawny Mouse to Superman with markers in between labeled Pantywaist, Nice Lady, Weight Lifter, Popeye, Sampson, and Captain Marvel.

"Step right up, folks! Measure your strength! Ring the bell, and win a prize!" the carnival barker had yelled. He was a large, ruddy-faced middle-aged man dressed in a red suit with white patent leather shoes. A limp, olive green tie hung around his thick neck, clashing with his wrinkled purple shirt. His hair, plastered down with hairspray, was an unnatural yellow color and styled in an obvious comb-over.

Moe Bacon, a brawny star athlete at Central Ashe High School, had just given the High Striker a try. Moe had reached the Captain Marvel level, but had not rung the silver bell. I had once seen Moe hit a baseball almost four hundred feet, so his failure at the High Striker game convinced me that some, if not all of the carnival games were rigged.

"Dad gummit!" shouted Moe. "Somethin' ain't right here!"

"Nice try, son," chuckled the barker. "You ain't as stout as you look. Now run along and eat a bunch of spinach like Popeye does. You can come back later and give the Striker another try." Several men joined in the barker's laughter. His hands stuffed in his jeans, Moe, looking humiliated, hurried away from the crowd gathered around the game of strength. A good-looking, fair-haired high school girl at the carnival's popcorn stand had motioned for Moe to join her. He did, and soon both were munching popcorn and smiling.

"Tank, why don't you try your hand at this game?" Pudge had asked. He grinned as he pointed to the bell perched high atop the High Striker. "If Tankus Giganticus can't ring that bell, who can?"

"Grandpa Charlie," I said.

I reminded the guys that Grandpa Charlie had rung the High Striker bell several years before. It had happened when I was only eight years old, and I still remembered how proud I was of my grandpa. He chose a Swiss Army knife as his prize. Grandpa Charlie still carried the multifaceted tool in a pocket of his bib overalls.

"Go ahead, Tank," Gene had urged, staring at the heavy mallet resting on the High Striker platform. "I'd ring the bell myself, but my gizzard is kindly queasy from eatin' them two candied apples a while back."

The carnival barker looked at Tank and smirked. "Come on, big boy. Show the crowd that you got some muscle under all that flab. Are you scared, son? You ain't just a big fat chicken, are you?" The barker began walking around flapping his arms and clucking like a hen. He bobbed his head up and down like a chicken pecking corn.

"That's enough," said Tank. "I'll give this game a try."

The Tank reached deep into his jeans pocket for change and gave the barker two quarters. He leaned over and picked up the huge mallet and examined it briefly as Babe Ruth might've examined a new baseball bat way back in nineteen twenty-seven, the year he hit sixty home runs. Using both hands, Tank raised the giant hammer high over his head and slammed it down with terrific force. The heavy black puck shot skyward and struck the glossy metal bell, sending it spiraling high into the air. After its short, arching flight, the detached bell landed with a thump near a cotton candy stand. Fortunately, no one was injured.

"Great God Almighty! Hellfire and damnation! I'm ruint!" screamed the crimson-clothed barker just after the shiny bell had been torn from its attachments and propelled into the sky. His eyes had followed the launched metal object from liftoff until it crashed onto the ground. He pushed his way through the crowd, sprinted over to the cotton candy stand, and picked up the bell. He wiped away the sawdust and, cradling the bell in his arms as a new mother might carry her baby, carried it back to the damaged High Striker.

"Sir, do I still get my prize?" asked Tank. "If so, I'll take the baseball glove hanging on the first row next to the black and white teddy bear."

"Hell no, Fatso! You don't get no friggin' prize!" growled the carnival man. "You've ruint my business! You've cost me over a hundred dollars! That's what it'll take to fix this High Striker! You don't get no baseball glove after what you done! Get your lard butt away from here and take your snickerin' buddies with you!"

Gene had doffed his black Hopalong Cassidy cowboy hat and said to the red-suited man, "Well, good evenin' then. Mighty nice to make your acquaintance, I'm sure."

Walking away from the game of strength, headed for the Ferris wheel, Pudge and I had congratulated Tank on his show of power, but Gene said, "Tank was just lucky. That ole bell was probly just hangin' by a thread. I wish I had give the High Striker a try before Tank tore it up. Then you boys woulda seen some real muscle."

As we continued up the broad path that led to the carnival grounds, I felt a sharp stinging on the side of my right little toe. I was sure that a blister was forming because I was outgrowing my sneakers. I stopped, bent down, and loosened my laces. I wiggled my toes as I pulled my right sock up higher. I walked on and discovered that the foot pain had subsided.

In contrast to Tank's flawless, fresh, snowy white sneakers, my used-to-be white Converse All-Star tennis shoes were smudged and showed considerable wear. My formerly white footwear had assumed a dusty brown shade. The bottoms of the shoes were getting slick, providing little traction on smooth surfaces like wet sidewalks and paved driveways.

I wore a chocolate colored, short-sleeved cotton T-shirt that my grandmother had purchased just days ago at Smithies Department Store. The store was having a big sale because there had been a small fire in one of the storage rooms in the rear of the store. My blue jeans, also purchased at Smithies, smelled of smoke and had grass stains on both knees from my playing tug-of-war with a neighbor's purebred German Shepherd puppy named Ike, the nickname of the man in the White House, President Dwight David Eisenhower.

For his size, Ike was the strongest puppy I had ever been around. His huge puppy paws indicated that he would grow into a large dog, perhaps as big as the movie star dog, Rin Tin Tin. The puppy's sharp primary teeth had left a few tiny puncture wounds on my hands, but the insignificant injuries were healing quickly.

So far, my face had been relatively free of the common teenage maladies such as zits, blackheads, and oily skin. I say relatively free, because sometimes a humdinger of a pimple would pop out on my face, usually near the creases of skin beside my nose or around the dimple on my chin. Occasional pimples would also visit the skin around the nape of my neck, just below my hairline.

I was in the throes of adolescence as were my three companions. Our bodies were changing rapidly according to Mother Nature's plan. We pubescent teenagers were dealing with oily skin, blackheads, pimples, uneven growth spurts, and sprouting underarm and pubic hair. Our voices were beginning to change. Already, Gene, in a single sentence, could sound like both Johnny Cash and Patsy Cline.

Tank, Pudge, Gene, and I were suffering the slings and arrows of outrageous youth. But it wasn't all that bad. During the last year I had grown a few inches taller and my shoulders had broadened considerably. Sinews and muscles had replaced baby fat on my arms and legs. My chest and stomach had firmed up, and the fatty tissue on my sides, my "love handles," had virtually disappeared.

Shortly after I was born, my parents named me Halbert Joseph Grayson. Now everybody calls me Hal, and I like the name Hal much better than Halbert. Who wants to be called Halbert? Not me. My Grandma Grayson sometimes calls me Halbert, but only when she's fussing at me for not doing my chores or not cleaning my room. Yesterday she said, "Halbert Joseph Grayson, you take this broom and sweep out your room. The floor's so dirty a'body could grow a crop of corn in there without usin' no fertilizer."

My grandparents on my father's side, the Graysons, were raising me because my parents had divorced. I never talked with anybody, not even Pudge or Tank and certainly not Gene, about my parents' divorce because talking about the split-up always made me feel sad and blue. Growing up, I had visited my mom and dad on my birthdays, on holidays, at Christmas time, and on long summertime breaks from school. I took turns staying with my parents.

My mom and dad loved me, but they didn't love each other. I guess they *did* love each other at the beginning, when they first got married, but their love turned sour after a few years. However, I never heard my mom say a bad word about my dad, and, in my presence, Dad never spoke an ill word about Mom. When my parents first separated, I used to pray that they would get back together. That didn't work, so I gave it up. I guess God didn't think it would be a very good idea, or He had more important things to do.

My two grandpas, Grandpa Charlie Rufus Franklin and Grandpa Morgan Ambrose Grayson, agreed that I was growing up to be at least a halfway decent and an almost normal person. Grandma Jetta Ellen Franklin concurred, but Grandma Nancy Trula Grayson wasn't so sure. She thought I should take my church attendance and my Sunday school lessons more seriously. I had overheard the four of them talking about me about three weeks ago. I was sitting at the top of the stairs reading a *Tales from the Crypt* comic book, but they thought I was napping in my room. I had stayed very still. You can learn a lot by eavesdropping.

Grandpa Charlie and Grandma Jetta no longer lived together. They were separated, not divorced like Mom and Dad. They'd managed to maintain a friendship, but they lived in different houses and had for a long time, more than ten years.

One morning when we were in the fifth grade, Gene had stopped me at the classroom door and had said, "Lemme get this straight, Hal. Your grandpa and grandma, the Graysons, is raisin' you, but you visit your mama for a week or two in the summertime, and then you go to see your daddy for a spell? I know you stay with your other granny, Jetta Franklin, on some weekends. Grandpa Charlie's cabin is within walkin' distance of the Grayson's house, so you spend a lot of time there, too. Stayin' at all them places, don't it get kinda hard, tryin' to figger out where your real home is?"

I didn't answer him. I went inside the classroom, sat down at my desk and opened my reading book. I pretended to read until Gene passed by, heading for his desk. Using my textbook, I slammed him on the seat of his pants as he sauntered by. He had staggered forward, almost falling down. I was mad at Gene, but I had been unable to explain my reasons to the teacher when she confronted me.

"Hal, you've given me no excuse for your behavior," said my teacher. "I can't allow you to strike another student. This is so unlike you."

"I'm sorry, ma'am."

"He didn't hurt me much," said Gene in my defense. "My daddy whups me a whole lot harder. Why, my butt has stopped stingin' already. It ain't no big deal."

"Hal, I will think about your punishment and let you know tomorrow morning," said our teacher. "Now, you boys return to your desks."

Her solution had been to keep me in for two recess periods. Missing one play period would've been enough to get the teacher's point across; for a fifth grader, missing two recesses bordered on cruel and unusual punishment. I was miserable as I sat in the vacant classroom while the sound of my classmates playing softball outside drifted in through the open windows. I heard a loud pop as a player struck a softball firmly with the distinctive sound of the fifth grade's heaviest wooden bat. Someone huffed and puffed as he rounded the bases. No doubt, Tank had hit another of his prodigious home runs.

From the playground, Gene had screeched, "Foul ball! Foul ball! That ball was hit foul by over three foot. Make Tank bat again with two strikes. What? *What?* That was not a fair ball! Cheaters! Cheaters! Cheaters!"

Tank, Gene, and Pudge sometimes called me "Curly" because I had curling dark brown, almost black hair that twisted into tight coils with the slightest hint of humidity, making me look as if I were wearing a brown Brillo pad toupee with a teenage face under it. I tried to comb my hair straight back from my forehead like Elvis Presley and James Dean, but the effort was useless. Within seconds after combing, my individual hairs would spiral back into their original corkscrew shapes with the longer strands falling forward onto my forehead. My eyes were a common brown color with just a twist of green, and I spent too much time wishing they were blue like most of the male movie stars and teen idols of the late fifties.

I enjoyed sports, especially baseball and basketball and fancied myself a decent athlete. My favorite baseball player was Dodger centerfielder, Duke Snider; my favorite basketball player was Bob Cousy of the Boston Celtics. I was right-handed, but when I played baseball or softball, I tried to bat left-handed like the powerful Duke of Flatbush, and when I played basketball, I tried to throw slick, no-look, behind-the-back passes like the Celtics' point guard who was called the Houdini of the Hardwood. The "Cooz" was amazing with his revolutionary passing, unorthodox dribbling, and his clutch scoring. Like the Duke, Bob Cousy was fortunate to have a great supporting cast of teammates around him. Among other first-rate Celtic teammates, Cousy had Bill Russell, Bill Sharman, and Frank Ramsey. Duke Snider had Jackie Robinson, Roy Campanella, Pee Wee Reese, Don Newcombe, and Gil Hodges, to name a few distinguished Dodgers.

Only last week, Pudge had mused, "Hal, do you think the players on the Dodgers, like Duke Snider, Jackie Robinson, Roy Campanella, and Pee Wee Reese were pals like you, me, Tank, and Gene?"

"I think they were buddies," said Tank. "Before Robinson retired and Campy got hurt, they won a lot of games together and even a World Series."

"I've seen pictures of them in sports magazines and newspapers," I said. "They sure looked like pals. In one picture, they were standing side-by-side, holding up their baseball bats and grinning."

"I say they ain't pals nor buddies," blurted Gene. "They can't be. No way!"

"What?" I questioned. "Why not?"

"Them Dodgers is too old to be pals. My daddy says that after you turn twenty, your pals and buddies becomes your friends, just friends. Daddy ain't got no pals nor buddies no more, but he has lotsa friends. Grown-up folks ain't got no pals nor buddies; they just got friends."

"We won't be like that, guys" said Tank. "We'll be pals even when we're old men."

"We'll be racing our wheelchairs down the halls of the old folks' home," I laughed.

"We'll be sword fighting with our canes and crutches," grinned Tank.

"Buddies forever!" said Pudge, grinning from ear to ear.

Gene said, "How dang immature can you fellers get? I'm the only mature one in the bunch, and from now on you fellers ain't my pals nor buddies, you're just my friends, good friends, but just friends, nothin' else. I can't help bein' more grown-up and sophisticated. Don't take no offense."

Tank winked at Pudge and proffered his hand in Gene's direction. "None taken. Let's shake on it, little buddy."

"Okay, pal," Gene had said, beaming as his slender hand disappeared into Tank's huge paw.

My interest in girls, especially older, high school girls, had reached a fever pitch at the conclusion of my eighth-grade year. However, I had enough sense to know that, as a rising freshman, I didn't stand a chance with a junior or senior high school girl. Still, a guy can dream, can't he?

In reality, I was hoping to see two special girls at the carnival tonight. One girl was in my class and was almost exactly my age since we were born in the same month, and the other was a couple of years younger than me. On the last day of school, the younger girl had slipped a carefully folded note into my hand as I boarded my school bus, number 29.

"Don't read this note until you get home, Hal," she had whispered through rosy lips. I stuffed the note into my jeans pocket. She smiled, standing there in her pink dress, lime green scarf, and black Mary Jane shoes. She pushed her long dark hair out of her face, exposing her gorgeous green eyes. Then she turned away, swirling her dress upward, and ran back to her school bus, number 42. Before she climbed her bus's steps, she looked back at me and blew me a kiss.

Her gentle, windblown osculation was right on target and almost bowled me over. My legs felt all loosey-goosey. My stomach began oscillating. My tongue curled tightly inside my mouth, making speech impossible. Indescribable warmth flooded my body, causing unusual tingling sensations from head to toe. Fresh teenage testosterone, coursing through my veins, reached the boiling point. My heart had bumped against my rib cage as if searching for a way to escape. My breath came in rapid gasps. *Wow!* A secret folded note and a blown kiss were hot stuff when you had just graduated from the eighth grade and were still a few months from high school.

Already I thought of myself as a ninth grader, or more specifically, a freshman in high school. The young lady who had pressed the note into my hand would be in the seventh grade when school started in the fall. In age, we were two years apart. In reality, we were light years apart because she would stay at Healing Waters Elementary School, while I would go on to Central Ashe High School. I was going to miss seeing her in the elementary school's hallways almost every day.

CHAPTER 2

Still reeling from the effects of the blown kiss and the top-secret note, I had tripped as I climbed up my orange school bus's steps and had fallen forward into the aisle, landing on my knees and hands. My blue notebook slid down the bus's aisle and rested a few feet in front of me. I hit the heels of my palms hard on the floorboard, and I was sure that in a few seconds, my hands would be oozing blood.

While on all fours, I raised my head. In this position, I was at eye level with Sally Sue Carpenter's perfect, tanned knees. She always sat in the front bus seat directly behind the bus driver with her friend, Bertie Mae Wallace beside her. Sally Sue was not a classic beauty like Elizabeth Taylor or Grace Kelly, but more of the cute blonde type, like Tuesday Weld or Sandra Dee, with the upturned nose, the big blue eyes, the gleaming white Colgate toothpaste smile, and the long ponytailed hair. She was the reigning homecoming queen and head cheerleader at Central Ashe High School.

Sally Sue had looked down at me and laughed derisively at my eighth-grade clumsiness. Her knees had opened slightly, ever so slightly. On my hands and knees, I was mesmerized by her dimpled knees and the feminine mysteries that lay just beyond my field of vision. Was I dreaming, or did her knees separate faintly, almost imperceptibly, again?

Then Sally Sue turned to speak to a girl in the school bus seat behind her. When she did, her skirt rose higher and her knees spread open even more, displaying her flawless, lean thighs. From my vantage point I could see that Sally Sue was wearing lacy black panties. Sally Sue turned back around and caught me, still on hands and knees, intently looking up her dress. Embarrassed, I smiled broadly and foolishly, like the proverbial mule eating briars through a barbed wire fence.

"The view is much better through the bus windows, Hal," smiled Sally Sue Carpenter sweetly, closing her knees. She had stared deeply into my eyes as if evaluating me as a member of the male gender. She continued, "Why don't you get up, grab your notebook, and take your usual seat in the back of the bus? You're holding up the line, you naughty boy. Move it, little man, move it." She was right. There were several kids behind me waiting to board the bus.

Sally Sue's seat mate, Bertie Mae Wallace, a brunette who was also a cheerleader and almost as attractive as Sally Sue, whispered something in Sally Sue's ear. I was close enough to overhear the whisper. Bertie Mae had said to Sally Sue, "Tell Hal he can look, but he'd better not touch!" The two eighteen-year-old girls reverted to girlish third-grade giggles.

Sally Sue's father, Bartholomew Carpenter, was a deacon at Healing Waters Baptist Church and taught the young adult Sunday school class. I would've bet a hundred dollars that Mr. Carpenter didn't know that his daughter was running around in black frilly underpants. I was half a mind to tell him next Sunday after Sunday school class, but I couldn't think of a way to broach the subject of his daughter's lacy lingerie to my middle-aged Sunday school teacher.

Feeling both aroused and humiliated, I had picked up my school notebook with my report card inside, dusted myself off, and had scrambled to the back of the school bus where I took my customary seat. I examined the palms of my hands and decided they weren't going to bleed after all. The skin was roughed up, but there was no blood.

I looked toward the front of the bus and saw Sally Sue Carpenter's flouncing ponytail. She was obviously flirting with the bus driver, Central Ashe High School senior and basketball star, Monty Dale Lewis. I knew for a fact she was going steady with Monty's best friend, Billy Dean Robinson. If Sally Sue Carpenter cared for Billy, why was she engaging in this flirtation with Monty? Monty was no innocent bystander in this flirtatious affair, because he flirted right back with the perky cheerleader. Once, Monty Dale looked up into his broad rearview bus mirror and winked at Sally Sue. Seated right behind him, she giggled and put her knees up against the back of his driver's seat. She pushed Monty Dale's seat forward and back rhythmically for about half a minute. Older teenagers, like Sally Sue, Monty Dale, and Bertie Mae, fascinated me. I could never quite figure them out.

I live in a strange, sometimes incomprehensible world, I thought to myself as I sat in the backseat of the rumbling school bus. Don't get me wrong, I knew a few things about life—after all, on this last day of school, I was a graduate of the eighth grade—but I was slowly beginning to comprehend that life was complicated, far more complex than it was back in the sixth grade. I wondered if my buddies, Tank, Pudge, and Gene, had noticed the new intricacies and fresh convolutions of teenage life.

Almost halfway home, I settled down in the backseat of the school bus, watching through the multiple half-open windows as Ashe County's variegated scenery flashed by my eyes: the fertile farms with rich, plowed chocolate-brown soil; the verdant pastures with herds of grazing, rust-colored white-faced cattle; the glistening blue waters of the meandering New River; the forested green landscapes; the many-hued wildflowers growing alongside the road; and, of course, the surrounding azure haze of the Blue Ridge Mountains. The afternoon was hot and sultry. I got out of my seat to lower a few bus windows. For safety, all the school bus windows would go only halfway down, so they didn't provide much relief from the heat. I made sure all the windows were down, but the outside air streaming through them was just as hot as the air inside the bus. I went back to my seat and settled in for the long, sweaty ride home. From time to time, the bus would stop to let a single student or groups of students descend the vehicle's three steps and head for home.

Gradually, I felt a pang of uncertainty. A sense of disquietude spread over me, like when it's your turn to stand in front of the class to give a book report and you haven't even read the book. I felt as if I had forgotten or lost something important. I checked for my billfold and found it safe and secure in my back pocket. Next, I patted my jeans pocket where the secret note should have been safely tucked away. My jeans pocket was empty.

"Damn!" I muttered to myself as I rapidly checked all my pockets, even my shirt pocket. I must've lost the note during my head-first sprawl as I entered the school bus. I peered toward the front of the bus, and sure enough, I saw the note resting unnoticed on the bus's floor just behind and almost touching Sally Sue Carpenter's bright white tennis shoes. Sally Sue reached down to scratch her slender ankle. I held my breath. Her fingers were just inches away from my note, but she didn't notice it.

I knew that it would be an unthinkable, calamitous disaster if Sally Sue discovered the note resting next to her tennis shoes before I could grab and flee with it. She would undoubtedly read the secret note out loud to Bertie Mae and Monty Dale. She might read the message aloud to the remaining fifteen or sixteen kids on the bus. She might even take the note to church and pass it around the young adult Bible study group. I had to retrieve that note before anyone else saw it, but how? My mind worked feverishly on the problem.

If I could make my way to the front of the bus without the note having been discovered, it would be the work of an instant to kneel down, reach under Sally Sue's seat, and secure the note, but I had to be careful, very careful.

I decided to walk nonchalantly to the front of the bus, on the pretext of talking to Monty Dale. He lived not far from me and our families were friends. We visited each other often, especially after church on Sundays. Monty had a basketball hoop nailed up in his father's wide barn and he practiced on that rusty hoop until he became a great shooter, especially from the top of the key. Monty had taught me how to shoot a jump shot. He taught me to leap as high as I could, and then as I started my descent, use my wrist to flick the ball toward the basket. Monty had stood under the basket and thrown the basketball back to me as I practiced. Then he and I played a game of Horse. I had won, but I think Monty let me win. In fact, I'm *sure* he let me win. Monty was that kind of guy.

I made my way slowly forward down the bus's narrow aisle toward Sally Sue, Bertie Mae, and Monty Dale. I held onto the metal safety bars at the front of the bus and chatted briefly with Monty about the baseball season and the Brooklyn Dodgers who were now the Los Angeles Dodgers. We were both fans and lamented the Dodgers' move to the West Coast. Monty's favorite player was first baseman Gil Hodges. Monty also liked the Dodgers' two young pitchers named Sandy Koufax and Don Drysdale.

"Too bad about Campy," said Monty, referring to the Dodger catcher Roy Campanella, who after a tragic automobile accident in Brooklyn had been paralyzed from the shoulders down. Campy had won three most valuable player awards while in Brooklyn. Now, the stocky catcher watched Los Angeles Dodgers games in a wheelchair.

Suddenly, a brand-new, red nineteen fifty-nine Chevrolet Impala driven by Central Ashe senior, Billy Bob Baker, whizzed past the orange school bus. There was a long blast from the Chevy's horn. Monty and Billy exchanged waves. Soon, the red Chevy was out of sight.

"I think the new fifty-nine Chevy Impala is the prettiest car ever built," said Monty. "I dig those crazy tailfins!"

"I have to disagree, buddy," I said. "The nineteen fifty-six Mercury Montclair has my vote. I like smooth lines more than tailfins. I hope to own a Mercury someday, maybe a fifty-six Montclair."

Monty kept his eyes on the road as we shot the breeze. I wasn't supposed to be standing at the front of the bus, but Monty didn't seem to mind. He was a good driver. I kept my eyes on the note under Sally Sue Carpenter's seat. Monty shifted gears smoothly as the bus rumbled through the hilly terrain. The bus rounded a curve, and the note slid a few inches toward the aisle. I decided to make my move.

"Talk to you later, Monty. I'm going back to my seat."

"Okay, Hal," said Monty, gearing down for an uphill climb. The bus's engine whined.

As I had turned to return to my seat, I knelt down and grabbed the confidential note that rested on the floorboard near Sally Sue's seat. I stooped down to grasp the note just at the precise instant that Sally Sue pulled up her skirt and examined a bruise on her slender tanned thigh. She massaged her thigh in a slow circular motion, and as she did her skirt rose higher. Kneeling there beside Sally Sue's bus seat with the secret note clutched in my hand, my nose was no more than six inches from the bluish bruise on her thigh. Sally Sue's lacy black drawers were again in my sight. I felt a woody beginning to form in the crotch of my jeans, but my denims, thank God, were so tight in my kneeling position that blood circulation to my pubic region was virtually blocked. Thankfully, like a flower left too long in the sun without water, my erection wilted.

Holding the note tightly and thinking rapidly, I stood up and said, "Excuse me, Sally Sue. I dropped my pen."

"My, but you're the persistent one, aren't you, Hal?" said Sally Sue, smiling and still rubbing her exposed thigh. She lowered her skirt. "I like that in a man, but the difference in our ages is just too great. I'm sure you understand; now run along kid, you bother me."

"Yeah," echoed Bertie Mae. "Run along kid, you bother us."

With the bus rounding increasingly sharp curves as the vehicle descended Fairview Hill, I staggered back to my seat, holding onto the bus's seat backs to prevent another fall. I plopped down in the back of the bus and stuffed the secret note deep into my jeans pocket.

The school bus turned off the paved road onto a gravel road. I looked out the window as we passed a vacant house with broken windows. The empty house was the one that Mom, Dad, and I had lived in until I was five years old. I felt an old, familiar pain as a memory or two came calling. I closed my eyes and reminded myself that my parents were divorced and were never getting back together.

The bus clattered over a low-water bridge with a few loose boards. I folded my arms, put my knees up on the seatback in front of me, looked out the bus windows, and watched as a sudden soft rain made dimples in the slow current of the New River. We were almost at the Grayson farm. Through the bus's windshield, I could see the barn and the white two-story house in the distance.

The best thing about growing up on Grandpa Grayson's farm was the proximity of the New River. I could stand on the front porch and throw a rock almost halfway across the river. My summer days were filled with wading, swimming, and fishing. The worst thing was the number of chores involved. I hated weeding the garden and hoeing corn, but I didn't mind feeding the livestock or gathering fresh eggs from the henhouse.

One morning while finishing my chores in the barn, I discovered that our best milk cow, Pet, had delivered a little black and white bull calf. Pet had licked her hours-old calf as he stood beside her on trembling legs. Grandpa Grayson let me name the calf. I named him Elvis.

CHAPTER 3

I had been sorely tempted, but I didn't open my young lady's folded message until the school bus dropped me off at my house. Ignoring my joyfully yapping eleven-year-old dog, Jingles, I trotted up the porch steps and hustled through the screen door, which slammed noisily behind me. Taking the steps two at a time, I sprinted upstairs and into my room. I locked the door, creating my very own Fortress of Solitude. I sat down on my bed and carefully opened the young lady's note, which had been folded several times. As I unfolded it, a delicate perfume floated upward on its way to my nostrils. I read the message and smiled. I lay back on my bed and devoured it over and over again.

Since I believed myself to be a young country gentleman and not a cad, I'd never shared the contents of the young lady's note with anyone; but suffice it to say, the written communication piqued my ninth-grade interest in the seventh-grade young lady and aroused my curiosity about her. Yes, I was only hours out of the eighth grade, but already I considered myself a high school freshman, a more cosmopolitan individual, and a broad-based man of the world. After all, I seldom missed the six o'clock news broadcast on WBTV in Charlotte. I skimmed the *Winston-Salem Journal* on a regular basis, especially the sports pages and comic strips, and in my home, there was an almost complete set of *Encyclopedia Britannica*. Only two volumes were missing.

I read the note one last time. I had gotten notes and valentines from girls ever since the third grade, but never any communications like the one I had opened in the privacy of my room on the last day of school. I hid the subtly perfumed note in an old copy of *Boys Life* magazine. Then I stuck the magazine under my bed where it joined other magazines and comic books amid a wide-ranging collection of dust bunnies, tiny desiccated bug carcasses, and ancient spider webs.

Far back under my bed, in the darkest recesses where only the bravest of insects and spiders dared go, cleverly hidden under an old Sears and Roebuck catalog, was a *Playboy* magazine. Gene had given me the *Playboy* after helping his uncle, Shade Barlow, clean out Mr. Barlow's garage. Gene had found a virtual treasure trove of the forbidden magazines in a box behind a stack of old, slick tires in a darkened corner of the garage. Gene absconded with ten of Hugh Hefner's prohibited publications. Only after reaching the age of eighteen years old could a guy buy *Playboy* magazines at the drugstore in West Jefferson. Gene had given me one of the magazines instead of paying me the seventy-five cents he owed me. He also gave copies of the magazine to Tank and Pudge. He had kept seven *Playboys* for himself. We were standing behind the Healing Waters Elementary School's gymnasium when Gene handed me an innocuous brown paper bag containing the provocative, lascivious magazine.

"Hal, this here *Playboy* magazine is worth a lot more than the fifty cents price marked on the cover; it is worth a whole lot more than the seventy-five cents I owe you. I guarantee that this publication will provide hours and hours of readin' pleasure. The magazine sure opened my eyeballs. I'm doin' you a favor, a big favor, Hal. Just remember, you owe me a favor in return. Fair is fair, ain't it?" reasoned Gene.

"Okay," I said, as I pulled the periodical from the paper bag. My eyes devoured the cover of the illicit magazine. A partially clad lady much older than me, maybe twenty-one or twenty-two, smiled up at me. I couldn't resist smiling back at her. I stuffed the *Playboy* back into the large paper bag, and headed for my school bus. I knew that Grandpa and Grandma Grayson wouldn't approve of my having the publication, but I managed to get the *Playboy* magazine home in my book satchel, sneak it upstairs into my room, and hide it under my bed.

"Hal, is that you shufflin' around in your room, or has the squirrels got back in the attic?" my grandmother had called from the living room below.

"It's me, Ma'am," I hollered.

"Well, come downstairs and at least say howdy to me and your grandpa. Where's your manners, young'un?"

"I'll be right down," I called, lifting a flashlight from my dresser drawer.

Using the flashlight, I checked under my bed to make sure the *Playboy* was completely hidden. It was. I replaced the flashlight. Satisfied, I descended the steep stairs. Grandma Grayson was seated in a rocking chair near the living room's picture window, which framed her flower garden. Grandpa was resting in his recliner with a newspaper covering his face.

"Morgan, look how tall Hal's gettin' to be," she said. "He's 'bout as tall as you are, maybe taller. He's more like his daddy with ever' day that passes."

Grandpa lifted his newspaper and squinted at me. "Yep, he's growing up, and that just makes me feel older. He'll grow up to be a little taller than average, like me and his daddy. Now you two be quiet and let me finish my nap." He replaced the sports pages over his face, and within minutes he was snoring comfortably.

Grandma and I had grinned at each other. I went outside and sat on the sun-warmed porch steps. Our gray female cat, Foggy, the mother of seven newborn kittens, came up to me and rubbed against my ankles. I leaned over and scratched her behind the ears. She purred and stayed with me until she heard her kittens mewling under the porch. Several of them were orange and white indicating that Tangerine Snow was the father.

The mama cat had bounded down the wooden steps, pausing on the bottom step. With soft green eyes, she looked back at me as if to say, "A mother's work is never done." With another bound, she had disappeared under the porch. The kittens' mewling ceased, replaced by the contented maternal purring of Foggy.

Occasionally during the summer months, I had taken the young girl's note out from under the bed and read her message again; the words, written in a delicate, feminine, cursive style, always made me smile. Her sentences stoked a small fire in my abdomen. At the bottom of the note, she had drawn a small heart with our initials inside.

The scent of the perfume had long since disappeared, and, unfortunately, the amorous note had taken on the aroma of my room consisting of a malodorous blend of river-soaked tennis balls, fermenting tennis shoes, a rotting apple on the windowsill, a blackened banana peel partially hidden under my dresser, and a growing pile of sweaty socks, grass-stained blue jeans, and unwashed underwear.

Also, anyone with sensitive nasal passages would've detected the unmistakable canine scent of Jingles, my old dog, a prime example of the Heinz 57 multi-breed variety. The short-haired dog, mostly brown with a few white spots on his chest and flanks, was slightly overweight at thirty pounds. His milk chocolate muzzle was flecked with gray hairs and his short, thick tail acted as a rudder when he swam in the river. For his undersized body, the mixed-breed dog had enormous ears that stuck straight up when he heard another dog bark or when he fancied that something unusual was going on outside the house. Squirrels infuriated Jingles and they were the primary reasons for his lengthy barking spells.

Jingles had slept at the foot of my bed for years. Only on the coldest nights would Jingles sleep downstairs next to the kitchen stove or, rarely, by the fireplace. Once I had dropped Sophia's note and Jingles grabbed it. I had to chase the dog around my room to get it back. The small letter was wet with canine saliva but undamaged.

I always read the secret message three or four times before returning it to its hiding place under my bed. I tried my hand at writing a note for Sophia, but when I read my composition critically, I decided it was too mushy, so I tore it up. I collected the torn pieces of my schmaltzy note and wadded them into a ball. I shot the paper ball toward my wastebasket across the room. I had missed my goal on the first try but had hit the second attempt. The tightly compressed paper ball had rattled around inside the metal wastebasket.

"Cousy scores from the top of the key!" I shouted. "There's the buzzer, fans! Celtics win! Celtics win!"

CHAPTER 4

I hadn't seen Sophia all summer, but there was a good chance I would see her tonight at the carnival. We wouldn't see each other much in the coming school year because she would be a seventh grader at Healing Waters Elementary School, and I would be a freshman at Central Ashe High School.

Thinking about her milky skin, flowing dark hair, and bright green eyes, I began to whistle softly and dreamily as I continued my journey up the steep path leading to the carnival. I could picture the unfolded note in my mind. I concentrated on her signature at the bottom: *Yours truly, Sophia.* Instead of dotting the 'i' in her name, she had drawn a tiny heart above the letter. Her message had been written in blue ink, except for the heart, which had been drawn in red.

I felt lightheaded just thinking about Sophia Bishop.

My footsteps were wavering and I absentmindedly wandered from left to right, still whistling and daydreaming. My feet got tangled up, and I bumped into Tank and rebounded into Pudge's shoulder. Pudge, walking beside me, eyed me curiously, and then he elbowed me hard in my side. I grabbed my side. I stopped whistling and began walking in a steady, predictable, unchanging gait. For a little guy, Pudge packed a powerful punch.

"He's daydreamin' about that Bishop gal, ain't he, Pudge?" laughed Gene. "Hal needs to wake up; hit that lovesick hillbilly again, a little bit harder this time."

"I'm awake! I'm awake!" I said. Pudge socked me lightly on the shoulder anyway.

Richard James Hawkins, nicknamed Pudge after a friendly Chihuahua-sized mutt owned by his grandfather, was small for an eighth-grade graduate. His green eyes twinkled beneath a shock of red hair that was combed neatly, except for a large, unruly cowlick that stood up defiantly at the crown of his head. Pudge wore a yellow, short-sleeved T-shirt and khaki trousers that were a bit too short with yellow socks that showed above his black sneakers. He possessed an easy, friendly, and exceptionally wide grin. His freckles and his innocent, childlike face made him look like Opie Taylor, Sheriff Andy Taylor's son on *The Andy Griffith Show*. There was a touch of *Mad Magazine's* Alfred E. Neuman in his visage when he smiled, which was often. A single, ripening pimple dotted the center of his forehead. His more than ample ears were sun-burned and one ear, the right one, twitched occasionally, especially in stressful situations.

Not much bigger than a teacup, the pint-sized Chihuahua from which Pudge got his nickname had died when we were in the third grade. On a warm spring day with misting rain, Pudge's grandfather had backed his truck over the old dog while it was sleeping peacefully under the vehicle. Pudge said the little dog was thirteen years old and was probably deaf. Tears had welled up in his eyes as the human Pudge told me about the canine Pudge's passing.

"I'm sure gonna miss little Pudge," the third grader had said. "He was my first playmate and my first real friend. I remember when I was five years old and learning to tie my shoes, the tiny dog would grab my shoelaces and pull them loose. That crazy dog liked to play tug of war with my shoestrings. Once, little Pudge pulled my shoe off and ran under the bed with it. I got down on my hands and knees and put my head under the bed, but I still couldn't reach my shoe. The dog growled and barked at me, and I growled and barked at him. I crawled all the way under the bed and got stuck. Mom laughed until she cried." Pudge had reported the dog's death as we sat at a table in the Healing Waters Elementary School's lunchroom. As he concluded his somber announcement, two tears fell, one from each eye. The tears tracked their way down his freckled cheeks and he wiped them away with the back of his hand.

Our third-grade teacher passed by our table, monitoring our class for any signs of misbehavior. She noticed Pudge's tears.

"Is anything wrong, Pudgie?" she asked.

"No, ma'am," snuffled Pudge. "I got allergies."

Pudge and his grandfather had buried little Pudge under a tall weeping willow tree, one of many growing along the New River's banks not far from the Hawkins' house. The tiny dog's corpse fit into a shoebox coffin. Pudge's grandfather even put up a little stone marker under the willow, and Pudge placed wildflowers on the dog's grave.

Pudge had taken me to the grave site exactly one year after the passing of little Pudge, and he and I had spread bright yellow dandelion blossoms in a heart shape around the grass-covered grave. The wind rustled; the river babbled around large rocks near its shoreline; and from far away up the river, a dog barked, not an angry bark, but a lonesome bark. Gradually, the deep-throated bark became an extended howl.

"Rest in peace, little Pudge," said my redheaded friend, kneeling beside his namesake's grave. Pudge bowed his head. His uncontrollable cowlick stood at attention, and the willow tree's drooping, green-leafed branches swirled in a gentle wind.

I said, "Amen," then made the sign of the cross as I had seen a Catholic priest do on television. Pudge stood up and solemnly shook my hand. His eyes were wet.

"I always counted that little dog as my best friend. I guess you're my best friend now, Hal," said Pudge, raising his right hand to shield his eyes from the bright sunshine. He grinned. The sunlight turned his red hair to burnished bronze.

I had nodded, but I was reluctant to assume the responsibilities of being a best friend. I wasn't sure I was up to the task of being anybody's best friend. What would I do if bigger kids started picking on Pudge? I suggested that Tank might be a better choice.

"Tank is a lot bigger and stronger than I am," I explained. "If you got into serious trouble with an older kid, Tank might be a better friend than I could ever be."

"Then I could have two best friends, you and Tank," Pudge had said resolutely. He smiled broadly. "I'll tell everybody that my two best friends are Tank Banner and Hal Grayson."

I felt better after he included Tank in his best friend deal. I told Pudge I would be his best friend, and we shook hands on it. I knew, even back then, that I could count on Tank to share the manifold duties of friendship. Sometimes it seemed that Tank was everybody's best friend, even Gene's.

"Hal, do you reckon there's a heaven for animals?" Pudge had asked, standing close beside me as we stared down on little Pudge's grave.

"I don't know," I mumbled. The question made me feel uneasy somehow, like when people asked me about my parents' divorce. From listening to adult conversations, I had learned that Grandpa Grayson wasn't sure there was a heaven for people, let alone animals; Grandma Grayson, however, was convinced there was a heaven full of winged angels, beautiful flowers, and streets of gold. She once told me that in heaven, huge lions and tigers would lie down beside little goats and lambs.

"My Grandma Grayson believes there will be animals in heaven," I said.

Pudge turned away, picked up a smooth, flat stone, and skipped it across the New River. For a while, using an old, cut-off broomstick that Pudge's mom had given us, we hit strawberry-sized rocks into a creek that fed into the much broader river. We managed to hit a few stones all the way across the creek. Those stones plunked on the far bank instead of splashing in the stream. If we cleared the waterway, Pudge and I counted those blasts as home runs. Pudge pretended he was Yankee centerfielder, Mickey Mantle; I pretended I was Dodger centerfielder, Duke Snider. Mickey Mantle won our make-believe home run derby five to four.

After the derby, Pudge and I walked down closer to the slow-moving, wide river, took off our tennis shoes and socks, rolled up our jeans, and waded out until we were almost knee deep. In the clear water, fifty or more tiny, dark minnows congregated about our feet, then scurried away at the slightest movement. The river bottom was sandy and the sand felt good between our toes. We didn't stay in the river long because the water was too cold. We splashed toward the riverbank where the warm comfort of our shoes and socks waited. My toes were numb by the time we reached the shore.

Donning our socks and shoes, we decided to walk back to Pudge's house, about a mile away. On our way, we encountered a tall tree with low branches, just right for climbing and I challenged Pudge to a contest.

"I bet I can climb higher up that tree then you can," I said, pointing toward the tree's topmost branches.

"No thanks, I don't like to climb up high. Something happened to me when I was a little kid. I don't even like to climb up on ladders," said Pudge. "You can climb that tree, Hal. I can wait."

"Nope, I'm getting hungry and thirsty," I said. "Let's go back to your house, and see if your mom will fix us some peanut butter and jelly sandwiches with grape Kool-Aid."

"Okay," said Pudge. Then he added, "When you see him, tell Grandpa Charlie I say 'thanks.'"

"What for?" I asked.

"He made a dream catcher for me," said Pudge. "I was having real bad dreams, almost nightmares. Mom hung the dream catcher over my bed. It's made of a willow hoop decorated with beads and feathers."

I knew that American Indians made dream catchers to trap bad dreams and let good ones pass through. I had no idea Grandpa Charlie knew how to make one. That old man was full of surprises.

"Did it work?"

"Yep, the bad dreams stopped," Pudge said as we continued our walk. "I don't need the dream catcher anymore, but I keep it in my dresser drawer just in case. Be sure to thank him for me."

"Okay, I will."

I had felt a twinge of jealousy because Grandpa Charlie had never made a dream catcher for me. Then I realized I seldom had bad dreams, so I didn't really need one.

As we walked farther along the dirt road, a big, handsome collie, the television *Lassie* type, surged out of the green woods and trotted beside us for about five minutes. The dog's prancing gait was graceful and balanced. Now and then, the large dog, wagging its tail, would look up at Pudge and bark the collie breed's high-pitched bark. The dog gave all his attention to Pudge, hardly noticing me. I tried to pet the collie, but he shied away.

The collie's long shiny coat was tricolored with subtle shades of black mixed in with the golden brown. The white ruff that circled the dog's neck was almost blinding in the bright spring sunlight. When we got in sight of Pudge's house, the big dog lowered his head, grabbed Pudge's tennis shoe laces, and tugged them loose. While Pudge knelt to tie his shoestrings, the collie whined and licked his face. Then the dog turned, barked, and bounded back down the road toward the sun-dappled, winding river. Soon, it had disappeared around a bend in the gravel road.

"Whose dog is that?" I asked. "He sure is a beauty!"

"I don't know," Pudge said, looking back down the road to where the dog had vanished. He scratched his red head. "I've never seen that dog before."

CHAPTER 5

On this late afternoon, as we four teenagers climbed Seagraves Hill, we could now see in the distance some of the carnival rides waiting for us. Pudge's lips tightened a bit as he caught sight of the giant Ferris wheel looming above the lesser carnival rides at the top of the hill. His right ear was twitching like crazy. Was that dread or excitement in his eyes? I couldn't tell.

Pudge walked closer to me and Tank than to Gene, always keeping Gene at an arm's length. Tank and I had earned Pudge's trust over our elementary school years. Gene had not. In fact, no one trusted Gene completely, not even his own mother.

I had spent a few nights at Gene's house during elementary school. If I had correctly interpreted Gene's mother's eyes during my visits, Mrs. Ethel Clodfelter didn't trust her son entirely. I saw worry in her eyes. Gene could be unpredictable and impulsive; his mom knew it, and so did I.

Currently, as we made our way farther up the Seagraves Hill, I noticed that Gene's thin, perpetually oily hair was mussed up and a few conspicuously ripe, white-topped pimples were scattered randomly across his face, testifying to his headfirst plunge into the depths of puberty. Gene had battled blemishes, zits, and blackheads since the sixth grade, but his mild case of teenage acne didn't bother him.

Gene's nose, broken as a child, pulled sharply to the left. His grandmother had broken his nose with her fist after a long and tumultuous day of babysitting. The six-year-old Gene had pushed his grandma to the brink and beyond, and she lashed out with uncharacteristic violence. Gene told me all about the incident. Tank enjoyed Gene's story about his grandmother and his broken nose so much, he asked to hear it again and again. Tank liked the way Gene imitated Granny Clodfelter, shaking his finger in the air for emphasis and making his voice all whiny and scratchy. Tank always beamed as Gene began his impersonation. Pudge liked Gene's account of the nose incident, too.

The following is what happened on the day his nose was broken, according to Gene. He tells it better than I do. I'll try not to leave anything out, but I wish you could hear Gene tell the story. He sounds just like his granny.

"Don't call on me to babysit that young'un no more, Ethel," Gene's granny had said to his mom. "Why, Jesus Christ hisself woulda beat the tar outta that boy if He'd went through what I been through today. First off, Gene hid my glasses so I could barely see to get around the house. When I looked in the kitchen, I couldn't see my hand in front of my face and almost stepped on the boy's little dog, Snapper. When noontime rolled around, I found my glasses in a mayonnaise jar while I was fixin' Gene a 'mater and onion sandwich.

"After our meal, the little devil spread my dippin' snuff all over the ground outside the kitchen, and then little Gene unzipped his little pants and peed right on the snuff, I mean all over my dippin' snuff. I couldn't salvage none of it. The anger welled up in me. I cut myself a switch and I chased after him, but I couldn't catch him. He's a runner; that child is quick as a deer. I got all out of breath and had to lay down on the couch for a spell. My heart valve was botherin' me again. I was wheezin' somethin' fierce, for asthma hits me hard this time of year. My breathin' finally settled down. The radio was playin' a purty song, soft and low.

First thing I knowed, I was sound asleep and dreamin'. My nap didn't last for no more than ten minutes, but when I woke up Gene was nowhere to be found. I commenced to search for him, for I knowed it didn't take him long to get into meanness. I was right about the little turd.

"While I was sleepin', Gene hammered nails into all four of his daddy's car tires. Now, all four whitewalls is flatter than a flitter. His daddy will have to keep drivin' his old pickup for a while, I reckon.

"Sometimes I can't believe Gene is one of my grandbabies. There ain't nobody else on my side of the family like him. Oh, his brother Jackie is mean, but nothin' like Gene. If he didn't look so much like his daddy, I would swear he was a woods colt. No offense, Ethel.

"Well, later on, in the middle of the afternoon, when him and me walked down to the apple orchard, he rocked a wasp nest, causin' the waspers to swarm out and sting us three or four times apiece. We run inside the house to get away from the wasps. I looked in the hall closet to see if I could find some salve to put on our stings. Then the little bastard—overlook my language, Ethel—pushed me into a closet and propped a dinin' room chair under the doorknob so I couldn't get out. I was fit to be tied and could feel the fantods comin' on. Gene left me in there for nigh on to thirty minutes with me needin' to pee real bad for the last fifteen. It was pure torment. My bladder was about to bust. I thought I was gonna make water right there in the closet. I had to bribe him with a Almond Joy candy bar to get out. As soon as the little turd let me out, I throwed him the candy bar from my pocket book, and I run like a wild woman to the outhouse.

"And last but not least, while I took another nap in the late afternoon from plain ole tiredness, Gene cut my hair real close to my scalp usin' your pinkin' shears. I was so wore out that I slept right through the hair cuttin'. When I woke up, I felt my head, found some blood, and then run to a mirror. God Almighty! I looked like I'd been scalped by a wild Injun.

"Through the lookin' glass, I seen Gene, standin' right behind me snickerin' and grinnin' like a dang possum. I seen red! The anger welled up in me and took control. The devil in me took over. Lord forgive me, I struck little Gene across his face with my balled up fist when I seen what he had done to my hair; I admit it! I struck the young'un, and I'd do it again! But I'm right sorry, Ethel, that I broke his nose and knocked it kindly out of kilter."

As most grandmothers would, Gene's grandmother had forgiven Gene for his antics, and he had forgiven her for the punch that rearranged his nose. The only significant change Gene noticed from his broken nose involved his sleeping habits.

"Ever since Granny broke my nose, I snore like a chainsaw cuttin' down a dead locust tree," Gene had said. "My snorin' don't bother me none 'cause I'm asleep, but it does sometimes wake up other people in the house. It's funny, when I sleep on my stomach I don't snore."

If I remember correctly, we were fifth-graders when Gene first told me that story about how his nose got broken. That was a long time ago.

As we slowly climbed the Seagraves Hill, Gene peered at Pudge and chuckled darkly. I was sure he had plans for Pudge during this evening's carnival outing.

Gene Clodfelter's dark, piercing eyes were set widely apart and were quite mobile. His condition could be described as walleyed, according to Grandpa Grayson. Chameleon-like, his left eye could move independently of his right and vice versa. His nose displayed a strong preference for the left side of his face thanks to the punch thrown long ago by Granny Clodfelter. And although Gene was not smiling, a few upper teeth protruded from between his thin lips. His long-sleeved button down was originally black, but many washes had turned the garment to a smoky gray. His shirt pocket held a pack of Lucky Strike, his current favorite brand of cigarettes. His shirt was a size too large and his shirttail fluttered like a flag in the slightest breeze. Gene was slender and tall for his age and his long legs were thin, with sharp, bony knees. His jeans were tight with swollen pockets in which he carried everything from a cigarette lighter to a Swiss Army knife.

Once Gene had brought to Healing Waters Elementary School, in his distended pants pocket, a live, good-sized bullfrog freshly scooped out of the New River. Gene had christened the frog Ferdinand after a bull he had read about in a children's story book. He placed the large green amphibian on the floor beside his school desk and it bounded away, seeking freedom. Our teacher screamed and climbed up onto her chair as the creature hopped under her desk. Reversing his direction, Ferdinand bounced down a row of shrieking girls and laughing boys. Ruthie abandoned her desk and ran out the door, headed toward the principal's office. The bullfrog caused quite a classroom sensation until the principal came in and corralled the slippery amphibian.

"Don't hurt Ferdinand, Mr. Church," Gene hollered. "In the short time I've knowed that frog, we have growed to be good buddies."

Mr. Church put the frog in a big pasteboard box with a large bowl of water. The frog had tried, but he couldn't jump out of the container. After school, Mr. Church had returned the creature to his watery New River home.

On our march upward toward the carnival, Gene wore black, scuffed cowboy boots and carried a black cowboy hat, two sizes too large. He shifted the hat rhythmically from one hand to the other as he sauntered along. Now and then he placed the cowboy hat on his head and squinted, hoping some teenage girl would notice his rugged good looks. To the best of my knowledge, no teenage girl ever did. The son of a Baptist preacher, Gene had been, hands-down, the meanest kid at Healing Waters Elementary School, although his older brother Jack had given him a run for his money until Jack left elementary school and moved up to Central Ashe

High School. Jack had been held back in school many times, so he was several years older than his classmates. Jack used to brag that he had learned twice as much as most kids in school because it frequently had taken him two years to finish a grade.

Jack Lionel Clodfelter was currently a nineteen-year-old sophomore at the high school and had calmed down considerably since he met and started dating Edith Jane Culpepper, the daughter of one of the more prosperous men in Jefferson, a town just a few miles east of West Jefferson. Of course, Edith Jane's parents (he was a lawyer; she was a teacher) didn't think Jack was good enough for their daughter; therefore, the budding romance was forbidden.

Edith Jane and Jack had solved that problem by sneaking out on dates. The Culpepper parents had caught their daughter with Jack several times, resulting in more than a few big fusses. Eventually, after a long, weary struggle in which middle-aged concern and parental authority battled teenage desire and adolescent angst, the Culpepper parents just gave up and let Edith Jane and Jack date one another in public. Jack and Edith Jane got engaged after two months of public dating, but broke up a few weeks before their wedding date.

The reason for the canceled nuptials was that Jack had been cheating on Edith Jane with her precocious younger sister, Shirley Lou Culpepper. The flapping tongues of county gossips had gone into gleeful high gear in passing along the story of the triangular Culpepper-Clodfelter-Culpepper romance.

Gene had said, "If Jack married Edith Jane, her married name woulda been Edith Jane Culpepper Clodfelter. It's a right purty soundin' name, but that ain't no reason to get married, 'specially when a good-lookin' sister of the future bride gets involved. My brother just couldn't resist that bad little Shirley Lou Culpepper. I don't blame him none, for she's awful purty. Jack ain't seein' neither one of them Culpepper gals now. He's glad to be shed of 'em. Besides, Jack ain't ready to get married; he ain't sensible nor mature like me."

A wide, dusty, rock-strewn path led Pudge, Tank, Gene and me forward and upward through green pasture land on either side. We plodded along like movie zombies with lifeless eyes. I lifted my head and cupped my ear. I could distinctly hear the music of the carnival carousel, as we drifted along the meandering trail. The melody encouraged the four of us and we picked up our pace. Up ahead, I saw the long shadows of tombstones as the sun nestled lower on the mountain tops.

There was a large fenced-in graveyard on the left side of the path surrounded by pastureland. Within the protective white fence, elaborate, modest, and old, worn-out gravestones encircled a single mausoleum in which the dusty bones of an influential and wealthy lawyer rested. I can't remember the lawyer's name, but my grandpa, Charlie Franklin, could tell you about him and how he helped bring the railroad to the county, and more specifically to the town of West Jefferson. With the railroad came jobs, trade, and money. The town of West Jefferson grew larger and more prosperous than its neighboring towns and villages. The influential lawyer—I wish I could remember his name—became a rich man, wealthy enough to be laid to rest in a mausoleum.

Sometimes, Tank, Pudge, Gene and I, when we were a few years younger and were feeling brave on a Halloween night, would climb up and across the graveyard fence and try to peek into the lawyer's tomb through a tiny window on the heavy sealed door. In the moonlight, shadowy figures appeared to move behind the thick glass. Invariably, someone would make a noise or hear a strange sound, and we Halloween trick-or-treaters, infected by contagious terror, would hastily scramble back over the wooden fence and run away at top speed, fearful that we were being pursued by the lawyer's remains, followed by other long-buried ghouls hungry for human brains and flesh.

The wooden white fence around the cemetery was sturdy enough to keep cattle and horses from pushing through and walking on the graves. Only last week, before the carnival workers had come to set up the rides, tents, and booths, white faced, rusty red cattle and a few work horses had grazed lazily beside our path and drunk cool water from the rocky stream far below. The cattle and horses were gone today, transferred to another fenced pasture until the carnival left town.

Now and then, we and our fellow carnival goers encountered cow manure as we ascended the trail. The circular bovine droppings were carefully avoided because some of the manure was relatively fresh. Cow piles were sometimes called cow pies, cow patties, or meadow muffins by farmers who raised cattle in our county. Stepping in a fresh cow pie could be a major, stink-filled calamity. Stepping in some horse biscuits, even fresh ones, was much less catastrophic.

Through trial and error, Gene and I had discovered that a dry, rounded horse turd could be kicked along a gravel road several times and for quite some distance before it disintegrated into desiccated particles of equine excrement. Back when we were sixth-graders, Gene had invented a game that was much like kickball using horse biscuits. When we got a little older, he invented a game involving horse turds and fence rails that was much like soccer. I got to be pretty good at the soccer-type game, but I learned quickly not to wear my Sunday-go-to-meeting shoes when I visited Gene at his house.

"You're a natural born manure kicker, Hal," Gene had declared after a hotly contested game. "I ain't never seen nobody that can kick a horse turd as far and as straight as you can!"

I had felt a sense of pride at the time, but not so much nowadays.

CHAPTER 6

The folks descending the trail and leaving the carnival grounds seemed tired, but happy and cheerful. Fathers and mothers carried sleepy children who rested their chins on their parents' shoulders. The youngsters had spent the afternoon riding kiddie rides, tasting treats, and playing games. Greetings passed back-and-forth between those descending the hill and those climbing upward toward the carnival. Apparently, the yearly festival was having a successful opening day. The carnival gates had opened at three o'clock and would not close until midnight if they kept the same schedule as last summer.

Tank, Pudge, Gene, and I knew that at the top of the hill the land would flatten out. The hilltop was flat enough to provide space for a baseball field and two smaller softball fields. The bases, backstops, and fences had been removed temporarily, providing ample space for the carnival's tents, rides and concession stands. The concession stands were filled with hot dogs, hamburgers, sugary treats, and soft drinks. I could hardly wait to sample the funnel cakes and cotton candy.

An exuberant crowd surrounded us and swept us upward. The adults chatted, laughed, and greeted old friends with handshakes and hugs. Small children tugged at their parents' arms and sleeves, trying to speed up the adults. Several teenage couples were walking up the steep path hand-in-hand. Younger teens and older teens without dates skittered around in groups of three or four.

Tank's formidable size—he was not quite obese but several laps beyond corpulent—caused people to step aside and give him room. Pudge, Gene, and I followed in his wake.

The July twilight marked the beginning of the end of a hot, muggy day in the North Carolina mountains as a soft high-country breeze did little to provide relief from the heat.

"I'm glad we don't live in Charlotte," panted Tank. "The weatherman on the radio said the temperature down there would reach one hundred degrees tomorrow." Perspiration dotted his forehead as the Tank wiped his brow with a white handkerchief for the second or third time.

"Hot weather don't bother me none," said Gene, "'til the temperature gets up around eighty-five degrees. Then it bothers the dickens outta me."

"Whew! I wouldn't want to take all that Piedmont heat and climb a hill like this," said Tank, folding his dampened handkerchief and putting it back into his pocket. "This weather feels like a heat wave to me."

"Well, at least it's not raining, and hasn't for days," said Pudge. An expansive smile repositioned his abundant freckles. "I think the weather is getting back to normal. Usually our summers here in the mountains are great with not too much or too little rain. We can pull out our short sleeve shirts in May and not put them back up until mid-October when the leaves begin to color. I wouldn't want to live anywhere else."

Three teenage heads nodded in agreement.

Tank, Pudge, Gene, and I were old enough to appreciate the typically mild temperatures of spring, summer, and fall in North Carolina's Appalachian Mountains. The winters, however, could be harsh and cold with deep snows, howling winds, and solidly frozen creeks and rivers; but wintertime also provided snow days with no school, good sledding, and slowly melting snowdrifts offering plenty of ammunition for snowball fights. In the icy cold of January and February, rhododendron leaves clenched like arthritic green fingers partially gloved by white snowflakes left behind by the most recent snowstorm. Occasionally on windless days, soft snow spiraled straight down in great, fluffy flakes. These cottony snowflakes settled on the leafless trees, covering the bare limbs and trunks with delicate silvered garments. The towns, farms, and woodlands snuggled comfortably under a silver and white blanket. Chimneys from cabins and farmhouses puffed gray smoke skyward. If the soft snowfalls were deep and then followed by strong winds, simple objects, like mailboxes, wheelbarrows, and fence posts took on unusual shapes—sometimes comical, sometimes eerie.

Tall evergreen trees, mostly hemlocks and white pines, were appreciated for their green color during the cold winter months because the other leafless winter trees turned to a dismal, tombstone gray. In early winter, the fallen leaves from deciduous trees lost their color and became dull, brown, and dry. The early winter wind gusts whirled the crisp leaves around in crazy, zigzagging flight patterns. After a few cold rains or significant snows, coupled with below freezing temperatures, the leaves blackened and clung to the frosted ground, challenging even in the strongest winds to loosen their clammy grip on the frozen earth.

If the winter weather conditions were just right, the crests of the mountains frosted over and looked like giant hoary cupcakes topped with fresh white icing. Bright sunlight caused the frosty mountain summits to shimmer and sparkle. Below the frost line, the landscape, except for a sprinkling of evergreens, maintained its somber gray color, refreshed from time to time by the bright whiteness left by snowstorms.

Winter birds added some bright colors to the drab wintertime scenery, for red-crested woodpeckers, noisy blue jays, and bright scarlet cardinals stayed in the North Carolina mountains during the cold months.

Sometimes in the coldest of southern Appalachian winters, after a hard freeze with below zero temperatures and prolonged temperatures that hovered in the lower teens, the ice covering the New River would become substantial and solid enough to allow foot traffic. I didn't know anybody who owned ice skates, but kids skated on that thickly frozen New River with their slick-bottomed leather shoes and boots. I had done so myself, several times.

CHAPTER 7

Below freezing temperatures and deep February snows seemed so far away on this hot, increasingly muggy July evening. I hoped the rising humidity didn't signal the chance for more rain. A carnival in the rain is no fun at all.

My companions and I were sweating more profusely with each step up the trail. Today's high temperature of ninety-two degrees was unusually warm, even for the month of July in our high country. Ashe County citizens rarely experienced temperatures above eighty-five degrees, even in July.

The whole county was in the midst of a rare mountain heat wave and the still air was sticky and stifling. Insects buzzed and hummed in the oppressive air. In contrast, I remembered that during last year's carnival, the nights had been so cool that most folks wore jackets and sweaters in mid-July. This year, carnival goers were sweltering although it was almost sundown.

The sinking orange sun created long cartoonish shadows as Gene, Tank, Pudge, and I climbed the path. Gene's shadow resembled a great blue heron stalking fish from the sandy banks of the New River. Pudge and I had relatively normal silhouettes with the exception of having extremely long legs, but Tank's shadow resembled an elongated beach ball sporting a flattop haircut.

Gene slapped at the back of his neck. "Damn mosquito!" he said, whacking his neck again. "Got the little son of a bitch!"

Gene regarded the tiny broken gray body and a miniscule crimson droplet in his palm briefly, and then wiped his skinny hand on his jeans. He resumed the climb upward, and in fact took the lead. Outpacing the rest of us for the moment, Gene's long legs carried him effortlessly forward. I saw Gene smack his neck again and heard a muffled curse. I slapped my forearm and flicked a deceased mosquito away. I slapped again and again sending more mosquitoes to meet their maker. Tank, because of his corpulence, had more exposed skin than any of us, but the big guy was capable of ignoring the thirsty insects. For some unfathomable reason, the bloodsucking parasites avoided Tank while attacking Gene, Pudge, and me.

"Bloody little vampires!" said Pudge. Using both hands, he slapped the air near his head as the mosquitoes whined and buzzed around his ears. Usually mosquitoes, because of our freezing winters, were no problem in our North Carolina mountains, but a mild winter, coupled with a wet spring, and a warm, sticky summer had increased the mosquito population tremendously.

We continued our ascent with long-legged Gene still leading the way. We found the air becoming fresher and crisper as we moved higher up the trail. The number of mosquitoes decreased markedly as we reached a slightly higher elevation. We stopped for just a moment for Tank to remove a pebble from his tennis shoe. He placed a beefy hand on my shoulder, using me to steady his balance, then the big boy removed his tennis shoe and shook out the tiny offending stone.

"Ah, that's much better," sighed Tank staring down at his tennis shoe clad foot. "It's funny how a little irritation can bother you so much."

"Are you talking about the pebble or about Gene?" I asked, rolling my eyes toward Gene. Gene stopped in mid-stride and froze for a second with his boot in midair. He clamped his oversized, Hopalong Cassidy cowboy hat fiercely onto his head and then whirled like a gunfighter to face me. Gene's beady eyes gleamed under the hat brim, but I could tell that he wasn't really angry. He was itching for a battle of wits, a form of verbal fisticuffs.

Gene scowled at me in mock animosity. He pulled his black cowboy hat down until the hat almost covered his eyes. Then he made a fist, shook it vigorously, and gave me the finger. His middle finger, rising above the others, was long and slender, and at the end of the digit, I saw greasy dirt under the scruffy, un-manicured fingernail.

"Take that, you mangy, curly-headed polecat!" bawled Gene, holding his offensive finger high.

"I see that you know the state bird of Tennessee, Gene," said Pudge.

"Huh?" grunted Gene, turning toward Pudge.

"Your 'bird' reminds me of the 'dirty bird' you carved on your desk in sixth grade and the cartoony birdie you scrawled on Mrs. Bender's chalkboard when her back was turned," said Tank, observing the skinny guy's upraised digit.

"Mrs. Bender never did catch me drawin' that nasty bird," boasted Gene. "Yep, I drawed the dirty bird on the blackboard when her back was turned, or when she was out of the room. I was purty slick, and I knowed nobody wouldn't tell on me, not in our class. I outsmarted that ole bag many a time."

"Sometimes your educational achievements astonish me," said Pudge. "The intellectual progress you've made since we first met in primary school is truly breathtaking. From your crude drawings on several school desks, I gathered you had an artistic flair; but it amazes me that using only your raised hand with an extended finger, you have created an amazing replica of the Volunteer State's favorite bird."

"What do you mean the favorite bird of Tennessee?" demanded Gene. He whirled toward Pudge, assumed the sword-fighting posture of the Mexican hero, Zorro, and swiftly gave the redhead the finger with his left hand. Gene continued to give me the finger using his right hand. In the act of obscene gesturing, Gene was ambidextrous.

Silhouetted by the sunset's soft, rosy sky, Gene, with his hands raised and with his dark cowboy hat resting atop his head, had the stance and profile of Doc Holliday, wielding his two six shooters before the classic gunfight at the OK Corral. There, the gambling, gun-fighting dentist had taken out one of the Clanton brothers as Doc fought beside the legendary Earp brothers. Like the lightning-quick gunslinger, Holliday, Gene was fast on the draw when giving someone the one-finger salute.

A scowling middle-aged man walked by in a light gray summer-weight suit. The man glowered at Gene's upraised hands. The gentleman hurried his wife and his two teenage daughters forward, pushing them gently ahead of him and up the trail toward the carnival. As the man passed close by the skinny cowboy, he gritted his teeth and glared at Gene one more time. Gene lowered his hands and crossed his arms defensively over his scrawny chest. Two "Tennessee birds" took flight and disappeared.

The skinny guy raised one eyebrow and stared at Pudge.

"I asked you about the Tennessee bird, Pudge," said Gene, "and I expect answers, clear answers. No bullcrap nor foul language, please. As you know, I can't abide rudeness nor foolishness of any kind."

"Okay, I'll tell you. My dad and I rode over to Mountain City, Tennessee, last week in the old family Ford," Pudge stated, "and we saw the hand signal that Dad called the 'Tennessee bird' rather often. The signs we saw were exactly the same as the signs you threw on me and Hal."

"Go on," said Gene.

"The reason the Tennessee bird was flipped so often could've been my dad's driving. You see Dad had been drinking, and he always drives real slow when he drinks, especially if I'm in the car. The clutch was giving him trouble, making the Ford lurch forward from time to time, especially when the stoplights turned green. The car's signal lights weren't working and the horn started blaring every time Dad tapped the brake. This infuriated more than a few of the Mountain City drivers and pedestrians, several of whom flipped us the bird. One old, gray-haired lady, pushing a baby carriage on the sidewalk gave us the finger, and like you, she used both hands."

"Sounds like your Ford's wires got crossed up real bad somehow; I am a Chev-uh-lay man myself. Gen'ral Motors makes the best cars. You can't beat a Chevy," said Gene. "Still, the Mountain City folks was rude to your daddy and you, and as you fellers know, I can't abide ill-mannered folks of any kind."

Tank and I laughed out loud at Gene's outlandish statement. The slender guy lifted one of his eyebrows and narrowed his eyes, assuming an expression of patronizing superiority. As he stared at us, a condescending smile stretched his thin lips.

"Go on, Pudge," said Gene. "Tank and Hal don't know how to engage theirselves in a serious, well-mannered conversation. If they don't shut up right now, I'm considerin' slappin' the hell out of both of 'em! Don't you scowl at me like a that, Hal Grayson; I'll mash your mouth!"

Pudge continued, "Anyway, while we drove at a snail's pace through Mountain City, I learned that Tennesseans are very proud of their Tennessee bird and often place the gesture on display with one hand, while honking their horns with the other. The Tennessee drivers were impolite to me and my dad. Then again, I guess they had their reasons. But you're right, Gene. Something is seriously wrong with the electrical system in our old Ford, not to mention the clutch. This morning Dad took the car to the Ford place to be worked on. Dad hopes the car will be fixed in a couple of days, and he can drive it. Now, while the car is in the shop, he will have to catch a ride to work with Emory Phipps, one of the barbers at the Country Clipper Barbershop."

"Maybe it wasn't your dad's drivin'," laughed Gene. "Could it be that those Tennesseans just recognized you, Pudge? Your reputation as a doofus has prob'ly spread throughout Tennessee and other states surroundin' North Carolina."

"Perhaps the signs those Tennesseans threw at you were just estimates of your IQ level, Pudge," ventured Tank, grinning. Pudge laughed along with the big guy.

"Pudge, I can't allow you to put down the great state of Tennessee," I added sternly. "My great-grand pappy on the Grayson side was born in the Volunteer State. The University of Tennessee is a prestigious university in the city of Knoxville. The state of Tennessee is full of good colleges and universities. I might apply to one someday. Ryman Auditorium in Nashville is the undisputed home of country music. Grandpa Charlie listens to Nashville's broadcast of the Grand Ole Opry on the radio every chance he gets. And don't forget the famous train called the Chattanooga Choo Choo and Miss Patti Page's version of 'The Tennessee Waltz.'"

"Patti Page sings like a heavenly angel. That woman has the purtiest and smoothest voice on the radio," said Gene, interrupting my minor tirade in support of Tennesseans, "next to Tennessee Ernie Ford, that is. I like it when Tennessee Ernie sings 'Sixteen Tons.' His deep voice is just right for that coal minin' song."

Ignoring Gene's interruption, I continued to lecture Pudge. "Also, I read that Elvis Presley, the King of rock 'n roll, loves the city of Memphis, so don't spend your time criticizing Tennessee or Tennesseans. I have kinfolk, mostly aunts, uncles, and cousins in Tennessee, and mostly living in Mountain City. If you continue to degrade Tennessee, Pudge, I will tear a branch off that little tree over there, and frail the hell out of you!"

"Oh boy! Looks like we're liable to have a dog fight!" snorted Gene. "I'm placin' my bets on the redheaded Chihuahua." He pointed at Pudge who ignored him and addressed me.

"Get off your soapbox, Hal," declared Pudge. "I'm not putting down Tennessee; I'm just telling you what happened to me and my dad over in Mountain City. I have relatives there, too. And

I like Elvis, rock 'n roll, and country music just as much as you do—maybe more. Besides, it was Grandpa Charlie who first told me that the raised fist with the extended middle finger was the 'Tennessee bird.' You ask your grandpa if you don't believe me. You'll find out you're not so smart, after all."

"Oh, ole Curly ain't too smart; that's something we can all agree on," laughed Gene. Turning to me, he said, "Hal, I'll bet you a dollar that you don't even know what North Carolina's state bird is. Most educated folks, like me and my kin, consider you a complete ignoramus. If ignorance was catchin', you'd have to be quarantined. Come on, birdbrain, what's our state's official bird?"

"I wouldn't want to take your money, pal. You'll need it for the carnival," I replied confidently. "Everybody knows that our state bird is the..."

"Yellow-bellied sapsucker. I think it's the yellow-bellied sapsucker," Tank interjected hastily. "And for just a moment, may I discuss this colorful North Carolina woodpecker, and in doing so, may I liken the distinctive yellow-bellied sapsucker to our buddy Gene?"

"What? You ain't tryin' to insult me, are you, Tankus Giganticus?" asked Gene truculently. "I don't never deal in insults, and I can't tolerate folks who do."

"By all means, Tank, go right ahead and make your comparisons," I said. I enjoyed watching Tank needle Gene. "Give Gene his comeuppance. He certainly likes to dish it out, but can he take it?"

Pudge nodded his assent as Tank pointed his index finger at Gene. While Tank spoke, Gene grimaced, bearing his tobacco stained teeth. He spat on the ground and rubbed the toe of his boot in the spittle.

"The yellow-bellied sapsucker looks amazingly like a small version of our friend Gene," Tank explained. "Take a close look at Gene, guys. Imagine him covered with feathers. Visualize red and yellow feathers and a beak between his eyes. Picture him sitting in a large bird's nest with peeping hatchlings surrounding him."

With his eyes closed, Pudge said, "In my mind's eye, I can see Gene with feathers. I see him perched in a tree beside a huge nest filled with wide-mouthed baby birds. Gene's feeding one of the chicks a woolly worm. Great Caesar's ghost! You're right, Tank. He's the spitting image of a yellow-bellied sapsucker."

"Dammit, Pudge!" said Gene raising a clenched fist. "You keep talkin' like that, and I'll warp your frame!"

"Of course," said Tank, "our pal is much larger and far less attractive than the small woodland woodpecker; however, Gene's general shape and nature mirror the sapsucker's characteristics almost exactly."

"You're treadin' on mighty thin ice, Tank," said Gene. His eyelids constricted. "Are you still hungry? How about a knuckle samwich or would you like a fist burger instead?"

Undaunted, Tank persisted, "Look now at Gene's shadow on the ground. Is that not the shadow of a bird? More than that, Gene's shadow matches perfectly the shadow of the yellow-bellied sapsucker."

"My shadder don't look nothin' like no bird's shadder!" Gene screeched.

"The woodpecker differs from Gene in only two minor respects," Tank continued. "First, the sapsucker has beautiful plumage and second, the creature is widely known as one of the most intelligent of North Carolina birds."

"I think Gene is smarter than the average yellow-bellied sapsucker," I said. "Of course, I could be wrong. If only there were an IQ test for birds, then we could know for sure."

"Are you fellers comparin' my vast and mostly untapped brainpower with that of a lousy bird, a woodpecker that bangs his head up against dead tree trunks all day long?" asked Gene.

"Certainly not, Eugene, Hal and I would never offend one of our avian friends," said the Tank casually. "But here is the true comparison: Because the sapsucker can severely damage trees here in our mountains, the feathered creature is often considered a pest. Can you imagine this colorful woodpecker, which you resemble in so many ways, being considered a pest?"

"Tank, are you indirectly calling my friend Gene a pest?" Pudge asked. Tank smiled and nodded. "If so," Pudge continued, "I feel I should defend my long-time buddy. The truth is that Gene can be an annoyance, a nuisance, an irritant, a bother, a troublemaker, a scalawag, a horse's hind end, a jerk, and an all-around king-sized pain in the rear, but my old friend Gene is certainly not a pest. How dare you even suggest that he is?"

Tank shrugged his shoulders, pointed at Gene, and rested his case.

"Thanks, Pudge, for defendin' me," said Gene. "You're a real buddy, you are, and you too, Tank."

"I remembered to say horse's hind end, didn't I?" asked Pudge.

"Yep, you didn't forget, and I ain't gonna forget neither," Gene said darkly, as he adjusted his hat. "Maybe I can figger a way to pay you back for your good words and kind-heartedness, good buddy. I'll be studyin' on my payback, while we walk on up the hill."

Gene rolled his eyes back in his head until they turned a frightful white. His wide jaws opened, presenting his discolored teeth. Then he emitted a bone-chilling, bloodcurdling laugh. Tiny hairs along the nape of my neck raised and straightened themselves. Few men, outside of those wearing straitjackets in padded cells deep inside the bowels of institutions devoted to the care of the criminally insane, could've produced such crazed laughter. I had heard the same sustained, demented laugh several times before, but only in horror movies.

Pudge, unconcerned, said, "Come on, Sapsucker, give me some credit for not mentioning dipstick, dork, shmuck, windbag, stumblebum, and rat fink."

"Cut it out guys. Let me clear one thing up. Our state bird is *not* the yellow-bellied sapsucker," I said. "As you know, Tank, our North Carolina state bird is the northern cardinal, but for insisting that our state bird is the yellow-bellied sapsucker, look closely at my right hand and you will see the Tennessee bird materialize before your very eyes. Take that, Tankus Giganticus!"

I threw the sign on him, and Gene joined me, but the Tank only smiled good-naturedly and said, "I know that the state bird of Tennessee is the mockingbird. I memorized almost all the state birds when we were in Mrs. Bender's class. I bet you guys remember the sixth-grade reports we gave on North Carolina bird species. After she read my report on the Carolina wren, Mrs. Bender said I might become an ornithologist someday."

"Ole Bender told me I might become a convict someday," chuckled Gene. "She sure did! When we were sixth-graders, she was convinced I'd become a prisoner, a jailbird!"

"She may be right, Gene; only time will tell," Pudge said solemnly. "Frankly, I trust Mrs. Bender's judgment."

At that point, a small flock of crows landed in a tall tree beside the trail. The dark fowls began cawing raucously and flitting from branch to branch. Gene picked up a rock and hurled it into the noisy tree. The crows scattered like ebony leaves seized by a powerful updraft. Flapping away into the deepening twilight, the dusky feathered creatures squawked angrily as they disappeared into the orange sunset.

"Crows ain't nothin' but rats with feathers. I can't abide a corn-eatin' crow," said Gene.

"Come on, guys, let's get on up this hill to the carnival," I said impatiently. "I've heard enough about birds and seen enough of Gene flipping the bird. Let's forget about Tennessee birds, yellow-bellied sapsuckers, northern cardinals, jailbirds, and crows. Let's go, I hear the carnival calling my name."

"Onward and upward!" yelled the Tank.

CHAPTER 8

We were now close enough to the carnival grounds to hear and distinguish some of the songs that were playing through the loudspeakers at the various concession stands, rides, and booths. One amplifier, louder than the others, blared out Bobby Day's version of "Rockin' Robin." According to the song, the robin was the best bopper in the avian kingdom.

Suddenly, Gene removed his dark cowboy hat slapped his skinny thigh, and started bopping around, bobbing his head, flapping his sharp elbows, and loudly mouthing the words to the hit song about birds dancing in the treetops. Gene's voice indicated that he was painfully tone deaf, but he could dance. Tank jumped in, and lowering his voice to a resonating bass level, sang along with Gene and Bobby Day.

Pudge and I joined Tank and Gene in the reverie as we frolicked among the more restrained and sedate carnival goers. We dodged, danced, and cavorted. Pudge had briefly stopped singing because he was laughing so hard at Gene's improvised dance steps, which resembled the jitterbug or the boogie-woogie. I was moving forward while dancing to my version of "The Twist" with Hank Ballard's music playing inside my head. Suddenly, Tank burst into the "Rockin' Robin" song again and began doing his adaptation of the dance called the Bop. Dust flew up around his tennis shoes.

His movements were easy, quick, and nimble; the big guy was light on his feet.

Pudge started clogging, country style, and when he did, a female teenage dancer dressed in light blue short shorts displaying long, tanned legs, a broad white belt emphasizing her narrow waist, and a pink, sleeveless blouse exposing her tan shoulders and slender arms, joined our entourage. Her white tennis shoes cast a silvery glow in the twilight. The girl was Ruthie, one of the two girls I had hoped to see at the carnival.

"Gentlemen, may I have this dance?"

Ruth Caroline Cornett was the most athletic, funniest, prettiest, and smartest girl in our class. My opinion might have been biased, because she had been my major crush in both sixth and seventh grades. I learned on this carnival night that she was also a versatile dancer.

Ruthie clogged with Pudge, twisted with me, and bopped with the Tank. She threw her head back, tossing her chestnut-colored hair, and laughed with the pure joy of being young and dazzlingly alive. Then Ruthie joined in with Gene and his more intricate dance steps. Gene swiveled his knees and hips to the rock 'n roll backbeat playing inside and outside his head. Gene was, in fact, a pretty good dancer. Ruthie followed his moves perfectly; she didn't miss a beat. Gene was her Fred Astaire—she was his Ginger Rogers.

"Rockin Robin" was followed, oddly enough, on the loudest carnival loudspeaker by "Somewhere Over the Rainbow" from *The Wizard of Oz* movie. Drifting down Seagraves Hill, Judy Garland's voice was soft and lilting, with perfect pitch, but Gene would have none of it. He began his even louder version of "We're Off to See the Wizard" from the old 1939 movie. Instead of 'wizard,' he would occasionally substitute the word 'lizard' or 'gizzard.' Naturally, Ruthie, Pudge, Tank, and I joined in.

The four of us guys were improvising very different dance steps as we boogied forward and upward, but we sang in harmony, except for the tone-deaf Gene. Ruthie had picked up the simple lyrics of "We're Off to See the Wizard," probably after hearing the tune on television, and she sang along with us.

The adults in the carnival crowd smiled graciously and let our goofy dancing parade pass through. One stooped old codger lifted his cane high in the air and shook it enthusiastically. He shuffled his brogan-clad feet and gave us a toothless grin. Several younger children began clapping their hands, made sticky by cotton candy and candied apples. Toddlers, carried by their parents, waived uncertainly and gave us curious, clueless smiles. A few high school teenagers sang along with us as we passed.

Pudge, Tank, Ruthie, Gene, and I began capering and gamboling around in the crowd like the Cowardly Lion, the Tin Man, Dorothy, the pup Toto, and the Scarecrow. Of course, Ruthie was our Dorothy; however, the other parts would have been difficult to assign.

Longing for the experiences that the carnival might provide, the prizes we might win, the adventures we might share on this midsummer night, we accompanied our pretty ingénue upward along our gritty, dusty, twilight trail.

"Watch out for that big ole cow pie and that pile of horse turds, Ruthie," warned Gene. "The cow pile looks awful fresh."

Ruthie pirouetted gracefully around the manure in the path.

"Thanks for the warning, sweetie. You are my very own guardian angel, Gene. I feel so safe when you're around," giggled Ruthie. She curtsied with her right foot behind her left foot and her hands holding her imaginary skirt out to her sides. Gene blushed and bowed from the waist.

"My dear, I am considered one of the few Southern gentlemen still livin' in these here mountains," bragged Gene, tipping his cowboy hat. Ruthie reached up and patted his cheek. "Ruthie, I shall safely ekscort you up this here hill. Don't you worry about nothin'."

"Oh Gene, you're so dashing, brave, and downright cute! My sister Cleta says you're 'ruggedly handsome' and I agree," Ruthie gushed. "I do believe you are the tallest boy in our class. You're almost as tall as Ernest Potter, and he's a junior at Central Ashe."

Having Ruthie's complete attention energized Gene. The skinny guy began cavorting and barking in high-pitched yaps like a little dog. Leaping up and down, he circled our teenage troupe moving in a counterclockwise direction. Suddenly, he changed directions and scampered around us going the other way. He woofed, yowled, and yelped. For a minute, I thought Gene was going to get down on all fours, growl ferociously, and nip anyone he perceived to be a relative of the Wicked Witch of the West.

Tank proffered his powerful arm and Ruthie took it at the elbow. Then she grabbed Pudge's elbow and standing between them, allowed the big boy and the redhead to escort her onward and upward. I trailed behind them, as did Gene.

"We're off to see the carnival! The wonderful Stephens Brothers Carnival!" exclaimed Ruthie. While Tank and Pudge shuffled along, Ruthie's dance steps replicated Judy Garland's skipping footwork in the movie.

In an infrequent flash of teenage insight, I realized that we five teenagers were climbing, on this sultry evening, our very own, very steep yellow brick road. But our road was made of dusty gravel, scattered sawdust, and gritty dirt. The darkening pasture path was flecked with cow patties and horse manure on either side. The magical ruby slippers were replaced with Ruthie's clean white sneakers. Wind-shaped trees cast creepy shadows on the yellow dust of our rocky trail. The carnival's illuminations that beckoned us upward were no less enticing than the lights of a glowing Emerald City.

I knew we would soon see, crowding around the merry-go-round, laughing children no taller than munchkins. Also, I was sure the carnival's Tilt-A-Whirl would spin its riders around like a Kansas tornado. And last year, the carnival had a small zoo in which were caged separately an ancient lion, a scrawny, flea-bitten tiger, and a bulky, muzzled black bear that danced and did tricks. A lion, a tiger, and a trained bear. Oh my! I wondered if we would meet anybody tonight, male or female, as despicable as the Wicked Witch of the West or as wise as the great Wizard who lived in the green, glowing city called Emerald City.

Looking around, I smiled as I reminded myself that this wasn't the wonderful country of Oz; this was the mountain county of Ashe; this was the quiet little town of West Jefferson, North Carolina; this was the small, tawdry Stephens Brothers Carnival; this was our slice of the real world. Only yesterday Gene had reminded me and the guys, "Nothin' never happens around here, leastways nothin' important, nothin' excitin'. And nothin' don't never seem to change. It's damn borin', if you ask me."

Just as Gene's words were echoing in my mind, we saw at a distance one of the town policemen descending the path that led up to the carnival. Moving down the trail, the tall lawman eventually emerged from the thin exiting crowd, a sparse crowd when compared to the vast migration headed upward. He was dressed in a khaki uniform with a gun belt supporting a holstered pistol. He was as slender and gangly as Ichabod Crane.

When the police officer came closer and into clear view, I could see his face more distinctly. I was mistaken. The officer wasn't one of the town policemen. The lawman was a county deputy, Deputy Luke Shumaker, second-in-command to Sheriff Brownlow Bailey. The officer said nothing, but stopped his descent and looked at us teenagers curiously.

We probably shouldn't have, but we continued our boogying and bopping. All of us were reasonably subdued, except for Gene who was hopping around as if he were on an electrified pogo stick. Luke Shumaker squinted his eyes and raised his hand to scratch his chin. When the deputy frowned darkly, our dancing and singing ceased.

Ruthie adjusted her short shorts which had ridden up a bit during her dancing and were displaying a little more thigh than she thought appropriate. Still frowning, the deputy stared at

Ruthie's long, tanned legs and grunted. Ruthie smiled sweetly at the deputy.

We paused and stood behind her as she spoke to the deputy. He replaced his glare with a grin as she stepped forward.

"Excuse me, officer," asked Ruthie, in her soft Southern drawl, "but have you seen my father? I've lost him in this crowd. He's wearing bib overalls, a mostly red plaid shirt, and a dark brown cowboy hat with a rattlesnake hatband. Dad walks with a cane. You might have passed him. He's walking up the hill to the carnival grounds."

"No, honey, I ain't seen nobody of that description on my way down," said the deputy. "I'm sure I woulda noticed a crippled-up, funny lookin' cowboy in a loud shirt. Maybe you and me should form a search party of two, sweetie. I bet we could find your daddy after a while, no need to rush. We could start lookin' over there behind them carnival trailers."

Ruthie lowered her eyes and shook her head. "No, thanks," she said. "I think I can find him without your help."

The deputy smirked and tipped his hat. "Just trying to be of service, honey. I didn't aim to suggest anythin' unseemly."

Ruthie took a few steps closer to the Tank. Her shoulders slumped. Her bright smile had disappeared, replaced with a glum frown.

"That singing and dancing was fun, guys, but I can't stay with you much longer. I gotta find my dad and my sisters," sighed Ruthie, smoothing her hair and glancing fearfully at the deputy who had stopped walking down the hill toward town and stood only ten feet away from us with his hands on his hips.

Coming up the hill, another deputy arrived, and he and Luke Shumaker began an animated whispered conversation. I heard the name "Zeke Sheets" mentioned, but I couldn't understand anything else. The new lawman pointed toward the carnival on top of the hill and then gestured down toward the town of West Jefferson. The younger officer handed Deputy Shumaker two sheets of blue paper which the deputy perused then folded and stuck in his trouser pocket. The whispering commenced again and continued until both men laughed heartily. Then the new deputy turned and continued his journey up the hill.

With the proximity of law enforcement, Pudge, Tank, Gene and I had assumed the comportment of law-abiding, upstanding, respectable teenagers. Gene removed his cowboy hat and slicked back his thin oily hair. Our postures improved; our facial expressions exuded innocence and virtue; our eyes oozed goodness and teenage incorruptibility. The four of us would've been readily welcomed into TV's Nelson family as friends of David and Ricky; similarly, Ward and June Cleaver would've been overjoyed to let Wally and the Beaver hang out with us.

I fully expected the deputy sheriff to pass us by and, perhaps, give us a salute or at least a nod of appreciation and approval, but the deputy had begun a conversation with a smiling man in a gray seersucker suit. Now and then the deputy grinned and glanced in our direction. Then he pointed at Ruthie and both he and the seersucker man smirked.

Suddenly Ruthie blurted out, "My dad's calling for me to catch up with him and my sisters. I can hear him. Bye!" Ruthie hurried away and disappeared into the ascending carnival crowd, followed by her flowing ponytail and her pert derrière.

"*Mmmmmm!* Boy, oh boy, oh boy! What a gal!" Gene exclaimed, staring at Ruthie as she evaporated into the ever-thickening, hill-climbing crowd. Tank, Pudge, and I needed no translation of Gene's feelings about Ruthie. We understood and agreed with his assessment of our pretty classmate.

For a minute, the four of us just stood there on the desolate, noisy path, hoping that we would see Ruthie again up on the carnival grounds. Her departure left us suddenly lost, sad, and forlorn. The teeming trail seemed empty without her. She had taken with her some of the dwindling sunlight.

"Bye, Ruthie," whispered Pudge. We stood silently beside the trail for a few more minutes. Tank leaned back, resting against the trunk of a giant oak tree. We were all glad we had seen Ruthie, even for a brief encounter, though I was still hoping that Sophia Bishop was somewhere in the carnival crowd.

After several moments, we all stepped back into the swelling, jovial crowd and renewed our upward trek toward the carnival lights and merry-go-round music. After a few steps, we met a teenage couple, rising seniors at Central Ashe High School, drifting slowly down the path as they left the carnival. Although the twosome didn't know me, I knew both of them since the teenaged boy played basketball for Central Ashe, and the girl, whose skintight jeans seemed to be spray painted on, was a Central Ashe cheerleader. Esmeralda Cook and Moe Bacon were leaving the carnival to attend to more pressing teenage business.

Blonde Esmeralda was as stunning to the male gender as Al Capp's comic strip creation, the statuesque and beautiful Stupefyin' Jones, a female who could literally freeze men in their tracks with her overwhelming good looks and red-hot sex appeal. Stupefyin' Jones appeared occasionally in Capp's *Li'l Abner*, a strip I read almost every day in the *Winston-Salem Journal*. Abner Yokum was a gullible hillbilly living in Dogpatch, USA. The country boy was surrounded by beautiful, curvaceous Dogpatch women and more than a few unusual characters, male and female, such as Daisy Mae Scragg, Moonbeam McSwine, Earthquake McGoon, Hairless Joe, Jubilation T. Cornpone, Lonesome Polecat, Evil-Eye Fleegle, and Appassionata Von Climax. Abner Yokum ended up marrying sweet, innocent, and persistent Daisy Mae. She had pursued Abner for years, and I think most of the comic strip's readers breathed a sigh of relief when they finally got married.

"I don't b-b-believe Esmeralda Cook was wearing a b-b-brassiere under her b-b-blue sweater," whispered the Tank breathlessly. He sounded like Bugs Bunny's pal, Porky Pig, the stuttering cartoon character whose girlfriend was the pleasantly plump Petunia. Tank's hands were trembling. His mouth hung open, and his eyes widened. The tips of his ears turned a bright red. His huge legs were pressed together at the knees as if he were in a hurry to take a leak.

As I turned to follow the hypnotic movements of the curvaceous Esmeralda while she descended the path with her longtime boyfriend, Moe Bacon, I noticed the couple's intimacy. I envied their relaxed closeness. Moe, the muscular, dark-haired senior boy, had his strong, slightly sunburned right arm wrapped snugly around his blonde girlfriend's slim waist with his hand cupped just under her full right breast. Esmeralda, in turn, had her left hand affectionately tucked into the left back pocket of her boyfriend's snug blue jeans. Esmeralda squeezed Moe's butt slowly but rhythmically as they descended the trail.

"Ain't young love a beautiful sight; ain't it grand; ain't it charmin'?" asked Gene, who had also stopped to watch Esmeralda Cook saunter seductively down the path. "That Moe Bacon is one lucky guy. I wish I could trade places with him tonight, or maybe forever."

"Someday, I'm gonna have a girlfriend like Esmeralda Cook," Pudge promised himself aloud as the attention-grabbing teenage couple disappeared into the downhill crowd.

"In your dreams," laughed the Tank. "Girls like Esmeralda Cook go for the muscular, athletic types like me and Moe Bacon."

Tank straightened his back and made a terrific effort to pull in his ballooning gut. He stood there posing like a bodybuilder, with his plump but muscular arms flexed, his massive fists clenched tightly just above his corpulent shoulders, and his heavy chest pushed out. His powerful but chubby biceps enlarged and trembled. His flexing had caused his T-shirt to rise five or six inches, revealing a wide expanse of portly belly. He sucked in his fleshy stomach as far as he could. The effort turned his face bright red.

Tank looked like a severely overweight Charles Atlas, a bodybuilder who advertised mostly in comic books. Broad-shouldered Charles Atlas, in an ad beneath his picture, claimed that he could take any teenage ninety-pound weakling and, by using his "dynamic tension" program, transform the teen into a hulking Hercules. There was an unsubstantiated rumor around Healing Waters Elementary School that Gene had ordered the

Atlas program through the mail. However, I never noticed any change in Gene's slim physique.

"Uungh, uungh," mumbled Tank, clamping his eyes shut and straining mightily. His thickset ribcage continued to expand. His midriff quivered. His belly button suddenly disappeared behind numerous tightening folds of quaking flesh. As a result of swelling his chest and tightening his mid-section, Tank's waist, receding within his voluminous trousers, looked considerably smaller than usual.

Had she been present, Esmeralda Cook might have been attracted to the overweight, flat-topped, red-faced, form-shifting Adonis who stood posing and flexing beside the trail; but, as they passed by on the broad path, several older teenage girls laughed derisively at the Tank. This prompted the big fellow to suck in his juddering gut even more.

At that point, Tank discovered that the immutable law of gravity would not be denied, for his jeans began to drop, revealing the upper portion of his expansive white Fruit of the Looms. The trousers fell almost a foot before the Tank could grab his capacious pants and adjust his denims back up around his normal bulging waistline.

"Uh, I'm considering a diet starting next week, possibly sooner," Tank confessed to Pudge. Pudge and Tank laughed as the big guy continued fiddling with his trousers and his belt. Tank was sweating, panting, and puffing.

A lukewarm breeze wandered down the trail, providing no relief from the high temperature.

The heat and humidity had caused Pudge's damp shirt to stick to his back. Pudge pulled the damp T-shirt away from his skin, leaving the tail of the moist T-shirt outside his jeans.

Turning away from our two friends, Gene and I stood on our tiptoes looking over the crowd and down the hill, hoping to get one last tantalizing glimpse of the undulating backside of Esmeralda Cook. It was no use. The alluring Esmeralda and her beau Moe had disappeared into the throng walking down Seagraves Hill.

CHAPTER 9

After the departure of Esmeralda Cook and Moe Bacon, Gene and I, stretching our necks for one last peek at Esmeralda, had whirled around quickly to proceed back up the hill, worried that Tank and Pudge were getting ahead of us. Actually, Tank and Pudge had paused momentarily and were waiting nearby. Tank was kneeling to examine his tennis shoes. Pudge was checking his wallet. I saw them out of the corner of my eye.

When I turned to continue my climb, I bumped into the chest of a man wearing a deputy sheriff's badge. His shiny metal badge was level with my nose at the moment of impact.

Whump!

The deputy staggered back a step or two and cursed. He grunted and dropped his right hand to his holster.

"Ouch! Dang it!" I cried out. "That smarts!"

I grabbed my stinging nose. I was afraid that the solid collision was going to cause my nose to bleed. There was no blood yet, but there was a sharp, stabbing pain. My eyes watered.

"I'm sorry; I didn't see you, officer!" I said, apologizing to Deputy Luke Shumaker as I rubbed my throbbing nose. Fortunately, no blood appeared on my hands. My nose was going to be all right, thank goodness.

The deputy grabbed my shoulders and shoved me hard. I reeled as my knees buckled. Unstable after the push, I lost my equilibrium and fell backward into Pudge, knocking him sideways into Gene who lost his balance and fell rearward toward the Tank. Pudge, Gene, and I were collapsing like dominoes until the Tank caught the three of us in his massive arms. In a second, thanks to the big guy, we were upright and had regained our steadfast footing.

The deputy looked at us sourly with his facial features constricting, especially the skin around his narrow eyes. The deputy said nothing but continued to eye us suspiciously. His feet were spread wide and his hands rested on his hips. His holstered revolver hung just a few inches from his right thumb, and he began tapping the weapon with his forefinger. The deputy continued staring at us and began shaking his head as we tried to pass by him.

The four of us looked longingly up the hill toward the carnival lights and took a few more steps forward, hoping that we could continue upward without dealing with the deputy; but we froze in our tracks when an authoritative voice bellowed orders from behind us.

"Hey you boys, hold it right there! I say halt! Halt, dammit! Don't make me unholster my weapon. Turn yourselves around right now! Come back here! Yeah, I mean you four scalawags."

Deputy Sheriff Luke Shumaker was pointing the long finger of the law right at us. We obeyed.

"That's better," he said. "You gents move over there. Get out of the way of the crowd so people can go on up to the carnival. Make it snappy! Move it! That's right, get off the path and stand over yonder next to them three big cow piles restin' there in the grass. Now, don't move no more! I need to have a word with you young bucks."

Following the deputy's orders, Tank, Pudge, Gene and I left the crowd, which continued hustling on up the wide pathway like a flowing river made of people. We stood in the green grass just beside the dusty path, facing the tall, lanky deputy who began waving his hands emphatically to punctuate his speech.

"I seen you young fellers at this carnival last year. Yep, just one year ago you all was ridin' all the rides, yellin' at one another, laughin' real loud, and screamin' your fool heads off. You was gallopin' around like wild ponies from one ride to another, and gen'rally makin' yourselves a nuisance, a bother, and mostly creatin' a pain in ever'body's ass, includin' mine. That was *last* year. Things is gonna be different *this* year, a whole lot different. Mark my words: your conduck is gonna change if you want to enjoy the carnival. Now, let's talk about this year at this here carnival."

"Yes, officer," said Pudge. His face whitened but his hands were steady.

"Just a few minutes ago, I seen you little pests dancin' and singin' and frolickin' around; and before the dancin', I seen you boys throwin' lewd gestures all around in the crowd like you owned the place."

"There ain't no law against havin' a little fun, Deputy Shumaker. We didn't mean no harm," said Gene amiably. Gene winked at the deputy, which was the wrong thing to do.

Luke Shumaker's face tightened even more, and he grabbed Gene by his scrawny shoulder. Gene winced in pain and twisted away, escaping the deputy's firm grasp.

"Listen, you boney little son of a bitch, I can smell the stink of trouble a mile away and you got the smell of trouble all over you, from head to toe."

The deputy wrinkled his nose as if he had just sniffed a foul broccoli or pinto-bean fart, and then he directed his attention to Tank, Pudge and me. "You other boys don't smell like no bouquet of roses, neither. I just got a whiff of you three. I got a nose like a bloodhound. You might say I am a law dog, and I'm trained to sniff out trouble! You four boys has got my nose all clogged up with the stench of pure, unadulterated trouble. Don't make me put you on my list of undesirables."

"We don't want any trouble, officer. We just want to get on up the hill and ride a few carnival rides," said the Tank.

"Shut up, Lard Butt!" shouted the deputy. "I didn't ask you no questions, did I? Speak when you're spoken to, Fatso. I don't cotton to no interruptions nor disruptions. I can't even stand commercials on television interruptin' my fav'rite shows. Buy this; buy that! Smoke this; smoke that! Eat this; eat that! Why can't the Charlotte TV station just let a man watch all of *Gunsmoke* or *Have Gun—Will Travel* without stoppin' ever' five minutes for a damn commercial?"

"You're right, officer," said Pudge. "I agree completely. There are far too many commercials on TV. It's outrageous. It's unheard of. I agree with you totally. Something should be done. Perhaps we should start a petition."

The deputy stared at Pudge, and a look of confusion traversed his face. His eyes looked skyward, and I could tell he was collecting his thoughts. Deputy Shumaker took a deep breath. He hitched up his pants using his belt and belt loops, took off his deputy's cap, and scratched his head. His dark hair was just as oily as Gene's but much thicker except right on top, where his hair was thinning. Grandpa Grayson would've called the deputy's hair loss "male-pattern baldness," a malady that stalked many a cap-wearing mountain man. Luke Shumaker reached up and massaged the location of his future bald spot.

"Dammit, boys, don't mess with me. I got a short fuse this evenin'. I been workin' this carnival all day, standin' out in the hot sun, sweatin' like a hog. The heat got so damned fearsome around two o'clock, I felt my flesh was gonna melt right off my bones. I woulda give anybody a dollar to throw a big bucket of icy water right in my face. When I couldn't take the heat no more, I bought two Nehi orange pops and drunk 'em right down, both of 'em at once, one right after the other. Them big orange drinks was lifesavers."

The deputy replaced his hat and stroked his chin. He wiped some spittle from his orange-stained lips with the back of his right hand. He tapped his foot, creating a miniscule dust explosion. The microscopic particles were whisked away by a stray breeze.

"Now where was I? Oh yeah! All four of you young heathens, listen up 'cause here's this year's carnival deal—no more runnin', no more dancin' and no more singin', and no more throwin' of them disgustin' signs or what us experts in law enforcement calls 'obscene gestures.' Oh yes indeed, I seen you throwin' them hand signs around! The gestures was as obscene as they come! Don't deny it!"

"Is the deputy referring to the Tennessee bird, Pudge?" whispered Tank.

"I'm not sure, but I believe so," said Pudge, grinning.

Deputy Shumaker looked at us as he might regard dirt scraped from beneath his fingernails after cleaning out a backed-up septic tank. His nose wrinkled and the pupils of his eyes became tiny dots of flame. He gritted his prominent teeth. Then he hitched up his trousers again, high enough to show several inches of his black socks. His brown, tightly laced shoes were polished, but were very dusty from walking the trail.

The deputy barked, "There is women and children, not to mention ole folks in this here carnival crowd, most of them bein' fine church-goin', upstandin' Christian people, such as myself and my kin. I won't have you intimidatin' the residents of this fair county by pushin' 'em around, by knockin' 'em down, and by throwin' indecent signs on these here patriotic, flag-wavin', taxpayin' United States citizens. By God, I'll not have you givin' 'em the finger or hollerin' out cuss words, or vicey versey, as the case may be!

"In this county and in this state, there is laws on the books against the stuff that you boys was doin' just a few minutes ago," he continued. "As a sworn-in deputy, I promised with my hand on the Bible to support the Constitution of these here forty-eight United States, North Carolina bein' one; and I just won't stand for no lawbreakin' or illegal funny bizness whatsoever under no circumstances. That's why I stopped you young sons of bitches— pardon my French."

"I can't see that we broke any laws, officer," I said, surprising myself with my boldness. Startled by my audacity, I stepped back and decided to shut up. I promised myself I would say nothing more to the deputy. I knew, however, that I often broke promises, especially those made to myself.

The deputy folded his arms across his chest, hiding his badge with his forearms. In the diminishing sunlight, a golden wedding ring flashed on his left hand. Deputy Luke Shumaker was married. Instinctively, I pitied the poor woman.

"Let me tell you somethin', Curly," said the deputy, addressing me. "Of the many laws set forth in our North Carolina Constitution, there is one that strictly forbids the givin' of any man, child, or woman the finger or throwin' any other obscene gestures or signs on any person in a public place, in a rest home, in a domestic dwellin', or in a drive-in movie theater. Didn't know that, did you, Mister Smarty-pants?"

"No, sir," I said.

"It's the law of the land found in section thirteen, article five, and verse twelve of the state constitution," he said, his tone both proud and condescending. "The only exception to the Obscene Gesture Statue, commonly known as the 'throwin' of signs law,' is when the offenders is consentin' adults who is either married, divorced, or engaged to one another. Even then, with fully consentin' adults, those lewd actions must be done only in the privacy of a citizen's own home, inside his parked vehicle after dark, or inside his local motel room and not out here in public where ever'body can see what he or she is doin'.

"The key adverb here is the word 'consentin' as defined by Daniel Webster in his best-sellin' dictionary. Now, I didn't hear no consentin' goin' on amongst the carnival crowd when you boys was runnin' around, with ever' last one of you actin' like a dadgum fool. I didn't heard no consentin' whatsoever. Did you boys hear any consentin'?"

We stared blankly at the officer.

"I, for one, didn't hear nobody say, 'Hey, I'm a consentin' adult and so is my wife, so why don't you four young scamps throw a big ole obscene gesture or two at us! We sure would appreciate it if you fellers was to give the two of us married folks the finger! And here's my young teenage daughter, how about throwin' one of them indecent signs on her, too.' Did you boys hear anybody in the carnival crowd say that?"

Gene grinned and began nodding yes, but quickly joined Tank, Pudge, and me in shaking our heads from side to side solemnly. Heads down, we stared at the ground. A June bug landed on my tennis shoe, crawled along the shoestrings, and then buzzed off again.

"I didn't think so!" said the deputy. "And do you immature bastards, do you young whelps consider yourselves adults, consentin' or otherwise?" asked Deputy Luke Shumaker. "Do you? Answer me!"

"No, sir," I blurted, forgetting my promise to myself to say nothing and shut my mouth. "We'll just be in the ninth grade when school starts up. We're not adults and we don't know much about the laws and statutes of our state."

"Well then, I may have to introduce you young scalawags to laws and statues that your school teachers don't teach you. Let's see now, first off, I bet you whippersnappers ain't never heard tell of such laws as commodus operandi, in loco appendicitis, ipso fatso, squid pro crow, and corpus crispy, not to mention the new rigor mortis law. Most of them laws is talked about in the North Carolina Constitution!"

"I ain't never heard about a single one of them laws, except maybe rigor mortis," said Gene, scratching his head. "I've heard tell of rigor mortis once upon a time somewheres, but I can't remember what that law is about. I just can't recollect the definition of rigor mortis. I'll keep thinkin' on it. Maybe it'll come to me. Them other laws might be brand new laws, I reckon."

"Nope, they ain't new laws, they was wrote down a long time ago, and I sure do hope ignorance ain't catchin'. You ain't heard of them laws because them's legal terms, gents, words you might hear in a court of law; and if I have to drag you little snots to the courthouse and put you in front of a judge, I ain't scared to use all them legal sayin's against you. If necessary, I'll use even more of them fancy French words which I've learnt in law enforcement school. I don't mean to brag, braggin' ain't my style, but right now there's a certificate, taped on a pasteboard square and thumbtacked up on my office wall, statin' that I've been successful in completin' two weeks of law school trainin' down in the city of Raleigh. You heard me right—I said *Raleigh*. I ain't no hick; I been to sev'ral other big cities like Charlotte, Greensboro, and Asheville. Sheriff Brownlow Bailey picked me out special from all the other deputies for extra schoolin' in the field of law enforcement. The county paid for my Raleigh motel room while I was studyin' the law down there. In Raleigh, I learnt how to deal with lawbreakers like you."

"We're sorry, officer, we didn't mean any harm by our actions. We appreciate the warning. We won't do it again," said Pudge, pushing his hands through his sweat-dampened hair. In the midst of his more composed and relaxed hair, his unruly cowlick stood up like an indecent red finger.

"Well, that's more like it, Red. I reckon you got more common sense than these other three hoodlums, but I hope you ain't tryin' to brownnose me, son. I can't abide a brownnoser, and the good Lord knows we got several of 'em workin' down at Sheriff Brownlow Bailey's office. Them brownnosers is tryin' to get promoted ahead of me."

"Pudge, ain't no brownnoser, Deputy," said Gene. "He ain't sunk that low—not yet anyways."

"Look Skinny, I didn't ask for your opinion, and if I have any more trouble out of you fresh bastards, I'm gonna take you four fellers to the police station downtown, interrogate the hell out of you, get you to confess to somethin', and then call your parents to bail you out—that is, if you got any moms and dads who'll claim you. I know I wouldn't claim you boys as kin! I got a young son about your age by the name of Larry, and I just hope and pray he don't turn out like you teenage retards."

The deputy focused on the Tank. "Tubby, I could take your lard bottom into custody right now on four counts of ipso fatso, and I'm mighty tempted to do it if you don't straighten up and fly right."

Tank shrugged his broad shoulders and smiled. Then Deputy Luke Shumaker turned to me. I could feel his hot breath on my face. My perceptive nasal passages told me that the deputy had recently eaten a hot dog with mustard, onions, and relish. Also, the faint odor of Pepto-Bismol hovered in the air around the officer complemented by the pleasing scent of Aqua Velva aftershave. Grandpa Grayson used Aqua Velva so I recognized the smell.

Deputy Luke Shumaker said, "Do you want to say anything more, Curly?"

"No, officer, I think we all understand," I said. "I believe I have a better understanding of the North Carolina Constitution and North Carolina's statutes and all that stuff, thanks to you. I wish I knew more about the law. I don't even understand how laws are made. I guess we'll learn about the government in high school."

Gene, Pudge, and the Tank nodded gravely in agreement. We were anxious to leave and resume our climb, but the deputy wasn't through educating us.

"Well, at least I made you young numbskulls understand just a little bit about our state constitution," said Deputy Luke Shumaker, rocking back and forth on his toes and heels. He cleared his throat and scratched at his Adam's apple. Tank, Pudge, Gene, and I braced ourselves. "We have a fine state constitution here in North Carolina. The original copy stays down yonder in Charlotte, our biggest city, which is the state capital, I reckon; but the national Constitution, the big daddy of all constitutions, is kept up yonder in Warshington, D.C., hid underneath the Liberty Bell and guarded by the Warshington State Highway Patrol.

"This guy is a lunatic," I whispered to Tank.

"He's a basket case," Tank whispered back. "He should be in a straitjacket down at the funny farm."

"He's nuts, but we'd better go along with him and not antagonize him. After all, he's the law," muttered Pudge.

The deputy, full of himself and evidently enjoying the sound of his own voice, heard nothing of our confidential conversation. He blathered on.

"Our Constitution was writ by four fathers who lived right outside of Boston, New Hampshire," the deputy continued, holding his chin high. "Them fellers was all good fam'ly men, accordin' to the history books. They had thirteen children altogether, six boys and seven girls. Well, these fathers all knowed one another and was right friendly, and they liked to get together after work and play cards and drink a few shots of moonshine whiskey whilst their wives had tea parties. One night, they was about half drunk and was bored with card playin', so the four fathers decided to write out the United States Constitution. They laid out sev'ral sheets of paper right on their card table, found a few ballpoint pens, and commenced puttin' pen to paper. When they was done with the writin', they read the words out loud to one another. Ever'thin' sounded good to 'em. They was right proud of their brand-new Constitution, so they signed their John Hancocks down on the bottom of the last page."

"Moron," whispered Pudge.

"What did you say, Red?" asked the deputy, his eyes narrowing.

"Go on, I said 'go on.' This is interesting stuff," replied Pudge. The deputy smiled.

"Well, one of the four fathers spoke up and said, 'The words we slapped down on these here papers tonight will be the underpinnin' for all the lawmakin' in this new country. Let's run this here Constitution down the road to George Warshington's house and see what he thinks.'

"Well, ole George liked what they had wrote a whole lot and asked Ben Franklin, who spent a lot of his time flyin' kites, inventin' electricity, and writin' in his almanac, to print up sev'ral copies of the Constitution and spread 'em around amongst the people. Back then, most people was ignorant and couldn't read, so they didn't give a damn one way or another, but them what could read liked the Constitution and commenced makin' laws right and left."

"That was in the olden days," said Gene. "What about lawmakin' in these here modern times?"

"As I understand today's current, up-to-date lawmakin' process," resumed the deputy, pushing out his chest and steepling his long fingers, "it goes this way. Ever' now and then the elected president, bein' real careful so as not to tear the pages, pulls out the nearly wore-out, dusty ole Constitution from under the Liberty Bell and runs the document over to the Capitol and reads it out loud to folks in Congress, of which some is called 'sinators' and the rest is called 'reprehensibles.'

"One president, I can't think of his name, mighta been that big lard-ass president named Taft. Anyway, one of them ole-timey presidents got in a big way of talkin' to Congress, stompin' on the Sinate's marble floor, and slingin' his arms about, and was so clumsy that he knocked over the Liberty Bell, which he was standin' right next to, and it hit the floor with a bang, causin' a big crack in it. In fact, the crack was so big that you could see the clapper inside the bell right through the fracture. It was bad broke.

"Davy Crockett, who was a reprehensible from Tennessee at the time, tried to patch up the Liberty Bell, but Davy didn't do no good at fixin' it. Nobody give him no credit for tryin', neither. Some even said he had made the crack a whole lot worse. A few of the other reprehensibles just poked fun at him and laughed at his buckskin clothes and his coonskin cap."

"Imagine that—laughin' at Davy Crockett, a man some folks still call the King of the Wild Frontier," said Gene removing his cowboy hat and brushing some dust off the brim.

"Anyways," said the deputy, "Ole Davy was so pissed off that he told ever'body in Congress to go straight to hell in a handbasket, and he took right off, headin' for Texas and the Alamo to fight a Mexican saint named Anna. She must of been a awful stout woman 'cause accordin' to the history books, Saint Anna kilt Davy with a Bowie knife and throwed his carcass into the Rio Grande river.

"That ole Liberty Bell is still cracked. It's still put to use once in a while, but I hear tell it looks awful and don't ring good. I reckon nobody but Davy Crockett has had the guts to even try to fix it."

"I heard all about Davy Crockett and the Liberty Bell in a song one time," said Gene. He smiled and puffed out his chest, reveling in his knowledge of American history. "I learnt more from 'The Ballad of Davy Crockett' than I learnt from any ole history book. Did you know Davy Crockett was borned on top of a mountain over yonder in Tennessee? My uncle, Shade Barlow, showed me the very log cabin where his mammy birthed Davy. There wasn't nothin' left but the fireplace, the chimbley, one wall, and a few rotten logs layin' around."

The deputy frowned because Gene had interrupted him. Still, he resumed his lesson without missing a beat.

"Now, you boys ort to know that there is three branches of government: Congress, the president, and the Extreme Court. As I told you before, Congress is composted of sinators and reprehensibles. Sinators live in the Sinate Buildin' and make laws, when they ain't out raisin' money so's they can be re-elected and stay in Warshington another six years. Reprehensibles does the same thing, except ever' one of them has to find his own place to live, and they is elected ever' two years. As soon as them boys gets settled in Warshington, they, like the sinators, commence raisin' money for their next campaign.

"But the good thing about bein' a reprehensible is this: All them reprehensibles or their good buddies gets to draw lines on maps markin' the places in their states where people is friendliest to their way of thinkin'. These map places is called districts, and if a man is good at drawin' maps, leavin' some voters in and some out, he can be voted back into Congress year after year, 'til he dies, I reckon. It may not sound fair, but as long as we are livin' under a democracy, it's all right by me."

"Me, too," said Gene enthusiastically. "Me and my fam'ly is awful patriotic. Of course, Daddy won't let Mama vote 'cause the Bible says a woman ort not vote. Daddy's terrible strict about follerin' the Bible's teachin's."

"Your daddy is a mighty smart man," said the deputy. "Most womenfolks is too e-motional for politics. Now I say 'most of 'em,' not all. Some women is near about as clever as a man. Them that's clever gen'rally can't cook."

"My mother's a college graduate, and she votes in every election," said Tank, rather proudly. His mother was a nurse at the county hospital. "Also, my mother is an excellent cook."

"I don't doubt that, son, not one bit," said the deputy, poking Tank's midsection with an elongated finger.

"I'm considering a weight loss program," said the big boy, rubbing his paunch.

"Could you tell us some more about them six-year senators?" asked Gene. "Six years in Congress makin' laws seems like a mighty long time to me."

"Six years is a long time," drawled the deputy, "but we got to foller the Constitution and that's what it says—six years, not five, not four. Sinators, these days, is awful smart and important because they is elected by all the big electoral colleges and universities. Ever' state has two sinators except for big states like New York, California, Texas, and Rhode Island. Them big states can have three or four sinators voted into office by the electoral colleges and universities located in their home states. I reckon the small colleges gets one vote and the big universities gets two."

"That makes sense," said Gene. "What about the other lawmakers?"

"Ever' state gets to have a whole bunch of reprehensibles. Why, they're as common as flies on a road-killed possum seven days dead. You can't walk through Warshington without bumpin' into one. Reprehensibles is not near as important as sinators, 'cause just anybody who is a law-abidin' citizen can vote for 'em—except maybe black folks."

"Wait a minute, black citizens can vote. Mr. Church told us so. And I believe every citizen has the..." said Tank, but the deputy shushed him with a harsh scowl and proceeded.

"After the elections is done, all the Congress fellers—there ain't many women folks up there in Congress, thank God!—get together and argue about the Constitution, which, you know, was writ by them four fathers that I talked about, who was all good husbands, I reckon. I ain't never heard no different. Well, sometimes them sinators and them reprehensibles gets real mad at each other and even gets into fist fights about how to pay the insurance on the domestic tranquilerty, how to provide all the generals with welfare, how to peel a more perfect onion, and how to give the blessin's of liberty and justice to the well-to-do and their prosperity which means all their small children and little grandbabies."

The deputy took a handkerchief out of his back pocket and dabbed at his eyes. "Excuse me, fellers. I'm awful softhearted when it comes to babies, grandbabies, and little children." He blew his nose, snuffled, and stuffed the soggy handkerchief back in the rear pocket of his uniform trousers.

The deputy's tears were real, and it struck me that the deputy had a warm spot in his heart for babies and small children but not for teenagers like us.

"Now where was I? Oh yeah. Fin'lly, after a month or two of quarrelin', them sinators—most of which is old, feeble, and sick—well, they gets kindly homesick and decides it's time to go back home to their wives, young'uns, and grandyoung'uns for a spell, so they takes a vote on all their lawmakin' at once. Ever' dang one of them laws has to be considered and voted on in just one day, usually on a Thursday, except for Thanksgivin', of course. If I ain't wrong, the laws has to get at least sixty sinators to vote 'aye' for the laws to pass mustard.

"But the lawmakin' ain't over yet, not by a long shot. Them sinators has to carry the bills they made a way over across the town of Warshington to a big fancy brick and marble buildin' called the House of Reprehensibles, and sometimes called the People's House, to see if any laws has passed over there in that buildin'. If the reprehensibles in the People's House has passed somethin' kindly like what the sinators has already passed, and then if this feller named Bill O. Wrights says it's okay with him, and all the sinators and all the reprehensibles agrees, the laws they passed together becomes the laws of the land, with no exceptions, no buts, and no maybes."

"No exceptions at all?" asked Pudge. "Mr. Church, our principal, says that he's found there are exceptions to almost every rule, even rules set up by the county board of education."

"Well, there is one exception, Red. The president could throw a torpedo on the bill and stop the law dead in its tracks. The president seldom torpedoes a bill because the Sinate could ride over the torpedo easy if they can find sixty people walkin' around on the streets of Warshington, D.C., who agrees with the Congress and thinks the bill the sinators and reprehensibles has passed should be the law of the land. Them sinators can usually round up sixty fools who agrees with 'em so very few law bills gets torpedoed."

"What if a law gets passed and it turns out to be a bad law, a law that hurts people?" asked Tank.

"I'm glad you asked that, Fats. You're thinkin' ahead of these three ignorant hillbillies," said the deputy, gesturing to Pudge, Gene, and me. "Our four fathers—I just now remembered their first names, Matthew, Mark, Luke and John—but for the life of me I can't think of their last names. I think one of 'em was a Miller or maybe a Jones. Anyways, them four fathers that I mentioned before set up a Extreme Court to handle bad laws and fix 'em. Our country's four fathers was right smart and awful good fam'ly men, as I said before.

"Some folks bring a case to the Extreme Court to try to get a new or old law they don't like turned over and fixed, but the judges in that court is so old, frail, and deaf that they usually won't even hear a case about any law—good, bad, or indifferent. One time, the Democrats voted to buy all ten of them Extreme Court justices hearin' aids, but the Republicans voted no, sayin' it would cost too much taxpayer money comin' mostly out of the rich folks' pockets, so now it's awful hard to get a law changed, even a bad law. The Extreme Court judges either won't hear a case, or they can't hear a case because they is so hard of hearin'. So once a law becomes a law these days, it's usually the law of the land forever and ever, amen."

"Amen!" echoed Gene. The vocal, knee-jerk response was automatic. His father was a part-time Baptist preacher.

"That's how laws is made up there in Warshington," said the deputy. "As soon as the final votes is over, the president grabs up the Constitution and slides it real careful like back under the Liberty Bell for safekeepin', and the sinators and reprehensibles goes home to wherever home is, except the president don't go home. He stays right there in Warshington because he has a year-round job bein' the president and a part-time job fixin' up cabinets and whitewarshin' his great big house."

"Astonishing! I wish our teachers knew as much about the law and the Constitution as you do, Deputy Shumaker," said the Tank, staring at the deputy in open-mouthed wonder. "You have educated us, especially on legal terms and the lawmaking process. I'll not soon forget what you have said. Truly amazing!"

"I've learned so much my head hurts," said Pudge, winking surreptitiously at me. "My head is packed with new knowledge. You should teach a course at Central Ashe High School."

"I appreciate you sayin' that, son. Us peace officers don't get the credit and respect which we deserves, considerin' how much law stuff we got to learn before we can go out and start handcuffin' and arrestin' people," said Deputy Shumaker. The deputy's eyes softened. A smile curled corners of his mouth.

"I figger I won't have to send you young hoodlums back down the hill toward town, after all. I reckon I'll let you fellers go on up to enjoy the carnival," said the relenting deputy.

"Thanks a lot," said Tank.

"We appreciate that," said Pudge.

"Much obliged," declared Gene.

I smiled but said nothing. I didn't want to thank this grown-up buffoon in a county deputy uniform for anything. I couldn't fathom how Luke Shumaker ever became a deputy sheriff.

"Yep, you young sons of bitches is in luck. My shift is mostly over and I don't get paid for no overtime. I'm leavin' shortly, but remember this: the sheriff will be sendin' two more deputies to patrol the carnival grounds. Sheriff Brownlow Bailey would be here at the carnival hisself, but he's over near the Wilkes County line 'cause some damn fool is threatenin' to commit suicide by jumpin' off the Jumpin' Off Place. The sheriff is tryin' to talk the shif'less bastard out of jumpin'."

"Well, that's his job, isn't it?" asked Tank.

"Hellfire, I say let the dumb hillbilly jump and leave his body on the rocks below for the bears and the buzzards. There'd be one less drunk for us in law enforcement to worry about. One thing is for sure, nobody ever jumped off the Jumpin' Off Place and lived to tell about it!"

I noticed that Pudge's hands trembled slightly, and he winced at the mere mention of the Jumping Off Place. Then I remembered that about five years ago, Pudge's much older second cousin, Barton Hamby, had committed suicide by leaping from the high rocks at the Jumping Off Place.

Gene had been there with his father who, as a minister, had tried to convince Barton Hamby not to take his own life. "Daddy took his Bible and prayed for Mr. Hamby a long time, but it done no good," Gene had said. From the information Gene provided, I pieced together the story of Barton Hamby's last minutes on earth.

With three empty liquor bottles at his feet, Barton Hamby had stood on the Jumping Off Place's upper ledge for about an hour before he jumped. He cursed at the small crowd that had gathered near the outcropping. He threatened to jump several times, but always pulled himself back from the overhang. His wife, Mavis Hortense Hamby, kept repeating the Lord's Prayer and imploring him to come back from the edge. Mr. Hamby had told her to shut up.

"Mavis, if it wadn't fer you I wouldn't be up on this here ledge," he'd shouted. "You wuz the one what drove me to drink. You wuz always criticizin' my smokin' two packs a day, spendin' my hard-earned sawmill dollars on trashy jewelry, and findin' fault with ever'thin' I done. Losin' my job at the sawmill wuz the last damn straw. It wuz yore daddy what fired me, Mavis. I'm a desperate man! I can't take it no more, so I'm tellin' you and ever'body here goodbye, kiss my ass, and have a nice day!"

Then Barton Hamby leapt out into space and plummeted to the rocks far below. Gene, an eyewitness to the suicide, said that Barton Hamby clawed the air and screamed all the way down. His body, on the rocks below the ledge, was twisted and torn, especially his face.

"One of his eyeballs was found three foot away from his corpse," Gene had said. "His broke arms and legs was turned and bent ever' whichaway."

Barton Hamby's casket was kept closed at his well-attended funeral. I went to the funeral with Grandpa Charlie, but Pudge didn't show up. I was surprised, because the redhead's mother and father were at the memorial services.

"I reckon Pudge has got his reasons for not bein' here," Grandpa Charlie whispered as the preacher spoke from the pulpit. "Don't pester him with no questions when you see him at school."

On the drive home from the cemetery, Grandpa Charlie had told me that over the years, there had been a few alleged murders committed by pushing people over the ledge at the Jumping Off Place. He had said that he couldn't remember hearing of any convictions, although two men had been brought to trial.

"If a dead married woman or a dead married man was found down on the rocks below the Jumpin' Off Place ledge, and the law had no clues, no proof, nor witnesses, well, that kind of death was called a 'mountain divorce' in the ole days," Grandpa Charlie had said.

Deputy Sheriff Luke Shumaker took his hat off and looked at his wrist watch. He shifted his weight from right foot to left foot and back again. He scratched his head and spat on the ground. The deputy looked at his watch again and replaced his hat.

"Before my shift is over in about ten minutes, I'm gonna give the other deputies, includin' Deputy Farmer, a description of you teenage asswipes. I'm meetin' two of them deputies at the foot of the hill. They'll inform Deputy Farmer; don't you think they won't. It'll be easy for the other deputies to spot the four of you 'cause all of you are kinda funny lookin'. See that you fresh bastards behave from now on, or they'll be hell to pay. You fellers had best know this: You boys is the grass, and I'm the lawnmower, understood?"

"Yes, sir," said three of us.

I didn't hear Gene say anything, but then he spoke directly to the deputy. Gene was smiling and that worried me. Sometimes, Gene went too far, refusing to leave well enough alone. At times Gene just couldn't resist an opportunity to antagonize someone, usually Tank, Pudge, or me. It troubled me that he was about to add the deputy to his list. My concerns were valid. Gene saw an opening, so as usual, he took it.

"Deputy, I don't think that rigor mortis law that you was talkin' about a while ago ever passed the North Carolina Gen'ral Assembly," said Gene, smiling smugly. "Some kinda 'Rigor Mortis Act' might become law next year unless the governor vetoes, I mean torpedoes it, but right now the rigor mortis law ain't no law at all. You might say it's 'in limbo.' I'm positive that law ain't gone into effect this year. In fact, I firmly believe that the rigor mortis law will be tested in court, if it ever becomes a real law, because the punishment is too stiff. Now I ain't no lawyer, don't claim to be, but I think the law might be found to be unconstitutional by the North Carolina State Supreme Court. At the very least, the rigor mortis law ain't carved in granite. The law ain't set in stone as you suggested earlier, Deputy Shumaker. Rigor mortis might set in someday, prob'ly will, but not yet. As of right now, there is still some doubt concernin' that law. Maybe it'll come to be the law of the land, and maybe it won't. If anybody was to ask me, I'd tell 'em to pay no attention to the Rigor Mortis Law 'cause it don't amount to nothin'."

"Are you disputin' my word?" said the deputy angrily. The deputy's back stiffened. His face hardened. He tapped his holstered gun. Gene stood boldly before him with arms crossed stubbornly.

"I ain't disputin', I'm merely disagreein'."

"Laws gotta be obeyed. They ain't no flexibility in that rigor mortis law nor any other North Carolina law! Laws is set in stone, and rigor mortis is the law of the land," insisted Deputy Shumaker.

"It ain't set in yet," Gene maintained.

"Rigor mortis has done set in. The law is up and runnin', and that's for sure, you skinny little snot! I'll guaran-damn-tee you that. There ain't no escapin' it. At least it's the law here in North Carolina. I don't know about all them other states. In this state, them that commits rigor mortis has got to serve time in one of our state prisons. The guv'nor didn't torpedo a single damn bill last year. Rigor mortis set in about two months ago, purty soon after they first opened up the Gen'ral Assembly to make new laws. I remember that one of them sinators in Raleigh tried to make rigor mortis a capital offense, like suicide and homicide is."

"Suicide and homicide ain't the same thing. To think so is plain foolishness," insisted Gene, raising his voice. "Homicide takes at least *two* people—the killer and the victim. Suicide takes only *one* person actin' alone, all by hisself."

"For your information, sonny boy, suicide and homicide is *exactly* the same thing—the takin' of a life belongin' to a human bean," said the deputy, his falsetto voice increasing in volume. "I, for one, support makin' homicide, suicide, and the crime of rigor mortis punishable by death in the electrical chair. Dammit, I just remembered that I got a bunch of papers in my bottom desk drawer about that rigor mortis law. Lord, I wish I had brung 'em with me."

Using the back of his hand, the deputy wiped several droplets of sweat from his forehead. He adjusted his gun belt. He looked longingly down the trail toward the town of West Jefferson.

"You four knuckleheads is just wastin' my time. Talkin' to you young'uns is like talkin' to a fence post. You boys don't know nothin' about the laws of North Carolina, nor the Congress, nor the Sinate, nor rigor mortis. I got a foxhound named Chaser that knows more about the law than you fellers. My shift is over, or will be by the time I get to the foot of the hill. I'm outta here. I'm gone, gents. I'm gonna make like a horse turd and hit the trail!"

"Well, good evenin', then," said Gene, lifting and lowering his Hopalong Cassidy hat. "It's been a pleasure makin' your acquaintance and talkin' to you. Give my regards to your fam'ly."

As Deputy Luke Shumaker turned his back to us and strode away in his long-legged gait, Gene gave him a quick two-handed, double dose of the Tennessee bird. The deputy disappeared into a swarm of carnival goers, never noticing the indecent signage that Gene was throwing on him.

"Take that, copper!" Gene said in a low raspy whisper, with the middle finger of each hand held high in the air. Gene sounded like a defiant George Raft, an actor known for his deep, gruff voice, who appeared in many black-and-white gangster films shown at the Parkwood Theatre way back in the thirties and forties. Some of those old gangster movies were being shown again on TV. I watched one on channel three, the Charlotte station.

"You dirty rat! You stinkin' rat! You'll never take me alive, law dog!" Gene emphatically promised the deputy in a rapid-fire, staccato voice, replicating the voice of James Cagney, another actor who had many gangster roles in old black and white movies. Gene's skinny arms and scrawny hands were still upraised and waving his twin Tennessee birds. His voice had become angrier and shriller, although Deputy Luke Shumaker was well out of hearing distance, thank goodness.

CHAPTER 10

Our farm-girl debutante, Ruthie, had long ago disappeared into the carnival crowd, and the dancing, laughing, and singing was over, at least for the moment, thanks to the interruption of Deputy Luke Shumaker. Far from tiring us out, the revelry with Ruthie and the extended lecture from deputy Shumaker had revived us. We were breathing normally and sweating less.

We felt reinvigorated. We laughed and joked. Even the unnerving encounter with Deputy Shumaker—a cartoon version of a police officer, a man whose warped, unschooled understanding of history and politics had left us momentarily stupefied—hadn't dampened our unshakable, unsinkable teenage spirits. The deputy's words and warnings were like water off a duck's backside.

Tank suggested we leave the main trail and take a brief detour onto a smaller pathway that led out to a rocky projection overlooking the town. Tank wanted to check out the twilight view of the West Jefferson town lights.

"Let's go!" I said. "I'll race you guys!"

I sprinted down the narrow path ahead of the other three, but came to a sudden stop when I saw that there was a drop of more than twenty-five feet over the edge of the rocky outcropping. It was, in fact, a miniature version of the Jumping Off Place out near the Wilkes County line just off Highway 16.

"That's it! Easy does it!" said the trotting Tank, who was breathing heavily when he arrived. "You wouldn't want to go over the ledge, Hal!"

As Gene approached the outcropping, he carefully stepped over a strangely-formed rock resting in the middle of the wide ledge. Gene continued slowly and carefully toward the edge of the precipice. He peered over the cliff. The sharp gray rocks below were turning black with the approach of nightfall.

"Dang! That's quite a drop!" cried Gene. "Watch out, Pudge!"

Pudge, jogging just behind Gene, stepped directly onto the misshapen rock, causing him to lean back and forth, searching desperately for balance, as he tried to stabilize his unsteady footing. He lurched sideways then forward, his arms waving in the air in an attempt to regain his equilibrium. His knees buckled awkwardly and his feet stumbled, sending him ever closer to the rocky edge of the ledge.

Gene and I stood motionless, watching like open-mouthed statues. Unless he regained his balance, Pudge was going over. Twenty-five or thirty feet below him, on sharp gray rocks, awaited certain injury and perhaps death. For a few seconds, he wavered between balancing and falling. Then he faltered and fell forward. Arms spread, Pudge pitched headlong into the fresh mountain air.

He had just begun his descent to the lethal rocks below when the Tank, moving like a lightning bolt, leaned over the outcropping, thrust out his powerful hand, and grabbed Pudge by the wrist, jerking him upward and then heaving him back to safety. Pudge landed on his chest with a thump and rolled over. He moaned softly.

Meanwhile Tank danced unsteadily along the edge of the precipice like a man walking a tightrope. He teetered and wavered, then threw himself backward toward the safety of the ledge, landing on his backside. For a moment, he struggled to breathe. Then he stood up and took a deep lungful of air.

"Where's Pudge? Is he all right?" Tank asked.

"I'm okay," wheezed Pudge from behind him.

From his pocket, Tank withdrew a Butterfinger candy bar and consumed it in two bites. "I'm powering up in case I'm needed again," he said.

Pudge stood up and wiped bits of debris from the seat of his trousers. He was safe, but his foot had somehow come out of his left tennis shoe. We waited as he knelt down and stuffed his foot back into the shoe. Then, with shaky hands, Pudge carefully tied his laces.

"I... I... I'm all right, guys," Pudge said. "Just let me rest for a minute."

"Are you sure you're all right?" I asked.

"I'm fine. Couldn't be better," said Pudge, leaning back against a massive, moss covered rock and giving us his reassuring Alfred E. Neuman smile.

With the redhead out of harm's way, Gene, Tank, and I stood on the ledge in the deepening twilight and viewed the twinkling lights of West Jefferson and the surrounding communities. Several house lights flickered on as several downtown business lights were turned off. The whole scene reminded me of lightning bugs, flashing on and off in a summer hayfield.

"Let's meet up here on the week before Christmas if it's not too snowy and cold," said Tank. "If the weather cooperates, this would be a fine place to check out the downtown Christmas lights." He waved his arm over the glittering scene below us.

Tank knew the merchants and townspeople of West Jefferson went all out and put on quite a show with their Christmas lights. Red, blue, and green lights would be intertwined with pine roping and suspended above the town's streets, and every downtown store window would sport a shining Christmas tree.

I looked down from the ledge, remembering the town's jeweled holiday glow.

Pudge stepped forward. He inched his way almost to the edge of the rocky shelf, glanced down at the town of West Jefferson, and said, "Guys, let's walk back to the main trail and head up to the carnival. We don't have too much farther to go. I can smell buttered popcorn, and I can hear the carousel music."

"Yeah. Let's not waste no more time," said Gene.

The four of us left the outcropping, marched back down the narrow path, and joined the crowd on the main trail. We then resumed our upward trek toward the carnival lights with Pudge and Tank walking side-by-side. Gene and I followed close behind them.

"That was a close one back there, Pudge. I almost missed when I grabbed for your hand. I thought you were going over for sure," whispered Tank. "You could've fallen twenty feet or more onto those rocks below!"

"Nah, not close at all," said Pudge. His quivering hands belied his confident words. "I really didn't need your help, Tank. I was ready to reach out and grab the ledge with my hands. My hands are strong. I could've held on. Besides, what's such a big deal about falling twenty or twenty-five feet? I read about a guy in Winston-Salem who fell off the roof of a five-story building and didn't break a bone."

"I read the same story about that man in the *Winston-Salem Journal*. Did you read the whole article, Pudge?" asked Tank.

"Nope, I only read what was on the first page and then I turned to the comics section. I read *Peanuts* every day. I read that comic strip as religiously as some people read their horoscopes."

"The news story was continued on page three of the paper with more information," said Tank. "The Winston-Salem man didn't break any bones, but the next day he died of internal hemorrhaging."

"What does hemorrhaging mean?" Gene asked. "I ain't never heard tell of that word."

"It means bleeding, bad bleeding," Tank said.

Pudge stopped walking and looked back at the outcropping. He drew in a long breath and slowly released it. Pudge's shoulder movement was almost imperceptible, but he shuddered. When he turned back to face Tank his face was ashen, and his hands were trembling again.

I could remember only one other time when I'd seen Pudge's hands shake like that. It was way back in sixth grade in Mrs. Bender's classroom. Pudge was reading aloud his book report on a book he'd never read. The book was called *Sled Dog of Alaska.* I was sure Mrs. Bender knew Pudge had never read that book. He was so nervous and shaky as he stood in front of the class with a blank sheet of notebook paper in his hand. I expected her to challenge him, but Mrs. Bender never did question him about the book report, not in in front of the class anyway. I meant to ask Pudge if Mrs. Bender ever confronted him privately, but I never did.

CHAPTER 11

Tank, Pudge, Gene and I were looking forward to starting high school. We had considered ourselves top dogs as eighth graders at Healing Waters and knew that wouldn't be the case at Central Ashe, but we anticipated new classes, new teachers, new friends, and new adventures.

At Healing Waters, the eighth-grade class ahead of us had never really bullied us when we were lowly seventh graders as had become the custom with previous eighth-grade classes at the small school. At the time, I had guessed the reason for the lack of intimidation was that we had, as seventh-grade classmates, Tank and Johnny Knight, the two strongest boys in the whole school. Or it might've been because our pal Gene was the meanest kid in school, capable of devilish pranks, sadistic settling of scores, and sudden bursts of hot-tempered violence. Anyway, the eighth graders, from time to time, picked on us seventh graders but not to any great extent. There had been a few rare confrontations, but nothing serious. However, the detente was fragile, and hostility on both sides lurked just beneath the surface.

For a short time back in seventh grade, three eighth graders had gotten in the habit of chasing Pudge down at recess, holding his hands behind his back, and pulling his nose. Pudge was no pushover, but there were three eighth-graders against one seventh-grader. The nose-jerkings had happened about four or five times before Johnny Knight and Tank intervened and put an end to the yanking of Pudge's pained proboscis. The redhead was mighty grateful. Pudge rubbed and poked his nostrils until his enlarged nose returned to its normal shape.

Once during our seventh-grade year, Johnny Knight, Tank, and I had entered the boys' bathroom and had found three eighth grade boys forcing Gene's head up and down into a commode. Water splashed everywhere and the walls of the restroom stall were dripping. Tank brushed those eighth graders aside like January snowflakes swept from the shoulders of a dark winter coat. He stepped into the stall to check on Gene.

"Good grief!" exclaimed the Tank. Gene had slumped to his knees on the stall's floor and was clinging to the toilet bowl as if it were a life preserver. Water dripped from his head into the commode.

"Howdy, Tank," snuffled Gene, raising his drenched head. "How you doin', pal?"

"Stand back, eighth-graders!" ordered the Tank. "Keep an eye on them, Johnny. Don't let them leave."

Dragging his bony classmate from the stall, Tank picked Gene up, held him high in the air, and shook him. At first the scrawny guy was as limp as a wet dish rag, but then Gene began coughing up water and kicking at the Tank's midsection. The half-drowned, skinny-as-a-rail seventh grader was all right, except he was soaked to the skin. Tank set him down on the tile floor and turned to face the three eighth-grade bullies. Gene's tormentors rushed toward the exit door.

"Oh no you don't," said Johnny Knight with his broad shoulders barring the restroom door. "Everyone stays right here."

Big Johnny Knight, whose strength rivaled the Tank's, restrained the three eighth graders who were trying to leave the restroom. He shoved them away from the exit door. The three older boys stumbled toward the Tank.

"What's going on here?" demanded Tank, eyeing the eighth graders suspiciously. "Gene, are you all right?"

"Do I look all right, Tankus Giganticus?" coughed Gene, sitting in a puddle on the restroom floor. "I feel like I am next of kin to a New River catfish, 'cept I ain't never learned to breathe through my gills. Are these eighth graders tryin' to teach me to swim in this here commode? And ain't they the same boys that pestered Pudge by stretchin' his nose?"

"They are indeed," Tank said. He scowled at the older boys.

"Whew!" gasped Gene. "My lungs feel like sponges. I can't hardly breathe. I may need mouth-to-mouth resusertation; call Ruthie right away and have her on standby."

"Okay, eighth graders, let's hear your side of this little misunderstanding," said Tank.

Gene spat up some more water as the eighth graders explained what Gene had done to them; it was something involving a dead snake and sandwiches at the annual eighth-grade picnic. I didn't hear all the details, because I was taking a leak at one of the urinals.

All I know is after checking to see that the commode in which the eighth graders had been plunging Gene's head had been freshly flushed and that Gene was in no danger of drowning, Tank and Johnny Knight decided not to interfere.

"Gentlemen, you may proceed," said Tank, addressing the eighth graders.

The leader of the eighth-grade group was Roscoe Darnell, a tall, heavyset fellow who spent most of his spare time bullying younger kids and confiscating their lunch money.

"Boys, go ahead and stick Gene's head into the commode a few more times," commanded Roscoe, addressing his two cohorts. "I told you the Tank and Johnny Knight wouldn't stop us once they learnt what the little bastard done to us."

"Ain't you gonna help me, Tank?" whined Gene. "I'm pert near drownded."

"Nope, not yet," said Tank, folding his arms over his broad chest.

The splashing and spattering began again as Gene's head was forcefully submerged. Water droplets flew everywhere, producing an indoor rainstorm. I felt sorry for Gene who was beginning to look like a soaked rat, but I knew I couldn't stop the three eighth graders alone. Tank and Johnny Knight could, however, and easily. Nonetheless, the two strongest guys in the seventh grade stood motionless, seemingly powerless, watching Gene's head as it was submerged repeatedly in an oft-used toilet bowl.

"Why don't you put an end to this, Tank? You have big Johnny to back you up," I asked. I didn't want to witness Gene's drowning, and besides that, Gene owed me a dollar, which he had promised to pay on Monday for sure.

The Tank turned to me, put his hand on my shoulder, and said, "Hal, put yourself in their shoes. How would you like to bite into a ham sandwich at the eighth-grade picnic, only to discover you were chewing and eating pieces of a road-killed, partially dried out, venomous copperhead?"

"Copperhead?" I repeated. The milk I'd had for lunch began to curdle in my stomach. My belly heaved, splashing stomach acid and bile halfway up my esophagus. I had seen several road-killed black snakes and garter snakes. The squashed reptiles, oozing blood, were far from appetizing. The thought of eating a flattened snake, especially a venomous copperhead, was nauseating.

Roscoe Darnell raised his right hand, a signal that Gene was to be given a temporary respite to catch his breath.

"Okay, boys! Put him under water again!" yelled Roscoe. Gene's stringy-haired head disappeared into the swirling toilet bowl water. Many seconds later, gasping for air, he was lifted up. After a few seconds of frantic breathing, his head was plunged back into the water.

"Gene deserves the splashing he's getting and maybe a bit more," said the Tank. He shook his head and glared at Gene who had come up for air. After a few heartbeats, Gene's head was thrust into the pot again.

"I agree," said Johnny Knight, standing like a muscular statue next to the globe-shaped Tank. "Secretly feeding anyone a dried-out snake is just beyond the pale in my book."

Gene's head broke the surface of the toilet bowl. He had a look of desperation in his eyes. His fingernails were turning blue. He addressed Roscoe.

"It was only a little bitty (cough!) squished garter snake, Roscoe," Gene wheezed. "Harmless (cough!) as a tater chip, at least that's what I thought the reptile was!"

Gene gasped, shaking his head and slinging water about. Almost immediately, his head was thrust back into the porcelain mouth of the commode by his eighth-grade oppressors. Seconds passed and then Gene surfaced yet again, sputtering and coughing.

"It weren't no garter snake, Gene," bellowed Roscoe Darnell directly into Gene's saturated right ear. "I bit into my samwich, chewed a little, and spit out a whole snake's head. The copper-colored head was broad with a little scrawny neck. That's the sign of a poison snake. The snake skull had two long fangs in front and lots of little bitty teeth on both sides goin' way back in its mouth. That reptile was a copperhead all right and a big 'un, too. I have kilt rattlesnakes and copperheads in the woods around our farm. Dammit, I know what a copperhead looks like. Thanks to you, I know what one tastes like!"

Roscoe Darnell's two hoodlum companions, strong but short in stature, could best be described as adolescent thugs. The duo grunted their assent as they held Gene firmly by his shoulders and elbows with powerful, stubby fingers. Once again, the two hooligans pushed Gene forward, and his head was dunked into the commode's depths. His face was underwater for a bit longer this time, and he began to flail his arms. Gene was then lifted into a standing position, and his assailants vigorously shook him. Water sprayed into the air, and like Gene, his two persecutors were getting soaked.

Hirsute and apelike, Roscoe's two brutish cronies in Gene's punishment were chinless Gaither Callaway and stubble-bearded

Blue Barton. Roscoe, Gaither, and Blue had been involved in the intimidation of younger students at Healing Waters Elementary School for years. Both shaggy accomplices were just a shade over five feet, and they looked at their leader, Roscoe, with dull brown, often uncomprehending eyes. The two wore heavy brogan boots, bib overalls, and flannel shirts that were soaked up to the armpits with toilet water. Gaither's red shirt, doused by the water, had turned a deep burgundy color. Blue's damp shirt was a dark forest green. Roscoe was similarly attired except that his flannel shirt was yellow and not nearly as wet.

Gaither and Blue, held back in school numerous times, were probably four or five years older than their eighth-grade classmates. A rumor persisted around the school that Gaither Callaway was married and had a child. As far as I knew, the story was mere speculation.

Both Gaither and Blue had disheveled thick black hair and sloping brows. Blue, the heavier of the two, had a prominent chin with many short black whiskers sprouting out in various directions. His nose was unusually small with tiny nostrils, and the elfin snout didn't fit with the rest of his broad face. In the middle of his sun-darkened forehead rested a nickel sized blue-gray birthmark. Blue's eyes were large, dark, and bulging, and part of his left ear had been bitten off in a fight with his uncle, Eustace Barton—or so I had been told.

Gaither, the brawnier of the two, had a lower jaw that receded into his corded neck. His Adam's apple was more prominent than his chin. He was clean shaven and lacked any trace of facial hair except for his dense eyebrows, which almost hid his shifty, coffee-colored eyes, and an abundance of wiry black nose hair sprouting from the wide nostrils of his large, hooked nose.

If you've ever seen one of those novelty Groucho glasses with the attached plastic nose, the bushy eyebrows, and the fake mustache, you have a good idea of what Gaither Callaway looked like, except Gaither didn't wear glasses nor did he have a mustache. There was no more than an inch and a quarter of forehead separating his hairline and his bushy eyebrows.

Blue Barton's brow was even narrower. When Blue frowned, the bluish birthmark on his brow virtually disappeared, hidden by three deep wrinkles. When he smiled, which was seldom, he displayed an expansive pink gum line with only two upper front teeth. His lower gums exhibited three widely separated teeth, one of which, the middle one, was almost completely broken off, forming a tiny, sharp fang.

"I had et nearly half of my samwich, thinkin' it was a country ham samwich with sliced maters and onions, 'fore I noticed that I was chompin' on the hind end of a good-sized snake," said Gaither, scratching his nonexistent chin. "When I come to figger out what it was that I was chawin' on, I throwed that picnic samwich, snake and all, down on the ground. When the samwich hit the ground, the snake carcass skittered along through the grass for about four foot. Then a little bitty squashed, partly-digested mouse flopped out of the snake's innards.

"My gizzard started flip-floppin' around inside my chest like a drunk buzzard tryin' to fly through a bob wire fence. I didn't puke, nor nothin', but I did gag off and on for nigh on to five minutes. I woulda felt a whole lot better if I had of puked. I stuck my finger, this one here, way down in my throat, tryin' to make myself vomick, but it weren't no use.

"I couldn't get to sleep that night, just thrashed about in the bed, burpin' and passin' ass gas, 'til Mama made me drink some corn likker with a little honey mixed in. After that, I slept like a log, but I woke up powerful cornsterpated. I still ain't over it. I ain't near over it. Just yesterdy, I set in the outhouse and strained for ten solid minutes 'fore I done any good. Strikin' sev'ral matchsticks, I peered down into the lit-up toilet hole. That's when I seen bright red blood in my droppin's. Daddy says I got the piles. Imagine that, a feller my age with the piles! I figgered the piles was a very ole man's disease. Now, thanks to Gene, I got a bad dose of the sickness."

Grandpa Charlie would've sympathized with Gaither because now and then the old farmer suffered from hemorrhoids.

Whenever I saw him sitting on a big pillow at his small dinner table, I knew that he was having a hemorrhoid attack. "Thank the good Lord for Preparation H," he would say.

Gaither's eyes saddened as he continued, "I can still picture that poor little mashed-up gray mouse with little pink ears, couldn'ta been no more'n a baby." Gaither snuffled and wiped his substantial nose on his wet flannel sleeve.

Then the stubble-chinned Blue spoke up, "I et the whole dang samwich, which helt the middle part of the snake, the part with most of the guts, I reckon. Together with the mashed copperhead's belly, my white bread samwich was stuffed with great thick slices of country ham and a few mater slices, and it didn't taste half bad to me. The samwich had a nice sourness to it, kindly like buttermilk has a sour taste to it. I like buttermilk. After I done finished off what I had thunk was a ham samwich and had swallered ever' last crumb of it, I got unusual thirsty and drunk about a quart of lemonade, that purty pink kind that the cooks was servin' at the picnic. After I drunk that lemonade, I felt kindly queasy the rest of the evenin', but I didn't get sick till I went to bed that night.

"Like Gaither, I didn't get no rest. I was up and down all night pukin' from one end and squirtin' from the other. I was awful thankful that my ma keeps a slop jar under my bed. That slop jar come in handy, mighty handy, that night. Ma got up to see about me sev'ral times durin' the nighttime. She said that she hadn't never seed no young'un sicker than what I was."

"Blue, keep a good holt on Gene," said Gaither. "He's gettin' as slippery as a red sallymander in muddy water. Help us, Roscoe. Get aholt of his neck. Come on, let's push his ornery head under water some more!"

After Gene had been immersed a few more times, Tank shouted, "All right, that's enough! Gene is beginning to turn blue. He's not getting enough oxygen. Stop! Stop the dunking!"

"Aw, Tank, let us dip him just a few more times," said Roscoe. The Tank scratched his chin and rolled his eyes toward the ceiling, signaling that he was at least considering allowing Roscoe, Gaither, and Blue a few more plunges.

Gene blinked at Tank with watery eyes. There was a look of desperation in his sunken orbs. His eyelids were water puffed. Commode water streamed from his ears and nose, cascading downward and making small puddles on the restroom floor. His wet hair was plastered to his head. Hugging his arms across his chest, Gene began to shiver. Gaither and Blue gripped his shoulders and pushed his head slowly toward the commode.

"Gack! Gack!" Gene squawked as he resisted. He arched his spine and threw his shoulders back, keeping his head away from the watery bowl. Gaither and Blue tightened their powerful grips.

Fortunately for Gene, at that moment, Mr. Church who, in addition to being the school principal, was also our basketball coach and our seventh-grade teacher, walked into the boys' bathroom to check on the splashing that could be heard from the hallway. Smiling uncomfortably, the eighth graders unhanded Gene as Mr. Church approached them.

"Good mornin', Mr. Church!" said Blue amiably, although it was midafternoon.

As he stood with his black wingtips in a wide puddle of commode water, the principal surveyed the scene. Mr. Church frowned and scratched his head. The seven of us stood sheepishly in front of him as he looked from boy to boy with his eyes finally settling on Gene.

I was certain he considered Gene the major player in this little drama. Also, I was positive Mr. Church would use the word "gentlemen" when he spoke to us. He often repeated the word hoping that at least a few of us boys would someday become gentlemen. Mr. Church was an optimist through and through.

The principal, wearing a dark blue suit with a light blue tie, then folded his arms and said, "Look at this mess! The floor and walls are soaked. Gene... my goodness, are you all right? You're so pale. Gentlemen, am I witnessing horseplay or attempted murder?"

"Murder? Horseplay? Nothin' of the kind," replied Gene brightly, stepping forward and throwing his spindly right arm around Roscoe Darnell's broad shoulders, dampening the eighth grader's shirt.

"I call it friends helpin' out another friend, Mr. Church," Gene continued. "You see these wet fellers was helpin' me win a bet. I'm in the practice of makin' wagers now that I'm almost growed up. My uncle Shade Barlow is learnin' me the ins and outs of gamblin', and these three eighth graders, which for years has been some of my closest and dearest friends, promised to help me out. They done been mighty gen'rous, too. In their spare time, these here boys— Roscoe, Gaither, and Blue—has been tryin' to help me win my bet. Why, I love these fellers as much as I love my brother, Jack."

Gene's words left Roscoe dumbfounded. He turned and stared at his two befuddled buddies who gazed back in slack-jawed confusion. Blue slid his hand down into the backside of his bib overalls and began scratching his behind; Gaither began vigorously picking at his nose. Soon he was at least two knuckles deep in his left nasal passage. All the while, Gaither and Blue looked closely at Roscoe and mirrored their leader's several bewildered facial expressions, although they continued scratching and picking.

Gene explained to Mr. Church that he had bet several eighth graders a quarter each that he could hold his breath underwater for at least a minute. Catching on to Gene's subterfuge, Roscoe, who was no fool, nodded in agreement.

Seeing Roscoe nod, Gaither and Blue began nodding exuberantly at each other. Blue nodded so rapidly that his face became a blur. Gaither cackled, and Blue, in return, emitted high, ear-piercing giggles. Gaither clamped his hands over his ears and began jumping up and down, stomping his brogans on the soaked floor while he bounced enthusiastically.

"Snake eater!" hollered Gaither, pointing at Blue and stamping his feet in the standing water. His splashing brogans imitated the rhythmic steps of the dance called clogging, a folk dance popular in the Appalachian Mountains. The sound of Blue's snickers increased by several decibels as he joined Gaither in the clogging dance. Water droplets filled the air around them, as the two skipped, pirouetted, and stomped.

Roscoe put a calming hand on Gaither's shoulder and squinted sternly at Blue.

"Quiet down, fellers," whispered Roscoe. "Calm yourselves. We don't want to get into no trouble with Mr. Church."

The ear-shattering giggles ceased. Gaither and Blue settled down, staring forlornly at their damp brogans. The restroom was silent except for the dripping of a leaky faucet.

"Tell me more about your gambling and your bet, Gene," said the principal now that he could be heard, "but before you do, I have decided on your punishment. The janitor will need help cleaning up this minor flood. The boys who are soaked will stay after school and assist Mr. Eller. His helpers will be Roscoe, Blue, Gaither, and Gene. All of you live within walking distance of the school, so getting home should be no problem. Tank, Hal, and Johnny, you have relatively dry clothes. I assume you three were merely observers."

"Yes, we were just watching, and trying to figure out what was going on," said Johnny Knight.

"Well, Gene, I'm waiting for an explanation for all this water, if there is one. Why is the boys' bathroom practically flooded? What do these soaked floors have to do with your bet?"

"Mr. Church, I was just practicin' for the bet I made, and these eighth-grade buddies of mine was helpin' me out. With their unwaverin' support, I stand a good chance of winnin' two, maybe three dollars," said Gene. "Good money in these hard financial times." He ran his fingers through his thin, wet hair, causing several strands to stand straight up like weeds missed by a lawnmower. Gene smiled with divided, cigarette-stained teeth. Water continued to drip from his nose and chin, forming tiny pools on the tile floor.

"These eighth graders was helpin' me by timin' me while I held my breath under water. We was usin' Roscoe's watch," he said. "When I come up for air, I slung water all around. I come up for air sev'ral times while practicin'. I reckon I was splashin' water ever' time I come up to breathe. I'm sorry for the mess. How long did I stay underwater that last time, ole pal, ole buddy?"

Gene addressed Roscoe whose hands were still dripping. Roscoe glanced quickly at his watch and then hid his dripping hands behind his back.

Gaither and Blue stood next to Roscoe like Neanderthals, with their hairy knuckles hanging barely a foot from the floor. Judging by their expressions, they were baffled by Mr. Church's arrival and wanted to get back to the task of soaking Gene's head. An ant that was crawling across the bathroom floor caught their attention. The two were transfixed. The ant was carefully avoiding water puddles. The creature's gyrating antennas, like a car's windshield wipers on a rainy night, were working overtime. The bug stopped crawling to inspect Blue's brogan. Blue lifted his foot, aimed the shoe, and stomped down on the hapless insect, flattening it.

"Flat as a flitter," said Blue. He grinned at Gaither. Captured by the joy of the moment, the two began their nodding and giggling routine, only softly this time, barely noticeable.

When Roscoe spoke, their subdued bobbing and snickering ceased, and they jerked their heads toward their leader.

"You stayed with your face and nose underwater in that toilet bowl for nearly a minute, Gene. You done real good, buddy. I'm right proud of you," said Roscoe, who, unlike Gaither and Blue, had been held back in the eighth grade only once. Roscoe had some obvious smarts, but was retained due to pure, unadulterated laziness. He had refused to do any homework and often had refused to take tests. However, he was shrewd enough to go along with Gene's gambling ploy because he said to Mr. Church, "I guess sev'ral eighth graders is gonna lose their bets after all. I don't care because them boys ain't my friends like Gene is. Do you want to have the real contest tomorrow, Gene? I reckon you'll be ready by then."

"Nope. The real contest will take place here in this very bathroom stall on Monday mornin', bright and early," announced Gene. "It is against my religious upbringin' to gamble on Fridays, Saturdays, Sundays, and on any night when there is a full moon overhead unless it is a blue moon. Blue moons have always brung me luck."

Then Gene turned to the school principal. He coughed, clearing out his water-logged voice box. His raspy speech dripped with sincerity.

"I sure would appreciate it, sir, if you would meet us here on Monday mornin', and be the official timer and the official judge," said Gene. "Ever'body knows you're a fair man, a truthful man, and a law-abidin' man. I don't want to hear no eighth grader say I cheated on this here bet. I plan to win fair and square."

Mr. Church frowned. "Gene, you know we don't allow students to make gambling bets at Healing Waters Elementary School, so this contest, if that's what it really is, is hereby canceled. It will not take place, not on Monday, not on Tuesday, not ever. The school board has a policy against gambling on school grounds."

Gene scowled and looked disappointed. He folded his arms across his chest and said, "You mean all this practicin', all this holdin' of my breath underwater was for nothin'? Tarnation! Here I am shiverin', soaked to the bone, nearly drownded, and it's all been for nothin'."

"I'm sorry, Gene," said Roscoe. "You was gettin' awful good at holdin' your breath, but I reckon Mr. Church is right. Besides, some folks say gamblin' is a sin."

"My gamblin' days is over!" Gene exclaimed. "I'm done with it. This is a sign sent from up above, maybe from Jesus hisself. I ain't gonna bet nor gamble no more! Not never!"

In truth, Gene was a habitual gambler. He gambled more than any other kid at school. He would bet on televised ballgames, checkers, Monopoly games, coin flips, and H-O-R-S-E basketball shooting contests. He knew how to shoot craps, shoot pool, and play poker. Unfortunately, he recently had experienced a string of bad luck in all of the above. He owed a total of four dollars to various students in the seventh and eighth grades. Four dollars was a small fortune in our crowd. I'll say this for him—so far Gene had always paid his gambling debts—*eventually*.

Mr. Church touched his smooth, shaven chin and looked at the water-splashed stall, the dripping bathroom walls, the puddled floor, and the drenched commode. The principal shook his head and walked over to Gene, placing his hand on Gene's thin shoulder. The tall principal bent over, until he was eye to eye with Gene. Mr. Church's clear blue eyes showed genuine concern.

"In addition to the gambling, Gene, there is another matter that needs attention. It is a matter of cleanliness and sanitation," said Mr. Church, glancing again at the dripping commode with its rusty bolts holding the fixture to the stained tile floor. He knitted his brow as if he had the beginnings of a migraine headache. "Tomorrow, Ashe County's school nurse will be visiting our school. I'm going to set aside some morning time, Gene, for you and Miss Gentry to discuss personal hygiene."

"Well, I do know somethin' about personal hygiene 'cause we studied on it last year in Mrs. Bender's class. I hope I can call to mind all that I learnt," said Gene. "Let me think on it."

Gene put his thumbs under his belt and hoisted his soggy jeans. He sidled over to a sink and leaned his skinny frame against its front side. Using the school's rough, grainy soap, he washed his hands thoroughly and dried them on a paper towel which he then dropped into a nearby wastebasket. At that point, with both hands, he wrung the tail of his T-shirt and a pint of commode water dripped to the floor. He released the T-shirt and lifted his right hand to his face. Gene stroked his chin as if deep in thought. Again, he lifted his jeans to the point where three inches of bare ankle showed on each leg above his shabby, sockless, soaked tennis shoes. Through a slit in his left tennis shoe, his little toe, capped with a blackened nail, was visible.

Gene pushed his wet hair to the left using his right hand. His hair clung to his head, producing the comb-over hairstyle often used by balding men in their forties. His eyes, which usually operated independently of one another, were both focused and locked on his reflection in the mirror above the restroom sink. His mouth assumed a confident smirk as he sniffed the air three times, inflating his chest. Then Gene's mouth softened into an engaging, toothy smile, his eyes brightened, his nostrils widened, and his eyebrows leapt skyward. He turned and swaggered forward confidently and stood with erect posture in front of Mr. Church. Once more, he hauled up his heavy, waterlogged jeans which had sagged down well below his naval this time, almost to the point of embarrassment.

"I'll be glad to talk with Miss Gentry, Mr. Church," said Gene. "In fact, I'm mighty proud you picked me out special to speak to her. Mom will be awful pleased when I tell her this evenin'. But to tell you the truth, the school nurse has always seemed awful neat, nice lookin', and clean to me. I have never seen a spot of dirt on her white uniform, and I have never once considered talkin' to her about her personal hygiene. But if I must, I reckon I must. Thank goodness I learnt a lot about personal hygiene and sanitation last year. Mrs. Bender took a personal interest in ever'body's personal hygiene, 'specially mine. Well, I just hope I don't mortify Miss Gentry by bringin' up the subject of keepin' clean. Womenfolk gets embarrassed awful easy, you know."

Mr. Church shook his head slowly and then smiled down at Gene. He was a man of great patience. The principal opened his mouth to speak to Gene, but decided not to discuss further the matter of Miss Gentry's personal hygiene. He sighed then stood up straight and tall. Mr. Church was at least an inch over six feet.

The principal rode his eyes around our small group of seventh and eighth graders, making sure he made eye contact for a few seconds with each of us. Then he looked at his watch and said, "When the last bell rings, Mr. Eller will meet with his helpers here in the restroom. Follow his instructions. He will have buckets and mops for the four of you."

"I'll be here," promised Roscoe, "and I'll bring Gaither and Blue with me."

"Me too," said Gene. "Me and these ole boys won't quit until this here restroom is spick-and-span. With all four of us cleanin' and moppin' it won't take us no time. We'll have this here bathroom floor so clean a'body could eat off it."

"All right, I want all of you students to go back to your classrooms now. Remember that there will be no bets or wagers made at our school. You have about three minutes before the bell is scheduled to ring. On your way! And Gene, tomorrow morning I'll remind you of your meeting with the school nurse."

"Okey-dokey!" said Gene. "And don't you worry none, Mr. Church, 'cause I'd wager fifty sawmill dollars, if I had that kinda money, that I'll have our school nurse practicin' habits of good hygiene in no time. She looks like a fast learner to me. I'd gamble a bunch of money on Miss Gentry's progress, that is if I was a bettin' man, which I ain't, not no more! I'm swearin' off gamblin' from now on. Somebody fetch me a stack of Bibles."

Mr. Church could hear the telephone ringing in his office. I suspected he wanted to stay and talk some more with Gene, but he had no secretary and sometimes got important calls from parents or school officials at the central office. The superintendent of schools called him at least once a week. Mr. Church must have decided he'd better answer the telephone because he disappeared back inside the school. The phone rang two or three more times, and then stopped.

When Mr. Church exited the boys' restroom, Roscoe Darnell breathed an audible sigh of relief and looked at the dripping, coughing skinny guy with newfound respect, thankful that no one had been expelled or severely punished for what came to be known among our seventh-grade classmates as Gene's "head-in-the-commode adventure" or the "copperhead sandwich tale."

Among Healing Waters Elementary School students, Gene's reputation was enhanced by the telling and retelling of his watery restroom exploit.

Mr. Church's departure left Gaither Callaway and Blue Barton in a state of confusion. Slapping their hands on their chests, they grunted a few times in bewilderment. Gaither began picking at his nose again, and Blue stuck his pinky finger deep into his ear and rotated the digit several times. He withdrew a dark chocolate-colored wad of ear wax. He stared at the brown globule on his little finger with a smidgen of pride in his dull, vacuous eyes. He grunted softly. Gaither's nasal diggings also proved successful as evidenced by a green dollop of semi-solid mucus resting on the tip his extended forefinger.

"Looky here, Gaither, this wax was disturbin' my hearin'," said Blue, rolling the wax between his thumb and forefinger. "Now, lemme see what you got."

Gaither and Blue displayed their findings to one another. Their eyes narrowed good-humoredly, and they chuckled conspiratorially cuffing at each other in an almost apelike fashion. Blue slapped Gaither on the ear, and Gaither grinned although his ear reddened. Gaither smacked Blue on the nose, and Blue snorted and giggled. Blue's nose turned a rosy pink on its tip. Blue slapped Gaither again, a bit harder than before.

"You ain't hurtin' me none! You ain't got the stren'th I got!" one of them exclaimed. I couldn't tell which one.

Wiping his damp hair with a handkerchief supplied by Johnny Knight, Gene whispered, "Watch them two ole country boys, Hal. They're fixin' to get into it!"

Steadily, the slapping increased in velocity and intensity until the blows devolved into a full-fledged fistfight. Wildly thrown jabs and roundhouse punches often missed, but occasionally the blows landed and bounced off the muscled bodies of the evenly matched pair.

"Oof!" grunted Gaither as Blue slammed a powerful fist into his friend's midsection.

In return, Gaither landed an upper cut on Blue's prominent chin causing his buddy's eyes to cross momentarily. Hearing some sort of internal clock, they suddenly stopped swinging and began bumping their chests together. Round one ended in a draw.

As they stood toe-to-toe and chest-to-chest, now glaring at each other with their lips drawn back in snarls, both fighters emitted strange high-pitched yipping sounds through their clenched teeth. The yipping turned into a mournful yodeling duet as the primitive pugilists drew back their right fists, preparing for round two.

"Stop it! Dammit! Stop it!" shouted Roscoe. "Calm your asses down! Now both of you—take a deep breath. Gaither, you come over here and stand by me. Blue, you go over there and stand next to Hal Grayson."

Dutifully, Blue shuffled over and stood beside me. He grinned at me and pointed to his nose, which was beginning to bleed. He snuffled.

"My nose is bleedin' a little, but it don't hurt none," he confided.

"Okay, if you pint-sized heathens is settled down and ready to go, let's get back to the classroom. I consider us damn lucky not to be settin' in the principal's office right now. Come on now and foller me," said Roscoe, exerting his leadership. Roscoe's two troglodyte followers nodded in assent and shadowed Roscoe to the restroom's exit.

Once outside, they made a hasty retreat, heading for their eighth-grade classroom. Roscoe broke into a dead run, while Gaither and Blue, making guttural, simian sounds, scuttled along behind him.

As Gene exited the restroom, Tank grabbed him, picked him up, and placed him on Johnny Knight's shoulders. Laughing all the way, they galloped toward our classroom door. I followed several yards behind. Johnny Knight, carrying Gene's extra weight, still won the race. At the classroom door, Tank had lifted Gene off Johnny Knight's shoulders, set him down, and congratulated him.

Tank and Johnny each gave Gene a good-natured slap on the back, causing him to cough up about a cup of water.

"That was an Oscar-winning performance if I've ever seen one! Old Marlon Brando couldn't have acted out that restroom scene much better than you did, Gene!" Tank had said, slapping Gene on the back one more time.

We stood just inside the school room door, waiting for the bell to ring. Gene coughed again as Mr. Church entered the room. The school bell rang. By the time Mr. Church had begun taking the roll, Johnny Knight, Tank, Gene, and I had already taken our seats with the rest of our class.

While our teacher was putting math problems on the chalkboard, Tank leaned over the arm of his desk and whispered to Gene, "Did you mean it when you said you were making no more bets?"

"Yep, I meant ever' word," said Gene. "I done lost too much money this year, and therefore I have done swore off gamblin' for keeps. Gamblin' is a fool's game, anyways. I ain't makin' no more bets."

"Oh, you will gamble again, Gene; I'm sure of it. You're a gambler. You're addicted to gambling," Tank said.

"No, I ain't," Gene countered, retrieving his math book from under his desk. "No more gamblin' for me. I ain't addicted to nothin'. Sure, bettin' on things is a big temptation, but I got the strength to resist."

"Your next gambling experience will take place this very afternoon because you're hooked, my friend," said Tank, looking at his wristwatch. "Yes, I think within the hour. In fact, I'm willing to wager one dollar right now that you will gamble again, and soon," Tank stated, reaching for his billfold.

"You're on!" Gene snapped.

Sure enough, Gene wound up owing Tank a dollar. All of the guys, Pudge, Gene, and me, owed Tank much more than that. The big boy had a mischievous side, but generally he was steady as a rock. We came to depend on his strength, honesty, and friendship during our elementary school days. His moral compass, steady and true, helped guide us through the morass of homework, teachers, tests, bullies, scuffles, name-calling, and hurt feelings that were part of growing up. As the years passed, Tank became our protector. When Pudge, Gene, or I got into a scrape, he showed up, often in the nick of time.

CHAPTER 12

Fortunately for the rest of us, the two most formidable guys in our class back at Healing Waters Elementary School, Tank and Johnny Knight, were amiable and friendly. They were truly gentle giants. Never rough or domineering, they were more likely to break up a fight than to get into one.

I had once asked Johnny Knight who he thought was the stronger of the two. Johnny had wide shoulders, big biceps, and was the tallest guy in our class, next to Gene. His hands, hardened by farm work, were almost as large as Tank's. With his wavy black hair, Johnny looked like Superboy as he was drawn in the DC comic books.

"Tank is by far the strongest guy at school," said Johnny. "You may not believe this, but last year Tank picked me up and put me on a small table in the cafeteria, and get this, he then picked up my girlfriend Catherine and put her beside me on the table. After that, he lifted me, Catherine, and the table about three feet into the air. I couldn't believe his power. Boy oh boy, that Tank is something!"

Tank had wandered into our lives during the second week of school in our first grade year. His father had been transferred from Boston, Massachusetts, to Ashe County to manage Sponge Electronic and Engineering Company, a thriving manufacturing business in the county. Mr. and Mrs. William Banner had acquired a nice brick home near the New River and settled in with their only child.

Tank's given name was Douglas, Douglas Trent Banner. His mother's maiden name was Trent, he explained. Within three school days, all his first grade classmates were calling him Tank. Only the teacher called him Douglas.

In the first grade classroom, movement was a problem for Tankus Giganticus—the nickname that Gene, whose favorite dinosaur was the tyrannosaurus rex, had given him. As Douglas walked down the neat rows of desks, his great bulk shifting from side to side, classroom furniture and first grade children were rearranged. His immense posterior plowed into the art table, scattering our clay creations and finger paintings that were drying on top. By the end of his first day, a special desk had been brought down from the eighth-grade classroom to accommodate Douglas Trent Banner.

"The big boy moves like a tank," Pudge had cried. "Nothing can stand in his way. He's more powerful than a tyrannosaurus rex!"

"Douglas ain't stoppable. He's like a big ole brontosaurus movin' through trees and knockin' 'em down," said Gene.

Standing near the teacher's desk, Douglas Banner turned when he heard Gene speak his name. His voluminous posterior pushed the heavy desk aside. Reading books, sheets of wide-lined paper, and thick round pencils flopped to the floor. Our teacher gasped.

"Oh, my goodness!" said Miss Blevins, kneeling to pick up the fallen materials. "Oh, dear me!"

Her expletives were always mild.

"Man, oh, man, did you see that?" asked Johnny Knight. "Douglas moved Miss Blevins's desk with his butt. Wow! Oh boy, that's strength, that's power!"

"Well, I hope Douglas don't trip and fall on me," said Gene, eyeing the big boy warily. "It'd be like gettin' run over by a big ole Army tank. I reckon that's what we ort to call him from now on—the Tank!"

"He's not Douglas; he's the Tank!" exclaimed Pudge. In our young, developing minds, it was like saying "He's not Bruce

Wayne—he's Batman. He's not Billy Batson—he's Captain Marvel. He's not Clark Kent—he's Superman!"

"Look out, fellers! Here comes Tankus Giganticus!" bellowed Gene as we lined up for our lunch break.

Tank didn't wear a flashy costume, and he couldn't bend steel in his large hands. He certainly couldn't vault over tall buildings with a single leap. He couldn't change the course of the mighty New River, nor was he swifter than a zooming bullet—far from it. However, as we passed from grade to grade at Healing Waters Elementary School, Tank became our superhero—he believed in justice and fairness for all, even Gene; he was willing to risk his own safety to help his friends; he expected no rewards for his good deeds; and he was powerful, stronger than anyone I had ever met or known.

Of course, Douglas Trent Banner hadn't come from the extinct planet Krypton like the world's most famous superhero, but he had come from another place about a million miles away from Healing Waters Elementary School—the state of Massachusetts. When Pudge would kid him about being a Yankee, Tank repeatedly reminded the redhead that he had been born in *southern* Massachusetts.

CHAPTER 13

While we traipsed up the dusty path that led to the carnival grounds, I thought about how we'd met Douglas Banner in the first grade classroom so long ago. I wondered if he remembered his earliest days at Healing Waters Elementary School. I looked over at Tank, who was beginning to pant as the trail became even steeper. He paused briefly to consume a Milky Way candy bar pulled from his trouser pocket, then burped and smiled as he put the candy wrapper back in his pocket. Suddenly his nostrils widened, picking up the soft scent of cotton candy drifting down from the festival above us. He walked faster. When the steep, wide path leveled off, giving the four of us some relief, the big boy began to breathe normally.

As he strode forward with self-assurance, Tank hummed a Bobby Darin tune. Soon, the big boy stopped humming and tried to sing, but he didn't know all the lyrics to Darin's "Splish Splash."

"Split, splat, I was swingin' a bat!" warbled Tank. "Dadgum! I hit a home run."

"That's not the way it goes," said Pudge, who was a stickler for accuracy.

Nonetheless, the Tank, like a scratched record, kept chanting the incorrect words to Darin's hit over and over again, ad nauseam. Finally, Pudge got tired of the repetition and burst into a noisy vocal rendition of Lloyd Price's "Stagger Lee."

Amazingly, Pudge knew all the hit song's lyrics—and so did Gene. The two sang loudly, if not well. Tank stopped singing "Splish Splash" and listened to Pudge and Gene harmonize. When Pudge and Gene sang together, anyone could note that Pudge had a much better singing voice than Gene. However, as he sang, Gene threw in a few cool dance steps that he picked up by watching ABC's *American Bandstand*. His nimble dancing helped compensate for his poor singing. Gene became so intent on his dance moves that Pudge found himself singing alone.

"... men whooo gambled laaate," warbled Pudge.

The redhead sang on, finally reaching the point in the song where the deadly Stagger Lee had pulled his forty-four pistol on Billy, his fellow gambler.

"Take it, Gene," invited Pudge, assuming a vaudevillian stance with his arm thrown out in Gene's direction. He expected Gene to continue the words, but he was wrong.

Gene, who had stopped dancing, turned his face mournfully skyward and began plunking at an imaginary guitar like a solitary cowboy on the prairie surrounded by grazing longhorns. Atop Gene's head sat his large black cowboy hat with its broad brim that shaded his eyes. Back in third grade, his favorite television cowboy had been William Boyd's character, Hopalong Cassidy, and the silver-haired Hoppy always wore a black hat. Gene cleared his throat, adjusted his cowboy hat, and snuffed his nose a couple of times. He then sang out loudly, clearly, and off key.

"Dew nod foresnook me, my ole daahlin', on dis my marriage daaay!" warbled Gene, giving an inaccurate and painful imitation of Tex Ritter's rendering of the theme song from the movie *High Noon*.

Gene repeated the lyrics leering romantically at a seventy-five-year-old grandmother who descended the trail, leaving the carnival. The elderly lady wore a shapeless brown dress, scuffed orthopedic shoes, and wrinkled gray support hose. She passed close by, pulling behind her a reluctant five-year-old granddaughter. The granddaughter wanted to go in the other direction, back up the hill to the carnival grounds, so there was a mini tug-of-war going on.

"Dew nod foresnook me..." Gene continued.

The gray-haired grandmother stopped and stared at Gene, who, holding his nose, began to yodel miserably.

"Woo woo woo-whoopdee do! Woo woo woo-whoopdee do da! Oh, whoopdee da diddle do daay!"

The five-year-old clapped her hands to her ears, and scrunching her eyes, tightening her lips, and knitting her eyebrows, she made a face resembling a pink prune. Little prune face stuck out her tongue.

The grandmother spat snuff mixed with saliva onto the ground. The liquid puddled in the broad path's grit and dust. She eyed Gene curiously, perhaps thinking he was an entertainer hired by the carnival staff.

Gene pulled his large black cowboy hat down over his eyes until his nose, mouth, and Adam's apple were his most noticeable features. His broad, toothy grin was both amiable and disconcerting. He addressed the grandmother with a slow Western drawl.

"Howdy, ma'am. Yep, I'm a cowboy. Yep. Yippy yi ki yo! Ridin' the range, brandin' cattle, and all that western kinda stuff. Gittum up, Scout! Yer durn tootin'! A singin' cowboy is what I am. And, my purty little prairie blossom, I aim to make you my blushin' bride. Yes, you, dear lady. I knowed it the minute I laid eyes on you! You're my one and only. You're my heart's desire! You're the love of my life! You're my sugar dumplin'! We're gonna make beautiful music together west of the Pecos under a starry sky!"

Gene jiggled his prominent Adam's apple and licked his lips seductively.

"We'll ride off into the sunset together, just the three of us: you, me, and my trusty white mule, Diablo!"

The grandmother, whose hair was twisted into an iron-gray bun atop her head, looked Gene up and down through wire-rimmed glasses. A few strands of hair fell forward almost touching her spectacles and her thick, salt-and-pepper eyebrows slowly converged just above the bridge of her sharp nose. She constricted her eyes and widened her nostrils as she sized Gene up.

"You're a nut," she said, spitting dark snuff juice on the ground near his foot.

I could tell she used snuff habitually because her teeth, probably false, were stained with the powdered tobacco product. A slender twig about two inches long stuck out of one corner of her mouth. One end was chewed into a spindly brush used for dipping snuff. Both my grandmothers dipped snuff, so I was an expert at picking out old ladies who dipped.

"That's what you are, pure and simple. You're a nut," she continued. "You're just a young'un now, but when you get older, you'll prob'ly be a bigger nut. Then they'll put you in the nuthouse with all the other nuts. One of my closest neighbors, Fenimore Hodges, had to be put in the nuthouse. Started thinkin' he was the queen of England. Commenced dressin' the part. Wore big ole puffy dresses with his hairy arms stickin' out the sleeves. Painted his fingernails and toenails red, put on lipstick, and wore a big ole plastic crown on his head all the time. Demanded to be waited on hand and foot. His wife sent the old nut packin' off to the funny farm down near Raleigh as soon as she could get all the papers signed. Like Mrs. Hodges, Little Maude and me don't care for nuts, not of the human variety."

"I like some nuts. I like walnuts and peanuts on ice cream, but I don't like you," said Little Maude, kicking a few small stones in Gene's direction.

The old lady reached down and grasped her granddaughter's hand. The little girl looked up at her grandma and tugged her hand free. Then the child looked at Gene, folded her arms across her chest, and stamped her foot.

"You stop aggravatin' and pesterin' my granny, you little turd!" she bellowed and stamped her foot again for emphasis.

"Come along, Little Maude, let's go back to the truck. Grandpa Gunch will be waitin' inside the ole Plymouth truck. You can tell him that you saw a real live nut at the carnival."

With that, the grandmother and granddaughter turned and disappeared into the crowd.

"Well, good evenin' then," Gene called out. "Partin' with you is awful hard and filled with considerable sour tastin' but mostly sweet sorrow. Don't forget me, nor our faded love."

"Let's go, Kemosabe," said the Tank, grabbing Gene by his slender shoulders, turning him around, and shoving him gently forward. "We came here to ride carnival rides, not to disturb little old ladies with marriage proposals."

"You are right as rain, Tankus Giganticus, let us amble on up this dusty trail," sighed Gene. "My broke heart will mend with time. Like Gene Autry and Roy Rogers, I reckon I'd better just ride off into the sunset, knowin' that true love is so dang hard to find."

We continued our trek upward toward the carnival. After ten steps forward, Gene elbowed me and whispered, "Before Tank so rudely interrupted me, I was gettin' ready to foller that granny and ask her to the Central Ashe homecomin' dance this fall. Do you reckon I shoulda asked her?"

"That granny is much too young for you, Gene," I laughed.

Gene grinned back at me, shrugging his shoulders. He took off his cowboy hat and walked along, carrying it in front of him as he softly sang his off-key version of Ricky Nelson's "Lonesome Town."

CHAPTER 14

I had known Tank, Gene, and Pudge since the first weeks of the first grade. There had never been a kindergarten at Healing Waters Elementary School, so we were, during our first grade year, the youngest kids at the school. Our teacher, Miss Caroline Blevins, was a slight, bespectacled woman in her early twenties with shoulder-length chestnut colored hair. She was pretty, bordering on beautiful, and her glasses enhanced her beauty, like rosy sunsets during the fall leaf season could make the Appalachian Mountains look even more vibrant. Miss Blevins' smile was something to behold, and her laughter brightened up the classroom for all twenty of us first graders. In addition to teaching us, Miss Blevins seemed determined to find something likable and good in all of us, even Gene.

In short, Miss Blevins was the perfect teacher for her new and academically inexperienced students. I admit that I had a crush on her, and I even considered asking her to marry me. However, I realized, even at six, that the differences in our ages could present an insurmountable problem. I decided to bide my time. Perhaps, as I got older, the age difference would be less apparent and less important, but by fourth grade I had forgotten about Miss Blevins. By then I had an intense crush on my fourth-grade teacher, Miss Baker.

Tank, Gene, Pudge and I, as six-year-olds, had learned to read together using the traditional Dick and Jane reading books found in most schools. We students had small books at our desks and Miss Blevins had a giant book that she placed on an easel in front of the classroom. Our teacher often stood beside the easel and pointed out various words. I remembered in particular one of the earliest lessons in reading: "See Puff. See Puff run. Run, Puff, run. See Sally. See Sally run."

Gene, a curious first grader, raised his thin, pink hand, scratched his head, and inquired of Miss Blevins, "What the dickens are they runnin' for? Is there a big ole dog chasin' that little pussy cat? Is Sally tryin' to catch and protect Puff, or are they runnin' just for the hell of it?"

Miss Blevins seemed appalled and visibly shaken. Her high heels wobbled, and she grabbed the easel for support. She flushed and replied uncomfortably, "I think the latter, Gene. Sally and Puff are running for the fun of it. Yes, they are running for the sheer joy of running and being young and free. Do you like to run, Gene?"

"Damn straight!" Gene replied, waving his pencil. "And I can run fast as a rabbit! My daddy don't whup me much nowadays, 'cause I can gen'rally outrun him. My uncle Shade says that I'm the fastest runnin' little son of a bitch that he ever seen."

"Please watch your language, Eugene," said Miss Blevins. "We mustn't use…."

"And I ain't afraid to jump off the roof of the henhouse barefooted, neither!" continued Gene, unperturbed. "One time my cousin Toby double-dog dared me and Pudge to jump off, and I climbed way up on that chicken house roof and jumped. Pudge wouldn't even climb all the way up. Didn't hurt too much when I landed, except for my ankles. Uncle Shade said I durn near broke 'em! I limped around for two or three days, but I got to be all right."

Pudge fidgeted in his desk. His shoes began to tap the floor; his fingers patted his desktop.

"Pudge, the redheaded boy sittin' in that desk right over yonder close to the winder," continued Gene, "had come home with me from church, Miss Blevins; and he was afraid to jump off the roof of the henhouse, which ain't all that tall. Pudge wouldn't even climb three steps up the ladder. Pudge is a chicken, Miss Blevins. He's a scaredy-cat."

"Am not!" shouted Pudge. He sat up straight in his desk and raised his reading book to hide his blushing face.

"Are too!" said Gene stubbornly.

"Am not!" said Pudge from behind his book.

"Are too!" said Gene.

"Boys! No shouting. We must use our indoor voices. Now, I'm sure that Pudgie is brave in many ways, but we must return to our lesson," said Miss Blevins, smiling at the redheaded first grade reader.

"No, he ain't, Miss Blevins. Ain't no way he's brave. He's a chicken. At least he's a chicken about climbin' up and jumpin' off henhouse roofs!"

Pudge's face turned a bright red, and he put his head down on his desk, but he didn't cry.

"Anyway," Gene said, changing the subject quickly, "Uncle Shade, Cousin Toby's daddy, showed me, Pudge, and Toby how to tell a little boy puppy from a little girl puppy. It ain't hard to do if you know what to look for."

Although Miss Blevins knew that Gene's father was a Baptist minister, she did not know that Gene was strongly influenced by his favorite uncle, Shade Barlow, who was the county's most prosperous moonshiner.

"Did your uncle Shade show you how to tell a girl kitten from a boy kitten, Gene?" asked a pretty little girl named Clarissa Elliott, whose desk was behind Pudge's.

Gene replied, "One time Uncle Shade tried to show me and Toby about kittens, but I couldn't tell no difference between the two little kittens he picked up. He showed us their *things*. You know, the things betwixt their hind legs. Both kittens looked about the same to me. I couldn't see no real difference in them little cats. But I can tell right away whether a newborned calf is a boy or girl. All you do with a little calf is to look for...."

"Let's continue to the next page, students," Miss Blevins said desperately, turning the page of the large book on the easel; but Gene was not through giving the class information about himself, his family, and his farm animals.

The eyes of all us first graders were on Gene. We ignored our teacher, the small books on our desks, and the large book on the easel. We students were mesmerized by the skinny kid. Miss Blevins did not interrupt Gene, choosing instead to ride out the pedagogical skirmish. Or perhaps she, like us, was spellbound by the smallish first grader, waving his arms and gesticulating to punctuate his remarks.

"We got four baby calves on our farm, one boy and three girls, and my cat, Scratchy, had ten kittens, but one of 'em died, leavin' nine healthy kittens. We give seven kittens away, and we still got two, if anybody wants one," said Gene, looking around the classroom. Seeing no interest in the kittens, he moved along.

"And we have a three-legged Bluetick Coonhound that Daddy named Tripod, which sucks eggs in the hen house. Tripod don't kill chickens, though. Never has killed a single chicken. Daddy said if Tripod ever kills a rooster or a hen, he's gonna shoot him dead, but Mama won't let him. She loves that ole dog like fam'ly.

"I like cornbread and pinto beans and fried chicken and blueberry cobbler. I don't like peas much, but I do like corn on the cob. We feed the cobs and table scraps to the hogs."

"Gene, would you like to come up here and help me turn the pages in the big book? Would you like to be my helper today?" invited Miss Blevins. There was a tinge of desperation in her voice.

"Nope, you've been doin' a fine job of turnin' them pages, Miss Blevins. I'm gonna tell these young'uns a little about my fam'ly, and I know you're in a sweat to keep turnin' them big book pages, so I ain't gonna take long."

"All right. You may tell the class about your family, but please be brief."

"My grandpa wears red long johns under his bib overalls all year round," Gene continued. "Me and him like to pee off the back porch ever' night before we go to bed. My stream of pee is stronger than Grandpa's for he mostly dribbles."

Tank put his hand over his mouth and giggled softly during the remainder of Gene's monologue.

"My grandma keeps her teeth in a jar beside her bed. When I was little, I throwed her false teeth out the winder. Granny whupped my tail with a hickory switch. Stung like the dickens.

"My mama says that nobody should never pass gas at the dinner table when any of Daddy's church folks comes for Sunday dinner. Mama says it's a sin to pass gas durin' the blessin', so I'm workin' on getting' my gas passin' under control. Pass gas means *fart*, Miss Blevins. I reckon I'm through, Miss Blevins, unless you wanna hear about my big brother, Jack."

Ignoring Gene as best she could, Miss Blevins quickly flipped another page of the large reading book resting on the easel to reveal a picture of a small boy and his dog. All eyes turned to the big book perched on the easel. The interrupted reading lesson continued. Miss Blevins turned several pages in the big book, and the class read the short sentences on those pages successfully. We were halfway through the book when we came to the following sentences:

"See Dick! See Dick run! See Spot! See Spot run!"

At this point in the Dick and Jane story, Gene was waving his raised hand wildly, but Miss Blevins paid him no heed. Instead, she called on a pigtailed girl sitting in the back of the classroom.

"Janet, how many letters are there in the word 'run?'"

"Free!" said Janet Sunshine Summerfield, a dark-haired chubby girl who was missing a front tooth.

Since the response was close enough to its academic target, it was accepted by the teacher. She praised Janet who squirmed with pleasure. Then Miss Blevins called on Pudge who walked proudly up to the easel and pointed out the word 'run.'

"Very good, Pudgie," said Miss Blevins. A smiling Pudge, with head held high, walked proudly back to his seat. He stuck his tongue out at Gene as he sauntered past the skinny kid's desk. Gene returned the affront in kind.

Some of the teachers at Healing Waters Elementary School had insisted on calling Pudge by the infantile name "Pudgie" up until the time he finished the eighth grade and went off to high school. Pudge didn't like to be called Pudgie, in fact, he hated the name, but he never said anything to his teachers about it. After all, they were the teachers, the ones in charge. But I noticed that the principal, Mr. Church, always had called him Pudge, even way back in first grade.

Gene, who had settled down in his desk, pushed his first grade reading book aside, took out a small pocket knife, and began carving on his wooden desktop. Miss Blevins overlooked Gene as he whistled softly. Shavings appeared on the desk's wooden surface, and he brushed them aside. Gene was exploring his creativity as he carved what appeared to be a bunny rabbit, but I wasn't really sure what it was. Gene wiped the remaining wood shavings off his desk and onto the floor and then put away his knife. He stared silently and proudly at the carved rabbit—or fox, or dog, or whatever it was—as if his desk carving were on an artistic par with Vincent van Gogh's *Starry Starry Night*.

Miss Caroline Blevins' reading lesson had continued with only one other interruption. A piping girlish voice shattered the steady, incremental intellectual progress of our first grade classroom. Insistence was manifested by the shrillness in the little girl's voice. Everyone turned to look at her. She was so tiny that her desk almost swallowed her.

"Mister Blevins! Mister Blevins!" hollered the little blonde student who was much smaller and perhaps younger than the rest of us. Her name was Cindy Lou Winkler, and she lived way back in a mountain hollow, so far back in fact, that her family's three-room cabin couldn't be seen from the winding gravel road where the school bus stopped to drop her off. Cindy Lou's frayed clothes looked like hand-me-downs from older sisters or handmade dresses constructed by her mother with scraps of cloth and a needle and thread.

"Mister Blevins! Mister Blevins!" she continued. "Is that nice principal, Miss Church, gonna read us another one of them stories today?" asked Cindy Lou toward the end of our lesson. Miss Blevins smiled at Cindy Lou, but her brow was creased with tiny worry lines.

For some unknown reason, Cindy Lou insisted on calling Miss Blevins, *Mister* Blevins. Conversely, Cindy Lou called our tall, broad shouldered, male principal, *Miss* Church.

During her first grade year, Cindy Lou needed a bit more attention than the rest of us, so Miss Blevins gave her extra consideration, along with hugs, praise, and kindness. The principal, Mr. Church, often would stop by our first grade classroom for a short visit. On some days, he would stay longer and read us a story. Mr. Church spent extra time with Cindy Lou and her reading book. By the time Christmas break rolled around, Cindy Lou was reading and doing arithmetic as well as most of the other first graders in our class.

"Cindy Lou, please call me *Miss* Blevins. Yes, I believe *Mister* Church will be here at one o'clock to read us a story called 'The Lonely Pony.' When he arrives, let's all greet our principal by saying, 'Hello, *Mister* Church.' Will you help us Cindy Lou? Would you help us say hello to *Mister* Church?"

Cindy Lou smiled and said, "Yep, I will say howdy to the principal, and, Mister Blevins, can I please go to the indoor outhouse? I feel a peein' spell comin' on. Granny Graybeal says it ain't good to hold your piss."

"Yes, Cindy Lou, you may go since the girls' bathroom is right next door. Let's call it the 'girls' bathroom' or 'restroom,' not the 'indoor outhouse.' Don't be too long, dear."

Cindy Lou stopped before she exited the classroom door. The tiny girl smiled up at her teacher, wiggled the toes on her bare feet, and said politely, "Much obliged, Mister Blevins. I ain't gonna be long for it's a pee I'm in the need of, not a poop."

"Cindy Lou, dear, you don't have to tell us why you need to go to the bathroom, just ask to go to the bathroom. That's enough. Unless you're sick or your tummy hurts, you can just ask for permission."

"Okey-dokey, I reckon I can remember that," said the first-grade girl.

Cindy Lou grabbed the doorknob and twisted and turned until the door opened slightly. She looked back at her teacher.

"You know what, Mister Blevins?"

"No, dear, I really have no idea," Miss Blevins said, smiling bleakly.

"You're the best teacher I ever had—so fer!"

The little girl blushed, stepped through the classroom door, and closed it from the outside.

As promised, Cindy Lou's restroom visit was brief. She returned to the classroom and announced, "They ain't no Sears and Roebuck catalogs left in the girls' bathroom. I looked all over. All they got in there is real thin wipin' paper rolled up on little spools. We better tell Miss Church right away. I can bring one of them Sears catalogs from home tomorrow. We got sev'ral that ain't in use."

"It's the same in the boys' bathroom, Miss Blevins; us boys ain't got no strong wipin' paper like in my outhouse at home," said Gene. "I'll bring a Sears and Roebuck catalog first thing in the mornin'! I reckon Mr. Church'll be right proud of me and Cindy Lou!"

Miss Blevins sat down at her desk and put her head between her hands, using her elbows for support. She ran her fingers through her thick wavy hair. She uttered a soft sigh. In a moment or two, however, our teacher gathered herself, stiffened her spine, and finished the reading lesson.

CHAPTER 15

When Miss Blevins' very first reading lesson had been completed during the second week of school, Pudge put away his small Dick and Jane reader, leaned over his desk, and whispered to me, "That's the best story I've ever read."

"That's the *only* story you've ever read, Pudge," I reminded him, checking my Lone Ranger lunchbox to see if I still had an apple inside.

In the first grade, I was a Lone Ranger fan. That morning I gobbled down a big bowl of milk-drenched, sugar-sprinkled Cheerios, the Lone Ranger's favorite cereal, and the day prior Miss Blevins had taken away my Lone Ranger cap-buster pistol with the white plastic grip, and made me take off my homemade black mask. Tank had insisted in no uncertain terms that I stop calling him Tonto. The mask, the silver bullets, the great white stallion, and the Indian companion all added to the Lone Ranger's mystique. At the end of every television show, the masked rider of the plains rode away with Tonto, without accepting any thanks from the Western townspeople for their heroic deeds. On TV, Clayton Moore portrayed the Lone Ranger, and Jay Silverheels assumed the role of Tonto. When I was a first grader, I thought Jay Silverheels was the coolest name on the planet.

I still think it's pretty cool.

Moving up through the grades together Tank, Pudge, Gene and I had finger painted miniature masterpieces which, upon completion, were taped to classroom walls for prominent display. Back in first grade, however, we'd clutched the large, bulky pencils with inexperienced fingers in our initial, awkward attempts at writing. The four of us learned the alphabet and the alphabet song. Later, we studied our multiplication tables, and we learned to write in cursive style. Along with our fellow students, we learned to read and write and think at higher levels as we advanced to the upper grades.

At recess, we played kickball, dodgeball, and softball. Then, as the years passed, we progressed to baseball and basketball. We joined school teams and learned the importance of practice and teamwork.

On warm summer weekends, we swam in the clear waters of the New River. Truthfully, Gene only waded near the shore, occasionally throwing rocks at those of us in deeper water. Gene had an aversion to deep water, and he considered any water higher than his kneecaps "deep."

"You all can get drownded if you want to, but I hope to gracious that I'll live long enough to see better days," Gene would say as he waved from the river's bank.

Tank, Pudge and I took to the water like Labrador retriever puppies, and we learned to swim well. Tank had an advantage; his bulbous frame caused him to float like a cork on the rippling currents of the New River. There was no danger of drowning for the Tank.

I could swim faster than either Tank or Pudge. I had learned to ride the river's currents and let the flowing water assist in propelling me downstream. Like an otter, Pudge had mastered diving from the low riverbank and enjoyed retrieving shiny stones from the depths of the riverbed. He had a pair of goggles to help him see better underwater. The redhead could hold his breath a lot longer than I could.

Once, after staying underwater so long that Tank and I had become concerned, Pudge had broken the surface, gasping for air and clutching an 1880 silver dollar in his left hand.

"This silver dollar is older than my grandpa," said Pudge gleefully as he scrambled up the riverbank. "I can't wait to show it to him."

Another time, I think it was a few days after the Fourth of July, Pudge had ascended from a particularly deep river dive with a man's soaked billfold in his raised hand. The sopping black leather wallet had a damp twenty-dollar bill and a faded grocery list inside, but no identification. Pudge held the saturated twenty-dollar bill up in the sunlight to dry.

We wondered what might have happened to the wallet's owner. Had he drowned? Had he been murdered and tossed into the New River? Had he been a non-swimmer who slipped and fell to his watery death in the river's rocky depths? Was his partially fish-eaten corpse lodged between two huge rocks at the murky bottom of the river?

"Whoever owned that billfold prob'ly got drunk while fishin' and dropped his wallet from the big bridge up river. The wallet was washed down here by the strong current," said Gene. "I bet the man what lost that wallet is alive and well and is havin' hisself a few beers right now, this bein' Saturday."

Pudge tossed me the soggy wallet, and I examined it, checking for secret compartments and making sure it was empty. Gene was almost certainly right about the billfold's owner, but, nonetheless, we looked down into the deep, cloudy water, wondering what other secrets might be hiding below. Pudge decided to end his diving adventures for the day and Tank and I decided we didn't need to swim anymore. And Gene, who would only wade in the river, decided to remain on the shore. We didn't want to swim, dive, or wade in an area where a ghastly, waterlogged cadaver might be lurking somewhere underwater. From watching the horror movies at the Parkwood Theatre and reading *Tales from the Crypt* comics, we had learned that undead corpses were constantly hiding in the shadows, always seeking human flesh, blood, and especially brains.

We decided to walk down to the Riverbend Store, which was only about a mile down the dusty, wildflower-lined road. We passed Mrs. Virginia Grangerford's house, and, as usual, her big mongrel, Jake, barked ferociously at us from behind a sturdy fence. The elderly, widowed former teacher stepped out on her porch and said, "Don't worry, boys, Jake won't bite."

Still, the large black dog growled fiercely, leaping against the fence's gate again and again. His mouth foamed, his teeth were bared, and his canine eyes glittered. He was in a snarling frenzy, trying to get at us. We walked faster and soon the Riverbend Store was in sight.

"Somebody ort to put ole Jake out of his misery," said Gene as we entered the store.

At the cash register, Pudge exchanged the twenty for four fives. He then split the twenty evenly between the four of us. That's the kind of guy he was—generous and thoughtful.

We bought Moon Pies, Twinkies, chocolate ice cream cups with flat wooden spoons, and big orange soda pops. After we paid, I still had lots of money left over. I crammed the bills and loose change into my jeans pocket and thanked Pudge again for his generosity.

"You'd do the same for me, wouldn't you?" he asked.

I smiled but I didn't answer. I speculated on what I would've done as I opened my Moon Pie wrapper. I knew that Tank would've split the twenty; I wasn't so sure about Gene or me. I chewed on my Moon Pie and pondered the question. After finishing off a third of the Moon Pie and reaching no conclusion, I decided to forget about the question, a tactic I used often when faced with a moral dilemma.

We had eaten outside the store, sitting under a shady oak tree. Panting and wagging its tail, a lean brown dog that hung around the Riverbend Store for handouts joined us. Pudge broke his Twinkie in half and shared half his cream-filled sponge cake with the shorthaired mutt. The dog lay down beside Pudge, obviously enjoying a respite from the summer heat. A soft wind whispered through the oak's broad leaves and from high above in the green foliage, a chattering squirrel scolded us for trespassing on his property.

"If I had a rifle, I'd shoot that little gray son of a bitch," Gene said as he chugged the remainder of his Nehi orange soda.

Summers in our mountains had always seemed too short to me. Often spring days were chilly and rainy. Fall days could be downright windy and cold, especially after dark. Mountain people cherished every sunny summer day and every warm summer night lit up by the moon, stars, and lightning bugs.

My Grandpa Charlie once said to me, "You can always tell Yankees 'cause most of 'em call lightnin' bugs fireflies. Fireflies! Don't that beat all?"

After the farm work was done, many high-country families spent twilight time resting on their front or back porches. Often farm families relaxed outside on wooden swings. Homemade or store-bought rocking chairs rocked in rhythm to the chattering symphony of the insects in nearby fields. The singing, late-summer insects reminded mountain folks that after a brief, vibrant autumn, the extended cold, gray hush of winter would begin.

Although they activated Grandpa Grayson's pollen allergies and made him sneeze fitfully, Grandma Grayson loved the yellow flowers that lined the river banks in late-summer. However, her favorite wild flowers were the blue blossoms of early fall. The plentiful azure flowers, Grandma called them blue asters, caused no allergic reaction in Grandpa Grayson, so they were picked and then spread throughout the house in vases, pots, and bottles until our old house took on a soft blue blush.

"When them purty, sky-blue flowers comes out in early fall, it's a sign that the nights will be gettin' cooler," she said. "Yep, the days will still be warm but the nights will be gettin' colder. Mark my words."

When Grandma would see the light blue flowers blooming along the New River, she would put a folded woolen blanket at the foot of my bed.

CHAPTER 16

The final cool nights of late mountain summers signaled the beginning of each school year at Healing Waters Elementary School where Pudge, Tank, Gene, and I had been classmates for eight consecutive years. School began in a similar manner for all eight grade levels at Healing Waters—textbooks were passed out, seats were assigned, lunch money was collected, and library books were checked out. Students read silently or aloud from textbooks. In the upper grades, young readers gave book reports, students performed science experiments, and teachers administered the dreaded California Achievement Test at the end of the year. Teachers put blackboards to good use, especially during arithmetic classes, and kicked their mimeograph machines into high gear as the contraptions spat out thousands of monotonous, brain-draining worksheets. Then they'd pull out film strip projectors, dust them off, and plug them in to enhance their lessons. On rare occasions, our educators would take us to the school's auditorium where we'd view an educational film. Back in the classroom we watched wall-mounted clocks as everyone waited, sometimes desperately, for recess, bathroom breaks, and lunch.

The county's school nurse visited occasionally to give us the dreaded vaccinations needed to prevent childhood diseases. Lunchroom ladies prepared our lunches and cleaned up our messes afterward. Two busy janitors worked to clean the classrooms, the halls, the auditorium, the library, the cafeteria, the bathrooms, the principal's small office, and the gymnasium.

At Healing Waters, Tank, Pudge, Gene, and I had eaten cornbread and pinto bean lunches and giggled at the gassiness that would inevitably result later in the classroom. Toasted cheese sandwiches and vegetable soup produced far fewer farts. By sixth-grade, however, after years of practice, Gene had learned to control his flatulence so well that he could occasionally use farts to punctuate remarks made by our teacher, Mrs. Bender, whom he heartily disliked.

The feeling was mutual.

I wouldn't say Mrs. Bender and Gene hated each other, but there was no love lost between those two. I recall many times when they had clashed openly in the classroom, but I remember one incident in particular.

The ill-fated episode had occurred toward the end of the sixth-grade school year. Mrs. Bender had allowed us to do our math homework in class. The classroom windows were open all day, and birds were warbling outside. The countryside was awash in various shades of vibrant green. A gray squirrel with a peanut shell in its mouth came to the classroom windowsill and, flicking its bushy tail nervously, peeked in for a moment, until Mrs. Bender shooed him away. We students laughed quietly at the furry gray intruder. Mrs. Bender scowled at us and advised us to get back to our math assignments.

"I'm giving you students class time to complete your homework. You should be grateful," said Mrs. Bender. "Now continue with your work."

Our teacher walked around the room, occasionally bending over a student's desk to help him or her solve a problem. Whenever she bent over to assist a student, Gene would release, with faultless timing, a brief and barely audible burst of flatulence. This happened three or four times, maybe more, with each gaseous outburst increasing in volume. The last blast was obscenely loud and insolent.

Pfffft! Pifflesnit papfft! Pfffft! BLAAFT!

"The cease-fire is over," whispered Tank. "That last discharge sounded like an elephant stomping on a whoopee cushion."

"I knew the peace treaty wouldn't last," muttered Pudge, referring to the short-term truce between Mrs. Bender and Gene. There was disappointment in his voice.

Ruthie, sitting two seats behind Gene, quietly took a Kleenex from her desk and placed it over her nose, pinching each nostril. She continued doing her math homework, but I saw a smile beneath Ruthie's Kleenex, and I heard a stifled, almost inaudible girlish giggle. Our other classmates remained hushed and studiously pondered their math assignments. This was done not so much out of respect for Mrs. Bender, but out of fear of some sort of retaliation on her part. All twenty of her sixth-grade students had learned that Mrs. Bender had a temper, especially if her classroom authority was threatened or even probed.

Only a few weeks earlier, Mrs. Bender had punished the entire class because a pack of cigarettes had been taken from her desk. The perpetrator (it was Gene) would not confess, nor would anyone name the cigarette thief. I was surprised that none of the girls pointed out Gene, because they knew for sure that he had pilfered the cigarettes. Besides, he was the only kid in class who smoked. Mrs. Bender, of course, knew the offender was Gene, but she couldn't prove the theft was his doing. It seemed to infuriate her that no one in our class, not even the girls, would rat on him.

In her frustration, Mrs. Bender had lined the class up, boys and girls, along the classroom wall on which hung a colored portrait of George Washington and asked each student to hold out his or her right hand with its palm up. Like the rest of us, Lorraine, one of the smallest girls in our class held up her tiny, quivering hand. I noticed that the little girl's lower lip was trembling too.

Little Lorraine knew what was coming. We all did. This learning experience was not going to be a pleasant one.

Of course, Gene could've gotten us all out of the predicament by owning up to the fact that he was the one who had taken the cigarettes, but I knew he wasn't going to confess. Gene's uncle, Shade Barlow, had taught Gene one thing: never confess, even if the evidence against you is conclusive.

"Don't never admit that you done somethin' wrong. Leave a cloud of doubt restin' in people's minds. Reasonable doubt has saved my hide many a time," Shade Barlow had advised. Gene accepted his uncle's advice and urged us to do the same. He took that warning to heart because Shade Barlow had been arrested eight times for trafficking moonshine, but had never once been convicted.

"I'm giving everyone one last chance to name the guilty party who took my cigarettes," said Mrs. Bender. She put her hand to her throat and coughed a couple of times, as if something were stuck in her windpipe. She coughed deeply several more times before regaining her composure.

"If no one speaks up, then I shall have to punish each of you," she warned. "I would prefer not to do that, so I will give you students one minute to think about it."

Sixty seconds of uncomfortable silence began. Above the classroom door hung a black clock with a broad white face, and I watched the second hand as it moved past twelve. I had a sudden urge to run over to the electric socket and unplug the clock, but I couldn't dredge up the courage. No one moved; we students barely breathed. As Gene would state on the bus after school, "It was so quiet in that classroom, you coulda heard a bullfrog fart six foot under water."

The second hand of our schoolroom's clock reached the number six; we had thirty seconds left unless someone told on Gene. A soft breeze rustled leaves outside as Mrs. Bender stepped over to the windowsill and lowered one of the four open windows. Uninvited, a gentle gust entered our classroom and displaced a few papers on Mrs. Bender's desk. Like giant moths, silent white papers rose in the air and then fluttered to the floor.

At this point, I saw a cigarette roll out from under Gene's desk. The incriminating cigarette lay on the floor for a few seconds until Pudge, unnoticed by Mrs. Bender, stepped quietly forward and flattened it with the sole of his tennis shoe. Using the side of his shoe, he deftly flicked the flattened cigarette back under Gene's desk where it would remain until the school janitor swept up after school. The custodian who cleaned our classroom was a chain smoker, so the cigarette's eventual fate was sealed.

The second hand touched twelve and passed by. Time was up, and Mrs. Bender's punishment began. She grasped the first student's hand by the fingers, bending his fingers down and back, exposing the vulnerable palm. The bare palm was now unprotected and ready for several thwackings from a heavy wooden ruler. Mrs. Bender spared no one as she moved methodically down the line of students.

Thwack! Thwack! Thwack! After three smacks, it was the next student's turn. *Thwack! Thwack! Thwack!* And so the punishment continued unabated. *Thwack! Thwack! Thwack!* Janet was disciplined, then Cindy Lou. Johnny Knight was next. Mrs. Bender worked her way from student to student. However, Mrs. Bender stopped when she reached Pudge.

The redhead stood in front of his teacher, nervously expectant. He proffered his freckled hand.

Mrs. Bender's hand, holding the thick ruler, was raised when she hesitated. Breathing deeply, she lowered her arm, and with it the sturdy ruler. Like a Marine drill instructor, she looked Pudge up and down. She decided that out of all twenty of her students, Pudge was the most likely to break under pressure.

"Pudgie, are you absolutely, positively, and unequivocally sure that you have no idea who took my cigarettes? I want the truth."

"I have no idea, ma'am," said Pudge. His lower lip trembled ever so slightly. He looked at the floor, avoiding her eyes.

"You and I go to the same Baptist church, don't we, Pudgie? We have the same minister, don't we? We sing sacred hymns with our congregation. On Sundays, we worship together in our little church, don't we?"

"Yes, ma'am, we do," Pudge replied. His large ears blushed. Sweat moistened his upper lip.

"So, I'm asking you for the last time. Do you know who absconded with the pack of cigarettes that was in my desk? Give me his name, Pudgie," said Mrs. Bender, her voice rising. She raised the ruler with a shuddering hand. Her eyes spat fury. "Give me his name now!"

"I told you, ma'am. I don't know."

Thwack! Thwack! THWACK!

With his eyes closed, the redheaded kid stoically received his punishment. When it was over, Pudge rubbed the palm of his hand on his jeans. Standing nearby, I noticed that his hand was already swelling and reddening. The fair-skinned Pudge bruised easily. The next day, the palm of his right hand was black and blue.

Gene, of course, got the worst of it. I knew he would. So did everyone else.

Thwack! Thwack! THWACK! THWACKETY-THWACK!

Gene teared up and blinked his eyes, but he didn't cry. When the punishment ended, he shook his scrawny right hand until it became a blur at the end of his arm. Mrs. Bender glared at him and then moved on to the next student.

In line after Gene came the Tank. The big boy really didn't feel anything as Mrs. Bender's ruler smashed three times into his thickly padded palm. Tank's open hand reminded me of a catcher's mitt. The Tank smiled pleasantly at Mrs. Bender throughout the ordeal.

"Mrs. Bender, may I go to the library now? I have an overdue book to return," said Tank, grinning.

"You may not, Douglas," she said curtly.

After the Tank, finally it was my turn. I was last in line to get thwacked, and I hoped that Mrs. Bender might have run out of steam by the time she got to me. She hadn't. Dutifully, I raised my right hand and offered my palm. Mrs. Bender grabbed my upturned hand and pushed my fingers down hard. She lifted the ruler high as I closed my eyes.

Thwack! Thwack! Thwack!

The next day, I had a blood blister in the middle of my palm and could barely grip my pencil. I had been surprised at how much the smacking ruler hurt, and had lifted my right leg involuntarily on the third thwack. As I jerked my fingers from her vice-like grip, she narrowed her eyes and regarded me. I knew what she was thinking. Mrs. Bender was asking herself whether I had pulled my hand away in defiance or whether the pain had caused a spasmodic reflex. She must've decided on the latter, because she turned away from me and addressed the class.

"All right students, you may take your seats," said Mrs. Bender, her stare as cool as ice. She returned to her teacher's desk piled high with written book reports, tests, and homework papers, both graded and ungraded. She forced a smile as she faced the class. But then, as she slowly lowered her posterior down onto her plush, cushioned chair, there came a gently resonant, almost musical, yet rather extended discharge of intestinal gas. The protracted flatulent whining sounded like the wheels of a tractor-trailer truck out on the distant main highway.

Wwhhyyymph! Fuffleebuffee! Shrreepariiiff!

Of course, it was Gene. Who else? My classmates and I shuddered, and our spines stiffened. We feared more punishment from Mrs. Bender.

The gaseous sound produced was long enough to be judged as sufficiently insubordinate, but short enough and soft enough to signal a temporary truce that both Mrs. Bender and Gene silently accepted.

The constant tension between Gene and Mrs. Bender had frayed nerves across the sixth grade. Our teacher had become a frazzled bundle of tension, ready to lash out at the slightest provocation. Sometimes I felt sorry for her. Now, I sensed that peace would reign—at least for a while.

The whole class breathed a collective sigh of relief as a welcome respite came about in our classroom. All the students in Mrs. Bender's class, except possibly Gene, enjoyed the ceasefire. The wonderful accord lasted for almost three wonderfully tranquil weeks. Not one student in our class relished the bad blood that had built up between our teacher and Gene during that sixth-grade school year.

Despite it all, Mrs. Bender was actually a good teacher. She was creative, resourceful, and intelligent. She wanted her students to learn. She preferred projects over tedious worksheets, and she required her students to present monthly book reports, sometimes oral, sometimes written. We students got to choose the books from an extensive list that she had prepared, and I read more books during my sixth-grade year than any other elementary school year.

After lunch each day Mrs. Bender read a brief section of *The Yearling*. She had a pleasant reading voice, and even Gene enjoyed hearing her read. There was no flatulence during our after-lunch reading time. Mrs. Bender led interesting class discussions, and I found myself thinking more deeply about myself and the world around me.

Still, Mrs. Bender was far from perfect. As a teacher, she had two main problems: her flaming temper and Eugene Clifton Clodfelter. The skinny guy, a constant annoyance, a perpetual irritation, and an endless exasperation, was like a prickly burr under her saddle. Most of Mrs. Bender's students liked her—that is until Gene brought forth the blazing anger that dwelled somewhere deep inside her soul. Strangely enough, Gene got along with most of his teachers, especially Mr. Church. No one could explain why Gene and Mrs. Bender felt such animosity toward each other.

One rainy, uneventful Wednesday afternoon in the sixth-grade classroom, after I had packed all my books in my satchel, I took three dull pencils up to the pencil trimmer and trimmed them until their points were sharp. Mrs. Bender was writing on the chalkboard, and her students, including Gene, were sitting quietly at their desks, eyes glued to the classroom clock. The bell would soon ring and send us all to our school buses. For weeks, Mrs. Bender's classroom had experienced no interruptions, no outbursts from Gene. The days had passed by blissfully.

Returning to my desk with my sharpened pencils, I noticed a thick folded note resting on the desktop. "To Hal" had been scrawled across it in almost indecipherable penmanship, indicating that Gene was the author. I had opened it cautiously, not knowing what might be inside. When the message was completely unfolded, I read his boldly printed words:

The End Is Near! Hold Your Nose! Cover Your Ears! Heed This Warning!

Yours Truly,
The Fartman!

Oh no, I thought. This was not good. Gene, alias The Fartman, was soon to be back in business, wreaking havoc in our peaceful classroom. Why couldn't he leave well enough alone? I wadded up the note and stuck it in my jeans pocket. I could only wait and hope for the best.

CHAPTER 17

On a beautiful but fateful Thursday afternoon in sixth grade, while beginning work on my math homework assignment, I had discovered to my dismay that the short-lived truce between Mrs. Bender and Gene had ended. Once more my thin friend had begun coordinating his flatulence with Mrs. Bender's actions. Evidently for Gene the memory of the mass hand-thwacking had faded.

The recollection of the group punishment still festered in my brain like a splinter under a thumbnail. I opened and closed my right hand and a dull pain still pulsed in my palm, emanating from a spot near my lifeline. Oh yes, I remembered The Thwacking. I remembered it well. Now I feared Gene might get the whole class in trouble again.

The afternoon had been bright and warm with birds singing outside the classroom's windows. Mrs. Bender bent over Tank's desk to examine his math work, and he showed her the first six math problems as she perused his answers carefully.

"That's correct, Douglas; you remembered to invert and multiply. You have superior math skills, young man. Notice that number seven is a similar problem."

Tank grinned, appreciating the extra help. He went back to work. His pencil moved quickly across his paper, and as Mrs. Bender left to help another student, he called her back.

"I think I've answered number seven now. Would you check my answer, please?"

Mrs. Bender leaned over Tank's desk, pushed a wisp of hair out of her eyes, and bent closer for a better view of Tank's notebook paper. At that precise moment, from just a few desks away, Gene, his chin resting on his desk, discharged a booming broadside, an insolent volley over Mrs. Bender's bow. The temporary cease-fire had ended with a bang. Moments later, he had somehow reloaded and renewed his attack.

PFFFFT! FRAAFADA! Pfffft! **BLAAFT! GRUTHUNKA!** **PAPOOF! SPUURFONG!**

Mrs. Bender's back stiffened ever so slightly. Her nose wrinkled, sensing both odor and impudence, and as her eyes narrowed to mere slits, she bit her lips, leaving lipstick stains on her front teeth.

Uh-oh. I feared a potential all-out civil war between Mrs. Bender and Gene would erupt. I could foresee a conflict in which I might become a casualty, a victim of collateral damage. The recollection of The Thwacking burrowed deeper into my unsettled mind. My injured hand was still sore and I was developing a stress headache. I burped to relieve the building pressure in my stomach.

Truth be told, many of our classmates grudgingly admired Gene's faultless timing and seamless synchronization with Mrs. Bender's movements. Until our teacher's temper flashed, Johnny Knight and Ruthie Cornett found his antics tremendously entertaining. I was not among Gene's admirers.

FOOPAPHOOEY! MORFAVEEPH! **WHYYNIFLEEsssh!**

On this particular Thursday afternoon, the gassy sound effects, punctuating Mrs. Bender's movements, went on until Gene finally stood up and raised his hand. Mrs. Bender pretended to ignore him, as she had for the past ten minutes. I felt sure that she was seething inside.

"Mrs. Bender! Oh, Mrs. Bender!" cried Gene, standing on his tip toes. There was a tinge of panic in his voice and his already pale complexion was a whiter shade.

Mrs. Bender's back was to Gene, but I knew that she had heard the flatulent flare-ups. The last three of the skinny guy's eruptions, however, sounded unusual, like someone letting air out of a balloon submerged in water. Mrs. Bender slowly turned to face Gene. He was standing pigeon toed beside his seat, looking uneasy. His knees were held together, and he was sweating. For just a second, Gene and Mrs. Bender locked eyes.

Mrs. Bender's gray eyes flew open wide, and her pupils became small as pinpoints as she regarded Gene and his upraised hand. Her upper lip was curled, exhibiting her long sharp canine teeth.

"Yes, Eugene. I suppose you have to go to the bathroom now. Is that right?" asked Mrs. Bender. Gene often asked to go to the toilet in order to sneak a smoke. She had suspected his tobacco transgressions but could never prove the wrongdoings beyond the shadow of a doubt.

"No ma'am, I ain't got to go to the bathroom now... I think I already done soiled my britches! Yep, I done did it! I have gone to the outhouse right here in my underwear!"

"What?" Mrs. Bender asked, horrified.

"I have dropped a toilet turtle in my Fruit of the Looms. I have set free a brown sewer snake in my skivvies, and I sincerely apologize from the heart of my bottom."

Mrs. Bender stared at Gene as if he were an alien from the depths of space, somehow sent to earth to harass and annoy her until her nerves were completely unraveled.

"I didn't mean to do it, Mrs. Bender; a boy can't fight ole Mother Nature! It just natcherly happened and it ain't over, not by a long shot. Whoops! Aack! Wait a minute... Hold on. Woo! I really have to go to the bathroom—quick! Gotta go! Gotta go now!" Gene exclaimed, hugging his twitching abdomen.

There was a wispy, almost timid release of flatulence noticed only by students sitting near Gene as the skinny guy stood up straight, displaying his best posture of the entire school year. A look of consternation crossed his uneven facial features. Then suddenly, Gene's eyes crossed, and he grabbed the rear of his jeans. Clasping his butt cheeks with both hands, he waddled to the door. When he raised his right hand to turn the doorknob, the whole class could see that the hindmost portion of his jeans contained more than his skinny buttocks. Unnatural lumps, bumps, and protrusions were visible, filling the inside of his jeans between and below the back pockets. He groaned with discomfort as he pushed the classroom door open.

"Oh, Lordy." he moaned. "I got a nasty case of the dynorrhea! Nasty, nasty, nasty!"

Glancing back at his fellow students, Gene looked both pained and embarrassed as he exited the classroom. He slammed the door and we students could hear him running at full speed toward the boys' bathroom. His feet pounded the floor like the great horse Swaps' hooves had pounded the turf in the final stretch of the Kentucky Derby.

"Woo! Woo! Woo!" His shrill voice rang out and echoed through the narrow hallway. "Get out of my way, you second graders! This is a life-threatenin' emergency. Ouch! *Ouch! Jesus H. Christ!* I'm seekin' fast relief! You little kids better get the dickens out of my way!" squawked Gene as he careened down the hall at top speed. His rubber-soled sneakers squealed as he made a hard right in his mad dash to the boys' restroom.

Gene's screeching tennis shoes and his distressed cries released a torrent of pent-up sixth-grade glee. Our unchained delight, stifled for too long in Mrs. Bender's strict classroom, overwhelmed us. Pudge and Ruthie laughed out loud first, followed by Tank. Then the whole class joined in the boisterous gaiety. The classroom gushed with paroxysms of laughter. Backs were slapped; tears were shed; saliva was dribbled. A cloudburst of cackling engulfed us. Hilarity flooded the classroom and spilled out into the hallway through the open transom window above the classroom door.

"Gene's doin' the green-apple quickstep!" Johnny Knight guffawed, wiping drool from his chin.

"Hope he makes it to the john in time," roared the Tank whose belly laughs sent books flying from his desk.

Giggles, snickers, chortles, and guffaws blended together as the girls, usually quiet observers, joined the boys in outbursts of raucous merriment. Cindy Lou and Janet produced the shrillest laughter. Sitting close to the two screeching girls, I put my hands over my ears to prevent damage to my eardrums. Both Ruthie and Tank were almost hysterical as teardrops spilled down their bright red faces.

Mrs. Bender walked to the light switch and switched the classroom lights off and on twice, a prearranged classroom signal for absolute silence. However, the classroom merriment continued unabated.

During peals of laughter, Tank's great weight shifted back and forth until his over-sized desk began to creak and squeak. Two screws popped out, rolling under Ruthie's desk. Pudge and I were in stitches holding our heaving sides, as Tank suddenly came down with a severe case of giggling-induced hiccups which caused vibrations on the classroom's floor, windows, and walls. Johnny Knight's laughter came in tremors and fits as he, second in size only to the Tank, twisted about in his cramped desk.

The volume of the laughter doubled when Tank's desk cracked, splintered, and broke apart, sending him crashing to the floor. Surrounded by desk debris, Tank lay on the floor like a snickering walrus.

Next, Johnny slid out of his desk, and plopped on the classroom floor beside Tank. Johnny sat there letting the mirth spill out of his moist eyes and open mouth. There on the floor rested the two strongest boys at Healing Waters, made helpless by laughter.

As the jollity increased, any rational observer would've said that Mrs. Bender's classroom was completely out of control. Mrs. Bender, on the other hand, was as silent as a stone as her students' rising laughter surged like flood water, saturating the usually arid classroom. Mrs. Bender shouted a few stern commands, but her students' classroom revelry continued unabated. This sort of behavior had never happened before in her orderly classroom, and she had been teaching for well over fifteen years.

The closed door of Mrs. Bender's classroom had a small window. We sixth graders, except for Johnny Knight, had to stand on our tiptoes to look out that window. Standing outside the door, Mr. Church was looking through that small window into our classroom where the students were still in the midst of convulsive spasms of laughter. I saw him and I'm sure Mrs. Bender did, too. The principal frowned and scratched his head a couple of times and then disappeared.

Mrs. Bender, surrounded by bedlam, stood straight and tall, her clenched fists holding two freshly sharpened yellow wooden pencils, one in each hand. With a cracking sound, one of the pencils snapped in two. She cast the broken pencil into the wastebasket where the two pieces landed with a clatter.

Mrs. Bender's twisted face showed that her irritation had given way to a seething, barely controlled rage directed at the remaining nineteen students who were lost in helpless laughter. The teacher took a deep breath as purple veins bulged at her prematurely graying temples. The left side of her face developed a tic as her left eye opened and closed spasmodically. Mrs. Bender wiped her mouth with the back of her hand, pushing her carefully applied lipstick askew. She ran long fingers through her hair, giving it a Bride-of-Frankenstein effect. Several long strands of hair had fallen across her face, and she struggled for self-control as she addressed her class.

"Students! *Students!* This unseemly laughter must cease. Listen to me. It must stop, and it must stop right now. I warn you. You know the rules in this classroom. There will be consequences for this improper outburst. Listen to me! I can assure you there *will* be punishment. Oh, I can guarantee that you will all be chastised for this inappropriate behavior, all of you, boys and girls. As sixth-grade students, you must maintain some sense of decorum and...."

Just then, Gene reentered the room and slammed the door. Our disorderly laughter became more subdued as we watched Gene's entrance. Bright smiles greeted Gene along with a smattering of sustained giggles. About three feet of toilet paper clung stubbornly to the heel of his right tennis shoe. Dragging the toilet tissue, Gene swaggered over to the teacher's desk, turned his back to his classmates, and reached down into the rear of his baggy pants. About an inch of the stretchy band of his white Fruit of the Looms was exposed as his skinny hand disappeared into the back of his jeans. From his pants, he extracted a small red apple, a lump of coal wrapped in a soiled yellow handkerchief, a scuffed baseball, and a small bag of marbles his father had given him for Christmas. He set all of the items on Mrs. Bender's desk. Gene immediately picked up the apple, spat on it, and began shining it on the seat of his pants until the fruit glowed.

"This here apple is for you, teacher," he said, placing it back on Mrs. Bender's desk. She gagged and placed her hand over her mouth. Gene smiled amiably.

"Take your seat, Eugene! *Immediately!*" bellowed Mrs. Bender. Leaving the shiny apple, Gene quickly retrieved the other items and stuck them in his hip pockets. He sauntered back to his desk and sat down. He walked right past the smiling Tank, who was now pleasantly ensconced on the floor amidst the rubble of his shattered desk.

Back in his own seat, Gene lowered his head until his chin touched the desktop, then hoisted his butt about an inch above the seat. He closed his eyes tightly, wrinkled his brow, and pursed his lips. He strained mightily as if he were a constipated old man seeking long-postponed relief in his family's outhouse. Nothing happened.

Gene lowered his rear end onto the seat, but almost immediately raised his bottom again. He was not one to give up easily. The straining commenced again. I noticed that this time, in addition to his rigidly closed eyes, his deeply creased brow, and his constricted, hard-pressed lips, Gene had crossed his fingers on both hands. He held the crossed fingers on either side of his flushed face. His veined temples adopted a purplish-blue hue. Gene grunted in pain. His breathing was labored.

Gene's lower gut, just moments earlier in the throes of painful peristalsis-induced contractions, had provided a final, fateful push. Suddenly, a burst of sound filled the classroom from its floor to its ceiling. A single windowpane, loosened by the past winter's wind and ice, rattled testily. Gene had outdone himself.

FRAPPATAPPA! **ZOOIEEE!** *TADUMPHH ZOOIEEE!* **FRAPPATAPPA!**

Something about the extended, elongated discharge of gas reminded me of the William Tell Overture broadcast at the beginning of the Lone Ranger television and radio shows. I could almost hear, in addition to the rousing music, gunshots and the pounding hoof beats of the masked man's great white stallion, Silver. About halfway through Gene's brash, melodious flatulence, I felt the almost uncontrollable urge to call out a hearty, "Hi-Yo, Silver!"

The echoing bowel bomb was awe-inspiring. In short, Gene's soon-to-become legendary fart was a doozy. Mrs. Bender's students gasped at Gene's audacity.

Mrs. Bender staggered backward a step or two toward her desk, and, in her suddenly claw-like right hand, the second number two pencil snapped and then dropped. The eraser end of the halved pencil bounced softly on the floor, rebounded a few more times, and lay still as death. However, the pointed end landed on the floor with a click, fell over on its side and began to roll, first picking up speed, and then slowing down. Fascinated, my fellow classmates and I watched intently as it rolled across the floor. The pencil finally came to a stop under Gene's desk next to the white toilet tissue serpent affixed to his tennis shoe.

The sun, beaming through the classroom window, created a grotesque, fearsome shadow of Mrs. Benson; her dark silhouette shrouded the broad chalkboard. Our laughter, which had diminished to a few suppressed chuckles, stopped completely, mirth having collided with reality.

Tank rose from the floor and took a seat at the large project table in the back of the room. Johnny Knight quietly returned to his seat. A needle of fear pierced my brain, and I was not alone. Serious silence ensued. You could have heard a cotton ball drop to the floor as my classmates and I lowered our heads and silently studied our desktops.

After a moment, one by one, we raised our eyes to look at Mrs. Bender. She stood before us like a trembling scarecrow, gaunt and horrible. Mrs. Bender started to say something. Her frothing mouth formed a perfect O, but no sound came forth. She seemed frozen in time and space. Evidently, the pedagogy taught at Appalachian State Teachers College never prepared Mrs. Bender for a student like Gene.

A full ten seconds passed as Mrs. Bender stood speechless, and then, mercifully, the school bell rang, ending the school day. She lurched toward her seat and within seconds, almost all of her students had exited the room, leaving her there alone. Her sharp elbows rested on her broad desk calendar as her head sunk into her hands. As I left the classroom, I thought I heard her moan softly.

Gene made a beeline for bus 42, jumping up the bus's steps. He disappeared into the back of the bus where Pudge soon joined him in the backseat. Nearby, Tank sat as well, filling an entire bus seat that could have easily seated three riders. As the school bus pulled out of the parking lot, I could see Pudge through the bus's smudged rear window, slapping Gene on the back in a congratulatory fashion. They shook hands. Broad, toothy grins creased their faces. Gene waved to me through the bus window, and I waved back just before climbing aboard my own school bus. My bus ride home was anticlimactic, and I so wished I could've ridden home on school bus 42 with Pudge, Tank, and Gene.

CHAPTER 18

I had expected Gene to fail the sixth grade, and I told him so the next day in the lunch room. Gene and I were alone at the table since Tank and Pudge had finished their meals early and were now out on the playground tossing a baseball back and forth.

"Considering the way you've behaved this year, there's no way Mrs. Bender is going to pass you to the seventh grade, Gene."

I predicted this confidently as Gene gobbled down his second serving of pinto beans. He took a bite from a golden square of cornbread before commenting. Cornbread crumbs fell from his mouth onto his cafeteria plate, settling next to a single, neglected pinto bean.

"You like seafood?" Gene asked unexpectedly, leaning across the lunchroom table toward me.

"Yeah, I like seafood," I said.

In truth, Mrs. Paul's Fish Sticks were the only seafood I had ever experienced. I knew that a trout pulled from the New River didn't count as seafood. Seafood came from the ocean. I had never seen the ocean except on TV shows and in the movies. I had heard rumors of a place called Myrtle Beach where you could buy something called Calabash seafood, but I knew it would be a long time before I saw the Atlantic Ocean and the sands of Myrtle Beach. Grandpa Grayson didn't even drive a car, and I never knew him to take a vacation from the farm. Myrtle Beach and its seafood might as well have been located near Paris, France or Athens, Greece.

"Are you plumb positive you have a likin' for seafood?" Gene asked again. "I need to know."

"Sure," I said, because I certainly enjoyed Mrs. Paul's Fish Sticks covered with ketchup. According to Tank, ketchup made everything taste better.

"Yep, I like seafood," I said. "Why?"

Gene opened his mouth wide, so that I could "see" his food. I saw, in addition to crushed pinto beans and saliva-drenched cornbread, that his tongue was coated with a thin film of mucus. His teeth housed deep, black craters and his receding gums, which were inflamed by a chronic case of gingivitis, tentatively held his choppers in place. There were at least two empty sockets, and Gene's strangely premature wisdom teeth appeared to be growing in sideways. His gray uvula was covered with white spots indicating infection, and his oral cavity, festering and inflamed, was conceivably in the final stages of terminal halitosis.

Gene washed his partially-masticated cornbread and pinto beans down with a huge gulp of milk and then burped and scratched his skinny belly. He belched purposefully, and his bad breath engulfed me like a cloud of floating sewage.

"Gene, you could gag a maggot!" I laughed, leaning back in my chair, and we both snickered.

"Yeah, I reckon I could. I forgot to gargle with my Listerine this mornin'!" Gene cackled, holding his stomach.

"You should have chug-a-lugged the whole bottle of mouthwash," I suggested. We laughed together again.

Then Gene's mood turned serious and he pointed an accusatory finger at me. His countenance became wise and knowing. I had seen that facial expression often on teachers, but seldom, if ever, on Gene.

"Like most folks does, you underestimate me. Do you honestly think Mrs. Bender wants to put up with me for another school year? Do you, Hal? I, for one, don't think so. Nope, I will pass to the seventh grade with flyin' colors."

"Are you sure?" I asked.

"My grades may be low, but I'll pass along with you and the others. Throw away all of your doubts, ole buddy, and cast aside your misgivin's. When push comes to shove and the pressure is on, ole lady Bender will fold like one of them accordions on the Lawrence Welk TV show."

Gene had been right. Since at Healing Waters Elementary School each grade level had only one teacher, if Mrs. Bender chose to fail Gene, he would be with her in the sixth-grade classroom for another one hundred and eighty days next school year. When Mrs. Bender reached this stage of reasoning, Gene was home free. She passed Gene.

Had I been in her shoes, I'd have passed him, too.

Gene, along with Mrs. Bender's remaining nineteen sixth-grade students, had continued on to the seventh grade, where we encountered our first male teacher, Mr. Thomas Church. Mr. Church wore many hats at Healing Waters Elementary School. He was our principal, our seventh-grade teacher, and the coach of our seventh- and eighth-grade boys' basketball team. Mr. Church was a tall, lean man with thinning brown hair. He wore suits or sport jackets to school every day and always wore a tie. He laughed easily and often, although he was serious about misbehavior. He put up with no disruptions or shenanigans that interfered with the learning process, and no student wanted to be called to his office. In the seventh-grade classroom there was an extra door which led to Mr. Church's office.

Mr. Church had a gift for teaching, and I think all of my classmates enjoyed our seventh-grade year, especially Gene. His grammar and composition skills improved noticeably, along with his grades in every subject. Gene revered Mr. Church, and, as our basketball coach, Mr. Church had helped Gene develop a driving hook shot that was almost impossible to defend.

"Put the ball up softly against the backboard, Gene. Don't slam it. Good job! Now, let's try it again," Coach Church had said.

Giving our all for the Healing Waters Hawks, Pudge, Gene, and I won and lost as basketball teammates. Tank had discovered early that basketball was not his forte, but he was in the stands for every game, cheering us on. Our school was too small to field teams in baseball or football, so basketball was the only sport in which we competed with other schools.

Our gymnasium, constructed almost solely of wood, was old and compact. The floor of the basketball court creaked in places and its unevenness caused the basketball to take occasional unusual bounces. There were uncomfortable wooden bleachers on either side of the court, and both natural and electrical lighting brightened the place. A timeworn scoreboard displayed the scores, revealed the game's time in minutes and seconds, and buzzed at appropriate intervals. Just behind one of the baskets was a stage used for assemblies, plays, and graduation ceremonies.

On chilly winter days, the building was heated with two cast-iron potbellied stoves placed strategically within narrow recessed sections of the bleachers. Our basketball teams, boys and girls, practiced during planned physical education times. Our seventh and eighth grade basketball games were usually scheduled in the late afternoon rather than at night. A few of our games were played during the school day with students from the first grade through the eighth grade in attendance.

Once when we had played a much larger elementary school from an adjacent county, Pudge had heaved the basketball from the Healing Waters' midcourt line with just seconds left to play. The shot hit the backboard, the basket's front rim, the back rim, and then plunged through the twine. We had won the game 39 to 38. After the game, Pudge admitted that the shot was pure luck. He was treated like royalty for the next week. A first grader even asked for the redhead's autograph.

CHAPTER 19

On my way up Seagraves Hill to the Stephens Brothers Carnival, so deeply was I involved in musings about our past glory days at Healing Waters, that I tripped over my own feet, and almost plunged headfirst into the ample bosom of a female carnival goer who wore a blue and white polka dot dress. She was descending the trail as I stumbled upward.

"Look out!" cried Tank, grabbing my arm.

"Sorry, ma'am," I blurted. My nose was inches from her abundant cleavage when I regained my balance. I jerked my head back.

The polka dot lady was dragging behind her a crying child who obviously didn't want to leave the carnival grounds. Her navy blue high heels were coated with a film of dust, and she had trouble keeping her steadiness on the path's rocky surface as she and her son walked down the trail.

The boy kept screaming, "Mama, why? Why? I didn't hit him! I throwed that rock clean over his head. I just wanted to scare him a little. The rock never even came close!"

"You know perfectly well why, Jeffrey," the exasperated mother said, brushing back her thick, curly blonde hair. "You and I talked about this before we came to the carnival. I don't care if you didn't hit the gentleman! You must not throw rocks at the carnival workers. Now, we are going home! Remember, young man, you brought this on yourself. Our discussion is over!"

"Gee whiz!" muttered the boy. "I don't get to do nothin' that I want to do!"

His mother glowered, put her hands on her full hips, and hissed, "Jeffreee!" through clenched teeth. The small boy stood before her in grass-stained tennis shoes and a white baseball uniform trimmed in green. Emblazoned on his shirt front and on his baseball cap were the words, "Little Beaver." Jeffrey's lower lip trembled as he stared at the dusty ground. He looked to be barely nine years old.

"Better luck next year, kid," laughed Gene, looking down at the youngster in the green and white cap. Gene went into an elaborate windup and pretended to throw an invisible baseball.

"Keep practicin' with them rocks, Jeffrey, and always throw at their heads!" Gene instructed. "The carnival workers won't stand a chance next year! Remember, when you throw, aim for their *heads*. They're like zombies in the movies; you got to hit 'em in the head just right to do any damage. Aim your rock so you can hit 'em betwixt the eyes; most of the carnival workers is vulnerable there. But if you throw and miss, Jeffrey, turn around and run like the devil 'cause if they catch you, the carnival zombies will stick a straw in your ear and suck out your brains."

"No, they won't," said Jeffrey, blinking moist eyes. "Besides, they ain't no such thing as zombies. Maybe you mean vampires or, more likely, goblins."

"Don't talk to strangers, Jeffrey," implored his mother.

"They ain't zombies now, but wait 'til dark," Gene said. "That's when the change comes over 'em. At nightfall, they get dangerous, awful dangerous. That's why the carnival needs good rock throwers like me and you. We gotta keep them brain guzzlers in check."

The kid swabbed his teary eyes and grinned at the slender, crooked-nosed, buck-toothed teenager, but the mother spun and glared at Gene. Her protective maternal instincts accelerated to full throttle.

"Why, you impudent juvenile delinquent! How dare you plant such ideas in my precious little son's head? I'll thank you to keep your nose out of my Jeffrey's business, you ill-mannered, insolent young criminal!"

She snarled at Gene like a panther protecting her cub. Gene held his hands up with his palms toward her and took a step backward and away from the angry mother and her offspring.

"Look, lady, I threw rocks at the carnival workers when I was little Jeffrey's age, and I turned out all right," said Gene, who pulled his cowboy hat down until it covered his ears and most of his eyes. He rolled his partially-hidden eyes, each eye in an opposite direction, and then began picking his nose.

Horrified, the lady stared at Gene. She was transfixed and her mouth dropped open. Her expression consisted of one part fear and one part revulsion as Gene's forefinger all but disappeared into his cavernous right nostril. He retrieved a rather large, olive-colored booger encrusted with hard mucus and sprinkled with minute flecks of dried blood. In the dwindling sunlight, Gene held the mucus marble up to his eyes and examined the green globule as a jeweler might examine a precious gem to determine its value.

"Rather a nice snot samplin', but I think I got sev'ral at home that are even purtier. Jeffrey, I begun my booger collection when I was about your age," said Gene. He rolled the booger between his forefinger and his thumb. When he finished the rolling process, the nasal lump was about the size and shape of a plump, ripe blueberry. Gene continued to scrutinize the nostril discharge as if he were a Yukon prospector who had just unearthed a huge gold nugget.

Suddenly he frowned and sighed, indicating that this particular booger did not meet his high standards.

"Ma'am, I keep only the really large boogers. I store them in a glass jar by my bed along with a few other smaller crystallized nose samplin's that I find interestin' or unique. Mom always puts my booger jar out on the mantle come Christmas time. It has become a cherished fam'ly holiday tradition. Mom lights a candle behind the jar and the flickerin' flame, radiatin' through the booger specimens, casts beautiful, rainbow colored lights that gleam through the jar and onto the Nativity scene on her coffee table. With Yuletide carols playin' on the radio and snow fallin' outside, it's like havin' a little dab of Glory right there in our livin' room."

The polka dot lady put her left hand over her mouth as if fighting down her rising gorge. Her nose wrinkled as her eyebrows rose high on her forehead. A large diamond gleamed from her ring finger, lighting up her troubled face in the early gloaming.

"This here dried-up chunk of snot, however, is a throwaway, not a keeper," added Gene. "I only collect the really good ones!"

He flicked the berry-sized lump of hardened mucus toward the ground and it landed between the pointed toes of the lady's high heel shoes, where the solidified secretion seemed to glow eerily in the deepening twilight. Jeffrey's mother gasped in shock and stepped back, tottering on her high heels.

"Well, I never!" she spluttered, putting young Jeffrey behind her. The boy peeked at Gene from behind his mother's polka dot dress, pulling it upward and revealing more matronly thigh than many would have deemed appropriate.

"Well, like you, lady, I never did, neither. That is, I never did drink no moonshine whiskey, 'til I tasted Uncle Shade Barlow's good ole mountain dew. Deelicious! Best white lightnin' in Ashe County, bar none! Wilkes County likker can't hold a candle to Uncle Shade's corn squeezin's."

Gene looked furtively around, and then smiled knowingly at the unsettled lady. His eyebrows attempted a get-together just above the bridge of his crooked nose. He removed his cowboy hat and cocked his head as a sustained breeze lifted his long thin hair upward and over his forehead, nearly covering his eyes.

"Would you like a swaller, lady? I been drinkin' all day, but I think there's a little whiskey left. Uncle Shade says his corn whiskey will put hair on your chest and starch in your drawers."

Gene reached toward his hip pocket for a nonexistent flask. He relished teasing and making adults squirm.

"Good grief, Jeffrey, let's get out of here!" The lady grabbed the kid's wrist, then turned once more toward Gene.

"With drunken hoodlums like you running around, what will become of our county in the future?" she growled. She turned in a huff and marched down the trail toward West Jefferson with Jeffrey in tow.

"Well, good evenin' then. Mighty nice to make your acquaintance, ma'am, I'm sure," said Gene, tipping his hat.

Young Jeffrey dug his heels into the dirt, slowing his mother down long enough for the kid to turn and give Gene a jaunty goodbye wave. Then his small hand became a fist. Young Jeffrey locked eyes with Gene for a split second and then gave him the finger. His mother jerked him around and pulled him down the trail.

"That boy has potential," laughed Gene. His eyes crinkled. "Little Jeffrey reminds me a whole lot of me when I was his age, only he's not quite as good lookin'—nor as sophisticated!"

Fearing trouble with the polka dot lady, Tank, Pudge and I had walked on ahead, and Gene trotted to catch up with us. He was out of breath and beginning to cough when he reached us. We were approaching the top of the hill where the land would level out into a spacious meadow dotted with carnival rides, concession stands, game booths, and people—a growing mob of people.

The four of us paused near the top of the hill and saw below us the lights of West Jefferson flickering in the twilight. The Parkwood Theatre, in the center of town, produced the brightest lights. A car was stalled on Main Street, impeding traffic. Ten cars were backed up, and headlights flashed in frustration as hostile horns honked.

"I'm glad we're up here, and not down there," declared Tank as he strode toward the Stephens Brothers Carnival entrance. Gene, Pudge, and I followed.

Green, blue, and red lights flashed above a broad, makeshift wooden arch that marked the carnival's point of entry. Three flags hung limply at the carnival's entrance gate—North Carolina's state flag, the Confederate flag, and our country's Stars and Stripes. Above us on this sultry July night, the moon was a tangerine slice in a darkening, star-spangled sky.

We took a few steps forward, passed by a hand-painted sign that read, "No Charge to Enter," and crossed over into another world, another dimension.

CHAPTER 20

The carnival was spread out before us like a crazy quilt of flashing neon. Clowns walked among us, a lady wearing pink tights whizzed by on a unicycle, and a man dressed as Uncle Sam strolled by on stilts. A little fellow, no taller than Tank's belt buckle, strolled by in a tuxedo. He had a thick beard, as did the tall, voluptuous lady, dressed as a scantily-clad harem girl, who walked by his side.

The carnival's smells, sounds and lights filled our senses to the brim, reminding me of the moonlit, mid-October night a few years ago, when we camped out, roasted hotdogs and marshmallows, and told ghost stories by firelight on the leaf-strewn banks of the rushing New River.

Tank, Pudge, Gene, and I advanced into the milling throng of Ashe County citizenry, mainly farmers with wives and kids. A few furniture plant employees and several cheese plant workers, along with their families, were scattered about. The plant workers weren't as tanned as the farmers who worked outside under the sun. A few of the men had on light-weight suits and sport coats, and I thought they must've been bankers, undertakers, or lawyers. Most mountain men reserved suits exclusively for church services, weddings, and funerals.

Grandpa Charlie thought bib overalls were suitable for all social affairs. At a funeral, he had once worn a suit coat over his plaid flannel shirt and bib overalls. That was about as dressed up as I ever saw him. I looked around for my grandfather. Gene had said it would be easy to spot Grandpa Charlie in the crowd, but I didn't see him in the carnival's expanding multitude.

I did see Mr. Thomas Church, our former seventh grade teacher and principal at Healing Waters Elementary School, with his wife and small son Gregory. Mr. Church smiled and waved to us as Gregory tugged him toward the merry-go-round. Mrs. Church recognized us and waved, too, and we waved back.

Mr. Church's wife was not a teacher, but she was always around the school, helping out in the cafeteria, running errands for teachers, and encouraging students to do their best. She was friendly, petite, and very pretty. She knew the name of every student at her husband's school. I didn't know half the names of the kids who rode my school bus.

Each of us guys looked around the expanding crowd hoping to see Ruthie again. Well-liked and attractive, she had been the most admired girl in our eighth-grade class. Our eyes combed the crowd. No luck. Ruthie was either being closely chaperoned by her father and a couple of older sisters, or she had met an older guy, maybe a sophomore or a junior in high school, and was touring the carnival grounds with him.

Ruthie had begun developing curves in the latter half of the sixth grade. We sixth-grade guys barely noticed then, but now, as rising ninth graders, she, along with a few other pubescent girls, had our complete attention. Ruthie's smile lit up our old elementary school's halls and her laughter was infectious. One or two of the girls resented her popularity, but on the whole, she was popular with both guys and girls.

Ruthie was the best athlete in our class. She could hit a softball as well as any of the guys, but not quite as far, and she could run faster than any of her classmates. However, her greatest gift was her ability to play basketball. Ruthie always provided a lock-down defense against the opposing team's best player. She shot the ball well from any part of the court, she scored from any angle, and she did it all so gracefully, almost effortlessly. Her specialty was a running hook shot that banked softly off the backboard and plunged downward through the net, barely ruffling the twine. Her long legs propelled her upward for rebounds and an occasional blocked shot. Her lean legs were remarkable, but while watching her play against other schools, I found my eyes drawn more and more to her perky posterior.

"What a purty and amazin' butt on a young'un'!" Gene had shouted in an old man's voice once as we sat in the stands during a girls' home basketball game with Lansing Elementary School. Gene could make his voice sound just like Grandpa Charlie's and had even fooled me once on a telephone call. Ruthie heard him call out, and she turned her head in our direction, frowning ferociously.

Then, after receiving a bounce pass from teammate Cindy Lou Winkler, she lowered her head and dribbled toward the basket for a shot. Gene's yell might have caused her to miss her patented hook shot which bounced off the rim. Undeterred, she got her own rebound and went up for another shot as a Lansing forward crashed into her, sending Ruthie flying out of bounds.

The basketball spun around several times within the perimeter of the basket, tantalizing the Healing Waters' fans, and finally rimmed out of the goal. There was a collective groan from the wooden stands, but then the referee blew his whistle. Ruthie had been fouled by the tallest and heaviest girl on the Lansing team, Colleen Stump, who was first runner-up in the local spelling bee competition. In spite of the violent impact that sent her sprawling, Ruthie almost made the basket.

As Ruthie approached the free-throw line, our Healing Waters girls were one point behind with only one second on the clock. Ruthie had been fouled intentionally, causing her to miss her put-back jump shot. She was awarded two shots. The referee handed her the ball as Ruthie stood at the foul line with a look of determination on her pretty face. The small crowd was hushed and I crossed my fingers. So did Gene and Pudge. Tank, who sat beside me, closed his eyes.

Ruthie bounced the ball twice and then twirled it in her hands. Her fingers felt for the seams. She displayed the calmness and concentration of a gifted athlete. She held the ball in front of her eyes, took careful aim, flexed her knees, and then pushed the basketball forward. The ball rolled off her fingertips and spun backward as it arched upward through the air and then plummeted downward toward the goal.

Swish!

After Ruthie sank her one-handed push shot from the foul line, the score was tied. She then swished another free throw through the net to ice the game. The buzzer sounded as the tall Lansing forward, Colleen Stump, hurled a long desperation shot that missed its target completely. The whirling ball sailed into the stands where Gene caught it. He flung the basketball back onto the court where Ruthie grabbed it. She dribbled the ball as she, surrounded by teammates and fans, walked toward the girls' dressing room.

"Hot dang, you all, I swear!" Gene screamed, again imitating Grandpa Charlie's voice. Then Gene whirled like a highly caffeinated, coffee-drinking, slightly deranged dervish and pounded Tank and Pudge on their backs as the crowd of students, parents, friends, and neighbors stood and cheered. Ruthie paused at the corner of the basketball court and waved to her fans.

I cheered along with the enthusiastic crowd, and then left the stands to get dressed in my Hawks uniform. Gene and Pudge followed me. The boys' game was next.

"Good luck, guys," said Tank.

I was one of the starting guards on the boys' basketball team and our game with the Lansing boys' team followed. I had a terrible game, my worst of the season, scoring only five points. Pudge scored six. Gene had a good game, scoring fourteen points. I missed six straight shots, including a fast-break layup.

I remember looking up at the scoreboard when the final buzzer sounded. We had lost the game by fifteen points. There had been no cheers at the end of that basketball game, except for the shouts of the fifteen or twenty diehard Lansing fans in attendance.

During basketball season, sometimes I wished Ruthie could have played on the boys' team. She was that good.

CHAPTER 21

The carnival throng continued to swell as I looked in vain for Ruthie. Perhaps she was not among the carnival goers anymore. Conceivably, her father had taken her and her sisters home early. Ruthie's father was a farmer and most farmers in Ashe County got up early in the morning, sometimes before daylight. If Ruthie happened to still be at the carnival, however, it would not have shocked me to see her walking around with a tenth or eleventh-grade guy, enjoying the world of older high school men. After all, many of them had cars and drivers' licenses, which added to their standing in any teenage community.

I wondered if I would ever have a car of my own. Grandpa Grayson didn't even drive. He depended on neighbors, family, and friends for his transportation needs. Grandpa Charlie had promised to teach me how to drive, but said I wasn't quite ready. "Maybe next year," he said.

A miniature convertible clown car sped by with a green-haired clown driving. He beeped the horn, and Pudge leapt aside to avoid a collision. The tiny car missed the redhead by inches.

"Watch out!" shouted the clown. "Look where you're goin', ya stupid kid!"

The clown and his small-scale convertible disappeared into a huge gray tent. Another clown, riding a diminutive motorcycle, followed the convertible into the tent's opening. The second clown looked remarkably like Bozo, an orange-haired, red-nosed, always-smiling clown that appeared on television on Saturday mornings.

The revving engines inside the mammoth tent signaled that a race was about to begin. I wanted to buy a ticket and go inside, but Gene pushed me away. He spun me around so quickly that I confronted a myriad of whirling lights as he pounded me on the shoulder and pointed to the glittering Ferris wheel in the distance.

"Ain't that Ferris wheel bigger than the one they had last year, or is it the same one?" asked Gene.

"It's the same one," said Pudge without enthusiasm. "It's just decorated with more lights."

"I reckon you're right; it does have more lights this year. The new lights is colored, some of 'em. Wow! Ain't that Ferris wheel a purty sight!" breathed Gene, staring upward in open-mouthed wonder.

Now, if there was one thing that Gene loved, it was the rides at a carnival. He took special delight in riding with Pudge who seemed fearful of all but the most tepid of rides. Almost always Gene could find ways to increase Pudge's fright, especially on tall rides like the Ferris wheel and the highflying swings. Nevertheless, Pudge always rode with us, even on the most frightening rides—the rides that took your breath away, made you momentarily weightless, and left you feeling dizzy and drunk as you staggered toward the next one. Such rides were common at carnivals in the South during the late nineteen fifties. Poorly maintained mechanically, they were loud, rickety, and sometimes downright dangerous.

Suddenly, the Tank touched his nose which twitched and sniffed with ever-widening nostrils. His nasal passages were bewitched by the carnival's strong aromas of caramel candy apples, freshly popped popcorn, blue and pink puffs of sugar-spun cotton candy, and steaming corndogs-on-sticks. The big boy was pulled around, first in one direction and then in another, by the appetizing carnival scents. He was like a bloodhound, on leash, hot on the trail of an escaped convict. The enticing smells wafted tantalizingly toward us. I smelled hotdogs behind us and popcorn in front of us. The Tank snuffled and then sneezed. A look of overwhelming happiness darted across his broad face. Tank had found his version of El Dorado.

"Excuse me, guys. I'm famished and losing power. Gotta find food! Gotta refuel!"

Opening and closing rapidly, Tank's sensitive right nostril led him away from us toward a hotdog stand. As he stood in front of the stand, I saw him reaching for his billfold with his right hand and holding up three fingers of his left to indicate the number of hotdogs he wanted. When he was handed the roasted frankfurters on toasted buns, Tank slathered them with catsup, mustard, and relish. His eyes closed dreamily as he inhaled deeply the aromas of the warm buns, the steaming hot dogs, and the zesty condiments. He wolfed the wieners down with amazing speed and fervor. Then, he finished off a bottle of RC Cola in three swallows, pulled a clean white handkerchief from his back pocket, burped loudly, and wiped his lips. An expression of ineffable bliss passed across his plump face and lingered momentarily. Then he turned away from the fragrant hotdog stand, looking for us, and Pudge waved, signaling our location. The Tank hoisted his belt buckle to the center of his belly and ambled toward us.

As he rejoined us, Tank belched again, filling the air with an explosion of scents from his last meal. The odors, popping like invisible scented balloons in midflight, quickly dissipated except for the mustard and relish smell, which hung stubbornly in the air around the big guy.

"You guys should try the hotdogs at that hotdog stand," said Tank. "I give those frankfurters my highest recommendation. They are culinary delights, like manna from heaven. I may have a few more before the night is out."

"I don't doubt that," laughed Pudge. "Last year you ate six dogs."

"Seven," confessed Tank. "The last one was a corndog and I ate it with mustard and ketchup."

"Corndogs and hotdogs ain't got no dog meat in 'em," opined Gene. "The meat is mostly hog jowls, beef innards, and chicken gizzards. Good eatin' if you ask me."

It was at that precise moment that Sophia Cassandra Bishop, the girl who gave me the perfume-scented, top-secret note, strolled by, tossing her long, raven-black hair. She was accompanied by five family members. She passed so close to me that had I possessed more courage, I could've reached out and touched her hand. I could smell her delicate perfume, the same fragrance she had drizzled on the secret note.

Sophia walked with the fluid, graceful movements of young womanhood, as if walking in a frame-by-frame slow motion film. Her erect carriage emphasized her budding figure. Young Sophia had a certain polish and sophistication about her. A slight movement of her graceful neck turned her head toward me and for an instant, our eyes locked. An unseen electrical charge passed between us.

At that split second, the earth stopped its rotation. Time was put on hold and the noisy carnival multitude grew silent. Suddenly she and I were the planet's only two real inhabitants; others were blurry, insignificant ghosts floating around us. The carnival music was hushed. The flashing lights softened. Sophia's pupils enlarged and her mouth pouted. Her eyes were the color of Green Lantern's ring on the cover of a new DC comic book. She smiled, her rosebud lips parting almost imperceptibly. She touched the center of her ruddy upper lip with the tip of her pink tongue.

I grinned back at her, showing every tooth in my head and, more than likely, the rosy uvula hanging at the back of my throat.

Sophia was dressed in yellow Bermuda shorts, a white blouse, and brown saddle shoes with short white socks covering her slender ankles. Around her neck, she wore a gold and white scarf. She looked almost regal, even in yellow Bermuda shorts.

Unfortunately for me, Sophia was with her family, consisting of her father, who was a minister, her mother, her younger sister, Sandra, and two little brothers, Nolan and Larry. Each member of the family had fair skin and wavy black hair. Like Sophia, her mother and sister were beautiful, movie-star beautiful. They had the same green eyes, the same soft, smooth skin, and the same graceful movements.

Her father, wearing a navy suit, was tall and thin, almost gaunt, with hair blacker than anthracite coal. His dark, stern eyes were sharp and penetrating. He held Sophia's hand and his wife's elbow as he guided them through the crowd. Sophia's younger siblings followed behind. Once he stopped to turn and admonish his youngest son who was throwing small wads of cotton candy at his older brother. The tomfoolery ceased immediately, and the little boy apologized to his father.

"I'm sorry, sir. It won't happen again," said the boy.

Without question, Reverend Bishop was the ruling patriarch of the family.

As the Bishops walked away, Sophia, turned, and our eyes locked again. Her slender neck blushed. She lifted her hand and touched her throat lightly. We gazed at each other for as long as we dared. After all, her father was walking right beside her. Sophia was every bit as tall as her mother. She looked as if she could have been an eighth or ninth grade girl, but I knew she was only entering the seventh grade.

Before she and her family faded into the carnival's swirling human throng and disappeared, Sophia smiled her mysterious Mona Lisa smile, and, like a queen or princess, waved her left hand slowly, ever so slowly, almost undetectably. Then she turned away.

I stood lost in a teenage trance, beaming and waving goodbye to her. My broad, somewhat contorted, ear-to-ear smile rivaled the ghastly grin of the Joker in the Batman comic books. Warm saliva trickled to my chin. My jaw bone was beginning to ache when I noticed that passersby were staring at me. They probably thought I was part of the carnival's freak show. I had difficulty closing my mouth and ridding myself of the frozen smile.

"Sophia," I whispered dreamily, speaking to her gently perfumed spirit which still hovered in the air near me. I spoke her name softly, but Tank heard me and turned in my direction, as did Gene and Pudge.

My face flushed so severely that I was afraid my cheeks and Rudolph-like nose were shining in the gloaming. My perspiring under arms moistened my T-shirt, providing a pungent dampness to my newly-acquired but rapidly sprouting armpit hair. My palms sweated copiously, and I could feel a droplet of sweat forming between each of my toes.

At the mere sight of Sophia, a swift surge of testosterone had flooded my bloodstream. The powerful hormone, mixing with other unidentified adolescent hormones—and enriched by a nutritious teenage diet consisting, in recent days, entirely of honey buns, Tootsie rolls, Pet chocolate ice cream, and Butterfinger candy bars, all washed down with ice-cold Pepsi-Colas—had caused a sudden, intense heat to flash through my body, settling somewhat embarrassingly in my loins. Plunging my right hand deep into my jeans pocket, I surreptitiously adjusted the suddenly uncomfortable twist in my snug underwear.

The hormonal and digestive tract combination of ingredients bubbling throughout my bodily systems would, without doubt, contribute mightily to the formation of a huge, white-crowned, red and yellow monster zit that mysteriously appeared on my chin on the morning after the carnival.

Not to worry, for in the last few months I had become an expert at popping fearsome facial blemishes. Using my recently developed double-thumbed, pressure-pump squeeze, I could conquer even the most formidable pimple. After completing the squeezing procedure, I always staunched the resulting blood flow by pressing the afflicted area, usually my chin, with a tissue drenched in rubbing alcohol. The resulting short-lived stinging sensation was comparable to getting a vaccination from the school nurse. After a minute or two, my chin, except for a tiny red crater, was as fresh as a daisy.

Only a few weeks ago, in a discussion of teenage blemishes as the four of us had sat in the Healing Waters cafeteria drinking chocolate milk, Pudge had said, "Rubbing alcohol hurts, but it works. The pimples I had last week are gone."

"Now, I don't mind gettin' a few zits and pimples now and then," Gene responded, "but a dang boil is a diff'rent story. A boil is a serious infection. I got a big angry boil on my butt one summer, and it like to have kilt me. The thing swole up almost as big as a ping-pong ball and turned a whitish yeller on the very top. I could tell it was full of thick pus. Lord, was that carbuncle ripe and painful! I had to hold a mirror behind me and twist my head around to get a good look at the infection on my backside. I tell you it wasn't no purty sight. The only way I could rid myself of the swellin' was to take a sharp butcher knife and..."

"Shut up about lancing that boil!" Tank had shouted, slapping his hand on the cafeteria table causing his lemon-lime gelatin dessert to quiver madly. With alternating shots of root beer and chocolate milk, the big boy had been chomping on his third homemade livermush sandwich with ketchup, mayonnaise, mustard, onions, horseradish, and pickles. He fondled his other dessert, two large Reese's peanut butter cups in his shirt pocket.

"My stomach is easily upset, Gene. You know that. I'll not have you spoiling my appetite," said Tank, and he took another hearty bite. His condiments dribbled from his mouth corners and gathered on his chin, ready to make the leap onto the broad, chin-tucked napkin that protected his shirt.

CHAPTER 22

Sophia's arrival at the carnival, albeit a fleeting appearance, had affected me profoundly. My reddening ears had throbbed with each thumping beat of my heart. My trembling legs felt weak and loosey-goosey, and I began breathing heavily through my mouth. I strained to get one final look at Sophia before she disappeared. I stood on my tiptoes and got one final glimpse of the top of her head before she and her family vanished into the roiling multitude.

I hoped that the guys hadn't noticed my reaction to Sophia, but that was wishful thinking. Tank, Gene, and Pudge were smirking like drunken Cheshire cats.

Elvis Presley's recording of "All Shook Up" blasted out from one of the nearby carnival booths. The volume was turned up so loud that the very air seemed to vibrate. Using Presley's lyrics as cues, the teasing began. In the background, Elvis Aron Presley sang backup to Tank, Gene, and Pudge.

"My goodness, Hal, your knees are wobbling; your hands are shaking. Can you stand up straight? Can you find your feet? You're all mixed up, Hal! That pretty girl has you all mixed up!" warbled the Tank, slicking his hair back with a black comb and lifting his upper lip in a fair imitation of the most famous sneer of the nineteen fifties.

"Your tongue is tied and you're as shaky as Jell-O. When she says, 'hello,' you get all mixed up! The pretty girl has you all mixed up!" sang Pudge, grabbing his right leg which seemed to be quivering uncontrollably despite his efforts to steady it. Pudge had watched Elvis perform a similar move on the Ed Sullivan Show before televising Presley below the waist was prohibited.

"Hal, you're as wild as a June bug landin' in a fryin' pan! You're the man that's all mixed up! That purty gal has got you all mixed up! Our pal is all mixed up!" Gene chanted, taking off his cowboy hat and pushing his thin hair up into a pompadour. Gene began dancing around in a disorderly fashion as if he had jumping beans in his underwear. His hips jolted forward a time or two, as Gene gave his best Elvis the Pelvis imitation.

"He's in puppy love; he's a lovesick fool; hope she don't treat him cruel! Hal is all mixed up! He's all mixed up!" crooned Tank, adopting various Presley stances that he had seen on TV or in Presley's movies.

There was a ripping sound as Tank stretched to re-create an athletic Presley pose. Unfortunately, Tank had assumed a position that no one of his portliness should ever assume. The Elvis song ended as Tank searched for the tear in his jeans. Fortunately, the only damage was a minor split in the waistband; no serious damage was done to his pants or to his modesty.

"Tank's all right, no harm done; but, after seein' Sophia, your sugar booger, how are you doin', Hal?" Gene asked with a smirk.

"I'm a little confused, but I'm feeling okay! Well, really, I'm feeling better than okay, much better. I admit it! I admit it!" I laughed. "Anyway, guys, Sophia is only in the seventh grade, or will be once school starts. She's too young for me. Like you, I'm almost in the ninth grade. I prefer older women like junior or senior high school girls. You know, an older but wiser girl for me."

"You wish," said Gene. "Sophia Bishop is the only girl who ever give you a second look. Now you're talkin' about older girls, high school girls. Don't make me laugh. Them girls wouldn't even give you the time of day."

Then, trying to change the subject, I said, "Come on, guys, let's find that Ferris wheel. If we came here to ride, let's get started!"

I dashed ahead of them toward the distant Ferris wheel. As I ran, I heard Gene's shrill voice, not far behind me, call out, "My mama and my daddy got married when she was sixteen and he was eighteen. Six months later, my brother Jack was born. I reckon he was a premature baby. Haw! At least Jack wasn't no woods colt. When you're eighteen, Hal, and Sophia's sixteen, you'll be just right for one another. I'll be best man at your weddin'!"

"Maybe you two will get lucky and have a little son, just like Gene!" yelled Pudge.

Gene snorted with amusement. He threw his cowboy hat four feet into the air and then caught it on the way down. Pudge and Tank hooted with glee. Pudge was cackling like a banty rooster, and Tank was holding his heaving sides. I could feel my ears turning as red as Valentine's Day roses. I picked up my running speed, leaving the three teenaged comedians behind in the fairground dust.

As I ran from the mocking laughter, I dodged a couple of imminent collisions, one of which would've involved a clown with bright yellow hair, a purple suit, and huge green shoes. He stood at least six feet, five inches tall and sported an enormous potbelly. One of his white-gloved hands formed a formidable fist. He waved his clenched hand in the air.

"Watch where you're goin', you little son of a bitch," snapped the happy-faced clown with his painted-on smile. I paid him no mind and continued my run. Seconds later, I almost bumped into a very pretty, very pregnant lady who sang in the choir at Healing Waters Baptist Church, so I stopped running and began to walk through the crowd, still well ahead of my three cronies.

I started thinking about green-eyed Sophia. She was taller than most of the girls in her class, not *too* tall but just right for a guy of my height. Then I thought about her voice. It was always pure and calm. I had walked past her classroom one time when she was giving a speech in front of her class. Sophia was running for vice president. The classroom door was open and I stopped to listen. Her voice was musical and soothing. Sophia had pronounced each word in her speech clearly and crisply. Her thoughts were presented succinctly. I would've voted for her, but my vote wasn't needed. Sophia Bishop became vice president of her class that year. The following year she became the class president.

I had memorized her secret note and began reciting it silently as I moved through the carnival crowd. "Dearest Hal, I cannot begin to say all that I would like to tell you, but…"—and so forth. When I finished my soundless recitation, I realized I was thinking about Sophia too much. I furrowed my brow and closed my eyes, trying to concentrate on someone or something else.

I thought about cheeseburgers and french fries for a while. Then I thought about the lettuce, tomato, and mayonnaise I always ordered on any burger. I thought about Butterfinger candy bars and strawberry milkshakes. Switching gears, I thought about Boris Karloff's starring role in *Frankenstein* and Bella Lugosi's performance in *Dracula*. I thought about the fish-man in *The Creature from the Black Lagoon*. I thought about the bare-breasted statue of Pocahontas in downtown West Jefferson. I thought about President Eisenhower and his wife, Mamie. I thought about the Dodgers moving from Brooklyn to Los Angeles. Then I thought about Dr. Peppers, Creamsicles, and Moon Pies.

I remembered that Ruthie Caroline Cornett loved Moon Pies and often kept one in her school desk for a snack. Gene had snitched one when we were in the sixth grade. Ruthie caught Gene in the cloak room and kicked his shins until he returned her snack. After that remembrance, I began thinking about Ruthie exclusively. I had seen her in West Jefferson just last week, helping her father load groceries onto the back of his pickup truck. Ruthie had on shorts, short shorts to be exact. Those tanned legs! Those long, perfect legs!

I was still thinking about Ruthie when I stopped near the merry-go-round and waited for Tank, Pudge, and Gene to catch up with me. I watched the little kids ride monotonously around and around. Some children were so small that their parents had to stand beside them, riding along and holding them on their circling merry-go-round mounts; other youngsters, just a few years older, seemed comfortable in their saddles. On this night, those older kids were as relaxed on horseback as their television heroes, Hoppy, Gene, and Roy. A little blue-eyed girl with curly blonde hair was laughing and waving to her parents as she circled on a buttermilk pony with a black saddle. Her pony and the others were fixed in permanent up-and-down gallops.

A little boy, seated on a golden palomino and equipped with a Roy Rogers cowboy outfit complete with hat, boots, gun belt with holsters, and two shiny cap busters, was whimpering and twisting in his saddle. I wondered why. Then I noticed a melting chocolate ice cream cone under the prancing palomino he was riding.

"There he is!" shouted Pudge from behind me. I waved to the guys to signal my location.

Breathing hard from the run to catch up, the guys joined me, and for a moment or two we stood silently watching the little kids on the merry-go-round. Every painted steed had a fledgling rider. The familiar carousel music caused a brief moment of reminiscence and reflection.

"Gosh, it's the same one, the very same merry-go-round that we rode as kids," Tank said with a touch of wonder and nostalgia in his voice. The big boy wiped some carnival dust from his eyes.

"Hasn't changed a bit since second grade—or maybe it was first grade," said Pudge.

"Yep, I can pick out the horse I rode all those years ago. I named him Topper the same as Hoppy's horse," said Gene, pointing to a silver carousel horse with a dark brown saddle. The merry-go-round pony was currently ridden by a five-year-old boy who waved bravely to his parents as he passed by them, and then, when out of sight, the kid fearfully gripped the saddle horn for dear life as his shiny pony rose and fell, galloping slowly in a never-ending circle.

I looked more closely at the spinning merry-go-round. The guys were right. It was the same one that we had ridden when we were first graders. I could see no wear and tear on the ride. Evidently the money-making merry-go-round was well taken care of, unlike many of the other carnival rides, which were in a state of disrepair.

Rust, the cancer of outdoor machines, had metastasized throughout the carnival, targeting the older rides. The miniature roller coaster was in especially poor condition. The coaster kept jumping off its tracks as it came in to unload passengers at the end of the ride. No one was injured, but workmen were constantly trying to realign the roller coaster's wheels to its corroded tracks. That ride was an accident waiting to happen.

Nearby, the old but freshly-decorated Ferris wheel was creaking as it slowed down in preparation for unloading its passengers and picking up new riders. One of the great wheel's seats, locked in a fixed position, was labeled "Out of Order." The other seats swung freely as the passengers descended.

Overhead, gripping rusted chains, riders of the carnival's huge swing set circled in the night air, enjoying the thrill of centrifugal force. There must've been eighteen people, both guys and girls, flying high above us in a circuitous route. Soaring high, one teenage girl's repetitive screams almost drowned out the ride's steady metallic screeching.

"Hey Tank! Hey Pudge! Look up, you guys!" shouted one of the swing riders circling above us, his arms and legs flapping madly.

Tank, Pudge, Gene, and I looked up at the gyrating boy with legs flailing and waving arms circling above us.

"Who's that dang fool?" Gene asked.

"That's John Bowman," said Tank. "He's from Jefferson Elementary. Some say he's the smartest kid in the county. His teachers say he's gifted. He will be in our freshman class at Central

Ashe. John's mother and my mother are good friends. That's how I know him."

"I met him through the 4-H Club two summers ago," said Pudge. "I've been to his house a time or two. John really likes to play Chinese checkers and chess. He has an amazing comic book collection, and on one side of his bedroom there's a huge bookcase crammed with hardbound books, including the complete works of William Shakespeare. John calls Shakespeare 'Willie, the half-sprung Shake,' and he calls Einstein, 'Uncle Albert.' He wrote President Eisenhower a letter and the president wrote back. His mother framed the letter and it hangs in his room. The Jefferson Elementary principal, Mr. Otis Paisley, was overheard telling Mr. Church that John might be the most intelligent kid in the county school system."

I didn't know him, but I had read about John Bowman in the local newspaper. He had won the countywide spelling bee twice, the local 4-H Club's young farmer award, and the school superintendent's science fair for a project on honeybees. During the summer, he acted in *Horn in the West*, an outdoor drama about Daniel Boone presented over in the nearby town of Boone. There were several pictures of John in the newspaper. He was a skinny kid with very thick glasses. His crooked smile was both engaging and mischievous. He was a smart guy; there was no doubt about it.

Gene scratched his head and said, "Wait a minute! I thought one of you three guys was the smartest kid in the county. Now, which one of you boys was rumored to be the smartest? I'll have to put on my thinkin' cap to figger this out. Let's see, was it the Tank? No, it ain't Tank who's the smartest. The big boy is a numbskull who barely has enough sense to come in out of a lightnin' storm. He has trouble rememberin' his middle name. One time I looked up the word 'stupid' in the dictionary and seen a picture of Tank. That's not all. I seen his picture three more times—when I looked up idiot, imbecile, and moron. With that big, toothy grin of his, the big boy takes a mighty fine dictionary photograph. I will admit that."

"Thanks, Gene," said Tank, lifting his nose in the air and assuming his haughtiest expression. "I don't need intelligence, when I can get by on my remarkable looks and charming personality!"

Gene turned his attention to Pudge.

"Could it be that Pudge is the smartest kid in these here mountains? I reckon not! Pudge is a borderline idiot who crosses the border ever' now and then. The redhead spends his spare time sittin' in a dark corner pickin' his nose, scratchin' his crotch, and singin' 'Bye Bye Love' to a faded picture of Marilyn Monroe. The picture is that one where the wind underneath her is blowin' up her white dress and showin' off her fine legs and almost showin' her drawers. That photograph is also one of my personal fav'rites, but I don't sleep with it under my pillar like he does. Givin' him ever' benefit of the doubt, I have determined that Pudge is a dunce, pure and simple. That ain't no cowlick on top of his red head; that's where his head comes to a single sharp point. That's two numbskulls knocked down, Pudge and Tank, and one still standin'—namely Hal."

"I demand a recount!" said Tank.

"Me, too," said Pudge.

"Hard to believe, guys" said Gene, "but by the scientific process of extermination—I mean elimination, our pal Hal must be the smartest kid in the whole dang county!"

"I feel proud, humble, and grateful as I accept your award, Gene," I said, pulling a wrinkled slip of scrap paper from my pocket. "I have prepared a few brief remarks. My fellow Americans, I am honored to have been chosen the most intelligent..."

"Not so fast, Hal," said Gene. He turned to Tank and Pudge, and spoke conspiratorially. His voice became a whisper. I stepped closer so that I could hear.

"You know, guys, Hal suffered a bad concussion when he fell hard for that Bishop gal," whispered Gene. "In fallin' for purty

Sophia, ole Curly musta struck his head on somethin' solid like a cinderblock, a hard, unyieldin' wooden bookcase, or maybe the corner of his school desk."

"Perhaps a cafeteria table," suggested Tank.

"Perhaps a bench in the gym," added Pudge.

"Whatever," Gene continued. "Anyways, after his starry-eyed, moonstruck fall, Hal now spouts nothin' but gibberish as he grinds his choppers and drools all over his shirt front. He spends hours drawin' little hearts on notebook paper. I seen the hearts while I was tryin' to copy his science homework. He puts Sophia Bishop's initials inside ever' one of them tiny hearts."

"I can vouch for those little hearts; I've seen them in his notebook," said Pudge.

"And whenever his little ladylove comes around to hand out one or two of her purty smiles, Hal scoots across the floor on his hind end like a itchin' hound dog beset with a bad case of the tapeworms. And after the scootin' is done, he beats his head against any nearby wall while singin' Elvis Presley's 'Love Me Tender' at the top of his lungs," joked Gene, flashing his possum grin.

"I have noticed some changes in Hal recently," said the Tank. He patted me sympathetically on the shoulder.

"Worst of all," continued Gene, "Hal has lost all control of his bodily functions. Ain't you fellers detected that sour outhouse stink that floats in the air surroundin' the boy?"

Tank and Pudge nodded solemnly.

"The foul odor stops up my sniffer like a bad cold," said Gene. "My granny gets a case of the vapors ever' time he comes to visit us. Poor Hal, he had so much goin' for him before Cupid shot him through the heart. He's a mere shadder of his former self. I feel sorry for the boy, but the big question remains: If it ain't Hal, and it surely ain't; and if it ain't Tank; and if it ain't Pudge, then who is the smartest kid in these hills? Who? Who can it be?"

"Who indeed?" asked Pudge.

"Who, pray tell?" questioned Tank.

I said, "Don't keep us in suspense, Gene. Who is it? Who's the smartest kid?"

"Without futher ado, I gotta confess that I, Eugene Clifton Clodfelter, am the smartest young feller in these here mountains. In my own mind, there ain't no doubt about the deepness and broadness of my available intelligence—although in the last few years, my mental power has been untapped and therefore has gone mostly unnoticed. You see I ain't one to brag, not me. But I'll prove my brainpower to you guys and to this so-called smarty-pants, John Bowman, when we all get to Central Ashe High School."

"*See you at Central, Tank! You too, Pudge!*" screamed John Bowman, as he, with arms and legs wigwagging madly, hurtled through the air twenty feet above us in what must've been the twentieth rotation of the whirling ride. The carnival swings were going so fast now that the shapes of the riders were blurred—just looking up at the circling swings made me dizzy.

"Let's head for the Ferris wheel, guys!" cried Tank, waving at the gyrating John Bowman overhead. "We can ride the swings later!"

"Time's a-wastin'!" yelled Gene, who was currently the self-appointed smartest kid in the county.

Pudge took a deep breath, gauged the height of the Ferris wheel, and muttered, "All right, let's go. Let's get this first ride under our belts."

Gene, Tank, Pudge, and I almost always rode the Ferris wheel first because when we stopped at the top of the gigantic wheel, we could map out the other rides we wanted to try. As we struck out toward the distant wheel, a deep voice croaking from behind us stopped us in our tracks.

"Young'uns! Hold up a minute!"

CHAPTER 23

I didn't have to turn around—I knew it was my grandpa, Charlie Franklin, a man in his sixties who addressed everyone younger than fifty as a "young'un." He stood before us in faded blue bibbed overalls, a tattered yellow and red plaid shirt, and heavy farm boots which bore the stains of both mud and manure. He was bald except for thick gray hair growing around the lower back part of his head and his ears, creating a horseshoe formation. He had covered his baldness with a shabby Boston Red Sox baseball cap which he had found alongside the gravel road near his cabin.

"Without my cap, I look like I done been scalped by the ole-timey Injuns!" he had told me after plucking his windblown hat from a blackberry bush on a particularly breezy summer day.

His short, graying beard was neatly trimmed, but he needed a haircut or as he called it, "gettin' my ears lowered." White stubbly hair grew from the openings in his elongated ears, rivaling in length the stiff gray bristles peeking from his wide nostrils. His gray eyes were sharp and keen; he didn't have to use reading glasses as Grandpa Grayson did. His broad shoulders were slightly hunched. His coppery skin was wrinkled and leathery from many days of working outside in the burning summer sun and in the biting winter wind. The old man smiled broadly, showing most of his remaining yellowed teeth.

"I've still got sev'ral good grindin' teeth left. Eatin' corn on the cob is kindly tricky, but I can eat most anythin' else that I want without no trouble," he had told me after a meal at his cabin. "Thank the Lord for his boundless mercy and forgivin' nature. Would you like another servin' of deer meat and biscuits, Hal?"

When he gave anyone advice, solicited or unsolicited, the old man always raised his right hand and pointed a thick, gnarled finger, waving it back and forth like a magic wand to emphasize and punctuate his remarks. On his left hand, Grandpa Charlie was missing more than two thirds of his index finger, lost in a sawmill accident when he was only eighteen.

"I reckon that I zigged when I shoulda zagged," he had laughed when he told me of the accidental amputation.

He kept that severed index finger in a Mason jar filled with Wilkes County moonshine and a dash of formaldehyde. He told me that he had picked up the jar from his bedside table and looked at his disembodied finger every morning since the accident, just to remind him to be careful around farm tools. Over time, the digit had dissolved leaving only bits of gristle, fingernail, and bone.

Grandpa Charlie often kept his left hand in his pocket or pushed it up under the bib of his overalls when he was out in public. He had gotten tired of people asking him about the lost finger.

"Your mama bit it off!" Grandpa Charlie had yelled at a Pennsylvania stranger in Ray's Drug Store who kept pestering him with questions about his missing digit. The tourist walked away in a huff.

Grandpa Charlie Franklin and my grandmother, Jetta Franklin, were separated, but they had never bothered to get a divorce. Once, Grandpa Charlie had told me why they separated: "Jetta is a good woman, but I can't get along with her. She craves the excitement of a big town like West Jefferson or Jefferson. I crave the excitement of seein' a mother bear and her cubs splashin' around in the river or a bobcat comin' down the bank for a drink. That's why she lives up in town and why I live down on Grassy Creek Road, near the lazy ole New River. I like to wake up to the birds singin', not to cars runnin' up and down the street. Livin' out in the countryside gives me a peaceful, easy feelin'. Breathin' the clean mountain air and eatin' food comin' fresh from the garden makes me strong."

Standing about ten feet away from the tilt-a-whirl ticket stand, Grandpa Charlie took off his baseball cap to scratch his head. Colorful carnival lights played across his bald pate. Shielding his eyes from the Ferris wheel's flashing brightness, he looked up toward the top of the ride and then brought his eyes slowly down to see Pudge standing before him.

"Pudge, danged if your hair don't get redder ever' time I see you. I wouldn't be surprised if your head don't catch on fire one of these days!"

"If it does, I'll just douse my head in the New River," grinned Pudge. "How are you doing, Grandpa Charlie?"

"Purty good for a man of my years. I ain't puny nor feeble. I reckon I still could whip my weight in catamounts or black bears, whichever a'body might choose. Why, I'm near 'bout as stout as this big feller."

Grandpa Charlie gave Tank a playful punch on the shoulder. Tank pretended that he had received a jarring blow. The big boy staggered back two steps, holding his shoulder. Both he and the older man laughed. Grandpa Charlie liked all my friends, even Gene; but I think Tank was his favorite.

"Gene, I ain't seen you in a month of Sundys. You done growed some. I bet you're taller than your daddy right now. How you been doin', pardner?" asked Grandpa Charlie.

"Fair to middlin', nothin' extry," laughed Gene.

"What I wouldn't give to be your age again, Gene. Seems like ever' mornin' I wake up with a new ache or pain. This mornin', it was my knee. Yesterdy, it was my back. Nothin' serious. Arthritis, I reckon. Oh well, I'm feelin' pert tonight, and I'm determined to have me a good ole time."

Grandpa Charlie was obviously glad to see us, but then his smile faded and his expression became serious. He put an oversized hand in the air and waved his remaining index finger. His digit drew invisible circles in the air and then pointed at Pudge.

"Pudge, see to it that these three boys walk the straight and narrer line tonight. Don't let them get into no trouble," advised the old man. "I reckon I can count on you."

"I'll do my best, Grandpa Charlie," said Pudge, grinning.

"I hope you young'uns is watchin' yore money 'cause this carnival is just the place to waste it. How much money have you got?"

He swept his gray eyes across our faces and squinted. I knew he wanted to give us some extra money, but I wondered if he could afford such an act of selfless generosity. He was not a wealthy man, far from it. Grandma Grayson often referred to him as "poor ole Charlie Franklin."

"Hal, how much change is rattlin' around in your pocket?"

For me, it always was hard not to tell him the truth. I couldn't remember ever lying to the old man.

"Grandpa, we each have five dollars, and that should be plenty. You don't have to give us any extra money," I said.

"Four, is all I have left," frowned Tank who had dropped a dollar at the hotdog stand.

"I cashed my Social Security check today, so I'm gonna give each of you young'uns 'cept fer Tank, another dollar. Tank, I'll let you have two dollars with your promise to pay me back one dollar by next Friday, or you can pay me back fifty cents next Friday and the rest later. I trust you. You look like a downright upright feller to me."

The Tank nodded enthusiastically as he glommed onto the two dollars. He stuffed the bills into his jeans pocket and smiled broadly. He rubbed his stomach contentedly knowing that he now had more money for carnival sweets. Muffled digestive sounds, some pleasant, some ominous, came from Tank's innards.

"Gosh, thanks, Grandpa Charlie," belched Tank. The pleasant summer smell of grilled hotdogs filled the air around him. "Excuse me, sir. It's the carbonation in that RC Cola; I'll be burping all night."

Grandpa Charlie nodded understandingly as he doled out a dollar each to me, Pudge, and Gene. We were excited because an extra dollar meant additional rides and more carnival treats.

All of my friends, and most of the kids at school called my grandfather, "Grandpa Charlie." He volunteered two days per week to help the custodians at Healing Waters Elementary School. He enjoyed sweeping the halls and talking to students and teachers. The school's janitors and Grandpa Charlie kept the oil-soaked floors spotless. The old man and the principal were very good friends, though Mr. Church was at least twenty-five years younger than Grandpa Charlie. They had gone hunting and fishing together for years. Once, Mr. Church had driven Grandpa Charlie down to Winston-Salem to watch a college basketball game.

Grandpa Charlie enjoyed West Jefferson's Christmas lights, Fourth of July parades, carnivals, and an occasional movie at the Parkwood Theatre, but he didn't come to town too often. As a younger man he worked at the Dr. Pepper bottling company in West Jefferson. He told me that the job was "mostly part-time work." The wooded land around his cabin and the nearby river provided him with much of his food. Every summer he raised a garden. He invited me over for supper when he was fixing something special such as "oven-fried squirrel." Grandpa also cooked up wild turkey, venison steaks, and rabbit stew. Once we had servings of snapping turtle—the meat tasted like a combination of chicken and country ham.

"Be careful around snappin' turtles, Hal," he had said. "If one bites you on the finger or toe, the big turtle won't turn loose 'til the sun comes up the next mornin'."

"I thought a snapping turtle wouldn't let go until it heard thunder. That's what Gene's granny says," I replied.

"That sayin' ain't nothin' but a big ole wives' tale," Grandpa Charlie explained. "Don't believe everythin' you hear, son. Besides, ever'body knows that a snappin' turtle is deaf as a post. A snapper couldn't hear no thunder. Turtles ain't got no ears."

He usually spent his nights in his cabin, reading or listening to the Grand Ole Opry on his radio. His favorite singer on the Opry was Roy Acuff. Grandpa Charlie would sing along with the country music star. Sometimes he would pick his banjo, clawhammer style, to the tune Roy Acuff was singing on the radio. Grandpa Charlie knew every word of the "Wabash Cannonball" and "The Great Speckled Bird."

"I wouldn't mind leavin' this ole world ridin' on the back of a big ole speckled bird," he had once told me, turning up the radio so that Roy Acuff's voice filled the room and spilled outside through the cabin's open windows.

Tonight, facing the carnival's timeworn roller coaster, Grandpa Charlie said, "Boys, I want you to use the extry money I'm givin' you to ride the rides and eat carnival fixin's and have a bushel of fun. Yep, have a big ole time, but I don't want to see none of you around that there hootchy-cootchy show over yonder."

The nub of a finger on his left hand pointed to a ragged gray tent in front of which three scantily-clad, forty-year-old women on a platform rotated their pelvises to the Fats Domino tune, "Blueberry Hill." A barker shared the stage with the undulating women and shouted over Fats Domino, extolling the ladies' physical virtues and hinting that there was much more to be seen inside the tattered tent.

"Young'uns, I'm gonna hang around that there hootchy-cootchy tent and make sure you boys don't get near it. And if I was to go inside that tent and see ary one of you rascals watchin' the show, they'll be hell to pay. You boys understand me? Don't you dare try to sneak into that tent. I'll tell your mommies and daddies; don't you think I won't! Hal, I'll tell the Graysons on you. That there show is for a-dults only."

"Don't worry, Grandpa Charlie," I said. "We'll be on the carnival rides until we go home. Thanks for the extra money."

"You boys is as welcome as rain after a dry spell. One other thing, I'll give all of you a ride home when the carnival closes down. I figger that'll be around midnight. My pickup is parked downtown in front of Blackburn's Department Store. Me and Tank will ride in the front of the truck, the rest of you will have to ride in the back in the truck bed. It won't be too cold tonight, but it might get a little windy and airish. I hope you don't mind."

Pudge, Tank, Gene, and I didn't mind, in fact, if there was one thing we enjoyed in life, it was riding in the back of any pickup truck. With all four tires beneath the truck humming a merry tune, the streaming wind and fresh air were more rejuvenating. At night, the moon, especially a full moon, was more luminous; in the daytime, the sun overhead was brighter, and the distant mountains were bluer. The back of a pickup truck on a sunny day or a moonlit night was a country boy's Cadillac convertible.

"Now go spend your money and have some fun," chuckled Grandpa Charlie. "You will be young for only a brief spell. Enjoy the short stretch of youth while you can. Like you, I was young once, but my ole candle is about burnt out, and your candles has just been lit! Make your candles burn bright like the stars overhead, young'uns!"

Dumbfounded by this unprecedented financial turn of events, Gene, Tank, Pudge and I stumbled into the carnival crowd, again headed toward the Ferris wheel.

"Hey Pudge, would you come back here for just a minute or two. I want to talk to you about somethin'," called Grandpa Charlie.

"Sure thing," said Pudge. Dutifully, Pudge turned and walked back toward the old man. The old farmer put his callused hand on Pudge's shoulder.

I stopped to get some cotton candy at a nearby stand as Tank and Gene went on toward the Ferris wheel. The old man and the redhead were talking quietly. From where I stood, I could see Grandpa Charlie and Pudge and hear their conversation. I listened as I ate my cotton candy.

"Pudge," Grandpa Charlie began, "you remember sev'ral weeks ago, when you four boys was playin' ball on the school grounds.

Three softballs was hit up on the roof of the school and got stuck up there. You remember?"

"I remember," said Pudge. He lowered his head, as if he didn't want to remember.

"I brung a ladder around from the school's tool shed, and Gene and Hal scampered up the ladder to the roof like a pair of squirrels lookin' for the last acorn to be found in these mountains," explained Grandpa Charlie. He always had a way with descriptions. "I didn't let Tank climb that ladder for fear that the big young'un might break it down. After some searchin', Gene found them softballs restin' in those rusty gutters near the drain pipe. He tossed the softballs down to Tank, and then Gene and Hal walked over to the belfry to look at the view from way up there on top of the school.

"Now, I recollect Hal and Gene called for you, Pudge, to come up and join 'em on the roof, but you wouldn't do it. You wouldn't take one step up that tall ladder. I kindly wondered why, Pudge. That ladder was brand new and steady as a rock."

"I didn't want to go up on the roof at that time," said Pudge defensively. He looked down. His cheeks were flushed. "I just didn't feel like it."

Grandpa Charlie put his hands in the pockets of his bib overalls. His lips tightened, and he slowly shook his head.

"I'm just the same way, Pudge," he said. "If I don't feel like doin' somethin', it gen'rally don't get done. Well, I reckon I'll mosey over yonder and buy me a Coke. It's been nice talkin' to you, son." He turned to walk away, but Pudge's voice called him back.

"Did you know that you forgot about that ladder, Grandpa Charlie? You left it there, leaning against the school building. You forgot the ladder because you were telling Tank some big story about a copperhead snake, the one that almost bit you last year when you were stacking wood."

The old man nodded, "Yep, and I was remindin' Tank about always wearin' work gloves when he helps folks stack firewood."

My grandfather remained silent, waiting for Pudge to continue. Pudge smiled up at the old man. The teenager spoke with a trace of pride in his voice.

"What you don't know is that I went back and climbed that ladder after all of you had left. I made myself do it. I went up rung by rung slow as molasses, and when I reached the top, I touched the school's roof. I just reached over the guttering and put my hand on the shingles. I couldn't make myself look down at the ground. I tried but I just couldn't do it. I climbed down even slower than I went up. My eyes were closed. When my feet touched the ground, I stood still for a solid minute. Then I opened my eyes and put the ladder back in the shed for you."

"Thank you, Pudge, for returnin' the ladder after you had clumb it. I'm mighty grateful. The older I get, the more forgetful I get. I almost took a wrong turn at the Jefferson Esso station in gettin' up here to West Jefferson."

"Here's another thing you don't know, Grandpa Charlie," said Pudge. "Last summer, I went to visit my uncle Blaine who lives in Baltimore."

"Yep, I know Blaine, and I remember when he went up to Baltimore lookin' for work. Blaine said he couldn't find no jobs around here that paid good money. He ended up workin' for a big airplane company up there in Baltimore, didn't he? Does he still have to wear that back brace?"

"Yes, he does," said Pudge, frowning. "He works for the Glenn L. Martin Company. The company makes airplanes and airplane parts. He has an office job with a special parking place and everything."

"I always figgered Blaine would get a job workin' outdoors. I can't picture him workin' indoors all the time. When he was a boy, he was always outside, swimmin' in the river, huntin' in the woods, playin' baseball in a level pasture when he could locate enough boys to make up two teams. I reckon he can't do no hard outdoor work because of the accident. Am I right?"

"You're right, Grandpa Charlie. He still wears his back brace. If he takes it off, he has to walk with a cane. He can't do any strenuous work outside. Even at his office, he has to lie down on the floor for thirty minutes after lunch before he can return to his desk. He takes the brace off when he goes to bed, but sometimes the pain in his back wakes him. He has had two operations."

"I remember when Blaine had that accident. The ambulance takin' him to the hospital passed me on Highway 16 with its lights flashin' and its siren wailin'," said Grandpa Charlie. "Folks around here said Blaine was a mighty brave feller. I'd call him a hero. You know, Pudge, that he don't blame nobody for what happened."

"I'd rather not talk about Uncle Blaine's accident," said Pudge. He ran his fingers nervously through his red hair. "I will tell you he walks better than he used to, but he still has to use a cane or wear his back brace, sometimes both."

"I understand, Pudge," said Grandpa Charlie. "I'll bet you had a good time up there in Baltimore. Knowin' your uncle Blaine, I'd wager he had planned out some nice places to go and fun things to do. He always thought a lot of you, Pudge. You was always his fav'rite nephew. I hope you don't blame yourself none for that accident. You was just a little feller at the time and didn't know no better."

"I'd rather not talk about it," Pudge repeated.

Pudge bit his lower lip and looked away from the elderly farmer. Flashing carnival lights smeared the old man's tanned face with neon war paint. He raised his wounded hand to shade his eyes and better see Pudge who was standing with a drooping head and sagging shoulders.

"Did you like bein' in Baltimore?"

Pudge lifted his head, straightened his shoulders, and said, "Sure, I went with Uncle Blaine to an Orioles game; the Orioles beat the Yankees. I got to see Hoyt Wilhelm pitch. He throws knuckle balls that flutter all over the place. That game was fun to watch, but Uncle Blaine took me to one place I'll never forget."

"Tell me about it, Pudge. We both got the time. It's early in the evenin' yet. I bet the chickens ain't even gone to roost," smiled Grandpa Charlie.

"Uncle Blaine took me to a swimming pool in the city. He knew that I'd learned to swim in the New River. The pool was Olympic size and had one low diving board and one high diving board. I jumped off the high board three times. On the last jump I was terrified and almost climbed back down."

"Do tell," said the old man.

"I'm scared of high places; I'm always afraid I'm going to fall. I'm petrified. Sometimes I panic and just freeze! Somehow the fact that Uncle Blaine was there, watching me dive, helped me make that last leap off the board.

Grandpa Charlie became thoughtful. He examined his hand carefully, the one with the missing finger. He smiled at Pudge, and when he smiled, he didn't look so old.

Standing at the cotton candy stand, not far away from my grandfather and Pudge, I munched on my cotton candy. The treat was tasty so I ordered another. The spun sugar was sticky and sweet like the honey Grandma Grayson put on peanut butter sandwiches. Savoring the soft sweetness, I resumed my eavesdropping.

Grandpa Charlie cleared his throat and looked down at Pudge. I waited for them to return to their conversation. I was eavesdropping, but I didn't care. Grandpa Charlie scratched his chin and tugged at his ear. I knew he was going to weigh his words before speaking.

"Let me tell you somethin' about me that you don't know," said Grandpa Charlie. "You know Wallace Osborne's boy, Frank, is home from State College. Frank took me for a ride in his little red sports car. The automobile was a convertible type, and since it was a purty day, Frank and me talked it over and decided to take that car out for a jaunt. We was a-ridin' around in that convertible when it commenced to rain. The rain come down hard. It was pourin' the rain, a gully warsher and us with the top down. We was gettin' soaked, almost drownded, but we just laughed.

"Frank stopped the car. He went around back of the car grabbed that convertible top, pulled it up and over me and fastened it. We took off again, but I couldn't stand bein' inside that sports car with the top up. I felt all cramped up. I started gaspin' for air. My heart was beatin' real fast.

"Then I got scared that I might have a heart attack right there in front of Frank. I made him stop the car and let me out. I took shelter under a big oak tree. I was tremblin' all over, but I felt a whole lot better outside. I could breathe good again. My heartbeat slowed down. I told Frank to come back and get me when it stopped rainin'. He didn't want to leave me, but I made him drive off. I told him I would be all right. After about a half hour, the rain stopped and the sun come out. Frank come back and got me and took me home. The convertible top was down on the ride to my cabin, so I didn't have no problem. I enjoyed the ride to my cabin and told Frank so.

"Pudge, when the top was up, I wanted to claw my way out of that body-huggin' vehicle. That's when I realized I have got a bad case of closet phobia, which is, as most ever'body knows, gettin' scared in tight places. That ride with Frank made me positive that I had closet phobia and a dang bad case of it, too. It's terrible when the tight feelin' hits me. I can't hardly breathe. My heart starts poundin'. My skin gets cold and clammy. Whewee!"

"Closet phobia?" asked Pudge.

"That's right, Pudge, and it's happened to me sev'ral times before, that closet phobia thing. I was down in a big buildin' in Raleigh, and I got in one of them elevators. Now I can tolerate what they called a eggskuhlater, that thing with movin' stair steps—it don't bother me none—but a cramped-up elevator is a diff'rent story. I get eat up with fear 'til I can't hardly stand it.

"I was wantin' to go up to the seventh floor to see a lawyer feller about sellin' a little piece of land. I went inside the elevator, and I mashed the number seven button and the doors slid together and shut tight. When the doors sealed up, my heart dropped to the floorboard. I hollered, 'God Almighty!' as my toenails commenced tryin' to scratch their way out of my brogans.

"My closet phobia kicked in fierce, and I was shakin' all over. I banged on them elevator doors, yellin' for help. I musta scared this ole lady who was my feller passenger 'cause she started beatin' on me with her pocketbook. She was a whole lot stouter than what she looked, and she was bent on frailin' the hell outta me. She kicked like a mule and scratched like a bobcat. She didn't believe that all I wanted was out! Things got unusual wild 'til the elevator doors flew open. I jumped out and run toward the stairs. I didn't get on no other elevator in that buildin', nor any other since then. I have used the stairs goin' up and down from that time on. Closet phobia is a terrible thing!"

"You have *claustrophobia*, the fear of being in tight places," corrected Pudge.

"Yep, that's what I got, closet phobia," said Grandpa Charlie. "And I'll tell you how I got it."

"Go ahead," said Pudge. "I'm in no hurry."

I was glad Pudge encouraged him to tell his tale. This was the first I'd heard of Grandpa Charlie's claustrophobia. I wanted to learn more. I ordered my third cotton candy puff. I munched on the sugar-twirled treat and listened.

"When I was a boy, knee-high to a possum, my oldest sister Ginny was babysittin' me. I went outside and caught me a bumblebee and a wasp in a Mason jar. I punched holes in the jar lid, took the jar inside, and chased Ginny around the house with the wasp and bumblebee jar. I threatened to open the jar and turn them critters loose. That big yeller-and-black bumblebee was buzzin' and tryin' get out. The wasp was doin' the same—only not as loud.

"I run Ginny around the kitchen table a few times, still threatenin' to let the stingin' bugs out. She got tired of my foolishness and pushed me, holdin' the jar, into a closet and slammed the door. She locked the door. I dropped the jar and it busted. The glass shards spread ever'wheres. I was shut in a dark closet with a loose bumblebee madder than a hornet and a wasp even madder. I was barefooted and stepped on the broke glass and cut my big toe. It bled considerable. But my main problem was the wasp, not the bumblebee nor the sharp glass. The wasp stung me five times whilst I banged on the door. The bumblebee stung me one time, on the elbow. I hollered and hammered my fists against the closet door.

"Ginny fin'ly let me out and was sorry when she seen me. She put salve on my swellin' stings and a Band-Aid on my toe. My closet phobia musta come from that incident. I can't figger no other way that I got the disease. Do you reckon somethin' happened to you when you was little to make you scared of high places?"

"You're probably right about that, Grandpa Charlie," said Pudge. "What I have is called acrophobia. I think you know how I feel sometimes because of your problem with tight places. So, we both have irrational fears, fears that can't be explained easily."

"Yep, I reckon we're stuck. I get panicky in close spaces, and you get panicky in high places," said Grandpa Charlie, putting both his work-toughened hands on Pudge's shoulders. "What I don't understand is why, if you have this here acre-phobia, you're still here at the carnival ready to ride them big ole rides that take you way up in the air and then all of a sudden drop you down. You know that Gene will try to scare you on them tall rides, just like he done last year and the year before."

"I know," said Pudge, dropping his head again.

"Gene scares the devil out of Hal, too; and Hal ain't got no acre-phobia, not one smidgen of it. Give Hal a dollar, and he'd climb the tallest tree in the county. Still, Gene scares him when he gets way up on them rides. Pudge, you don't have to ride on them high rides with Gene and them boys. Nobody would blame you if you didn't."

"I'm trying to face my fear tonight, just as I did at the Baltimore swimming pool with Uncle Blaine; I'm trying to gain some control over my phobia," said Pudge. "Someday, I might want to travel in an airplane. I might even join the Army and have to fly overseas. Maybe I'll work on the tenth floor of a building in New York City or Charlotte. I don't want a crazy, senseless fear to hinder me. I'm going to try to overcome my fear, my acrophobia; and every year I get a real test on the carnival's high rides."

"You got pluck. I admire you for that, Pudge, because you're facin' yore fear and all. I really do, but to this very day, I just can't abide bein' in a tight space. At home I even put a little winder in the outhouse, and if I know they ain't nobody around, I leave the privy door wide open. That is 'til the flies gets too thick and start swarmin'. I reckon I ain't like you. I ain't got your determination. I ain't got your courage. I ain't never been able to face up to my fear of closed-in places."

Grandpa Charlie sighed, his shoulders slumped, and he stuffed both hands into the deep pockets of his tattered bib overalls.

"You know, Pudge, the Cherokee Injuns has got a sayin' about courage and fear. They say that inside ever' man lives the spirits of two big wolves. One wolf spirit is cowardly, wicked, sneaky, and awful dangerous. The other is brave, bold, above board, and unflinchin' in times of trouble. Them two wolf spirits is always fightin' with one another, tryin' to take over a man's soul. The Injuns say both spirits is mighty powerful and good fighters, alike in strength."

"Which wolf wins the struggle?" asked Pudge.

"The Cherokee say it's the wolf a man feeds."

Pudge smiled up at the old man. "That makes sense."

"Pudge, go on now, and find Tank, Gene, and Hal. Ride with them boys if you must. You know if Gene tries to scare you while you're up on a ride, Tank and Hal will prob'ly go right along with him. I got a feelin' that tonight them boys will make you face up to that acre-phobia of yours, 'specially that Gene. I ain't got no doubts about it."

"You're right," said Pudge, "but that's why I'm here. I'm trying to confront my acrophobia, one step at a time. I think I see Tank over by the Ferris wheel. The Ferris wheel will be our first ride, as usual. Just my luck. So long Grandpa Charlie, I might as well start this baptism by fire!"

"Good luck, Pudge," called Grandpa Charlie. "I believe you can whip this here acre-phobia that you got. If I was a bettin' man, I'd put my money on you! I got a whole lot of faith in you, son."

I finished off my cotton candy and ended my eavesdropping. I wiped my sticky fingers on the front of my T-shirt. Leaving the candy stand, I jogged toward Tank and Gene, waiting at the Ferris wheel. I heard footsteps. Pudge was running to catch up with me. He raced past and beat me to the ticket stand where our two friends waited.

"Me and Tank have been waitin' a long time. What kept you guys?" asked Gene, as he examined his blue ticket stub.

"Cotton candy," I said. "I was hungry."

"Grandpa Charlie," said Pudge. "He wanted to talk."

"Don't never start a conversation with that ole feller. He'll talk your ear off," laughed Gene. "You and Hal go buy your tickets. Get a move on; me and Tank have already bought ours. While you're at it, check out the lights on this contraption. The Ferris wheel has a whole lot more colored lights than it had last year. It's a thing of beauty, like somethin' you'd see in a magazine or a movie!"

CHAPTER 24

The multi-colored lights of the Ferris wheel mesmerized us. The tinted beams washed over the crowd waiting below, painting the people with multi-colored pigments and making them look like comic-book characters in a Technicolor cartoon. The huge wheel overlooked a weedy field far below where the brief golden flashes from hundreds of lightning bugs were competing with the gaudy carnival lights. We scanned the carnival grounds, surveying the other rides: the swings, the tilt-a-whirl, and the sad, rusty roller coaster whose tracks were, at their highest point, only twelve feet off the ground.

A sudden humid haze blew over the hill, partially shrouding the ominous shape of a new ride, perhaps taller than the Ferris wheel. Blurred blue lights flashed through the gossamer fog. The new ride, if that was what the apparition was, suddenly disappeared when its lights flicked off for several seconds. The blue lights blinked back on as the mist thickened, transforming the carnival ride into a shapeless, glowing, powder-blue cloud. We strained our eyes, but we couldn't quite make out its true form.

"Wonder what that ride over yonder is," mused Gene. Within an hour we would find out.

The "kiddie rides" were virtually invisible to us, except for our nostalgic visit to the merry-go-round. We had outgrown the slow, monotonous circular motion along with the repetitious rising and falling of miniature horses on the carousel and similar rides. We were young male sprouts looking for adventure and thrills. Also, we knew that conquering fast, somewhat dangerous carnival rides had become a rite of passage for seventh- and eighth-grade men.

Last summer, we had passed the carnival test with flying colors. We even rode the Ferris wheel three times. Some of my classmates thought that riding the Ferris wheel was no big deal, but they had never ridden the Ferris wheel with Gene. The skinny guy made every ride memorable.

We had to double dog dare Pudge to get him to ride the Ferris wheel for the third time, but eventually he did ride with us. At our age, the double dog dare was still a powerfully influential mechanism. The rarely-mentioned, all-powerful *triple* dog dare, like an atomic weapon, was seldom, if ever, used. Even Gene carefully avoided invoking the nuclear choice, the dreaded *triple* dog dare.

Starting around the fifth grade, it had been like this at Healing Waters Elementary School: If you were challenged to ride the roller coaster or the carnival swings, for example, and you refused, you became an object of derision, plain and simple. Being without funds was, of course, a legitimate reason for refusing the carnival dare. We all knew that money was scarce in many of the county's households. However, carnival-ride cowardice was not tolerated by the boys in our class. Non-riders became social pariahs for a couple of weeks or more, until their timidity had been fully forgotten and our evolving male brains turned to other matters like baseball, comic books, and girls.

Gene, Tank, Pudge and I clutched our tickets for the lofty Ferris wheel, waited impatiently in line, and finally were seated. At least Gene, Pudge, and I were seated. Tank waited for the next available seat. I sat between Pudge and Gene, hoping to mollify any problems that might develop between the two. I was certain that last year they might've come to blows had I not been the mediator.

The sweating carnival worker who seated us snapped our safety bar into place. The ride began as we lifted backward and up. When the Ferris wheel stopped to load other passengers, our seat swung back and forth, creaking loudly.

The Tank was now seated just below us as we rose upward, which meant he would be above us on the great wheel's descent. As usual, Tank filled his seat to capacity and then some. When the safety bar was snapped into place, the bar made an indentation that neatly divided his belly into an upper half and a lower half, like the equator divides the earth on a globe. Tank was secure, but after consuming three large hotdogs and a soft drink, the big boy was uncomfortable. He rubbed the upper half of his tummy as we lifted off.

When we stopped at the very top of the giant wheel, Gene, Pudge, and I beheld the magical world far below us—a world of merry laughter, constant motion, and whirling color; a world of sweet funnel cakes, salty pretzels, and sugar-spun cotton candy; a world of thrilling rides, tempting grilled burgers, and rigged games with cheap, made-in-Japan prizes. I was in awe of the carnival's gaudy majesty and so was Gene.

"I ain't never seen nothin' so purty and shiny in all my life," he said reverently. "It's like ever'body in the crowd way down below is lookin' up, smilin' with painted-on clown faces and holdin' up different-colored Fourth-of-July sparklers. The whole hilltop is lit up!"

"You can see the Parkwood Theatre lights from up here," Pudge said with his fingers wrapped around the safety bar. Gene and I looked way down toward the lights of the town below. Sure enough, I could pick out the Parkwood Theatre just off Main Street. An Elvis movie was playing. Many of Presley's movies had descended into the great Hollywood abyss, but some were worth the half-buck to get in. However, tonight it was the carnival, not Elvis, that drew people to the town of West Jefferson, and then on up to the fairgrounds at the summit of Seagraves Hill.

At the final jerking Ferris wheel stop, the ride's last customers, a junior girl and a senior boy came on board. Gazing into each other's eyes, they held hands, and they both knew—and even I had heard—about a tradition as old as Ferris wheel rides: when a guy and girl stopped at the top of the Ferris wheel, the girl had to give the guy a kiss. Also, the girl always determined the intensity of the kiss. The smooch might range from a mere peck on the cheek to a passionate French kiss.

Gene always referred to a French kiss as a "tongue twister" or a "tonsil tosser." Gene was not the most delicate soul, nor was he the most romantic of individuals.

Unlike Gene, one of Pudge's cousins, Tommy Wilson, five or six years older than us, had always been a hopeless romantic. Tommy had proposed to his girlfriend at the top of a Ferris wheel. He had hidden the ring in cotton candy and almost dropped the ring once when his girlfriend reached over to pull off some of the downy threads of spun sugar. Pudge said the ring had cost Tommy over one hundred dollars and that his cousin still owed seventy-five dollars on it at the time of the proposal.

Grace Godfrey, the potential bride-to-be, had been the valedictorian of her graduating class at Beaver Dam High School, and, as a senior in high school, she had been the reigning Miss Ashe County. She had won both the bathing suit and the evening gown competition, which had never happened before in the pageant's history.

Grace had earned a full academic scholarship to Woman's College in Greensboro, but most folks expected her to forget about college and marry Pudge's cousin, Tommy. After all, the two had been going steady for two years, and the rumor was that Tommy and Grace had once gone to Wilkesboro to look at mobile homes. In the North Carolina high country, a young man and a young woman shopping for a house trailer was definitely a sign of commitment. However, Grace Godfrey said 'no' to Tommy

Wilson, 'no' to the mobile home, 'no' to the ring, and 'no' to the rest of his cotton candy.

Nine months later Tommy was married to a short, stocky, dark-haired girl from Bristol, Tennessee.

Within three years, they were divorced.

"Tom Wilson married that Bristol woman on the rebound from Grace Godfrey. My daddy says them kinds of marriages don't never work out," Gene had opined one day in eighth grade as he, Pudge, Tank, and I stood in line outside the lunch room waiting for the seventh graders to finish. "When it comes to womenfolks, Tom Wilson and me is a whole lot alike, meanin' neither one of us ain't had no luck with the fairest sex. Not yet, anyways. Me and Tom is still lookin' for true love."

Moments later, as we sat at our favorite cafeteria table, munching on grilled cheese sandwiches, Tank said, "I'm sure I'll meet my true love someday. Maybe I'll meet her in high school or in college. I'm really in no hurry to meet my true love."

"My daddy says that true love don't never run smooth," Gene said as he dipped one corner of his grilled cheese into his bowl of vegetable soup. "My brother Jack can't seem to find his true love. His latest girlfriend just busted up with him, and he's feelin' lower down than a snake's belly." His older brother Jack Clodfelter, according to Gene, was enduring the sharp pain of one of his many high school breakups.

"Jack just mopes around the house claimin' that his insides hurt like he swallered a porkypine. He can't get his mind off Holly Maureen Hightower. He's really got a mess of the blues this time. I told him it's just like the record on the radio says, 'True love is a many splintered thing.' Them's the truest words I ever heard in a song."

CHAPTER 25

Tank, Pudge, Gene and I were suddenly weightless as the great Ferris wheel groaned, took us swiftly downward, and then began drawing circles of light in the darkening night as its riders rose and fell, rose and fell, rose and fell. Pudge and I laughed nervously as Gene studied our seat and its metal attachments to the big wheel. From the seat behind us, Tank burped loudly, and had a short hiccupping fit.

The noisy, wood and steel structure moaned and creaked as its passengers climbed and descended in the sultry night air. On the third revolution, Gene leaned forward suddenly, and then rocked violently backward, almost spilling us out of the Ferris wheel seat. Instinctively, I grabbed the metal safety bar. Pudge did the same. To maintain the equilibrium of our swinging seat, Pudge and I found ourselves leaning backward as Gene lurched forward and leaning forward as Gene rocked rearward. We neutralized Gene's movements effectively and preserved the balance of our seat.

Gene abandoned his efforts when he saw that Pudge and I were easily able to thwart his actions. After Gene ended his antics and settled down, the Ferris wheel ride smoothed out into the pleasant routine of lifting and falling. With the giant wheel in motion, the fleeting view from the top of the Ferris wheel was a kaleidoscope of color, shifting and changing below us. Pudge and I released our grips on the safety bar as the redhead pointed out the lofty carnival swings below us and suggested that we ride those next. Circling carnival swing rides always made me woozy, but I nodded my assent. Pudge was actually smiling. I had never seen him so relaxed on a carnival ride, except perhaps the merry-go-round rides of long ago.

I was just about to stretch my arms and yawn as the great wheel began its descent when I realized that Gene had been quiet too long—much too long. His silence was usually a prelude to trouble. I was certain he was formulating another tactic to make our Ferris wheel ride memorable.

"We don't need this!" cackled Gene as he released our seat's safety bar and flung it upward to his left. The bar careened wildly—up, down, and sideways. Both Pudge and I grabbed at the bar, missing badly the first time, but on our second try, we corralled it and held on for dear life, finally managing to secure it in place. Gene giggled insanely, with the same high-pitched laugh that had infuriated Mrs. Bender.

With the safety bar fastened securely, Pudge and I settled back to enjoy the remaining moments of the ride. The only bothersome thing now was the myriad of insects gathered in the tepid air. Attracted by the lights of the Ferris wheel, flies, moths, gnats, and other assorted flying bugs swarmed through the air around us. The living atmosphere droned, buzzed, and whirred. The insects seemed intent on finding shelter in our eyes, noses, mouths, and ears. The three of us swatted them away as best we could. In the seat behind us, Tank, also surrounded by a multitude of winged creatures, was having his own troubles.

In the midst of our descent through the insect hordes, Gene turned to me and stuck out his long tongue, which was coated with an unhealthy blue film. A large white moth landed on the fleshy organ and perched there for a second. Gene gulped it down and rubbed his belly as a June bug buzzed by, stalling in midair. Gene reached out and caught the hapless, hovering insect. Buzzing and wriggling, the large black critter followed the ill-fated moth down Gene's omnivorous gullet. His next victim was a lightning bug, then another. He emitted a self-satisfied belch. As Gene continued gorging himself on insects, Pudge, who had a notoriously queasy stomach, was beginning to turn a pale shade of gray.

"Insects' bodies is packed with protein, great nature's buildin' block, which is just what a growin' boy like me needs," said Gene. "Whoop-de-doo! There's a purty one!"

His next catch was a beautiful, lime-green Luna moth. The captured creature struggled for its freedom. Delicately holding the insect by its wings, Gene turned to Pudge. He arched a single eyebrow and looked directly into Pudge's eyes. Pudge gagged audibly and Gene snickered as he released the winged creature.

"Go forth flyin' critter. Be fruitful and multiply!"

Relief streamed over Pudge's face, bringing with it an almost normal facial color. The redhead slumped back into the seat. He closed his eyes and took a deep breath.

I thought that Gene's antics were through, but he was not finished. He turned to his left for a second and then back toward us.

"Did you hear that?" he asked. He was referring to a popping sound that occurred with each rotation of the great wheel. The sharp sound, steadily increasing in volume, occurred when our seat reached the uppermost point and then began its descent.

Pop! Poppa! Pop!

Something was definitely wrong with our seat attachment and the unnerving sounds were coming from Gene's side. I tried to check out the problem, but Gene's upper body blocked my view.

Suddenly, the skinny guy twisted toward me. His face was as ghastly as any rubber Halloween mask. His eyes were wide and his face was twisted with terror. His mouth was open, and his bottom lip was drawn down displaying uneven lower teeth, all suffering from various stages of dental caries. His shoulders shuddered, and his quivering fingers distended and then contracted into claw-like fists clinging to the safety bar.

My stomach reacted to Gene's panicked expression with a sudden pang of indigestion. A clammy fear nibbled at my gut. A voice deep inside me said that Gene wasn't faking. My heart began pounding against my rib cage. My breath came in gasps.

"Oh no, Pudge! Great God in heaven!" Gene screeched, as our Ferris wheel seat continued to snap, crunch, and pop with each revolution.

"What's wrong?" asked Pudge, rolling fearful eyes toward Gene.

"Holy moley, Pudge, the bolts is comin' loose from our seat!" he said in a panic. "Surely the three of us is gonna drop to our deaths unless I can fix this here problem. I just hope I ain't too late. Lord, help us! Give me some elbow room, Hal! I'm tryin' to save our dang lives!"

Gene pulled a medium-sized wrench from a bulging pants pocket and began working furiously on the bolts that connected our swinging seat to the framework of the Ferris wheel. Pudge was beside himself with fright. His white-knuckled fingers were locked around the safety bar, and his face was ashen. His eyes swelled and a pulsing purple blood vessel formed in the middle of his freckled forehead. The throbbing vein resembled rock 'n roller Bill Haley's famous spit curl. He leaned forward trying to get a better view of Gene's efforts. Since I was seated between Pudge and Gene, the redhead couldn't quite make out what the skinny guy was doing.

"Here, Pudge, hold this!" Gene shouted as he reached across me and handed Pudge a large, rusty steel bolt. Stunned, Pudge accepted the heavy corroded bolt and stared at it in horror as the object rested in the palm of his hand. As we were beginning our descent from the Ferris wheel's summit, Gene turned away; rose from his seat; and, leaning out toward the Ferris wheel frame, returned frantically to his work.

Pop! Poppa! Pop!

"One more bolt to go, and I'll have this here problem fixed— and just in the nick of time!" Gene exclaimed, brandishing his wrench like a crazed, water-soaked plumber attacking a spraying water pipe. "There now, one more turn is gonna do it!"

"No, you don't!" shouted Pudge, convinced that the single remaining bolt was the only thing preventing our headfirst tumble into the endless darkness of eternity. "Gimme that wrench, dammit!"

Pudge's right arm shot out, snatched the wrench, and tore the tool away from Gene's grasp. The realistic-looking wrench was made of plastic and crumbled in Pudge's grip. Bits of gray plastic fell onto his shirt and then into his lap. The redhead's eyes expanded as he struggled to fully comprehend Gene's prank, then having reached full understanding, Pudge seethed with fury. Casting the remaining pieces of the fake tool aside, he reached across me, and tried to punch Gene in the face. Gene punched back, and the skirmish quickly intensified. Our Ferris wheel seat pitched back and forth like a canoe caught in the rapids of the New River.

"Stop it, you guys! You'll tip us over!" I wailed. We were lurching at least forty feet above the ground and descending rapidly. A voice from somewhere deep inside me told me to calm down, relax, and take it easy. I told the voice to shut up.

Unlike the plastic wrench, the rusted bolt, which Gene had concealed in his blue jeans hours before, was real enough; and due to Pudge's sudden twisting and his striking at Gene with his fists, he dropped it. It clattered to the seat's floorboard, bounced around a few times, and then plunged through an aperture toward the dusty ground below.

The weighty bolt narrowly missed the blonde head of a pretty sophomore girl two seats below us as it plummeted downward and landed with a thump next to the carnival worker who had seated us. The worker picked the bolt up, eyed it curiously, and then tossed it over his shoulder. I smelled gas fumes as our seat passed by close to ground level.

The other carnival worker, manning the ride's controls, was oblivious to the hand-to-hand combat now taking place. Sitting between the two combatants, I was almost blinded by the blur of flailing elbows, flapping forearms, and flying fists. Gene had grabbed Pudge's elbow and was trying to bite it. Pudge seized a handful of Gene's hair and pulled hard. An anonymous fingernail scratched my chin, leaving a swath of raw skin. Pudge's tennis shoe flashed before my nose.

"No kicking!" I screamed as one of Gene's boots narrowly missed my left ear.

I decided to lean back and let Pudge and Gene carry on their no-holds-barred struggle without my interference. My maneuver didn't work, however, because I received several more sharp blows about my head and shoulders. Meanwhile, our seat was rising again toward the topmost portion of the massive wheel.

As the melee continued, Pudge grabbed Gene's cowboy hat, broke the flimsy chin string, and flung the hat, which soared like a gyrating Frisbee, into the night. At the loss of his cowboy hat, Gene spewed forth a boiling brew of blasphemies. His face blackened with anger and his voice became shrill. Reaching across me, he grabbed Pudge's wrists and held on.

"Dammit, Pudge! That was my Hopalong Cassidy hat! I've had that hat ever since I was a kid," he cried. "It's made of imitation felt with a reinforced plastic headband inside. Them hats ain't for sale no more. Now it's gone forever. You done messed up big time! Prepare to meet thy doom, you redheaded son of a bitch!"

"Not if I can help it, you broken-nosed, loud-mouthed, moth-eating bastard! Say your prayers because the end is nigh!" shouted Pudge, breaking free from Gene's grip. He landed a solid uppercut on Gene's chin. Gene counterpunched, striking the redhead firmly between his eyes.

Fists flew with newfound fury. Sitting between them and trying to constrain the teenage pugilists, I endured the brunt of their rage. A hard blow landed on my right temple, momentarily dazing me. For an instant, little yellow songbirds chirped and tweeted inside my head while bright flaming stars flashed and exploded.

When my head cleared, I began elbowing both Gene and Pudge as hard as I could. They returned the favor. To the crowd below, we must've looked like an adolescent version of the slaphappy Three Stooges. Our seat swung dangerously forward and back, nearing the tipping point.

Suddenly, the whole framework of the Ferris wheel began to shake as if an earthquake had struck. A surge of machine-made moans and groans reverberated through the Ferris wheel's steel and wood structure, and then an explosive sound, much louder than the rest, shattered the night air and caused a pain in my right ear.

The fighting ended and we froze in our seats as Gene, Pudge and I feared the giant wheel was ready to topple over. I was certain the collapse would deliver carnage and destruction to both riders and those unfortunate souls below. The three of us clutched the safety bar, rolled our eyes heavenward, and addressed the deity.

"Oh, dear God!" I whispered, as our seat juddered violently. "Help us!"

"Jesus!" Pudge cried out. "Jesus H. Christ! Have mercy! Please save us!"

Not to be outdone, Gene bellowed, "Great God Almighty! Sweet little baby Jesus! Glory be to God in the highest and to his Son in which I am well pleased! Wrap us up in them everlastin' arms! Hallelujah! Praise the Lord and pass the ammunition! God bless America! Amen!"

In spite of our requests for divine intervention, the great wheel continued to shimmy and shake. However, the disconcerting tremors were not caused by faulty Ferris wheel construction; the seismic activity was produced by the guffawing big boy, Tankus Giganticus. Lost in peals laughter, he snickered feverishly from his quaking seat now above and slightly behind us. Hoots, snorts, and cackles filled the air and signaled that the big boy was losing all self-restraint.

Tank, who from the beginning was in on Gene's prank, had been the skinny guy's co-conspirator for hours, if not days. Of course, Gene's earlier fear, involving the use of the heavy bolt and the plastic wrench as convincing props had been feigned, but neither Pudge nor I knew that. Tank knew. The big boy, seated in back of us on the great wheel, had a ringside seat to the all-out brawl that had developed between Pudge and Gene with me acting as an ineffective referee. Apparently, Tank had found the struggle and my efforts to stop it hilarious. I had seen Tank get extremely tickled before; he simply lost control of his immense frame. Atop a Ferris wheel, Tank's hysterical laughter could be downright dangerous.

When Tank laughed, his whole body pulsed. His ample jowls swung from shoulder to shoulder. His several chins rippled up and down like ocean waves touching the shore, hesitating, and then receding, again and again. His powerful chest rose and fell as his great, weighty gut shifted rapidly from side to side. Even the flesh surrounding his kneecaps and elbows jiggled. The Ferris wheel, absorbing his pulsations, shook like a soaked collie dog climbing out of the New River.

Gene's, Pudge's, and my eyes met in shared horror. There was a real chance that the vibrations caused by Tank's hilarity might cause the Ferris wheel to collapse. From below, there was an earsplitting cracking sound like a pistol shot. We held our breaths. The tremors continued undiminished.

"Stop it, Tank!" shouted Pudge. "Stop that infernal giggling!"

"Control yourself!" I yelled. "Right now! We're in danger!"

"Put a bridle on that laughin' or you'll kill us all," bawled Gene. He shook his bony fist in the air. "I ain't kiddin', Tankus!"

Tank heard us and concerned about the fate of his fellow passengers, he clamped his hands over his mouth to stifle his giggles. Red-faced and teary-eyed, he snorted noisily three times and then engaged in a sneezing spasm but finally managed to gain control of himself.

As Tank's powerful convulsions ceased, so did the Ferris wheel's shudders. The giant wheel steadied itself as if touched by an unseen hand, and, mercifully, the ride came to an end. A carnival worker was ready to help us dismount.

"Sorry 'bout the rough ride, fellers," said the worker. "The big wheel's motor has been givin' us problems, causin' the ride to be unsteady. I hope she didn't scare you when she backfired a couple of times. The noises damn near busted my eardrums."

"Nonsense," said Gene. "My redheaded friend here was just sayin' that the ride was delightful with a charmin' view, and, all in all, a most pleasin' experience from beginnin' to end. Ain't that right, Pudge?"

Pudge clenched his teeth and glared at Gene as we disembarked and set our feet on solid ground. A moment later, a beaming Tank joined us. We were all smiling, except for Pudge, who mumbled and grumbled to himself. His eyes were narrow, hateful slits. Suddenly, with both fists raised, he sprang at Gene. Gene pushed him away and began kicking at his shins. Tank muscled his way between them before any solid blows were landed.

Using his powerful hands, Tank grabbed their shirts just behind the collars and lifted both teenage warriors off the ground, holding them apart. They kicked and struck at each other ferociously but unsuccessfully because the big guy's wingspan held them far enough apart so that no damage was done. Soon, the two combatants realized that fighting was useless with Tank around. After less than a minute of flailing, their bodies went limp with fatigue. Tank lowered them slowly to the ground.

"Now you two can be friends again," said Tank amiably.

As soon as Tank released him and his boots touched the ground, Gene noticed that a tidy carnival goer had tossed his beloved Hopalong Cassidy hat into a waste container. The hat rested on top of a heap of garbage.

"Looky yonder—it's my hat!"

Grinning, Gene ran to fetch his headgear. After he wiped away some sticky candied apple residue, the western hat seemed as good as new, except for the broken chinstrap that could easily be replaced. Reaching deep into one of his seemingly bottomless pockets, Gene found a single long, thick shoestring. He repaired his hat and attached it firmly to his head. Even if the hat blew off on another ride, the shoestring would secure it. He flashed a yellow-toothed smile that was both offensive and endearing. Gene was satisfied with the hat's recovery.

Pudge, however, was still shaking with anger—or the remnants of fear. Sometimes with Pudge, it was hard to tell the difference. Tank put his huge hand on the redhead's shoulder, and he slowly began to relax as we walked away from the Ferris wheel. We strolled by the merry-go-round. The music, lights, and smells of the carnival soothed Pudge and his confidence returned. His posture improved and the drooping cowlick on top of his head stood at attention. The redhead didn't know it, but his greatest trial by fire was yet to come.

"You guys check out the rides and decide which one we're gonna ride next. I'll be back in a few minutes. I want to try out a few of the games," said Pudge. "Besides, I need time to think."

"Thinkin' requires brains, Pudge, and in that department, you are sorely lackin'," said Gene. "You'd be better off if you let me do your thinkin' for you, and I think you oughta buy me some popcorn and cotton candy!"

Pudge smiled and replied, "Thomas Edison once said, 'Five percent of the people think; ten percent of the people think they think; and the other eighty-five percent would rather die than think.' That means I'm in the top five percent. By the way, I learned about Thomas Edison in Mrs. Bender's class. She is your all-time favorite teacher, isn't she, Gene?"

With that, Pudge left us and headed toward a game that involved knocking over three hefty glass milk bottles by throwing a baseball. I was certain that the baseball-toss was the only game Pudge was looking for. He had been successful with that game last year. The game, like the one where folks throw darts and try to burst balloons, was a staple at most small southern carnivals. Pudge was either good or lucky at that pitching game. Sure enough, ten minutes later, while I bought a candied apple at a concession stand, I saw him standing in line at the baseball-toss booth.

He's going to try to win Ruthie another teddy bear, I thought to myself as I bit into my red candied apple. The apple's insides were mushy and brown. In the apple's soppy flesh, half a worm wriggled before my eyes. I spat on the ground and dropped the remains of the candied apple. I kicked at the candied apple, and it rolled along the ground like a baseball bunted toward third base.

CHAPTER 26

Pudge and I had tried the carnival's baseball-throwing game a year ago when we were rising eighth graders. We had been trying to win a giant Carolina blue teddy bear for Ruthie, the heartthrob of most guys in our seventh-grade class. Along with several other girls in our class, she loved collecting stuffed animals. Guys collected baseball cards and arrowheads; girls collected dolls and stuffed animals.

In the booth's prize section, the huge blue teddy bear hung among three stuffed giraffes, two stuffed tigers, and four stuffed black bears with pink noses. Other prizes consisted of cheap baseball gloves, dolls with open-and-close eyes, assorted knives, and miscellaneous headwear, including an out-of-fashion Davy Crockett coonskin cap.

The baseball toss, requiring a player to knock over three strategically stacked milk bottles to win, had looked easy, but it wasn't. Last year, I had thrown one baseball at the bottles with as much strength as I could muster. The baseball struck the milk bottles solidly, and I thought surely they would topple. Instead, the ball came whizzing back at me, forcing me to duck. It was as if I'd thrown that ball against a brick wall while standing at close range. After a few more throws, I admitted defeat. The bottles stood stubbornly upright in front of me. I turned to leave.

"Come on, kid. Don't give up so easy. You're awful puny, but

I'll bet you can knock the bottles down on the next throw. Just costs a quarter for three tosses. Take a gander at them prizes! A kid way scrawnier than you won a stuffed giraffe just a few minutes ago," wheezed the elderly carnival barker.

He must have been pushing eighty, and he looked it. His wrinkles cascaded downward from the bill of his Cincinnati Reds baseball cap, spilled around his nose and over his cheeks, and then formed thick, fleshy stalactites hanging under his chin. He took the cap off and ran his fingers through his thick silver hair. His large hands were twisted with arthritis and covered with liver spots.

"No, I'll lose my quarter at another game," I had said flippantly. The old man shrugged.

"Well, it's no skin off my ass, whippersnapper. Go home to mama. Have her change your diapers," the geezer had said mockingly, rubbing his sunken gray eyes. He displayed a few ancient teeth in a smile that was mostly a sneer.

I had a brief but almost overwhelming urge to flip the old man the Tennessee bird, but I fought down the impulse, knowing that neither Grandpa nor Grandma Grayson would have approved. Besides, there was a line of younger kids behind me waiting to flush their pocket change down the carnival's drain. Pudge had been among those who waited.

Having left Pudge to try his luck at the baseball toss last year, I had walked around for a while, carefully counting my money like a young Ebenezer Scrooge. From a teenager's perspective, I was close to financial ruin. I decided to use some of my leftover lunch money that I had saved during the school year. I opened my wallet to a secret compartment, and sure enough found two crisp one dollar bills. Bankruptcy had been temporarily averted. I decided I had enough money for a soda pop, maybe even a hotdog to go with it. I headed for a nearby concession stand.

While placing my order, I saw Pudge winding up for his first toss. He missed everything—didn't touch a single milk bottle with his throw. I chuckled, feeling a rare flush of adolescent superiority. Pudge was a poor pitcher. I knew for sure that he would never win baseball's Cy Young Award. I decided it would take nothing less than a miracle for Pudge to knock those bottles over and claim the coveted blue plush teddy bear.

I turned my attention to the steaming hot dog and the ice cold bottle of Pepsi Cola placed in front of me by the concession stand worker. Behind him, the grill, heated by glowing charcoal briquettes, sizzled with the drippings of circular meat patties. The sweating cook flipped the juicy patties. Globules of grease, like boiling raindrops, splattered into the air. An ineffective fan circulated the hot air within the sweltering concession stand.

The carnival's grilled hot dogs on toasted buns were always delicious. After scarfing the hot dog, I sipped my frosty Pepsi leisurely and looked around the crowd, hoping to see Ruthie, our seventh-grade femme fatale. She was nowhere in sight.

I strolled over and joined the crowd listening to a country music band performing on a makeshift stage. A pretty girl with a lilting voice like Patsy Cline's was singing "Walkin' After Midnight." I decided to hang around for a few minutes and listen to the country music. After the girl had concluded her song, a bluegrass band took the stage and performed "The Brown Mountain Lights," a song about the ghostly lights that can be seen on Brown Mountain near the town of Linville. I listened to three or four more songs.

Fifteen minutes later, after getting my fill of country music, I saw Pudge carrying a huge blue teddy bear with black button eyes. I was astonished. I was stunned. I had to blink my eyes to make sure they weren't deceiving me. Somehow, the redhead had become a winner at the baseball toss. The plush bear was at least three feet tall. I watched Pudge as he maneuvered through the crowd, his head turning from side to side, obviously looking for Ruthie.

Pudge found her near the carnival swings and gave her the huge, stuffed bear. Her eyes flew open wide. She reached out and grabbed Pudge's right hand while pressing the blue teddy bear to her rapidly developing chest.

"Oh, Pudge! You are the sweetest, kindest boy I know!" she squealed. "This bear is perfect. Thank you, thank you!"

"You're welcome," said Pudge, trying unsuccessfully to push his stubbornly erect cowlick down.

"Pudge, dear, we've been such good friends since the first grade. My goodness, you're getting so tall," Ruthie continued. "Can you imagine that when school starts, we'll be eighth graders? You and I must ride the Ferris wheel together tonight. We simply must for old times' sake. Wait for me here. I'll be back in five minutes or less. I need to tell my father where I'll be. You know how fathers are."

"I thought maybe we could ride the tilt-a-whirl or the..." Pudge suggested.

"Don't be silly. You know how I love the Ferris wheel. It's the most romantic ride at any carnival. The view will be marvelous. Besides, I might have a surprise for you if we stop at the very top," said Ruthie.

She fondled the teddy bear and looked up at Pudge with glowing eyes. Her Pepsodent smile was dazzling. She ran her fingers through her shining hair.

"This teddy bear will be part of my collection. In my bedroom I have eighteen stuffed animals and this will make nineteen. This blue bear is the biggest of them all. Thank you again, Pudge. You're such a darling boy!"

Ruthie gave him a hug and a peck on the cheek for his reward and then caressed the teddy bear as if it were a child. I remembered feeling a twinge of seventh-grade jealousy at last year's carnival as I watched the potential love birds from behind a sign that read, *See Smokey the Dancing Bear. Adults, one dollar—Children, fifty cents.* Ruthie squeezed Pudge's hand, turned, and disappeared into the carnival crowd, followed by her bouncing ponytail.

"Be back in a jiffy, Pudge," she called out from the crowd that encircled the carnival swings and a nearby popcorn stand.

True to her word, Ruthie bounded into the milling crowd, found her father, and rejoined Pudge in a matter of minutes. I noticed her lipstick was fresh and bright pink, making her supple lips look like an almost-ripe strawberry. That was the first time I'd seen Ruthie with lipstick on. She looked prettier than ever. I watched Pudge purchase their Ferris wheel tickets, and they were soon seated on the giant wheel, along with the Carolina blue teddy bear. At first, the teddy bear rested between them, but Ruthie moved it so she could sit next to Pudge. The big wheel turned and lifted them skyward.

There was a collective gasp from the crowd near the Ferris wheel as Smokey, the dancing bear, ambled by under the control and supervision of his trainer, a short bald man in an orange suit. Smokey was an overweight black bear wearing a thick leather muzzle. The bear tossed his large head from side to side as he shuffled through the carnival throng.

"Don't get too close, folks. Smokey ain't had his supper yet," laughed the bear's keeper. The crowd gave the ursine creature a wide berth. So did I.

"Smokey's show starts in fifteen minutes in tent number two," the trainer yelled. I was tempted to go see the bear perform, but decided to spend my money on hot buttered popcorn and another Pepsi instead. I found a quarter on the ground near the popcorn stand and pocketed it.

Ten minutes later, when I had caught up with Pudge, I asked, "Okay, how did you do it? I can throw harder than you, but I couldn't knock the milk bottles down. Tank throws harder than anybody, and even he can't knock the bottles down. How did you manage it?"

"Most guys play the game by throwing the baseballs at the milk bottles as hard as they can," Pudge explained. "I decided to put more spin on the ball, kind of like a slow curveball. Then I tried no spin at all, like a knuckleball. I picked the right spot, and I hit the stacked bottles softly, not hard. It worked for me. I won the stuffed bear; I gave the bear to Ruthie; and I rode the Ferris wheel with her," Pudge said. "By the way, when Ruthie and I rode the Ferris wheel, we stopped on top."

"What?"

"Yes, Hal, the very top."

Pudge smiled mischievously and pushed his hand through his hair. While the rest of his hair fell into place, his unruly cowlick stretched toward the stars. He had traces of Ruthie's bright lipstick at the corners of his mouth and on both cheeks. *Lucky guy*, I thought, *and just out of the seventh grade*.

"Mmm! I love the lingering flavor of ripe, red strawberries. Don't you, Hal?" Pudge asked. Closing his eyes, he murmured, "You know, that was the first time I ever kissed a girl. It was nice, very nice."

I had kissed a girl only once, and that was during a spin-the-bottle game at Cheryl Edwards' birthday party. The bottle had been spun and when it stopped, it was pointing directly at me. A female classmate and I rose from the circle and walked toward a door labeled "Kissing Closet." After a bit of innocent groping inside the pitch-black closet and feeling the pressure of a ten second time limit, I kissed my short classmate, Nancy Carter, firmly on the nose, missing my intended target completely while simultaneously she planted a smacker solidly on my dimpled chin.

Before Nancy and I could realign our noses and lips to prevent another mishap, the closet door was pulled open. Bright lights revealed our awkward embrace.

"Time's up, love birds! It's the next couple's turn!" Johnny Knight, our timekeeper, shouted.

The game ended without my getting another chance to kiss a girl. The partygoers sang happy birthday to Cheryl; she blew out her candles; and Mrs. Edwards sliced the cake. The cake's thick chocolate icing and moist yellow layers soothed away my first-kiss disappointment.

Under the flashing lights of the Ferris wheel on that night a few weeks before our eighth-grade year began, I had handed Pudge a clean napkin and said, "Wipe your face, Romeo. Get the lipstick off. Ruthie's daddy is right over there, and he's giving you some mighty mean looks. Did he see you kiss her?"

"I don't know, maybe."

Pudge and I turned away from the frowning daddy and distanced ourselves. His anger was probably imaginary on our part, but still we strode forward into the milling crowd. We ended up standing next to Tank and Gene at a hamburger stand.

"That makes four double cheeseburgers and five Dr. Peppers, Tank!" Gene had yelled. "Stand back ever'body! Take cover and say your prayers! Hold your dear ones tight to your bosoms! This big young'un is gonna explode any minute now!"

CHAPTER 27

The incident involving Pudge, Ruthie, the teddy bear, and the romantic Ferris wheel ride had been a highlight of last summer's carnival excursion. This year, Tank, Gene, and I were determined to ride any new ride the carnival might offer. Furthermore, Gene was determined that Pudge would ride every ride with us whether he wanted to or not. Unfortunately, there was only one new ride in the carnival's repertoire—the distant, mysterious ride shrouded in a blue foggy haze. The fog thickened and the ride disappeared like a ghost ship sinking in an azure sea.

We looked around for Pudge, but the redhead was nowhere to be seen. I even checked the baseball-toss booth, but he wasn't there. For the first time ever Tank, Gene, and I would ride without him.

"Dammit!" said Gene, disappointed that Pudge wasn't riding with us. "I bet he's hidin'. He is one sneaky redhead. Well, I ain't gonna waste no time lookin' for him. Now, which direction is that new ride? Hey, there it is, over there, shinin' through the fog. I see it! Foller me, boys!"

The three of us began walking toward the obscure, misty blue ride. Soon we were close enough to see the sign in front of the shadowy machine. The contraption was called "The Bullet." Taller than the Ferris wheel, the ride consisted of two spinning egg-shaped capsules at either end of giant, elongated metallic arms.

As we approached, The Bullet was slowing down. The capsules, encircled with blue and white flashing lights, were rotating slowly, about to stop. After the ride ended, the carnival workers unloaded the riders from the first capsule. The other capsule was suspended in the air. One rider, high in the air, waved a pale arm through an open porthole. The scrawny limb slithered back and disappeared inside the hanging capsule. The rider knew that he and his fellow passengers would soon be back on solid ground.

Two senior boys from Central Ashe High School were first to get off the ride. I had seen them around, especially at basketball games, but I didn't know their names. One senior seemed to have trouble walking. He had the stiff-legged gait of an old man. The other guy was rubbing his temples and coughing. With swirling lights flashing all around, I still noticed their pale skin tones. Their pants were rumpled, and their shirts were wrinkled and stained. Both boys were sweating. One kept wiping his nose with a handkerchief.

"How was that ride? We've never ridden it. Is it scary?" I asked, directing my question to the taller teenager. Tank and Gene stood behind me, waiting for his response.

"You boys are gonna love that ride," he said. "It's the best damn ride on these fairgrounds. Ain't that right, Jake? …Jake?"

"Huh? Oh yeah, yeah, right," Jake finally muttered. Jake was holding his stomach and his eyes were rolled back in his head. Jake began to hiccup and staggered away from us, presumably headed for the next ride. His friend, sporting a noticeable limp, followed.

Gene exclaimed, "Well, we just heard two heartfelt and mostly unsolicited testermonials. All right, let's go! It's time for us mountain boys to defeat The Bullet! Let's roll! Got your quarters ready?"

"Check out the sign," I said. "This ride costs thirty-five cents, not a quarter."

"That's an outrage! It's a shame and a disgrace! I'm mortified! I'm not made of money! No carnival ride should cost more than a quarter," said Gene. As he spoke, he pounded his fist into his palm, causing him to drop two quarters. He bent over and picked up his change.

"Sometimes you get what you pay for," Tank reminded us as he sauntered toward the ticket stand. Gene, still muttering about the ride's excessive cost, and I trailed behind him.

"If this ride ain't more excitin' and thrillin' than the Ferris wheel, I'm askin' for my money back," Gene promised.

Resting in the dirty sawdust near The Bullet's ticket stand, amid several candy wrappers, the upper portion of a pair of false teeth smiled up at us. I was undeterred as I felt in my pants pocket for my thirty-five cents, but I found the toothy, disembodied smile from the fake choppers unsettling.

In less than a minute, we had secured our tickets and were ready to board. Gene and I were seated in the front half of capsule number two. We were strapped in snugly with a single seatbelt that stretched across our abdomens and reached from one end of the missile-shaped capsule to the other. Then, a safety bar was clanked into place in front of our chests. This was the first time I had ridden a carnival ride that required both a seatbelt and a safety bar. I was somewhat unnerved by the security precautions.

Tank was to be seated in the back portion of our capsule. The capsule's halves were separated by a thick partition with no openings. The two workers were having trouble fitting Tank into the pod's space. Frustrated, they halted their efforts and scratched their heads.

"Snake, I can't get this kid into the seat. He's fillin' up three seats and still spillin' out. What we got here is too much kid and too little seat room. You push on his shoulder, Snake, while I push on his hip," said a short, wiry man who was just a shade over five feet tall. His lean arms displayed tough sinews and muscles. He and the much larger Snake pushed and heaved.

"Ow! Ouch! Watch where you're pushing," grunted Tank.

"Be careful, Clifford. Don't hurt the kid," said Snake. "We don't want no lawsuit like the one the carnival had over in

Allegheny County. That Sparta lawyer was one smart son of a bitch. The settlement cost the Stephens Brothers Carnival over two thousand dollars."

"All that money was paid out to that kid's mama and daddy because of a little ole broke wrist and bloody nose. I coulda understood if the kid had broke his back or his neck. It's gettin' so a carnival like ours can't make no money 'cause of lawyers and lawsuits," griped Clifford as he pushed Tank's distended belly with both hands.

After much heaving and shoving, Tank's body, like a hermit crab seeking shelter, slowly receded into his half of the capsule. Once completely inside, Tank laughed good-naturedly from the restrictive confines of his half of the capsule.

"Whew! He's in, Snake, but now I can't get the dang seat belt around him or the safety bar locked in place. Neither one of 'em will reach around the middle of this kid. He's liable to pop out on the turns."

"Don't you worry none, Clifford," said Snake, "that kid ain't gonna come out of the capsule. He's wedged in like a turtle in his shell."

Snake snorted and wiped his mouth with a greasy rag. When he laughed, he threw his head back and opened his mouth wide, revealing only two gleaming teeth, long, fang-like upper canines surrounded by pale, cottony gums. Snake dabbed some spittle from his thin lips, and I saw on his forearm a tattoo depicting a coiled rattlesnake ready to strike. Beneath the serpent were the tattooed words: "Don't Tread on Me."

"This big kid sure ain't missed many meals. That's for sure. Hey Snake, I just remembered that lady down in Wilkesboro, the one who lost her shoe and pocketbook on this ride. He's even bigger than what she was," said the diminutive Clifford, scratching his wiry arms with long dirty fingernails. In his cowboy boots, Clifford stood no taller than five feet, three inches. Snake, a brawny six-footer in worn gray tennis shoes, towered over his smaller friend.

"Ain't nobody on this planet bigger than what that Wilkesboro woman was, but most of her weight was spread out on her bottom. I did manage to get the safety belt around her and the security bar snapped in place. This kid does come close to her in size, and he ain't even full-growed," shouted Snake over the rising engine clatter as he manned The Bullet's controls.

Snake pulled the metal lever next to the droning engine and hollered, "Let's get this show on the road! Ladies and gentlemen, hold onto your valuables, includin' your family jewels and your loved ones. Get ready for a good long, highflyin' ride! The Bullet is ready to blast off!"

With blue lights flashing, the great machine growled and came to life like a hulking steel zombie rising from the grave. The Bullet emitted a long metallic moan followed by creaking reverberations similar to the ones we had heard while riding the Ferris wheel. Instinctively, I clutched the security bar.

Clank! Click! Clink!

Gene and I were suddenly hanging upside down, kept suspended by our seatbelt. Gravity caused blood to rush to our heads, flushing our faces. And then with another clank, we were seated with our backs parallel to the ground, facing upward. Squeezed into his section of the capsule and constrained by his massive frame, Tank was looking down at the sawdust a few feet below him. Gene and I could see the stars twinkling above, as the capsule rotated slowly and moved us skyward. Behind us, Tank watched the slowly spinning ground recede as he moved upward.

Clank! Clink! Clunk!

We were right side up in the capsule as The Bullet unhurriedly took us to its highest point. I felt like a jet fighter pilot sitting in a cockpit as I surveyed the glittering fairgrounds far below me. The cockpit's windows were open to provide a better view and fresh air. I took a deep breath. Tank, Gene and I waited for the capsule on the other end of the huge arm to be loaded with people who, like us, wanted to experience this new ride. Below us, two high school boys, wearing green letter jackets from Beaver Dam High School, came aboard The Bullet. Those two teenagers were the last in line.

"Check out the view from here! Look at those lights!" exclaimed Gene. "This here ride is way taller than the Ferris wheel, but it's so dang slow. It's slower than froze-up molasses. Pudge wouldn't even be scared on this ride. The Bullet moves like a snail. Mark my words, I'm gonna ask for my thirty-five cents back."

As he finished speaking, there was more movement from the tall steel contraption. There was an almost indiscernible vibration as the huge arms of the Bullet stirred sluggishly and deliberately, like a snapping turtle climbing onto a large sunny rock in the New River.

"Want some popcorn, Hal?" inquired Gene, pushing a red, white, and blue paper bag full of fragrant popcorn under my nose. I pushed the bag away.

"Thank you, but I'm not hungry."

Reaching into the warm popcorn bag, Gene flung a handful of popcorn, buttered and salted, toward his mouth with only a few puffy kernels missing their yawning target. Three popcorn pieces bounced off his chin and landed in his lap.

"This is mighty good popcorn, Hal. It's real buttery, and tastes like homemade. You can have some."

"No thanks. Not the least bit hungry," I said politely. My stomach was beginning to feel a bit uneasy, but I was still admiring the breathtaking view of the carnival lights. I thought I could make out Pudge's red head in the milling crowd beneath us. *He's probably looking for us,* I thought. *No, he's probably looking for Ruthie.*

"Okay, Snake! Time to let her rip!" Clifford's sharp voice drifted up from far below.

"Pedal to the metal, Cliff! They ain't nobody waitin' in line to ride The Bullet, so let's give these folks a long ride!" yelled Snake.

"Yep! Let's give 'em somethin' to write home about," cackled Clifford.

The Bullet's powerful engine began to roar and then whine.

The gears engaged and the engine emitted a single small puff of black smoke followed by another, somewhat larger gray puff. My nose wrinkled as the acrid smoke drifted upward. Gene sneezed.

Ka-chunk! Clunk! Ka-plunk!

Our revolving capsule swung precipitously downward and the solid ground appeared to be very far away. The ride continued placidly, and for just a few blessed seconds there was peace on earth, God was in heaven, and all was right with the world.

Then there was an unexpected surge in speed—ten, twenty, forty, eighty, one hundred and ten miles per hour straight up and then straight down!

I heard Gene gag on a handful of popcorn as the ride suddenly accelerated. Our heads and shoulders were thrown backward with backbone cracking force. Automatically, we reached for the safety bar, wrapping our fingers securely around it. On the second rapid turning of The Bullet's huge arms, Gene's paper popcorn bag exited our capsule and spun far out into the glowing carnival night, spewing puffy kernels and gyrating like a rapidly deflating red, white, and blue balloon.

"Dammit! There goes my pop..."

"Aaack! Aaack!" screamed Tank from behind us.

There was a neck-jerking, vertebra-snapping, mind-cleaving shock as the great machine changed the direction of each capsule. Gene and I found ourselves hurtling toward the stars, and just before going into certain orbit, our bodies, our very souls, were wrenched and whirled around. In a split second, we plunged downward. We discovered that the ground was moving toward us at the speed of light; and just before our premature burial deep in the fairground's firm sod, a gut-twisting, eyelid-yanking, lung-contracting turn sent us spiraling upward again at full throttle.

The mind-numbing, ass-jolting turns happened over and over and over. Far from enjoying the ride, I yearned merely for survival. Gene and I clung desperately to the safety bar. Silently, I thanked God for the snug safety belt.

Without warning, something whizzed through the cockpit window and clattered around inside the capsule. It was a pair of glasses with extremely thick lenses. I held my hands up to protect my eyes. I was afraid the lenses might crack, sending glass shards whirling everywhere, but on the next mind-rending turn the mysterious spectacles were ejected.

Whump-a-rump-a-dump-a-thump!

With every twisting turn, our rear ends slammed painfully into The Bullet's unyielding seat platform.

"Ouch! Ouch! Ouch!" yowled Gene. "Lordy, all hell is breakin' loose!"

"Eeeyah! Oh nooooo!" Tank shrieked from behind us. His voice echoed in the wind as The Bullet sliced through the night sky. The big boy was having major troubles. Filled with urgency, his bass voice had been transformed. His usual deep-toned speech sounded shrill, like a frightened girl shrieking after discovering a mouse in her bedroom slippers.

"No! Oh hell nooooo! Please! I'm too young to die!" wailed Tankus Giganticus.

Tank, seated with his back toward ours, was encountering dissimilar and opposite sensations from ours. In fact, his experiences were a reversal of ours. His immense body was rushing away from the earth backward as Gene and I headed face first toward the stars.

As he plunged rearward toward the earth, the stars Tank saw were rapidly receding points of light. Tank helplessly waited for impact and burial in the carnival turf. Just in time, The Bullet jerked the big guy upward again with the ground receding at super speed. The big boy's jolting, bouncing, repetitious flight was too rapid to be boring. His howls and moans indicated that his ride, although reversed, was no less terrifying than ours.

Beside me in our capsule, Gene, whose head seemed to be disappearing into his shoulders, alternated between loud, vehement cursing and almost inaudible praying. A pattern developed—Gene prayed with one hand raised as we hurtled toward the starry heavens, and he cursed profanely, shaking a fist, as we plunged toward the solid ground. One of Gene's hands was always firmly fastened to the safety bar. I feared a malfunction in the great machine would either send us skyrocketing toward the moon or plowing deep into the earth's molten core. Gene's alternating praying and cussing demonstrated that he would be ready if we reached either destination—paradise or Hades.

After the tenth revolution, both of Gene's hands clutched the safety bar in a white-knuckled death grip, and through clenched teeth, his speech, both prayers and curses, became incoherent. Gene's vocalizations were slurred, much like the rambling, incomprehensible baby talk of a toddler chewing on a pacifier.

"Gooph goo humph gursh! Snipple snarf poo poo!" Gene stated as emphatically as if he were delivering a portion of the Gettysburg Address. He looked at me seeking some sort of affirmation. His troubled, bloodshot eyes met mine in shared panic. His windswept orbs moistened and his chin trembled. His cowboy hat, secured by the single shoestring wrapped around his throat, had disappeared behind his shoulders and was, without doubt, being crushed by his shoulder blades into an unrecognizable mass. The hair on his head was so wind-twisted that I wondered if he could ever pull a comb through it again. The cold blue and white lights of The Bullet made Gene's hair look prematurely gray as his purple, swollen lips twitched in a desperate effort to communicate.

"Ruff snapple! Lurchen kaa kaa!" he declared with the conviction of a Baptist preacher in a revival tent, hell-bent on leading lost souls to Jesus.

Like a chicken flapping its wings in the middle of a barnyard hissy fit, Gene's emaciated arms and bony elbows began flailing up and down frantically. His eyebrows had lifted almost to his hairline and his sharply-tipped ears were flattened against the sides of his head. The wind shear had pulled his fluttering lips away from his tobacco-stained teeth, creating a ghastly, widespread grin. Gene's wind-tossed profile looked not unlike a braying mule that I had seen from my school bus's window just a few weeks ago. Without warning, Gene's elongated tongue protruded snakelike and flailed about in the whistling turbulence.

The Bullet had also changed my appearance. I was experiencing pure, unadulterated, open-mouthed shock. I may have screamed or yelled in terror during one of the first accelerated turns. Now the muscles of my jaw were solidly frozen. I must've looked like a rabid dog, with my lips drawn tightly back and a torrent of drool escaping from both sides of my gaping oral cavity. The saliva flood poured over the ineffective dam of my widely-spaced lower teeth, and soggy spittle spots decorated the front of my T-shirt.

Since there were no other patrons lining up to ride The Bullet, we were given the long ride Snake had promised. Relentlessly, the furious, mind-altering revolutions continued.

Like the Ferris wheel's lights, The Bullet's lights had attracted more than their fair share of insects. Moths, gnats, and mosquitoes hovered ominously in the stagnant air, pulsing like the Hindenburg airship. The Bullet's capsules carved through the cloud of bugs, and the cockpit's open windows gave the creatures a point of entry.

"Ghaack! Smarkle! Glurf!" gasped Gene, slapping ineffectually at the living fog of airborne creatures.

Since I couldn't close my mouth, I acted as a human vacuum cleaner, sucking up insects each time I inhaled. I swiped feebly at the insect air force. The attacking bugs were in my throat, my eyes, my nostrils, even my ears. I coughed up a buzzing June bug into my mosquito-covered hand. Miniscule kamikaze gnats whined in my ears as I closed my eyes and grabbed at the safety bar, renewing my grip and preparing for another bone-jolting turn.

However, the painful bump never occurred. Suddenly, the ride slowed its revolutions and the insect cloud lifted and floated away, leaving behind a few mosquitoes. The Bullet shuddered, gave a death rattle, and came to a stop.

I knew the Tank could withstand almost anything, so I checked on Gene. I grabbed him by the shoulder, and his spindly body flopped toward me. His face had assumed an eerie pallor; tight gray skin stretched across his countenance; his features were twisted into what could best be described as a frozen scream. At first, because of his stillness, I thought he was dead and wondered how we might explain his demise to his family; however, the bubbles forming around his purple lips indicated he was still breathing. His left eye opened and blinked.

"Gawd damp," he said softly.

I was almost certain he had cursed, and that was a good sign.

I checked my own pulse and found my heart was pounding furiously. I took a deep breath and, using my hands, I forced my mouth shut. I was grateful to be alive.

Gene and I had survived The Bullet.

Oddly, I remembered what the man on the six o'clock news had said after a recent hurricane flooded North Carolina's beaches, decimating many waterfront homes, "Fortunately there were no human fatalities." I repeated the newscaster's words.

Ashen-faced and trembling, with a flock of mosquitoes sucking the lifeblood from our bare arms, Gene and I attempted to exit the ride. First, I had to pry Gene's cold fingers from the safety bar. His hands fell lifelessly into his lap. He didn't thank me, but kept staring at me as if I were a total stranger. Gene seemed incapable of any voluntary movement.

"Lemme res jus a minnid," he mumbled. His chin dropped to his chest and he inhaled deeply.

"Boys, is ever'thin' all right?" asked Clifford, standing outside the capsule. He reached for my arm and gave it a pull. He pulled my left arm, the arm that had banged into Gene's skull several times on the jolting ride. I yelped, but the sharp discomfort in my arm subsided quickly. In the compartment behind me, I heard Tank moaning wretchedly.

With Clifford's assistance, I slowly escaped the confining capsule. I summoned up all my remaining strength, leaned forward and pulled my body toward the opening in the capsule's side. Slowly and painfully, I exited. Clifford held me by the elbow as the sole of my right shoe touched the ground, followed by my left. With both feet solidly planted on terra firma, I felt a sudden urge to kneel and kiss the soil; but I refrained, knowing that better things were expected of me after any carnival ride, even The Bullet. I stood like a statue because I knew I wasn't ready to walk, not yet.

Clifford turned to help Gene. Gene pushed Clifford's helping hands aside and swung himself nimbly from our compartment, but his knees buckled under him as he touched down. He knelt as if he were praying. He took several deep breaths and then rose to his feet. I watched as he lurched forward, reeling drunkenly from side to side. Gene ended his faltering journey about five feet beyond The Bullet's ticket stand. He lay down on the ground and assumed the fetal position. I thought he broke wind, but I couldn't swear to it.

"Tang ju, Jesup," he declared softly, looking upward. "Phrase Gop, fum hoop hall plessin's cump."

With a halting gait, I approached Gene. I sat down beside him and slapped at my arms, crushing the miniscule bloodsucking insects and leaving behind mosquito carcasses. I wiped my hands on my shirt. Gene mashed his mosquitoes by rolling over on his stomach with his arms beneath him. Then, struggling manfully, he sat up and held his head between his sweaty palms. Gene stared down at his scruffy cowboy boots. His left boot was turned sharply inward pointing toward his right ankle. I thought his left leg was broken, but he groaned and then stretched both legs into normal positions.

"I cane fill ma totes. Cane clost ma lef eye!" said Gene matter-of-factly. His tongue, virtually useless to him, dangled like a fat salamander from the right corner of his mouth, impeding his speech. I noticed that his skin had taken on a greenish tinge, perhaps from a lack of oxygen. Gene's right eye was closed, but his left eye remained grotesquely open and bizarrely mobile.

The eyeball looked up and down and from side to side, finally fixating on an empty popcorn bag near the ticket stand. The cloudy, bloodshot orb was swollen well beyond its normal size. A translucent blue film covered it.

Gene's thin, windblown hair stood straight up all over his head, reminding me of Larry Fine from The Three Stooges. He leaned forward. His misshapen, almost flattened cowboy hat, still secured by the thick shoestring, hung down his back between his scrawny shoulder blades. Spitting on both his hands, Gene ran his fingers several times through his disheveled hair, causing it to stick tightly to his skull as it usually did.

His face looked blurry and fuzzy, his features becoming more and more indistinct. I couldn't quite bring Gene into focus. Fleetingly, I thought something was wrong with him, not me.

"Stop moving your face," I commanded.

"I ain moopin' ma fades, nor nuttin' elf," Gene whispered hoarsely.

Through a murky gray mist, I saw that Gene's right eye remained tightly closed as if the upper and lower lashes on that eye had interlocked permanently. His singular functioning eye was opening and closing sluggishly. Gene's left eye continued to swell, reminding me of a picture of Cyclops I had seen in our eighth-grade literature book. The blinking eye watered. A clear teardrop the size of a fat green pea rolled down his gaunt cheek. His right orb stayed closed, sealed as securely as a Mason jar of moonshine. His thick, bluish tongue, which reached an inch below his chin, hung lifelessly from his mouth like a blacksnake carcass thrown across a barbed wire fence.

Sitting in the shadow of the ticket stand, I noticed I couldn't close either of my eyes, and there was a strange electric sound ringing in my ears. My shoulders were virtually immobile, my vertebrae crunched when I moved, and a few drops of blood fell from my nose onto my T-shirt. My left leg had fallen asleep and was practically inoperable. I felt pins and needles coursing up and down my right leg with every beat of my heart. I was as bad off as Gene, probably worse.

"Tonight, you're the lucky one. I may be ruined for life," I said to Gene who, like a magician reaching for a rabbit in his top hat, plucked a hefty wriggling gray moth from his ear. The insect circled Gene's head, briefly landed on his nose, and then flew upward toward The Bullet's bright lights.

"Mof go ub," mumbled Gene, grinning horribly and pointing to the fluttering creature as it disappeared into the flashing blue lights above.

Gene rose to all fours and crawled over to the ticket stand. He placed his back against the wooden wall and rested there. He sighed. Crawling on my hands and knees, I joined Gene and rested my aching back against the ticket stand with my legs sprawled out in front of me.

Shouts and curses, combined with a sharp, painful howl came from the vicinity of The Bullet. I had almost forgotten about the Tank. The big boy was trying in vain to disembark. He was imprisoned in the rear section of our capsule as Clifford and Snake attempted to assist his escape. One was tugging on Tank's left arm. The other grabbed his head and pulled. Desperation was etched on all three faces.

"Yeooooww! Ouch!" screeched the Tank.

"Well, that didn't work," said Clifford. "Let's try somethin' else. Grab him by the leg and pull."

"I'll try," huffed Snake. "One, two, three! Pull!"

"Ouch! Ow! Yeeooooww!"

"Sorry, kid," said Snake, scratching his head.

A small crowd had gathered to watch the two carnival workers extricate the Tank.

"They'll never get him out!" stated one bystander. Several men agreed with him. He continued, "That kid never should have been allowed on that ride."

"There's a crowbar in the trunk of my car," said another.

"Somebody better call an ambulance, just in case," ventured the shortest spectator, wiping his thick glasses with a handkerchief.

"I am bowin' my head and prayin' for that young'un right now," declared a blue jeans-clad, large-boned woman nearly six feet tall. "That boy needs a miracle from Jesus!"

She closed her eyes and lowered her head until her chin touched the front of her pink blouse. Other women in the crowd bowed their heads. The ladies mumbled multiple prayers on behalf of Tank, trapped inside The Bullet's capsule.

The men seemed more interested in the process of extricating the Tank.

"They keep pullin' on his arms and hands; they had ort to pull on his feet and legs," critiqued a male bystander who wore a blue jeans jacket and had a guitar slung across his back.

"If a'body could get a rope around him, we could pull him out with a horse or a tractor," said a lanky farmer. He spattered tobacco juice on the ground.

"Why you might break the young'un's back if you done that!" said a farmer with a thick white beard. "Be real gentle with the boy."

With the capsule's wide door flung open, I saw that Tank's abdomen was misshapen. Also his right shoulder seemed abnormally larger than his left. His ears were compressed against his head, and his hair was slicked back like Bella Lugosi's in *Dracula*. Tank's face was wind-warped, and his blue lips were contorted into a grinning countenance like an overly cheerful cadaver.

"Clifford, grab his other arm and pull. Pull hard! This kid's still alive ain't he?"

"Yep, he's still breathin'! Give us some help, kid. Don't just sit there like a flounder," said Clifford, who had begun to sweat. Patterns of perspiration showed under the arms of his blue uniform. The two men heaved, pulled, and wiped their brows. Then they repeated their labors.

"Come on, kid, push! Push!" hissed Snake through his fangs. "Help us or you ain't never gonna get out of this contraption!"

Tank wriggled like a butterfly extricating itself from a close-fitting chrysalis. He twisted his shoulders; he sucked in his gut; he raised one leg and stuck it through the cockpit's window. Gradually his body assumed its normal shape. At last he was pulled free. Snake and Clifford exchanged smiles as Tank teetered toward Gene and me as if in an alcohol induced stupor. His hands were shaking.

"Whew! That was hard work," said Clifford "I got two Budweisers in my cooler. I'll treat you to a beer after we unload them fellers in pod number one."

"Now you're talkin'! We deserve a break," grinned Snake. "It'll be a cinch to get them skinny boys outta their seats. Let's go!"

Tank, Gene, and I now sat together with our backs against The Bullet's ticket stand. We were battered and soon to be black and blue; however, we were in the recovery stage. I took a deep breath. Fresh mountain air filled my lungs. My heart was beating normally.

"Whee gop tuh..." Gene was indistinctly mumbling something. Neither Tank nor I understood him. The skinny guy's fugitive tongue withdrew into his mouth helped along by the fingers of his right hand.

"Dat's bettah," croaked Gene, "wid ma tonk pack hen ma mouf."

"What?" asked Tank, rubbing together his trembling hands. Gene grabbed Tank's T-shirt and pulled him closer.

"Gop tuh hun. Go fine, godda fine. Hun ever'wares! Mus pee year sumpwares. Search! Search! Hep fine! Whee godda fine!" croaked Gene, desperately clutching the front of Tank's T-shirt.

"Did you lose your billfold on the ride? Is that it?" asked Tank, reaching behind himself to secure his own wallet. I checked for my billfold, too. I felt the familiar flat bulge in the back pocket of my jeans.

"Gene, we'll help you look for your wallet," I said, scanning the landscape directly under The Bullet. I hoped he hadn't lost his Hopalong Cassidy billfold because the skinny guy would have us searching all night.

Gene's bloodshot eyes were frantic and pleading. "Ef only whee ain' too lade! Ho no! Whad if he's done gone? Whad if he lef early? Where's Grampa Sharlie?"

"Who? Grandpa Charlie? What are you talking about Gene? Did you hit your head on something inside The Bullet? You could have a concussion. You're not making any sense. Do you need a doctor?" asked Tank, who was now kneeling and massaging his own legs as if they were numb.

At least Tank was regaining control of his hands. That was progress. I was also feeling better. I was now able to close my eyes, and there was only a slight pain when I blinked.

Gene continued to mumble something incoherently, but on his next effort, Tank and I could finally understand him.

"Pudge! I'm talkin' about Pudge, of course, you dadgum idiots! We got to find him and get him on this here ride somehow!"

Gene pointed to The Bullet, outlined against the sky like a Colossus rising far above the lesser carnival Goliaths, including the Ferris wheel. In fact, the Ferris wheel looked puny in comparison.

"Pudge won't ride The Bullet with you, Gene, not after what you did to him on the Ferris wheel," I said.

"Not a chance," Tank added, standing up. Gene and I rose unsteadily to our feet.

Just then, as if ordained by fate, Pudge appeared, meandering out of the thinning crowd of carnival goers. He was finishing off a grape snow cone. Under his arm, the redhead held a giant chocolate-brown teddy bear, fully half his size, a prize from one of the carnival games, no doubt the baseball toss.

"Hey, Pudge," I yelled. We stepped away from the ticket stand.

"We're over here by the ticket stand," Tank called out.

"Have you guys seen Ruthie?" Pudge asked. "I walked all around and haven't seen her, her father, or her sisters. This stuffed bear is for her if I can find her before she goes home. If I can't find Ruthie soon, I'm going to give this teddy bear to some little kid. I'm tired of carrying it around."

"I haven't seen Ruthie since we saw her on the trail leading up to the carnival," I said. "She and her folks may have left early, or she and her family may still be here on the carnival grounds. One thing's for sure, this year she's more interested in riding the rides with tenth and eleventh grade boys than she is hanging around with us."

"We might as well face the cold, hard facts, guys—from now on Ruthie is going to be more interested in older guys," said Tank. "It's only natural, I guess. The silver lining is that one of these days, *we* will be the older guys, and younger girls will be interested in us."

Pudge nodded in agreement and then cast his eyes up toward the flashing blue lights of The Bullet. I saw a mixture of fear and resolve in his eyes. Pudge stuffed the brown teddy bear's head into his left armpit and held it there as he leaned back on his heels to get a better view. He raised his right hand to shield his eyes from the lights.

"Did you guys ride that?" he asked. There was a touch of wonder in his voice.

"Indeed, we did," said Gene, standing tall. He inhaled deeply, enlarging his chest.

The hulking ride stood ominously still and silent. There was no line at the ticket booth. Clifford and Snake sat on the ground, drinking from Budweiser bottles and eating popcorn from red, white, and blue paper bags. Snake started throwing puffy white popcorn kernels at Clifford who retaliated. The two men giggled and their laughter was oddly childlike. They looked like kids in a snowball fight.

CHAPTER 28

"We just got off The Bullet," said Gene gesturing back over his shoulder with his right thumb. "It's too dang slow. That's the slowest dang ride I have ever rode." Gene turned and looked at the metal monster towering above us and declared, "All looks and no action. It's big, but it ain't bad. I crave motion, danger, and speed. You know me; I'm always hankerin' for adventure! This slow ride has done broke my spirit. I'm plumb let down and feelin' like I wasted my money."

"It's a ho-hum ride, much too sluggish and dull," said the Tank. The big boy surreptitiously winked at Gene as he put his immense hand over his mouth, suppressing a giggle.

"Slow as molasses. Maybe we could get our money back," I added. "The ride shouldn't be called The Bullet; it should be called The Snail or The Sloth."

Pudge smiled.

Like double-dealing arachnids, Tank, Gene and I continued to spin a web of trickery around Pudge. Gene even yawned as he spoke, comparing The Bullet to watching the Lawrence Welk show with his grandparents. He did mention there was a spectacular view of the carnival grounds from the top of the ride. Our deliberate deceit had to be salted with a grain of truth to be believable.

Pudge said nothing. He just stood there observing the blue haze created by The Bullet's glowing lights. Gene shifted his weight from one foot to the other, becoming increasingly fearful that Pudge was going to avoid the ride. Gene's eyes moved from side to side, an indication that he was formulating a plan.

"I got a good idea!" Gene suddenly exclaimed. "Let's ride the Ferris wheel again. Forget about The Bullet. It's too dang slow. We got time for one more ride. They're prob'ly gonna close down all the rides in twenty or thirty minutes. Let's take our last ride of the night on the Ferris wheel. Let's go, Pudge!"

"You guys aren't getting me back on that Ferris wheel again. I can promise you that. But I will go on one last ride with you," said Pudge, checking his Timex wrist watch.

Looking up, Pudge considered The Bullet as the machine stood placid and serene amid the carnival's diminishing hustle and bustle. Moonlight softened its shape and the huge metal arms with the bulbous, egg-shaped capsules on either end were spread invitingly. The seductive blue and white lights blinked on and off merrily, but no one was in line.

From a loudspeaker, Perry Como crooned "Catch a Falling Star" to a dwindling audience. The merry-go-round had shut down completely, and the hotdog stand had turned out its lights.

"Tell you what," Pudge said, "I'll ride one more ride with you, if it's that one." He pointed to The Bullet with a steady hand. In his eyes was a look of determination mixed with resignation. A gust of wind ruffled his red hair, but his impudent cowlick pointed heavenward. Pudge readjusted the oversized teddy bear under his arm.

"Are you sure you ain't gonna ride the Ferris wheel with us again?" wheedled Gene. "You know how partial I am to the Ferris wheel."

Unseen by Pudge, Gene gave me the okay sign. The redheaded fly was very, very close to being inextricably snagged in the sticky web spun by his double-dealing friends. Pudge stepped toward The Bullet's ticket stand not knowing that he had been trapped.

"I'm positive! I have picked our last ride, and it will be The Bullet," said Pudge with unwavering determination.

I didn't like the way Pudge referred to The Bullet as our "last ride." My superstition kicked in completely when I saw Clifford and Snake petting a huge black cat under the ride's shadow. I reached into my trouser pocket and touched my lucky rabbit's foot keychain.

"This ride costs ten cents more than the Ferris wheel," said Tank. "Do you have the extra cash, Pudge?"

"I don't care how much The Bullet costs," said Pudge. "Let's go! Let's get this last ride over with!"

The redhead arrived at the ticket booth ahead of us and slammed a quarter and a dime on the counter.

In less than a minute, Pudge, Gene, and I had purchased our tickets and were being seated in the front section of The Bullet's forward cockpit. Pudge, with the huge teddy bear tucked under his arm, sat between Gene and me. Snake attached the single, long belt that held the three of us securely; Clifford adjusted the safety bar until it clanked into place. Tank was next in line. Just like last time, he was to be seated alone in the rear cabin.

"Not you again, kid!" exclaimed Snake, glowering at the Tank. "You must be a glutton for punishment."

Tank held up his red ticket between his thumb and forefinger and smiled broadly. His eyes crinkled merrily. His cheery face was bathed in azure light.

"Yes, I intend to ride The Bullet again," beamed Tank. He swung one immense leg into the rear section of the capsule.

"Hey, Clifford! The big kid is back! Gimme a hand here."

Clifford squinted at Tank and groaned audibly, but in less than a minute, most of the big boy's body was inside the egg-shaped pod.

"It's almost quittin' time," said Snake. "You take the controls this time, Cliff."

"All righty! I been lookin' forward to takin' The Bullet for a spin!" Clifford whooped excitedly. "I ain't been at the controls in a long time, must be over a year! Let's see if I can remember how to get this here machine started. First, I got to turn this here switch. Now, I know I got to pull these two levers at the same time while I push this here big pedal. Here we go!"

"Don't slam on the brakes at the end of the ride like you done the last time you was at the controls," advised Snake. "You're liable to cause damage."

The Bullet's capsule creaked and revolved slowly as the giant machine carried us upward toward the dark, star-flecked heavens. A menacing, droning sound I hadn't noticed before accompanied us as we lifted off. The cloud of insects was back and hovered for a moment beneath The Bullet's arms before drifting upward, seeking the bright lights.

"You were right about the view from up here. It's great!" said Pudge, clutching the brown teddy bear and surveying the dazzling scene below. His words were pleasant enough, but the redhead's voice sounded forced and strained as he peered downward. There was a clunking sound, and the capsule moved almost imperceptibly toward the ground; another louder clatter and we were hanging upside down. I was now familiar with the capsule's several positions preceding its upward climb and was eager to see Pudge's reactions when The Bullet blasted off.

"Does the ride go any faster than this?" asked the redhead as our capsule rose sluggishly skyward.

"Didn't go no faster last time," replied Gene. His eyes shifted away from Pudge as he wiped his nose on the back of his hand.

Pudge turned to me for corroboration. I nodded, fibbing in silence. At least I didn't lie out loud. While Gene had blatantly lied, I had merely fibbed. Really, I hadn't said anything. I convinced myself that my transgression was minor.

Then the ride began in earnest, but ever so slowly at first, like the second hand on a clock; then faster, like a powerful Kentucky racehorse; and finally picking up tremendous speed, like a supercharged hot rod Chevy roaring down the North Wilkesboro dragstrip. The velocity of The Bullet was almost unbearable when top speed was achieved.

"Yipes! God Almighty! Oh Mary, mother of Jesus!" yipped Pudge, hugging his teddy bear close. With his free hand, he seized the safety bar and held on with increasingly pale fingers.

"Yippee!" shouted Gene. Like a rodeo rider mounting the meanest bronc in Texas, he held the safety bar with one hand, while raising the other and waving it high in the air.

"Ride 'em, cowboy!" he bawled joyfully as The Bullet's capsule careened through the air like a wild mustang.

My fear of the ride had evaporated completely, and I was as cool as a cucumber. I noticed Gene was laughing out loud, and I hooted along with him. He whacked me on the back and cackled insanely.

Conversely, Pudge's panic was increasing incrementally as The Bullet slashed through the carnival night. The redhead's fear was so noticeable, so palpable, I could almost smell it. Gene and I watched him intently, drawing courage from his mounting fear.

"Ain't this a great ride, Pudge?" screamed Tank from his compartment behind us. His voice was partially muffled by the hurricane-force wind. Pudge did not answer. He placed the teddy bear firmly between his knees, touched our shared safety belt, and then, reassured that the belt was secure, clung with both hands to the metal security bar for all he was worth.

Pudge gasped as we hurtled downward at terrific speed. He gulped as the ride yanked us upward. Gene and I scrutinized Pudge's grimacing countenance as the arteries along his neck began pulsing, bringing new blood to his face. At first, his facial discoloration was a deep purple, then softened into a sickly, almost luminescent avocado green.

"Yaaagh!" Pudge hollered as the capsule twisted in midair, leaving us briefly weightless. Like the redhead, I hated the floaty sensation because it made me feel powerless. My pulse rate increased rapidly and I felt an invasive, unpleasant warmth surge through my body. A drop of perspiration fell from my nose.

Momentarily forgetting about Pudge, I paid attention to swiftly developing problems of my own. I was in pain and my discomfort was steadily increasing. With each vertebra-stretching turn, my battered spinal column, I felt sure, was becoming a boneless, jellylike mass. My palpitating arteries, I knew, were hardening prematurely, slowing down the crucial flow of blood to my vital organs, including my wounded brain. It seemed that one half of my brain had torn itself free from the other half and was spinning madly inside my skull. My thinking was muddled and my head throbbed with the aching of a self-inflicted migraine headache. I touched my face feeling for my eyebrows, which I was sure had been torn off in the last ferocious turn. Fortunately, I found both of them perching much higher than usual, but still attached to my forehead.

Pudge wailed pitifully as The Bullet's capsules rotated through the misty, moonlit mountain night. Although in pain, I smiled at the redhead's plight. I reveled in his predicament. From the darkest, most sullied part of my soul came a scornful chuckle, and I pulled one hand free from the safety bar to cover my mouth and hide my sardonic mirth.

I was dizzy, hurt, and confused, but I felt no real fear. I was too absorbed with Pudge's contorted facial features, his white-knuckled grip on the safety bar, his sweating, wrinkled brow, and his swelling eyes. All this revealed his mounting fright and I couldn't suppress my snicker.

An evil force, lying dormant in the reptilian portion of my brain, rousted himself and chortled darkly. A surge of superiority flooded my core; I became enormously proud of my fearless demeanor. Surely neither Gene nor Pudge could match my courage. Even the Tank would be hard-pressed to equal my valor. My brain's wicked gremlin applauded as the ride took another turn.

Fortunately, my better angels came to the forefront and shoved the malevolent force into the deepest recesses of my subconscious. I began to feel sorry for Pudge. I pitied the poor guy and had compassion. After all, I'd helped him get into this mess.

"Gack! Gork! Guffle!" coughed Pudge as The Bullet's topsy-turvy capsule descended into the insect throng. Biting, stinging, and bloodsucking ensued. The mosquitoes were particularly nasty. Lightning bugs and moths were not bothersome, except when they sought refuge in our noses and ears.

"Ah-Ah-Ah-Choo!" Pudge sneezed violently sending forth a miniature fireworks display of lightning bug innards.

Forewarned by our previous ride, Gene and I had clamped our hands tightly over our mouths and noses. Our ears, however, were vulnerable, and I felt the flutters of insect wings inside both of mine.

I noticed Gene was studying The Bullet's safety belt. He stretched the belt back and forth in front of his skinny belly. He looked past Pudge and winked at me. Surely Gene wasn't thinking of releasing our safety belt, not on this ride. In midair at our current speed, no one in his right mind would do that. But then again, this was Gene.

"Gene! Don't you dare!" I howled into the thundering wind generated by The Bullet's speed. Paying me no mind, he continued to finger the safety belt thoughtfully.

"Hey, Pudge! Can you hear me?" shouted Tank from the rear cabin. "Ain't this the greatest ride of all time?"

Suddenly, a tremendous vibration shook the cockpit from behind. The great machine shuddered from top to bottom, from stem to stern. My mind flashed back to the quaking Ferris wheel and the Tank's uncontrolled giggles.

Now skyrocketing aboard The Bullet, the mighty Tank could no longer contain his convulsive laughter, and his spastic mirth shook The Bullet to its foundations. A loud metallic pop, then another, arose from beneath our cockpit. The cracking sound increased in volume after every turn.

At this point a sliver of fear scrambled up backbones and wedged itself in my neck. My body stiffened. My shoulders hunched. I gritted my teeth and held on for dear life.

"Let's ride The Bullet once more before we leave!" cackled Tank into the gale-force winds. Gene, Pudge, and I could barely hear him, but his laughter continued to shake the ride. Our cockpit vibrated and whined. Then a deafening bang came from below as The Bullet's engine backfired with the power of a cannon's blast.

"What the dickens was that?" yelled Pudge. Crinkles of distress crisscrossed his face like lines on an Etch A Sketch.

Clutching at my innards and clawing at my bones, my terror grew. I shivered; I trembled. I was in misery and at the end of my rope. An agonized sob was welling up from my chest and I decided to pray. I hoped Jesus would listen because I didn't bother Him very often, only in extreme emergencies. I asked Jesus to sanctify and to strengthen our sturdy safety belt, and requested that He bless the metal bar that pressed coldly against our chests.

I ignored, as best I could, the lung-crushing blows from the safety bar, but I couldn't suppress the numbing sensation that had begun in my groin and now poured down my shuddering thighs and quivering calves. My toes bowed inside my tennis shoes, and my hair stretched out like a Halloween fright wig. My gut strained and I belched hot gas into the powerful, roaring wind.

Then I heard a ticking sound, like the first drops of rain on a tin roof. The nearby sound was soft and gentle, but somehow ominous.

Clickety, clack, tick, click!

"We don't need this ole strap," cried Gene as he unfastened our belt. "Now then, that's better!"

"You ass!" I bawled into the churning tempests. "You idiot! What have you done?"

"Great God Almighty!" screamed Pudge. "Put that belt back! Fasten it!"

Unrestricted, the safety belt rotated upward and spiraled like a demented python until at last it coiled around Pudge's right arm, which had been raised to strike at Gene. With the constriction from the strap, Pudge's fist turned a pasty, bluish white. He twisted around and struck ineffectually at Gene.

The giant teddy bear, released from Pudge's knees, whizzed out of The Bullet's cockpit and spun madly into the night air.

Flying high, like an intrepid superhero, the bear disappeared into the darkness.

Pudge's eyes, which had once bulged wildly, were now narrow, angry slits. Spittle formed on either side of his mouth, and his eyebrows were separated by two deep wrinkles I'd never seen before. He shook his arm free of the twisted security belt and gripped the safety bar with renewed determination.

Like Pudge, I had an iron grip on the safety bar. I called Gene a son of a bitch, but I don't think he heard me. I was certain Pudge would try to beat Gene's ass at the end of our ride. I decided I would help him. Meanwhile, Gene smiled gaily and shouted something into the roaring wind, but I couldn't hear him. Again, rocketing away from the earth, we hurtled toward the stars.

Whoops! Dang it! Gee whiz! Suddenly I realized I might have peed my pants. I wasn't sure about the urination, but my bladder definitely spasmed. At that moment, as I tore through space, I didn't much care. My real concern was simple survival, not damp, clingy blue jeans.

Then unexpectedly, The Bullet began to slow down, almost imperceptibly at first. With the slight decrease in speed, I noticed I was barely able to identify objects on the ground. Beneath us—was that a garish clown or a well-dressed young lady? Over there—was that the hotdog stand or the merry-go-round? I looked upward and couldn't find a single star.

Gradually, The Bullet's speed waned. I was rubbing my eyes with the knuckles of my hands when, mercifully, The Bullet came to a teeth-gnashing halt. A few aftershocks followed, then our cockpit was lowered slowly to ground level.

Like damaged, rusty robots, Pudge, Gene, and I clumsily exited our capsule and walked mechanically forward. All three of us were stumbling badly. We stopped at The Bullet's ticket stand where a sign read, "Closed," and leaned against the wall.

Through blurry eyes, I looked down at the crotch of my jeans.

The fabric was dry, thank goodness. Gene would have announced my bladder blunder all over Central Ashe High School. I might never have lived it down. Remembering my Baptist church upbringing, I silently thanked Jesus for keeping my jeans and underwear dry.

I knew it would take several minutes before our bodies began to rehabilitate themselves. I kept making fists with my stiff, claw-like hands, opening and closing them many times. After a moment, the cramps in my feet subsided as fresh blood brought warmth, and I was almost back to normal. Best of all, my usual 20/20 vision had returned.

Gene extended his arms and hands skyward, then bent forward in a futile attempt to touch his boots. His backbones made crackling sounds as he stretched. He straightened up and stood with much improved posture. Collecting himself, he took a single confident step forward and then stood as still and silent as the Pocahontas statue in downtown West Jefferson. Gene teetered forward, then toppled backward onto the carnival's turf, landing with a whumping sound. Luckily, his fall was cushioned to some extent by his Hopalong Cassidy cowboy hat. Lying on the ground, Gene blinked his eyes as he tried to focus on the stars above.

"Juss lemme catch muh breaf here on the groun for a little while, an I'll be all ride," Gene said in a shaky monotone. He breathed deeply for a few minutes, then he lifted his head and looked around. "Where's Tank? Is he all right?"

Tank was more easily extricated from the confining capsule this time. As the big boy wobbled forward, the two carnival workers, Snake and Clifford, stood shaking hands as they celebrated their success.

"What's buzzin', cousin?" Gene said glibly from his reclined position on the ground.

"High can't feel nuffin' on ma lef slide!" said Tank. The left corner of his mouth drooped downward, drooling spittle and his left eye was only half open.

"Don't worry, Tank," said Gene, sitting up. "After the first ride, I couldn't feel nothin' below my waist for about five minutes. It'll pass. Take a couple of deep breaths. Think about walkin' behind that purty Esmeralda Cook as she sashays down a dirt road next to the New River. Think about her bendin' over to tie her shoe. That'll make you feel better. Thinkin' about Esmeralda always improves my disposition considerable. How are you doin', Hal?"

"I expect to have feeling back in just a few minutes," I replied, kneading my distressed shoulder with stiff fingers. I knew that to feel better, I had to wait it out.

"Whew! You're ride, Sheen," slurred Tank with a misshapen grin. "High can now moof da punky finker on ma lef ham."

"I am beginnin' to feel a whole lot better," said Gene as he sat up and extended his arms. "If The Bullet wasn't closin' down, I'd go for another ride. I sure aim to ride it next year. How 'bout it, Pudge? Are you game?"

Pudge was hunched over like a pretzel with his head inches away from his knees. He groaned as he rubbed his knees with chalk white hands. We watched as Pudge slowly, ever so slowly straightened his back. All thirty-three of his vertebrae popped and snapped in defiance, but finally locked into their proper places. He grimaced, turned his head, and rode his eyes through ours, staring deeply. I felt uncomfortable, the way you feel when you hand your parents your wrinkled, messy report card after you've changed a few low grades.

"What's wrong, Pudge?" asked Tank uneasily. He put two fingers under the neck of his T-shirt and pulled downward as if he were loosening a close-fitting tie.

"I just want to know one thing: *why?*" Pudge asked. An uneasy silence followed his question. In the stillness he repeated, *"Why?"*

Just then a puff of wind lifted from the ground a dozen or more candy wrappers and tossed them about, exposing the false teeth I'd seen earlier. The estranged, earthbound dentures continued to smile merrily, unaware of the human confrontation that was developing.

Tank continued to tug on the front of his T-shirt. I tugged at my ears, grateful that their ringing had ceased. Gene picked up a half-eaten candy bar, removed the wrapper, and took a big bite out of the untouched portion. He cast the remaining candy aside.

Pudge's level gaze settled on each of us in turn, and then returned to the Tank.

"Tank, remember last summer when we climbed the water tower behind the hospital in Jefferson? Do you remember how I froze at the top, and you had to talk me down step-by-step? It took almost an hour. When we finally made it to the bottom rung, I confessed to you that I had acrophobia. I asked you not to tell anyone about what happened on the water tower. You gave me your word."

"I remember. I didn't tell anyone, Pudge, not even Hal," Tank said softly. The Tank lowered his head and stared forlornly at Pudge's tennis shoes. His massive shoulders were stooped. He started to speak and then changed his mind. The big boy squeezed his left hand with his right. His fingers reddened. For once, the mighty Tank looked small.

"What does any of this have to do with your dang acrophobia, your silly fear of spiders and bugs, Pudge?" asked Gene. "So you're scared of spiders, so what? Lots of people don't like spiders, I don't cotton to 'em myself, but I ain't seen no spiders tonight. Have you? If you see any spiders around, just call me, I'll squish 'em for you. Shucks, I'll even eat 'em for you. I ain't afraid."

"Arachnophobia is the fear of spiders; Pudge said he had *acrophobia*. That's an irrational fear of heights," I said, correcting Gene. I knew something about phobias thanks to Mrs. Bender. She taught us many things in spite of the strife Gene had caused her.

Pudge turned to face Gene, "Gene, remember two summers ago when we built that rickety raft and set sail on the New River like Huck and Jim did on the Mississippi? You and I poled the raft halfway across the river to where the current was deep and still. We were ready to head downstream when the raft developed a leak. I didn't think it was anything to worry about, but you begged me, pleaded with me, to turn around and head for the shore, which I did. When we got close enough to the bank, you and I abandoned the raft and waded to shore. We stood on the riverbank for a full ten minutes watching our wobbly, waterlogged raft before it broke up completely and sank. It came to me at that time that you might have at least a touch of aquaphobia or water fright. Some people call the unnatural fear of water hydrophobia."

"It's just 'cause I can't swim worth a lick, Pudge. I'd just as soon pick up a timber rattler as to get out in deep river water. You and Hal are good swimmers. Tank can float; he's unsinkable. My bony frame sinks like a dang stone, and I live futher away from the New River than you fellers. I didn't get the swimmin' practice you boys got. Now, ever' time I'm in a boat travelin' across deep water, I get edgy and downright petrified. Come to think of it, when I'm on a boat or a raft, I get just as fearful as you do up on the Ferris wheel, Pudge. I reckon we both got the same problem, only different. I ain't exactly afraid of the water; I'm afraid of drownin' in it. I'm a Baptist preacher's son, and yet I ain't never been baptized."

"So, it took some courage on your part to even get on that raft with me and drift toward the middle of the river where the water gets deep?" probed Pudge.

"I reckon so," mumbled, Gene. "I reckon it did take a smidgen of nerve. I mean I was purty dadgum brave, come to think of it. Not enough to brag about, though. As you fellers know, I ain't never been one to toot my own horn."

"Did you guys know or even consider that with my fear of heights, it's a struggle for me to ride the swings or even the miniature roller coaster with you, much less the Ferris wheel or The Bullet?" asked Pudge. "I try to block out the fear, but most of the time that doesn't work. When my acrophobia kicks in, I feel terror. Sometimes I can contain my fright, but I couldn't block out the fear tonight, not even on the Ferris wheel, let alone that instrument of torture they call 'The Bullet.'"

"Then why do you do it, Pudge?" I asked. I really wanted to know.

"Because you guys are my friends, and I enjoy being with you; but more importantly, it's because I believe I should face my fears. I'm trying to feed and grow what little courage I've got. That's why I ride. That's my answer. That's the truth. But the question remains for you three. *Why?* Why did you guys feel you had to trick me to get me scared on those rides? Really, 'scared' is not the right word. 'Terrified' is more like it. By the way, guys, you succeeded in scaring the dickens out of me tonight, if that was your goal."

"It was mostly Gene who scared you on the rides, Pudge," said Tank. The big boy looked sheepishly at Pudge and then admitted, "I guess Hal and I were in cahoots with Gene all along. We helped him hoodwink you. I'm sorry."

I started to deny my involvement in Gene's plots, but the Tank, as usual, was right. I was an accomplice, I was guilty, and I was finding it hard to look Pudge directly in the eyes.

"Why do you guys take my genuine fear of heights and double or triple my fear during the rides?" Pudge was relentless in his questioning, and we really had no responses. A period of uneasy quietness ensued.

"I'm really ashamed," said the Tank at last, breaking the silence, "because you told me about your acrophobia at the water tower. I saw you freeze at the top. Hal and Gene didn't know."

"I knew about your fear, Pudge," I admitted as my mouth went dry, and my face flushed. "I overheard your talk with Grandpa Charlie."

"That talk was supposed to be private," said Pudge, looking at me as if I were a stranger.

"How did you get this here acrophobia, Pudge? Was you born with it, or did it come on you over the years, a little bit at a time?" Gene asked.

"Maybe I was born with it. I don't know, but something happened to me when I was a little kid that may have caused my fear of heights. I never told my teachers, or you guys, or anybody about what happened to me, but I think Grandpa Charlie knows. Because I've always felt guilty, I've never talked with you three about the awful accident I caused."

"Guilty?" asked Tank.

"You caused an accident? Was it serious?" I asked, hoping he would tell us more.

"Do any of you guys remember my uncle Blaine?" asked Pudge, searching our eyes.

"I do," Tank said. "I remember him. He's the man who wore a heavy back brace. He worked in the office at Ore Knob Mine for a while. He had trouble walking, always limped around. I haven't seen your uncle Blaine around this county for years."

"Uncle Blaine lives up in Baltimore, now. He still has to wear a back brace, and it's my fault." Pudge paused and rubbed his chin. His eyes clouded and he turned away. He spoke again, his teenage voice splintering with emotion.

"No, I don't want to talk about Uncle Blaine anymore," he continued. "I've changed my mind. I've said too much already."

"Maybe it would be good to talk about it, Pudge," said the Tank, placing his weighty hand on Pudge's shoulder. "My dad says it's always good to get things out in the open. Dad says talking about one's troubles cleanses a worried mind."

Pudge nodded. His lips formed a tight line. He stared at us as if he were weighing, on a balance scale deep within his heart, our treatment of him on this carnival night against our many years of friendship. He seemed undecided.

"If Pudge is gonna tell a story, let's all sit down. My back is killin' me again. I thought I was over the hurt, but the hurtin' is back," said Gene. Tank and I joined him as he groaned and slowly sat down. Pudge remained standing, looking up at The Bullet. Then he slowly sat down between me and Tank.

"The carnival is closing down," said Pudge. "The workers will take everything with them. In a few days, things will be back to normal, and it'll seem as if the carnival was never here at all."

I looked around. There were only a few stragglers walking the grounds. The lights were dimming, unable to hold back the darkness any longer. A work crew, including Clifford and Snake, was picking up trash and placing it in thick cloth bags.

"Time to say good night, ladies," Snake jeered at us. "I think I speak for ever'body at Stephens Brothers Carnival when I ask you boys not to come back here next year nor any other year. You boys won't be welcome at our carnival, and that goes double for you, Fatso."

"Shut up, Snake!" yelled Gene. "Tank's mostly muscle, not fat. And not even countin' his strength, he's a better man than you or me or anybody else at this here carnival!"

"Shucks! I didn't mean nothin'," said Snake. "I was just teasin' the big boy and havin' a little fun."

"I can tease him 'cause him and me has been friends for years. You don't even know Tank, so keep your trap shut. Understand?" Gene glared at the large man.

Snake didn't respond. He bent over and picked up a partially eaten candy apple. He tossed the apple into his canvas sack, then picked up two popcorn bags.

"Don't bother with them young'uns," advised Clifford. "We got work to do if we want to get any shut-eye tonight." We ignored Snake as he and Clifford, along with the other workers, continued collecting carnival litter. Snake's large canvas bag was already half full.

Tank, Gene, and I kept encouraging Pudge to tell us about his Uncle Blaine and how his acrophobia might have come about. Finally, Pudge relented. As we sat in our circle of four, I was surprised that the ache in my legs had gone away. Pudge was hesitant and his expression was pained as he began the story.

CHAPTER 29

"I was only five years old, and Uncle Blaine was just seventeen," said Pudge as we sat in the sawdust. "There had been a family reunion that summer at my grandfather's farm in Chestnut Hill. There must've been over one hundred people there on the fresh-cut grass in front of the old white farmhouse. The gathering's food—fried chicken, ham biscuits, pork chops, creamed corn, green beans, baked bread, and mashed potatoes—was served outside on big tables. The big dessert table was covered with fruit slices, cakes, pies, and peanut butter cookies.

"I had just finished eating a slice of watermelon, and I remember looking around at all the grown-ups, wondering if I would ever be that tall. Some of the family members there hadn't seen each other in twenty years or more. My mom and dad were talking to an older couple, so I decided I wouldn't interrupt them. I was determined to explore the farm all by myself. I slipped away unnoticed.

"The barn was the biggest building on the farm, so I headed for it. My grandpa's barn was painted burgundy red and had a shiny new tin roof. There was a splintery, homemade ladder nailed to the side of the barn and I decided to climb up to the roof. I had no acrophobia then, in fact, I was a fearless climber. I climbed the ladder and managed to get up on the hot, slick roof. I tried to reach the peak, but I kept sliding back so I just sat down and held myself in place with my hands. The bright sun overhead was making the metal roof so hot that it almost burned my hands.

"Down below me, I could see Uncle Blaine shooting his basketball at a hoop on the side of the barn. He hadn't seen me climb the ladder and didn't know I was watching him. He kept practicing his jump shots and I noticed that he seldom missed a basket. I was amazed at how high he could jump.

"My dad had taken me to a high school basketball game to watch Uncle Blaine play. As we sat in the stands at halftime, Dad told me that his teammates at Lansing High School had voted Blaine captain of the basketball team. That night he scored twenty-five points in a win over Beaver Dam High School. During the game, he had scored eleven points on foul shots alone. He didn't miss a single foul shot! He had unbelievable hand-eye coordination; he hit baskets again and again from way outside, near the top of the key. And underneath the goal, he had blocked the shot of a much taller player, not once but *three* times.

"After the game, Dad had said that some coaches in the county thought Uncle Blaine might earn an athletic scholarship to a North Carolina college or university.

"From the hot tin roof, I watched him make two more buckets as the ball swished through the hoop, never touching the rim. I liked the sound of the basketball spinning through the net. On his next shot, he banked the basketball off the side of the barn and into the goal. The spinning ball soared through the air before it plopped into the basket and whooshed through the twine . One of his shots rattled around the homemade hoop before dropping through. He hit nine shots in a row, and I began clapping my hands. 'Way to go, Uncle Blaine!' I shouted.

"Uncle Blaine looked up and saw me sitting near the edge of the barn's high roof. He dropped the basketball and his tanned face whitened. His body froze like a statue. I waved to Uncle Blaine.

"That's when I slipped.

"I was sitting on my butt as I slid downward toward the edge of the tin roof. I couldn't stop. My slick-bottomed leather shoes provided no friction and I kept sliding faster. The seat of my little bib overalls caught on something, and that stopped my slide just before I went tumbling over the edge. I cried out because the tin roof was hotter near the edge and was stinging my hands. I was on the very edge of the roof with my feet dangling over. The ladder, only a few feet away, seemed unreachable, but I decided to try for it. I stretched my arms out and reached toward the ladder, but my five-year-old arms couldn't reach it.

"Uncle Blaine yelled, 'Stay where you are Pudgie! Don't move! I'm coming up to get you!' He sprang toward the ladder.

"He came up the ladder in a burst of speed. Uncle Blaine was at the top of the ladder and reaching for me when the nail that was holding my overalls released its grip. I slid forward a couple of inches onto a jagged section of the shining roof. There was a quick ripping sound, and I went over the side and began a freefall.

"Uncle Blaine dove from the ladder and grabbed me in midair. Now we were both falling. Uncle Blaine twisted in the air, and put me on his chest, holding me with strong arms. 'I got you!' he whispered."

"Jesus!" breathed Tank, putting his hand over his heart.

"I felt weightless," said Pudge, "like when you're in your seat, coming down from the top of the Ferris wheel. Uncle Blaine and I were falling so far, and so fast! Then I heard a shocking thud and a sickening crunch. Uncle Blaine's arms released me and fell to his sides.

"Although Uncle Blaine cushioned my fall, I felt a strong impact, and my breath rushed out of me. I gasped for air, but I couldn't breathe. On the fourth gasp, oxygen came rushing into me, filling up my lungs.

"People came running and gathered around me and Uncle Blaine. He lay there with his eyes open, not moving his arms or legs. Then, at last, he moved his right arm. His left arm remained motionless. He coughed. There was foamy blood around his nose and lips. 'Is he all right; is Pudgie all right?' Uncle Blaine asked.

"My mother, who had gathered me up in her arms, assured him that I was fine, and I *was*. I was just shaken up. I had no injuries thanks to Uncle Blaine.

"His father, my grandfather, knelt beside Uncle Blaine and began massaging his legs. Granddaddy kept asking him if he was feeling any pressure as he poked and prodded.

"Then Uncle Blaine said something to my grandfather that I'll never forget: 'I can't feel my legs, Dad! I can't feel my legs!'"

"Uh oh," whispered Gene, putting his hand over his mouth.

"My dad came running from the house and said, 'It's all right, Blaine. We've already called for an ambulance. It'll be here soon. Everything's gonna be all right.'

"But everything wasn't all right. His back was broken in several places. One vertebra was crushed. Uncle Blaine had a spinal operation and then intensive therapy for almost a year, but he never could walk as he had walked before that fall. Uncle Blaine had a limp that he couldn't rid himself of.

"His basketball career was finished because of me. His life was changed forever because of me. He had to take pain pills in order to sleep. Uncle Blaine had saved my life, but I had ruined his."

Tank wiped his nose, Gene coughed, clearing his throat, and I looked down at a shiny pebble on the ground. My eyes were burning from the dusty carnival air.

"I believe my acrophobia began with that accident," said Pudge matter-of-factly. He covered his face with his freckled hands. His shoulders sagged.

We were all silent for a while. Then Gene said, "Damnation, Pudge, I never heard that story about you and your uncle. If I had, I surely wouldn't have done some of the things I done to scare you on the Ferris wheel and then again on The Bullet."

"Neither would I," I said. I felt guilty about telling Pudge that The Bullet was a slow ride. "I'm sorry, Pudge. I should've been a better friend."

"I'm sorry, too, Pudge, real sorry" admitted Gene. "If I'd knowed about your phobia, I woulda done better by you. I'm apologizin'. I'm beggin' your pardon. I mean it."

I had never heard Gene apologize to anyone for anything he'd ever done, no matter how callous. I thought he was incapable of delivering an apology. His words of contrition stunned me. Tank's eyebrows lifted widening his eyes. A similar look of surprise swept over Pudge's face.

Tank leaned forward and said, in our defense, "Pudge, you were never in any real danger. Like you, I was almost scared to death tonight. You should've seen me after I got off The Bullet the first time. I was so nervous, I was shaking all over, and as you know, when I shake, I *really* shake. It's strange, but when we scared you tonight, it's like we lost some of our own fear. We transferred our fear to you. That made The Bullet easier for us."

"Good for you guys; bad for me," said Pudge.

"It was like a prank, Pudge," said Gene, removing his wrinkled cowboy hat. "People are always playin' pranks on other people, and most pranks are based on scarin' folks. People put on masks and hide in closets, just to jump out and scare their grandmaws and grandpaws—at least I do. And why do people go to scary movies ever' chance they get and go to haunted houses on Halloween? Why do kids like to hear ole ghost stories? Ever'one, even little kids, want to get scared. So causin' fear ain't such a bad thing. Ain't that right?"

Pudge's level gaze caused Gene to turn away. The skinny guy put his crumpled cowboy hat back on, stood up, and stuffed his hands deep into his pockets. He changed his mind about the position of his headgear and removed it, letting it fall down his back until the shoe string at his neck caught it. The black hat rested between his shaking shoulder blades as he rubbed his moist eyes and kicked at a stone.

Soon the four of us were all standing and stretching our arms skyward. I felt several of my vertebrae snap back into place. My aches and pains were subsiding.

"You're wrong about fear, Gene," I said, stomping my feet on the ground to aid circulation. My self-assurance was returning. My confidence morphed into cockiness.

"I, for example, have never known actual fear, not really," I continued. "The things that cause most people fright, I find laughable. Terror and I have never met face to face. We can never occupy the same space, for old man Terror knows that I am scarier, stronger, and tougher than he ever was. You wouldn't understand this, Gene, but fear does not occupy a place in my personal universe. My mighty strength, both physical and mental, overcomes all fear and trepidation."

"You lie like a dog, Hal. I seen plenty of fear on your face when we rode The Bullet, not just once but *both* times," said Gene. "No fear? It just ain't so! You're the biggest chicken-heart on this here planet. On The Bullet, I believe you was far more scared than what Pudge was, and you ain't got no phobias."

"Let me explain," I said, wagging a finger. "Sometimes I feign fear, just to fit in with you scaredy-cat guys and others far worse than you three, those in the lily-livered, sniveling, yellow-bellied category. My fear on The Bullet was make believe," I boasted, standing tall, puffing out my chest, and flexing my fourteen-year-old biceps, which were about the size and shape of two lemons.

"I wonder if there are any openings in the superhero line," I continued. "Just call me Captain Curly Courage, hero from the hills, mighty man of the mountains, protector of the possum, defender of the deer, bodyguard of the bobcat, guardian of the groundhog, and fearless fighter for freedom and justice!"

I assumed the stance of television star George Reeves during the introductory sequence of the *Adventures of Superman*. I stared stoically forward attempting to assume the noble facial features of the Man of Steel. I envisioned Old Glory waving patriotically behind me.

Just then, a large brown rat of the hefty Norway variety, with a candied apple core dangling from its sharp incisors, scurried between my legs and disappeared under the flap of a nearby concession tent. The hairless, snake-like tail was the last thing to slither under the tent and vanish. Startled by the unexpected rodent, I yelled and jumped about two feet into the air. Using both my hands, I cupped my private parts. Unfortunately, my usual manly yell sounded more like a woman's piercing shriek.

My teenage voice had begun to change and deepen with the coming of adolescence, but in that instant I squeaked like a girl who had just discovered a garter snake in her underwear drawer. The immense rat startled all four of us, and Tank almost lost his balance as he stepped backward clumsily. However, I admit I had the strongest response. I was getting ready to point out to the guys my exceptional reflexes, my jumping ability, and my instantaneous reactions when I noticed both Tank and Gene were pointing at me and laughing. Even Pudge was smiling.

"Musophobia is one of the most common phobias. It's the abnormal fear of rats and mice," smiled Tank. "Hal has a bad case of it, and if I know my psychology, our pal may need counseling. Guys, he needs our support. I hope he can be cured."

"Hal, don't you know a rat ain't nothin' but a squirrel with a clean-shaved tail," smirked Gene. "A rat might bite you if you tried to catch it same as a squirrel or snake would. Leave 'em alone, I say. This is the voice of experience talkin', for I caught a medium-sized rat behind our shed one time. The critter bit me three times 'fore I could turn the little bastard loose. Still, a rat ain't nothin' to be fearful of, unless you got a big dose of mouse-o-phobia, like Tank said."

"I'm not afraid of rodents. I was surprised, that's all. Give me a stick and let me at that overgrown rat!" I shouted.

There were no sticks around, thank God, and the rodent, probably a carnival hitchhiker, was long gone. I was glad I didn't have to tangle with the creature. The big rat looked as if he could've worn a size small in bib overalls.

"If that heavyset rat scared him so much, it's a wonder Hal didn't crap his pants when we rode The Bullet for the first time. I know I almost did. The Bullet is one helluva ride. I was as scared as I've ever been," confessed Gene. "Still, the ride had its good points. Durin' the first ride, Hal's expressions was hilarious! You shoulda been there, Pudge! I wished I had brought a camera!"

Pudge remained silent and unmoved. He stared at Gene until the skinny guy lowered his eyes. Gene studied the sawdust around his boots. He kicked at a Coca-Cola bottle cap. The top flipped over and over and landed near an abandoned wad of dirty cotton candy. Several insects were disturbed mid-meal and buzzed away.

Then Gene addressed Pudge earnestly, "The Tank is right. We was never meanin' to put you in no real danger, neither on the Ferris wheel nor on The Bullet. Besides, I believe ridin' these rides toughens you up. Like you said a few minutes ago, the rides make you face your fears. I know I got my own fears. Like you, I'm gonna face 'em. I'm gonna learn to swim someday soon, maybe this summer, and I think that little smidgen of success will take care of my aquaphobia, waterfright, hydrophobia, or whatever you called that dang fearful feelin' I get when I'm around deep water."

"I always think of rabies when I hear that word hydrophobia," said Tank.

"Grandpa Charlie says that a mad dog, a dog with rabies, won't drink any water because the disease paralyzes its throat muscles, so I guess the word hydrophobia fits with both rabies and Gene's fear of water," I explained.

Gene stared at me blankly, as if I were speaking a foreign language. He turned away from me toward Pudge. Gene reached behind him, and retrieved his dilapidated Hopalong Cassidy cowboy hat. He placed the rundown hat firmly on his head and tightened the shoestring strap under his chin. He started to say something to the redhead, but Pudge spoke first.

"I hope learning to swim takes care if your aquaphobia, Gene," said Pudge. "I really do. But I want to make you three guys a promise. Hal, Tank, and Gene, are you listening? I want to make this short and sweet. I will *never* ride another carnival ride with you three. Oh, I'll ride with other people in the future, maybe Johnny Knight or Ruthie, or my new friend, John Bowman, but not with you guys. Never again with you guys. My mind is made up."

"Pudge, you don't mean that," said Tank. "We four have been riding carnival rides every year since we rode the merry-go-round together in the second grade. I remember because Gene pushed you off your pony and you fell and broke your arm. I'd never heard a kid scream as loud you did. Mrs. Reeves was so concerned when you walked into the classroom wearing your cast. Am I right, Gene?"

"Yep, it was second grade," said Gene, "because Mrs. Reeves babied Pudge for most of the year. Made me sick at my stomach. 'Be careful around Pudgie. Be gentle when you play. Don't hurt his arm.' Pudge was the teacher's pet. He was always first in line for lunch, first in line for play period, first in line for ever' bathroom break. Pudge couldn't do nothin' wrong in the second grade with that cast on his arm, and she petted him for a month or more after it come off."

Pudge massaged his right forearm at the site of the broken bone that had been fractured so long ago. He had worn the cast for six weeks, an eternity for a seven-year-old.

"By the way, Pudge, I never meant to shove you off your merry-go-round pony. I was just grabbin' for some of your popcorn, and I reckon I lost my balance. I missed the popcorn bag and grabbed you. You fell off your horse and hit purty hard, but the grabbin' and the resultin' fall was purely accidental, a merry-go-round mistake, and nobody's fault," said Gene.

"I believe you, Gene, and I have never blamed you for my fall or my broken arm," smiled Pudge. The redhead seemed totally relaxed and in control, a far cry from his mood while he was careening through the air on The Bullet. His face was steadfast and calm; his hands, steady and sure. When he spoke, his voice was serene and cool.

"Look, guys, I don't even blame you for what happened here tonight. I got on the Ferris wheel and The Bullet of my own free will. No one put a gun to my head. The carnival rides tested me tonight. I wanted that experience. I needed it. I have to feel my fear to overcome it. Tonight I made progress, not much but some."

I told Pudge—actually my telling bordered on begging—to forget about this crazy carnival night; and that if he would ride with us next July when the four of us would be rising sophomores in high school, I would pay for two of his rides out of my own pocket. Tank offered to pay for three of his rides. Gene offered to make sure that all the safety bars and security belts remained in place at all times during all future carnival rides. He promised never to shake the Ferris wheel seats back and forth. He crossed his heart and hoped to die. That's how serious he was.

"I will do my dang best to make sure that you stay safe and secure on any upcomin' carnival rides with me, Pudge," said Gene. He raised his right hand. "I swear on my poor ole mother's grave!"

"Your mother is not dead," countered Pudge. "She's very much alive."

"That's a fact, but if she was dead I would swear on her grave or on a stack of Bibles, whichever you might pick," Gene continued. "And let me make this clear, I promise no more pranks or jokes on any forthcomin' carnival rides, especially on them rides that take you high up in the air. I swear on my great granddaddy's grave. He's dead, been dead a long time."

"Gene, you don't understand. This has nothing to do with pranks, money for rides, or my personal safety. Guys, I've been thinking about this for a long time, over a year now; and tonight, even before we got on The Bullet, I had made my decision. That's right, *before* we got on The Bullet, I had decided, and my decision is final."

"Come on, Pudge. You and I have been friends since the first grade. Don't let our friendship end like this," said Tank. He took a blue handkerchief out of his back pocket, and wiped his eyes.

"Lots of dust in the air around here," Tank explained as he put the handkerchief away.

"Don't worry, guys, we're still friends," said Pudge. "I guess we always will be. I hope so. But I will never ride another carnival ride with you three again. Not all together; not individually. Not next year. Not ever. The Bullet was our last carnival ride together. As I said before, I will face my fears in the future. I believe I can beat my acrophobia or at least keep it under control. I'll ride carnival rides, like the Ferris wheel and even The Bullet with others; but never again will I ride with you three guys."

And having known Pudge since the first day of school in the first grade, I believed him. Pudge had never broken his word to Tank, Gene, or me.

CHAPTER 30

The bright, festive lights were flickering and dimming, signaling that the carnival was closing down. Carnival workers were still picking up trash, made more difficult by mischievous breezes spreading wrappers and rubbish around. Vendors were counting their money, stacking the silver coins in neat circular piles.

A brown and white beagle with no collar roamed around the grounds, sniffing for discarded snacks. The dog found a half-eaten hotdog and wolfed it down. Then, trotting away with his nose close to the ground, he resumed his search for food.

A garbled recorded message, full of static, blared from the loud speakers thanking all of the carnival customers and wishing them a safe trip home.

"Well, that's it. Let's go," said Pudge. He headed for the exit; we followed.

We were among the several dawdlers trudging down the hill toward West Jefferson. We barely spoke as the moon overhead lit our path. We had to stop once on the way down while Tank knelt and tied his tennis shoe.

True to his word, Grandpa Charlie was waiting in his old Dodge pickup parked in front of the Blackburn's Department Store. Gene, Pudge, and I climbed up into the hard metal bed of the pickup. We found three empty burlap sacks and sat on them. Tank sat up front next to Grandpa Charlie.

Grandpa Charlie rolled down his window and called out, "Is ever'body ready? Okay. Now, don't nobody stand up whilst the pickup is movin'. Gene, I reckon we'll drop you off first."

He rolled his window back up and twisted the ignition key. The old pickup's engine sputtered to life, and we rode out of West Jefferson. One by one, my friends were dropped off at their homes, first Gene, then Pudge, then Tank.

"Thanks for the ride home, Grandpa Charlie," said Tank as he squeezed out of the passenger side of the pickup. Grandpa Charlie nodded and waved goodbye as Tank entered his darkened house. The big teenager closed his front door quietly so as not to wake his parents.

I climbed out of the pickup's bed and took Tank's place in the warm passenger seat. Grandpa Charlie backed out of the Banner driveway and pointed his truck down the main road. Assisted by the moon, its headlights lit up the dark paved highway. Soon we were riding along at forty miles per hour. I rolled down my window and let the fresh air wash over me. Grandpa Charlie rolled his window down, too. The old pickup chugged through the night on the asphalt ribbon of highway.

"Did you see your girlfriend tonight?" Grandpa Charlie asked.

"I saw Ruthie. I like her, but she's not my girlfriend."

"I ain't talkin' about Ruthie. I mean that purty young Bishop girl. Now what's her name? Cynthia? Nope, that ain't it. Sophia? Yep, that's what they call her. Sophia Bishop. Did you see her at the carnival?"

"I saw her," I said. Just thinking about Sophia increased my pulse and respiratory rate. My ears burned. My toes tapped an irregular beat on the pickup's floorboard.

"Did you get to speak to her? Did you get to hold her hand?" Grandpa Charlie teased.

"No, she was with her father and the rest of her family. I didn't speak to her, and she didn't speak to me."

"So, you was too scared to talk to her with her daddy around? Was both you and young Sophia afraid to speak to one another?"

Grandpa Charlie turned his head and looked at me. I nodded. He grunted. Laugh lines around his eyes deepened. A minute of silence passed.

"Hal, I can't believe you are of courtin' age," said Grandpa Charlie. "Time flies by when you get to be a geezer like me. Time's a fast movin' thing; after age sixty, the years skedaddle by on a feller. Seems like only a year or two ago that you was knee high and ridin' a shiny red Christmas tricycle around my cabin floor. Your daddy and me got tickled 'cause you could barely reach the pedals, and now you got yourself a girlfriend."

"I don't have a girlfriend, not really," I corrected him. "Besides, when school starts, I'll be starting high school, and Sophia will be in the seventh grade at Healing Waters. I saw Sophia and Ruthie tonight, but I spent almost all my carnival time with Tank, Pudge, and Gene."

"You boys has been close friends for a long spell now."

"Since first grade," I said. "We used to call ourselves 'The Four Musketeers.' In reality, we were more like Disney Mouseketeers, except for Tank, of course. I guess he could be a real musketeer, a real hero. When one of us guys gets into trouble, Tank comes to the rescue."

Grandpa Charlie grinned and nodded heartily. He slowed down and honked his horn at two whitetail deer, a doe and a fawn, grazing beside the road. The startled deer sprang up a steep bank and melted into the dense woods.

"Hal, I can't help but like them three friends of yours. Take Pudge, for example. He showed his pluck tonight by ridin' them big ole tall rides although he was scared half to death. He faced his fears like a growed man. I'm awful sorry he's got that acrephobia, but if anybody can whup it, he can. And what about your buddy, Tank? I ain't never met nobody with a better heart than what that big boy has got. He's stronger than two mules but as gentle as a newborn colt. I can't help but grin when I'm around that big young'un.

"He reminds me of Twig Bottomley, a good friend of mine from long ago. He was the strongest man in the county but mild as a little kitten. Twig left the county to work in the coal mines of West Virginia. Me and him used to Injun rassle. Some calls it arm rasslin'; I call it Injun rasslin'. I never could beat him."

"Do you think Tank could've beaten him?"

"Maybe, but ole Twig was awful stout."

I was certain that Tank could've beaten Twig Bottomley, but I didn't say anything to Grandpa Charlie. Nobody was stronger than the Tank. Nobody.

"Anyways, I'm glad you four boys is friends," Grandpa Charlie continued. "There's a sayin' about friends if I can recollect it. I heard the words at a funeral one time. 'Friends is like stars in the sky. They'll always be with you, even when you can't see 'em.' I reckon that's how it goes, somethin' like that anyways. I ain't no English teacher, but I think the sayin' means that if you keep your friends in your heart and bring 'em to mind ever' now and then, they'll always be by your side, so to speak, even when they're far away.

"I lost my best friend and huntin' buddy, Eustace Howell, sev'ral years ago. The lung cancer took him, but he ain't really gone. I keep his memory right in here." Grandpa Charlie patted his chest, right over his heart. "I believe you'll always remember Tank and Pudge like I'll always remember Eustace."

"You didn't mention my friend Gene," I said.

"I'm sure he's got sev'ral good qualities, but I can't think of none, right off hand."

Grandpa Charlie and I chuckled for a few seconds. Turning off the paved road onto the gravel road, he hit the pickup's brakes, and we slowed down to cross a low-water bridge. After we rattled across the bridge's planks, he said, "I know Gene don't always show it, but I reckon the boy's heart is in the right place. What do you think?"

"You're right about, Gene. At least, I think you're right. I hope you're right. He told Pudge that he was sorry for what he did on the rides, especially on The Bullet. He was sincere when he apologized."

"He did *what?* Well, boil my taters!" Grandpa Charlie seemed flabbergasted. The pickup swerved on the gravel road, kicking up dust. "Are you plumb sure? "

"Yeah, Gene apologized."

"Well, if that don't beat all! I reckon he fin'ly done the right thing by Pudge," said Grandpa Charlie. "I always thought there was some good in that tall, skinny young'un; he just keeps it well hid. It's easy to see the good in the rest of you boys."

Suddenly, for no apparent reason, I felt uneasy. My stomach burned with unexpected indigestion, and I wiped my sweaty hands on my jeans. I closed my eyes to catch a tear. Shifting carnival images of Ruthie, Sophia, Tank, Gene, and Pudge—especially Pudge—flashed in my head, and words I hadn't intended to say came pouring out of me like well water from a hand pump.

"Pudge said he wasn't going to ride any more carnival rides with Tank, Gene, or me, not ever. Not ever again. He said he would ride with others but not with us. He won't change his mind. Summer carnivals won't ever be the same. He meant it. Pudge meant every word he said. I know he did."

"You blame him?" asked Grandpa Charlie.

"Nope. The blame is on me and Gene, mostly. There's even some blame on Tank."

Startled by the bluntness of my reply, I felt a flush of shame as I recollected colluding with Gene to frighten Pudge on The Bullet. I was in cahoots with Gene while knowing Pudge had acrophobia. I knew about phobias; I knew they were potent fears that often left their victims feeling powerless. I tried to rationalize my meanness. I consoled myself by recalling that even Tank had been involved in carrying out Gene's schemes to scare Pudge on the towering rides. As it turned out, Tank also had prior knowledge of Pudge's irrational fear. I still felt mean and worthless. Tank was probably feeling the same shame.

Ironically, Gene, whom I considered the chief villain in the redhead's high-flying, fear-filled spectacle, did not know about Pudge's acrophobia. In that respect, he was far less guilty than Tank and I were.

"Acceptin' your fair share of the blame when somethin' goes wrong is part of growin' up, Hal, but sometimes it hurts. Take it from a feller who knows," said Grandpa Charlie.

As Grandpa Charlie's pickup pushed through the winding mountain road's sharp curves, I pondered the twists and turns of my new life as a teenager. My thoughts drifted back to two small boys, one with red hair and the other curly headed, standing on a shaded river bank. I recalled a promise made. I remembered having promised Pudge to be his best friend all those years ago when we stood near his little dog's gravesite on a green bank of the New River. Even as a little boy, I knew that best friends looked out for each other. A best friend could be counted on in tough times. Tonight at the carnival, I had let Pudge down.

Some best friend I had turned out to be.

CHAPTER 31

I had learned two significant things during my time at the carnival: Pudge suffered from acrophobia, and Grandpa Charlie suffered from claustrophobia. I was shocked because I had seen Grandpa Charlie work in tight places. He had helped Grandpa Grayson line the insides of two small closets with cedar wood to keep moths out. Also, one winter, after the water in the pipes under his cabin had frozen solid, he scrambled down into his narrow crawlspace to work on his plumbing. I helped the old man by handing him the tools he needed from outside the crawlspace. Working there on the cold ground, in the dark, confined space, Grandpa Charlie must have been terribly afraid.

Fog ghosts rose from the river and wafted across the gravel road. The pickup plowed through the floating mists and dispersed the vapor. The road up ahead was clear.

"Grandpa Charlie, I never knew you had claustrophobia," I said. "I can't remember anyone in the family ever mentioning it."

"That's because I ain't got no closet-phobia. I figgered that you was listenin' to my talk with Pudge. It took you a mighty long time to eat that cotton candy at the candy stand. I seen you lookin' over at us. You ort not to eavesdrop on people's private conversations, Hal. It ain't mannerly."

"But why did you tell Pudge that you had claustrophobia?"

"Hal, I told him I had closet-phobia 'cause I thought it might help the boy. You know I like that redheaded young'un. I made up the whole story inside my head. I didn't want him to think he was facin' his acre-phobia all by hisself. I tried to convince him that I had a fear problem, too. Maybe my words helped him some, and maybe they didn't. I knowed he wouldn't get much help from you young boys. I reckon I did tell him a lie about me havin' closet-phobia, but it was one of them white lies that the Almighty forgives a feller for tellin', if he didn't mean no harm. I hope my little lie done him some good."

"I think you helped him, Grandpa." I smiled and reflected. On this carnival night Pudge's best friend turned out to be, not me, not Tank, not Gene, but Grandpa Charlie. We tried to scare Pudge; he tried to help him.

"When you get a little bit older, Hal, you'll come to understand that any man, no matter how strong he is, needs some help along the way," said Grandpa Charlie. "Feelin' like you're all alone is a turrible feelin'. I've had them lonesome blues, and I've had to lean on my friends and fam'ly many a time. If I was kindly like a leanin' post in supportin' Pudge tonight, I was mighty proud to do it."

"I think you are a very wise man, and I'm proud you're my grandfather. Sometimes I wish I could be a better grandson; sometimes I wish I had your wisdom. I make a lot of mistakes. Like tonight, I really wanted to get Pudge up on The Bullet even though I knew he had acrophobia. I knew Gene would try to scare him, and I went right along with Gene's plan. Like Gene, I wanted to scare Pudge. I guess Tank did, too."

"You all was just boys bein' boys," said the old man, soothingly.

I knew it wasn't that simple, but I didn't contradict my grandfather.

"Not only did we scare the dickens out of him, we caused him to lose the big teddy bear he won at the baseball toss," I said.

"You say Pudge lost a big toy bear? Do you reckon he'll ever find it?"

"Nope, that bear's gone for good. He'll never see that bear again," I sighed, turning my face toward the darkness outside my open window. I listened to the pickup's wheels crunch the gravel. I matched the lyrics of a sad Hank Williams country song—I felt mean, ashamed, blue, lonesome, and lowdown all at the same time. "I wish I could be more like you, Grandpa Charlie, and try to help people, rather than hurt them. There's a meanness in me, way down deep inside. I've tried but I can't let it go."

Grandpa Charlie laughed, slapped his knee, and stretched over to tousle my hair.

"Son, when I was your age, ever'body thought I was as mean as a striped snake. My meanness showed up mainly at school. I got many a whuppin', and I quit school when I was thirteen years of age. I've regretted doin' that ever' day of my life. My partin' gift to the school was to set fire to the school's outhouse and burn it to the ground. I come back on the school grounds late at night, poured coal oil on the toilet buildin' and struck a match to it. The buildin' burned like a roarin' fireplace for a while. Whoopin' and hollerin', I danced in circles around that outhouse while she blazed. Then the little house was gone, nothin' but ashes left and a big stinkin' hole in the ground. A boy don't get much meaner than what I was back then. But I outgrowed my mean ways, most of 'em anyways, and you will too."

"I hope so," I said. I wondered if Grandpa Grayson, like Grandpa Charlie, had ever done any mean things when he was a teenager. I made up my mind to ask him.

"Reach up under your seat, Hal. I think you'll find somethin' interestin'. I hid it over there on the passenger side, under the seat. Tank didn't take no notice of it."

I felt under the seat and touched something made of a velvety soft fabric. The thing was firmly lodged underneath the seat. I tugged on the object and pulled out Pudge's missing teddy bear.

"Wow!" I exclaimed as I examined the bear looking for any damage.

Except for a dark ketchup stain on one ear, the stuffed bear was undamaged. I set the bear on the truck's bench seat between me and Grandpa Charlie. The pickup dropped its right front wheel into a large pothole. The jolt almost unseated me and the bear.

"I seen that teddy bear come flyin' out of The Bullet while you boys was ridin'. The bear landed close to the big hotdog stand next to a throwed away box of french fried taters. Ever'thin' around the carnival was startin' to close down, so I gathered up the bear and toted it down the hill to my pickup truck. I figgered I'd ask you what we ort to do with the stuffed critter."

"I never thought I'd see Pudge's bear again," I laughed. "We'll have to return it. Pudge wasn't going to keep it, anyway. He meant to give it to Ruthie."

Grandpa Charlie became animated, and he turned to me and said conspiratorially, "Wait 'til school starts up and then take the teddy bear to school. Give it to Pudge; it'll be a big surprise for him. Tell him you seen it floatin' down the New River. Say you swum out to the middle of the river and rescued that stuffed bear from drownin'. Let him know that you had to give that fuzzy critter artificial perspiration or whatever it is that brings drownded folks back to life. And tell Pudge it took three days of hangin' on a clothes line in the hot sunshine to dry the bear out."

"If he saw that bear again, Pudge would be surprised, but he'd know it's all a joke," I said.

"That's all right. Pudge likes a good joke better than any young'un I ever seen, unless it was you. Havin' a good laugh together won't hurt your friendship none, neither."

I looked closely at the teddy bear's ketchup-stained ear. A thorough scrubbing would remove the discoloration. Grandma Grayson took pride in her ability to remove stains from clothing. I was sure she could fix the bear.

"Grandma Grayson could clean this teddy bear up so he looks as good as new," I said.

"Yep, that woman could clean the dapples off a fawn, the spots off a bobcat, or the stripes off a skunk," chuckled Grandpa Charlie. "Hal, don't forget you got some other options with that teddy bear besides returnin' it to Pudge. You could keep it and give it to young Sophia, or you could give it to Ruthie. Maybe Ruthie would ride the Ferris wheel with you next year, if you asked her purty please."

"Nope, I'll return the teddy bear to Pudge. He won it at the baseball toss tonight. I wouldn't feel right keeping it."

"I see you don't believe in the ole rule of 'finders keepers, losers weepers' in this partic'lar case. Well, you're doin' the right thing, son, and growin' up right before my ole eyes."

"He wouldn't have lost the bear if he hadn't ridden with me and Gene on The Bullet. It belongs to him; he can do with it as he pleases. I reckon it'll end up in Ruthie's stuffed animal collection."

"Do you reckon, son?"

Grandpa Charlie let loose one of his belly laughs. He wasn't used to me using the word "reckon." It always tickled him when I used the word. He knew I thought the word was old-fashioned and outdated. I laughed along with him as he reached over the teddy bear, seated between us, and socked me gently on my shoulder. We laughed for at least a half a mile down the road.

"You'll do for a grandson, Hal. You make me proud of you more off-ten than not. You'll do right well, I reckon," he said, emphasizing his 'reckon.' Still chuckling, he said, "I wouldn't trade you for nobody else."

"Not even Tank?" I asked. Among my friends, I knew the Tank was Grandpa Charlie's favorite. Pudge was a close second.

"You know that big boy would eat me out of house and home, but I bet he could pull a plow as good as my ole mule, Jenny, God rest her gentle soul. Tank could be considerable help around the farm. I can see him throwin' up baled hay, two bales at a time, onto the bed of my truck. I wonder if his daddy would be willin' to trade you for him. Might be a good deal for me. Let me ponder about this here swap."

The pickup's cabin was silent except for the humming of the vehicle's engine. Lightning bugs lit up the grassy meadows on either side of the road, reminding me of the carnival's flickering lights at closing time. As we got closer to the Grayson farm, I could barely hear the murmuring river washing over ancient boulders on its expedition to join the warm waters of the Gulf of Mexico.

Traveling north, New River water would eventually splash into the Ohio River and then journey on to the Mississippi River, the confluence taking place at Cairo, Illinois. Traveling by boat on the mighty Mississippi from Cairo to New Orleans is a journey of over eight hundred miles. I learned much about the New River, the Ohio River, and the Mississippi River in sixth-grade geography classes with Mrs. Bender. Sometimes I wondered how much more I could've learned had she and Gene not been feuding and fussing.

After rounding a sharp curve, Grandpa Charlie adjusted the pickup's steering wheel to a straight stretch and said, "Nope, I wouldn't trade you for nobody, Hal, not even Tank! We're blood kin, you and me. As folks say, 'Blood's thicker than water.' I'm a mighty strong believer in that sayin'. Nowadays, fam'lies has got to stick together as best they can. In these changin' times, it keeps gettin' harder and harder to keep kinfolks together. People gets divorces, instead of tryin' to hold their marriages together; young folks grow up and leave the county for more schoolin' or better jobs; flatlanders and people from Floridy is startin' to buy up mountain land on hilltops and along the river so they can build big houses with purty views. In this day and age, some country folks can't make a good livin' here no more, so they head up north to a big city like Baltimore and get factory jobs. I've heard tell that they even give womenfolks factory jobs up there in Baltimore. Times ain't like they used to be. The ole times was awful good. I miss 'em."

I had heard similar statements from Grandpa Grayson. I wondered if all older people shared the desire to return to the past. But I knew Grandma Grayson wouldn't want to turn in her television set and go back to just listening to the radio. Neither would Grandpa Grayson.

"Oh, I almost forgot," I said. "Grandpa Grayson wanted me to tell you that Quincy Alexander is in the Ashe County Hospital. He said that you and he might want to visit Quincy this Sunday after church. Grandpa Grayson needs a ride. He said he would give you gas money."

Grandpa Charlie nodded and said, "You tell Morgan that I'll meet up with him after church and we'll drive to the hospital. I hope Quincy will be all right. I reckon he's had another heart attack. His heart has been troublin' him for years. Some folks gets to be all right after a heart attack and some don't."

The old man's face grew solemn as he spoke, "Quincy, Morgan, and me was in school together. Morgan Grayson took to book learnin' more than me and Quincy did. Morgan was one of the first boys that learned how to read real good in that little one-room school where we started. Me and Quincy laid out of school a lot when the weather was nice. We headed for the woods or the New River. Sometimes we rambled up a mountainside. Sometimes we hunted for arrowheads over near Ole Fields Creek. We didn't get much book learnin' accomplished, but we learned right much about the land around here. We tried to get Morgan to lay out of school with us, but he wouldn't do it. He liked his schoolin' and the school teacher a whole lot more than me and Quincy did. Lord, that was a long time ago."

"Grandpa Grayson still likes to read a lot," I said, "especially newspapers and farm magazines. Grandma Grayson reads the Bible every night before she goes to sleep."

"The Graysons is doin' a good job of raisin' you, son. They give you a home, and that's awful important. I reckon there ain't nothin' more important than havin' a good home. They've had you since you was a little shaver about five years of age. Like me, they ain't gettin' no younger. Help 'em out as best you can."

"I'll try," I said as the pickup rumbled on.

Already I helped Grandpa Grayson by carrying in wood and coal for the stoves. I stacked the heavy wood sticks on my left arm and steadied them with my right. The stacks were often so high I could hardly see as I staggered toward the kitchen door with the armload of wood. Grandma Grayson called my burden a "lazy man's load." She urged me to make more trips with lighter loads. In addition to bringing in the coal and wood, I helped Jingles fetch the cattle at milking time. After supper, I fed Jingles and the cats. However, for many of my farm chores, I had to be reminded, reminded again, and then *told* to get to work.

I can do better, I promised myself. *I'll try to do better.*

"Hal, I thought 'bout raisin' you myself, but when the time come, me and Jetta was still split up just like your mama and daddy was," said Grandpa Charlie. "To my way of thinkin', a man like me, all by hisself can't do no good in bringin' up a young'un, so I didn't cause no fuss when the Graysons took you."

I hoped Grandpa Charlie wouldn't bring up Mom and Dad again. He didn't. He knew I didn't want to talk about their divorce.

The pickup's headlights shone on the last low-water bridge crossing before Grandpa Grayson's riverside farm. In the distance I could see that Grandma Grayson had left the porch light on for me. The light illuminated the small gravel parking area where Grandpa Charlie would drop me off.

"You're almost home, son."

"Almost home," I repeated. I found comfort in the words.

"I recollect from somewheres a sayin' about what home really means, Hal. It goes somethin' like this: Home is a place where if a feller gets to the front porch and knocks on the door, and his folks answers the door and learns he's without money and busted up, sore and bleedin', needin' food and drink, and he's wore out and tired to the bone and near about dead—they can't run him off like they might a tramp or a stranger. They got to take him in, care for him, and help him 'cause he's come home to his kin.

Maybe the feller's been gone a long time, but he's come home, don't you see?"

"I've read something like that, too," I said.

"You realize that I'm just parrot-phrasin' that sayin' but tryin' to keep the meanin' of it. I reckon home means different things to different people. I like that ole sayin': Home is where the heart is."

"What does home mean to you, Grandpa Charlie?" I asked.

The pickup slowed to a crawl. The bright moon was reflected by the truck's dark hood where the motor cover wasn't rusted and discolored. Grandpa Charlie checked his rearview mirror. There were no vehicles behind us, so his slow driving was all right.

"When I was a young man, I ventured down to Raleigh to work in the construction industry," he said, pensively. "I got a job and was earnin' good money, so I thought I might make Raleigh my home. But the land was flat; the summers was too hot; and the air didn't smell fresh to me. I worked like the devil outside in the blisterin' sun, pushin' a wheelbarrel back and forth, and by quittin' time, my chest felt full and tight like my valves was all plugged up. I didn't even smoke no cigarettes back then. It was the city air, I reckon. The fumes from the cars, trucks, and factories left a bad taste in my mouth. On some evenin's, I would set on a park bench and listen to myself wheeze. I knowed I couldn't make my home in Raleigh. I was told that Greensboro and Charlotte was just more of the same, so I didn't try them two cities.

"I figgered that the beach might be a good place to make a home, so I took off down to Myrtle Beach, South Carolina, still workin' in the construction industry. Jobs was easy to find, for they was throwin' up buildin's right and left along the sandy beaches. I got work puttin' up drywall. The sun sparkled the ocean in the daytime, and the moon sparkled the sea water at night. The beach was good for walkin', night or day. The ocean air was fresh, and the food was good. I like to have foundered on fried oysters and boiled shrimps. But the beach sand was ever'where, and I mean ever'where. Sand got in a'body's shoes, in a'body's clothes, and even in a'body's underdrawers. I had gritty sand betwixt my toes, in my beard, in my ears, and up under my armpits—not to mention in my ass crack. When I was outside and the wind blowed, sand flew up into my eyes and nose. At night, it felt like I was sleepin' on sandpaper sheets. I come to the conclusion purty quick that the beach was not gonna be my home.

"I was surprised how much I missed the mountain people of my home county. City people don't smile as much as country folks. You'll never meet friendlier, kinder, gentler folks than those what was raised in these here mountains. Oh, they might gossip a little too much, but to me, as a growin' boy, they was always the salt of the earth as the preacher says. Besides, I reckon gossipin' takes place ever'wheres. I take part in it myself from time to time.

"Anyways, I got powerful lonesome for the mountains and homesick for my kinfolks when I worked down in Raleigh and Myrtle Beach. While I was at the beach, I'd wake up ever' mornin' with a hurtin' in my chest, the same kind of hurt I felt when I was a little boy and my daddy died. He was only in his middle thirties when he had that awful headache right after supper. He took sev'ral aspirin tablets, but they done him no good. Daddy went to bed holdin' his head and cryin'. I had never seen nor heard Daddy cry before.

"Mama couldn't get him to wake up the next mornin'. He was layin' on his left side, and she tried to roust him by shakin' him by his shoulder. It done no good. He was dead under the bed covers. Died in his sleep, I reckon. I touched my daddy's cheek, and it was cold and hard like a rock picked up out of the snow."

I shivered in the little truck's passenger seat. This was the first time I had heard a description of my great-grandfather's death. Pudge's big stuffed bear fell over to my left side, providing some warmth. The bear's button eyes shone soothingly in the moonlight.

"When I was workin' down in Myrtle Beach, I had a dream about Daddy," he continued. "It was like he was standin' at the foot of my bed all dressed in a shinin' white robe. His dark hair was longer than what I remembered, and his beard was shaved off, leavin' his face brown and smooth. He said, 'Go home, son. Go home to the mountains.' I blinked my eyes a couple of times, and he was gone."

"I would've been scared to death. What did you do?" I asked.

"I didn't feel no fear 'cause the spirit was my daddy. I just got up from my bed and commenced packin' my suitcase. I didn't have no real friends in Myrtle Beach, so I didn't have to say goodbye to nobody."

"Did you drive all the way home that night?"

Grandpa Charlie nodded, and a smile creased his leathery face.

"I was still drivin' my little rattletrap Ford when I seen the sun climb up over the blue mountains. The sky was all rosy and pink, and the lonesome feelin' deep down in my chest had done left me. I was wore out, but I just kept on drivin' up the steep mountain highway. I rolled the winder down and breathed in the cool air. Fin'ly I got home and knocked on the door. Mama cried when she seen me. She was awful glad to have me back home again. She needed me to help her around the farm. So, I come back to these mountains to help Mama and to farm the little piece of land that my granddaddy had left to me. I didn't miss Raleigh nor Myrtle Beach one little bit.

"When Mama passed away, I inherited more land. Your great aunt, Willie Lou, inherited the Franklin home place. I cleared my land and built my little three-room cabin—some folks call it a shack, I call it a cabin—and got married to a purty young gal. When the babies come along, includin' your mama, me and Jetta rented a big house down on the New River, just down from the Grassy Creek post office. Those was happy times.

"Me and your granny worked hard to keep food on the table. After the kids was raised, Jetta and I kindly got tired of one another, I reckon. I was forever findin' fault with her and she done the same with me. We separated and she moved to Jefferson town. I stopped payin' the rent on the big house and moved back into my cabin. That's where I've lived ever since. I expect that I'll die up there in that cabin one of these days."

The old Dodge pickup shuddered through three consecutive potholes. The moon drifted behind a cloud, and then popped out again brighter than ever. The countryside in luminous moonlight took on a twilight glow. Grandpa Charlie cleared his throat, making his voice sound younger and stronger.

"But I don't think of that little cabin as my real home; my home is a whole lot bigger than that. No, my true home ain't my cabin; it's too small for my soul. My real home is these Blue Ridge Mountains, deeded to me by the good Lord. The Almighty uses both ends of a rainbow to measure my propity. My livin' room stretches as far as the eye can see. My ceilin', so high that only God can jump up and touch it, is colored blue with a warm shinin' sun, a lonesome ole moon, bright yeller streaks of lightnin', soft purple sunsets, ever-changin' clouds of all shapes and sizes, and thousands and thousands of nighttime stars."

I closed my eyes so I could see the picture the old man was painting. "My floor, covered with a big green rug in the summertime and a big white carpet in the cold of winter, is made of leaf-coated forest soil, hardscrabble dirt were only weeds will grow, and the rich bottomland along the creeks and valleys where a man can grow corn way taller than his head. My big ole house ain't got no winders nor doors so rain, sunshine, wind, and snow can come right inside and be as welcome as a best friend you ain't seen for twenty years or more.

"My house pets is goats, cattle, horses, dogs and stray cats, of course; but also I claim bears, bobcats, beavers, foxes, raccoons, deers, groundhogs, skunks, and possums. I wake up at sunrise to a rooster alarm clock, crowin' way down in the misty holler; and then, while I work raisin' my crops and tendin' my livestock, I can listen to the songs of blue jays, cardinals, doves, and whippoorwills. Ever' now and then, a hummin' bird drops by to say howdy and take a drink from the wildflowers growin' beside my mule-plowed fields." The old man sighed contentedly, and a smile of satisfaction crept across his craggy features. "Yep, these wide-rangin' Appalachian Mountains is my real home, not that little ole cabin of mine, and I don't want to live nowhere else but right here in this high country."

"You love these mountains, don't you, Grandpa?" I asked, opening my eyes. I admired his affection for the rugged terrain. I wondered if I could love anyone or anything so deeply. "What you said was almost like a poem or a love song."

"I reckon I do love these rugged ole mountains and valleys. I've waded, swum, and fished in the New River for so long that its water has kindly seeped into my blood. My heart pumps a little bit of river water ever' time it beats. The mountain air has cleaned out my lungs since I quit smokin' them danged ole cigarettes. I don't cough no more like I used to. Pickin' up big rocks and carryin' them out of fresh-plowed ground has made my muscles stout. For my age, I'm as strong as any man in the county. I meant to try, one more time, that High Striker game at the carnival, but I couldn't find no such game on the grounds. They probly ain't got the game fixed up since Tank busted it last year."

I smiled remembering Tank's exploit. I hoped the High Striker would be repaired by next summer so that Tank and Grandpa Charlie could test their strength. When the carnival returned, I might even try the game of strength myself.

Sitting in the semi-darkness of the passenger seat, I felt my meager biceps. I wondered if I would ever be as strong as Grandpa Charlie. The large teddy bear sitting between us had bigger biceps than I had.

Grandpa Charlie took out his pocket watch and checked the time in the moonlight. He returned the watch to his pocket and pressed the accelerator. The truck rumbled, growled, and lurched forward at a slightly faster speed. Pudge said that my grandpa's truck had two speeds: slow and slower. To my knowledge, Grandpa Charlie had never gotten a speeding ticket.

Beside the road, a large tree branch, wind-torn from a tall maple, rested where it had fallen weeks before. The leaves, still firmly attached to the tree limb, were mostly dry and brittle, but some had assumed the many-hued tints of autumn. Grandpa Charlie looked closely at the parched branch as he steered the small truck around it.

"When the fall season comes around and the leaves change from green to bright yaller, flame red, and burnt orange, I think to myself that no man could paint a purtier picture than what I can see from my cabin's front porch," he said. "I like the changin' of the seasons. Cold as it is, even the winter season pleases me. I like to sit all snug and warm in my cabin next to the flickerin' fireplace while the snow falls and the wind howls and growls outside. A winter's day spent all by your lonesome is a good time to think, sing, and dream. I've spent many a pleasant day with no company except my banjer, my dulcimer, and one ole hound dog snoozin' by the chimbley corner. A cold spell don't bother me none."

"Doctor Jeremiah Plummer spends January and February in Florida," I said, naming the most well-known doctor in the county. Doc Plummer was semi-retired and worked only to help out his son Dean Plummer, another county physician, with his busy practice. There was talk of naming one wing of the county hospital after the old doctor."Doc Plummer said the cold mountain weather makes his arthritis act up, but he told Grandpa Grayson that he couldn't wait for late March to roll around so he could leave Florida and come back home to the mountains."

"Yep, Doc Plummer has got a bunch of money and could live anywheres he wanted to, even overseas if he was a mind to, but these mountains is home to him. Doc growed up over on Silas Creek. Lord, did that man like to hunt and fish when he was young. He was awful book smart, too. When he finished his medical trainin' down at the Chapel Hill medicine school, he come back to the mountains and set up shop in West Jefferson."

"Doc Plummer gave me my first shot of penicillin," I said. "I had a real bad sore throat and couldn't swallow anything, not even water, without sharp pains. I had a fever to go with the sore throat. Grandpa Grayson took a look at the back of my throat using a flashlight. He saw white spots. Grandpa called Doc Plummer and asked if he could drop by the house. That evening he came by and examined me using a cold stethoscope. After the examination, he took out of his briefcase one of the biggest, longest needles I had ever seen. He stuck it in my arm. The needle hurt like the dickens, especially when Doc shot the medicine into my muscle, but I felt much better the next day and went back to school the following day. He's a good doctor. Everybody says so. I'm glad he came back to the county."

"I knowed that he'd come back, felt it in my bones. I helped him set up his office in back of the town drugstore. Two years after he opened his office, Doc married a purty little Wilkes County girl from Trap Hill. Ethelene Fowler Plummer didn't have no college trainin', but folks said she had more common sense in her little finger than Doc had in his whole head. Her daddy was a Wilkes County moonshiner who never got caught, not once. I reckon she inherited her smarts from her daddy. I don't know nothin' 'bout her mama. The first time I met Ethelene, Doc and her was fishin'. It was fall of the year and colored leaves was floatin' down the New River. Both of 'em loved these mountains and that wide river. Whenever I met up with 'em, I could see happiness in their eyes. I never seen a husband and wife more comfortable with one another than what they was. Them two is old now, bent over and crippled up. Ole Doc and Ethelene might spend some of the wintertime in Floridy to ease their arthritis, but they'll come back to these mountains ever' spring just like the robins."

The pickup rounded a sharp curve, and the teddy bear slumped forward into the floorboard near my feet. I placed the stuffed bear back in his seat between me and Grandpa Charlie. His head and shoulders swung to the left, as if the bear were giving his full attention to Grandpa Charlie.

"When you start feelin' a strong likin' for this high country, you don't never want to leave, or if you do leave, you'll always be thinkin' 'bout comin' back," Grandpa Charlie explained. "Ole man Boyd Crabtree come back to the county after workin' forty years up North. I believe he spent most of his time in Chikahger, the windy city. Boyd is pushin' eighty now. He said he come back to the mountains to die. He told me the city ain't no place to die, too much noise, commotion, and way too many folks around. He wants it to be quiet and peaceful when he dies. The codger has a few good years left in him, I reckon. He's purty spry for his age, but when Boyd fin'ly passes, he wants to be buried in the Crabtree Cemetery with the rest of his fam'ly."

"That Crabtree Cemetery is on a hill overlooking the New River," I said. "I went to a decoration there one time with Grandma Grayson. We, along with people from our church, spread flowers over the graves until the whole cemetery looked like a flower garden. Some folks started singing hymns and we didn't leave until sunset. I remember that the sun sank down behind Black Bear Mountain, turning the sky pink and purple. Even the river water had a purplish glow."

"If you ain't careful, Hal, you'll fall in love with these ole mountains like me. Maybe Tank, Pudge, and Gene will, too. Maybe they already have. Wouldn't surprise me none. Many a time, I've seen you boys playin' down on the riverbank and then wadin' out in the water, happy as hound dog pups at feedin' time. I've witnessed you fellers hittin' rocks across the New River with cut-off broomsticks and ole ax handles, makin' believe you was Babe Ruth, Lou Gehrig, or Ted Williams, I reckon."

Actually, we were pretending to be Willie Mays, Duke Snider, and Mickey Mantle, I thought to myself, but I didn't interrupt the old man.

"I've seen you boys start traipsin' up a rough and rocky mountain trail, never knowin' where you all might end up and not carin' much one way or the other.

"One time you young'uns got lost, and I had to come lookin' for you with nothin' but a flashlight and a one-eyed hound dog. I found you boys, cold and hungry, sittin' on the bank of Catamount

Creek. I brought you some food and some drinkin' water. It was way after midnight when I got ever'body home, safe and sound."

"I remember that night. We had been hunting for chinquapins. We got off the Copperhead Trail and couldn't find our way back. Your old hound dog's name was Spirit, and you brought with you, wrapped up in wax paper, six big, thick peanut butter and jelly sandwiches, six Baby Ruth candy bars, and three canteens of spring water. Tank ate three of the candy bars and three of the sandwiches, and they were huge."

"Tank has one awful good appetite," said Grandpa Charlie, grinning broadly. "Over the years, many a time I have had to laugh out loud at you boys and at your mischief. You boys remind me of the friends I had when I was a young schoolboy growin' up in these here mountains. I've come to care for Tank, Pudge, and Gene almost like they was my own kin. My heart's gonna hurt when you all grow up and leave here. A lot of young folks leave and don't never come back."

"The guys and I won't be leaving for a long time; we've just finished eighth grade, and we have four years of high school ahead of us. Four years is a long time."

"When a'body gets to be my age, time passes awful quick," he explained. "Four years ain't nothin'. The Graysons is about my age, so time is passin' fast for them, too. You be good to them ole folks, Hal. They done give you a good home to grow up in. I'll try to give the Graysons a helpin' hand in raisin' you, when I can. But remember us ole people ain't gonna be around forever."

I nodded, not knowing what to say. The pickup puttered around the last curve before the gravel road straightened out. Green Grayson pastures, lit by moonlight breaking through wispy clouds, stretched out on either side of the road. The cloud-filtered moonlight, sifting through the broad branches of tall, thickly leafed trees, created a green fairytale glow on the waters of the New River. Grandpa Grayson's two-story farmhouse materialized like an apparition.

CHAPTER 32

"Well, we're here. Dang if I didn't almost hit that mailbox! I ain't the driver I used to be. Someday you might have to chauffeur me around," said Grandpa Charlie.

"I'll gladly take the job when I'm old enough to get my driver's license," I said. "How about trading this pickup in for a nineteen fifty-six Mercury automobile? Those Mercury's are the best-looking cars on the road."

Grandpa Charlie laughed and turned his pickup into Grandpa Grayson's small gravel driveway. He drove slowly and deliberately to avoid waking anyone. When the pickup stopped, I grabbed Pudge's teddy bear and got out, closing the passenger door gently. Behind me, the farmhouse's porch light bulb flickered, indicating it was about to burn out. Standing in the moonlight with the bear pushed up under my arm, I started to speak to my grandpa through the pickup's rolled down window, but I was surprised when he opened his door, got out, and came walking around his old truck to stand near me. He put his rough, calloused hands on my shoulders. I dropped the bear and it assumed a sitting position in the gravel with its head leaning against my knee.

"Son, I wish I coulda give you and your buddies some more money when we was up on the carnival grounds tonight. I know a teenaged boy don't feel comfortable when his pockets is empty."

"You gave us plenty of money. You were very generous," I said.

"When I was your age, if I had a quarter in my overalls, I felt like I was as rich as them Rockefellers up in New York City. You see, I ain't never had much money, same as my daddy, who was your great granddaddy, and same as my granddaddy Reeves Poe Franklin, who was your great-great-granddaddy. I make some farmin' money, and I get a little Social Security check mailed to me nowadays. That helps out right much. God bless President Franklin Roosevelt and rest his soul and Eleanor's, too. He done right by us ole folks. I never knowed that the president was crippled up with the polio 'til after he died. That man could keep a secret."

Grandpa Charlie admired President Franklin Roosevelt and his wife Eleanor. He had framed pictures of them on the fireplace mantle in his cabin. Also on his mantle over the oft-used stone fireplace, he had a picture of me and my mother taken when I was just a baby. I was holding a baby rattle and offering a toothless grin to the camera. There was a shadow in the photograph cast by the man taking the picture. The shadow belonged to my father, Howard Grayson.

"Thinkin' back on the hard times when I was a young'un, Hal, I can't remember ever havin' a birthday party. At Christmas time, I was lucky to get a ripe orange or a candy cane. Christmas gifts was plain and simple back then. Still, I growed up poor but happy and can count on one hand the number of times I went to bed hungry. One reason I growed up happy was bein' around Grandpa Reeves Franklin so much. I ain't never met a better soul. I wish you coulda knowed him. He was curly headed like you with coal black hair 'fore it turned steely gray and skin that looked tanned even in the wintertime. You and him got the same eyes. That ole man loved to laugh, joke, and play pranks. He was a big strong man but awful mild with children and livestock. Grandpa would start whittlin' on a tree branch or a stick of wood and turn it into a toy. He's the one that learned me how to hunt, fish, and play the banjer. I thought that ole man could walk on water if he put his mind to it.

"Granddaddy Franklin give me a special gift one time. When he give me the present, I was near about fourteen years of age, same as you, and thinkin' I knowed everythin' and Mama and other grownups didn't know nothin'. I come to understand the value of the gift as I got older. I ain't never got no better present since then, and I reckon I never will. Two weeks 'fore he died of the consumption, Granddaddy made me promise that if ever I had a grandson, I'd pass the gift along to him when he got old enough to be clear-headed and thoughtful about his life. That time has come, Hal. I reckon you're old enough."

I had seen a sturdy old Schwinn bicycle with a flat tire in the corner of the ramshackle shed behind Grandpa Charlie's cabin where he kept a few antiques and collectibles. In another corner, resting on a sawhorse was an old dust-covered saddle that resembled the saddle worn by Silver on the Lone Ranger TV show. Also in the shed, leaning against the back wall, was an ancient, seldom-used shotgun. I was hoping he was going to give me the bike or the shotgun or the saddle, maybe all three.

"Up 'til now, Hal, I ain't never give you nothin' but a whimmy diddle, sev'ral Cherokee arrowheads that I dug up accidental while plowin' my garden, and a bow with two arrows made of stout hickory wood. And I come by them presents mighty cheap, made the whimmy diddle and the bow and arrows myself. Didn't cost me nothin' but time."

"I still have all those presents," I said.

Grandpa Charlie looked up at the dark velvet sky with the moon and stars shining and invoked the name of my great-great-grandfather. "Granddaddy Reeves Poe Franklin, I hope you're listenin' up yonder in heaven. I hope you're peekin' out from behind one of them bright stars overhead and watchin' us. I'm keepin' my promise to you. I'm passin' your gift, the gift you give to me so long ago, on to this here boy. He is your blood kin, Granddaddy. Watch over him."

Grandpa Charlie stepped away from the old pickup truck and lifted both arms up toward the starlit sky. He spread his arms broadly as if he were encompassing the whole county. His wide shoulders, lately stooped with age, were thrown back. He turned in a complete circle and then stood still as a statue. With the moonlight illuminating the lines of his deeply tanned face, he looked like an old Indian chieftain of the Cherokee or Shawnee tribe. His profile reminded me of the Indian on the Buffalo Nickel. His voice was deep, resonant, and clear. His words flowed rhythmically, like a chant.

"Grandson, I give you all these rugged hills and all these rough mountains surroundin' us; I give you the rich bottom lands to be plowed, planted, and harvested. I give you the rocky green pastures where deers and cattle graze side-by-side. I give you the straight, tall trees reachin' for the driftin' clouds, the wind-twisted trees with their branches pointin' ever' which-a-way, and the green laurel hells, so thick with growth a'body can't hardly get through 'em.

"I give you this fresh, clean air—breathe in all you want, for there ain't no shortage. I give you cool, clear spring water, bubblin' and tricklin' up through damp rocks and tastin' so sweet that a'body would think sugar had been sprinkled in the water for flavorin'. I give you fast flowin' creeks and slow movin' streams made rich with silver fish. I give you the flashin' of lightnin' and the clappin' of thunder echoin' through the deep valleys. I give you the heavy rains that washes the land clean and fills the rivers and streams with fresh water. I give you rainbows that promises better days to come whilst hangin' their purty colors over faraway blue mountains after a big boomin' storm.

"I give you the flickerin' gold fire of a thousand lightnin' bugs on warm summer nights, and I give the roarin' of March winds in the chill of early spring, howlin' their sad goodbyes to the dyin' wintertime. And if your spirit gets troubled, I give you the chirpin' summer-night songs of the field crickets to calm your soul and to sing you to sleep with their peaceful hymns.

"I give to you green, shady trees of late spring like the weepin' willer, the blossomin' cherry, and the sarvisberry tree with its sweet purple fruit ripenin' with June's warm sunshine. I give to you all the thick, leafy shrubs, brushwood, and bushes, includin' the prickly, berry-bearin' bushes like the thorny wild blackberry with its ripe, thumb-sized berries drippin' from ever' branch, twig, and stem.

"I pass on to you windin' trails to explore, trails that was first made by the long-gone Injuns, elk, and buffalo; and I give to you this wise ole New River, which is whisperin' sayin's to us right now if only we was smart enough to understand the river's words.

"All this bounty is for you, grandson, and throwed in for good measure is warblin' songbirds of all shapes and sizes; wild critters, big as black bears and little as voles; bright green mosses soft as cotton to the touch; creepin' green vines twistin' and climbin' up both livin' and dead trees; and wild flowers, paintin' the land with the changin' colors of spring, summer, and fall.

"Also tossed into the mix is frosty gray mountaintops, lit up by mornin' sunshine; shootin' stars that streak across the sparklin' heavens and disappear behind the dark mountains; deep, driftin' winter snows that melts ever so slow while restin' in the wide, bitter-cold shadders of the big pine, hemlock, and fir trees; and I hand over the ice storms that pass in the cold night but leave behind their shiny, cracklin', rimy ice to decorate and color, with the comin' of the next day's sunlight, the gray, bare trees.

"All this is for you, Hal, and none of your other kinfolks won't never give you more than what I have give you on this night."

After his speech, Grandpa Charlie wrapped me up in a bear hug, lifting me off the ground. He hugged me so hard I could barely breathe. I felt his scratchy beard against my cheek. He smelled like newly plowed earth and dry leaves, mixed with the sweat of a farmer. I regained my footing as he lowered me to the ground and solemnly shook my hand.

"Good night, Hal," said the old man. In the moonlight, he raised his right hand with its palm toward me. "Look after what I give you tonight. Look after it always, my son. Keep the gift safe, and it could be that someday you can pass it on."

Then Grandpa Charlie got back in his dust-powdered Dodge pickup truck and drove away. The pickup's headlights, like spotlights, lit up the dark, dry gravel road. The red taillights blinked goodbye before they disappeared into the floating gravel road dust.

Suddenly, I remembered I hadn't thanked him for the gift. I took a few steps forward thinking I could run down the road and catch the old pickup. I stumbled and almost fell down. Then I realized the chase was futile. The vehicle was out of sight. The pickup's headlights showed up again as the little truck crossed a low-water bridge a quarter-mile or more downriver.

I'll thank Grandpa Charlie tomorrow; I'll walk over to his cabin and thank him, I promised myself.

I sat down cross-legged in the gravel driveway, facing the two-story Grayson house. I picked up a few pieces of gravel and threw the tiny stones in various directions. The teddy bear had fallen over and now rested nose down on the gravel. My old dog Jingles joined me and nuzzled my hand as I sat there in the moonlight. The dog whined, wanting some petting. I scratched him behind both ears. He emitted an almost human sigh, and then turned his attention to the stuffed bear, sniffing and pawing at it.

Inside the house the living room lights came on, and soon Grandma Grayson was standing just outside the screen door in her flannel nightgown. The flickering porch light sharpened her features. She adjusted her wire-rimmed bifocal glasses.

"Hal, that is you, ain't it?"

"Yes, ma'am."

"Did you see your friends at the carnival? I'm talkin' about Tank, Pudge, and that skinny boy with the broke nose and the cowboy hat," she said.

"You mean Gene? Yes, my three friends were there at the carnival."

"Well, I'm sure you all had a real good time ridin' them big ole rides, playin' them carnival games, and eatin' them candy apples. And Charlie Franklin has brung you home safe and sound. The good Lord answered my prayers. I prayed that nothin' bad wouldn't happen to you nor the other young'uns."

"Thanks, Grandma," I said and smiled.

"What's that thing settin' on the ground down there beside you and Jingles?" she asked.

"It's a big brown teddy bear. Pudge won it at the carnival. I'm keeping the bear for him," I explained.

"Jingles will tear the stuffin' out of that toy bear. Don't let that dog get aholt of it."

"I won't," I said, fingering Jingles' collar. The old dog sat stoically beside me.

"I heard Charlie talkin' to you, but I couldn't make out what he was sayin'. I hope he's not fillin' your head with his foolishness. Some folks say the Franklins has Injun blood in their lines from away back a long time ago, and that blood makes them kindly sorry. I reckon that's why he ain't never had no money to speak of and don't seem to care if he never has none. Some say he's just plain shiftless and lazy. He'd ruther hunt and fish than plow and plant. That too comes from his Injun blood, I reckon. Other folks say that Charlie ain't been the same since Jetta up and left him. Some think he has a broke heart that ain't never mended. I will say that the man has always been good to me and Morgan. One winter, before you was born, when we was runnin' low on meat, he provided us with fresh-killed venison and plenty of it. Morgan thinks the world of Charlie. It's almost like they was long-lost brothers. The ole man did talk sensible to you, didn't he, Hal?" she asked.

"Very sensible, very rational, and very wise," I said. I decided to tell her about the gift, hoping she would understand. "He passed on to me a gift, a gift of rich bottomlands, green meadowlands, the tall mountains, the rough hills, and this old river."

"Huh? Uh, well then… That's good, I reckon, but you know he don't own no propity except that little piece of land that his granddaddy left him, and when his mama died, he inherited a few more acres. His landholdin's don't amount to a hill of beans, just enough for him to scrape by," she said, pushing a strand of gray hair out of her face. "I don't see how in the world he could part with any of his acreage."

She didn't understand. I felt something akin to pity. I tried to explain.

"He didn't give me land that you could find on a deed or a map, like the Grayson property; he gave me a bigger place, an open space that you can see with your eyes, remember in your mind, and feel with your heart. You and Grandpa Grayson have given me a home here on the river and for that I'll be forever grateful. Grandpa Charlie has simply given me another home, a far-reaching, peaceful place where I can feel comfortable and safe."

"Well, I'll not have you spendin' all your time up there at his little shack, learnin' Injun ways, fishin' and huntin' the day away, and never learnin' how to work and save your money."

Grandma Grayson, I decided, would never understand Grandpa Charlie Franklin or the gift . They were from different planets or so it seemed on this night. Grandma Grayson believed Grandpa Charlie was trying to steal me away, to snatch me away from the Grayson farm, but in reality, he was encouraging me to stay, to make my home in this rugged, beautiful countryside. She bent forward, her eyes focused on me, her expression seeking reassurance.

"Don't worry, Grandma. I'll be growing up right here on the Grayson farm."

"Them words warms my heart, son. I don't never want you to leave us," she said, leaning back against the screen door. Inside the house, a grandfather clock chimed. "Goodness gracious, it's gettin' late, Hal. I got to get some sleep 'fore daylight comes. When you go up to bed, be real still and don't wake Morgan. He needs his rest. He chopped wood for the cookstove most of the day. He says he ain't, but I know he's wore out. You can bring Jingles in if you want to. Goodnight."

"Don't worry. I'll be real quiet, and I'll carry the chopped wood to the woodshed tomorrow. Grandpa can rest. I'll take care of Jingles. Goodnight."

Closing the screen door softly, she went inside the house. The living room lights were turned off. The porch light flashed and buzzed and then went out completely. The white frame house was enveloped in soft moonlight.

With a listlessly wagging tail, old Jingles left my side and gingerly climbed the porch steps and lay down in the moonbeams on the shabby mat in front of the screen door. In his younger days, I had seen him bound up those steps three at a time. He put his salt-and-pepper muzzle between his front paws and closed his eyes. The old grizzled dog looked like a sleeping puppy.

I stood up, wiped bits of gravel from the seat of my jeans, and lifted my arms skyward as Grandpa Charlie had done. I threw my shoulders back and expanded my chest, stretching my wrinkled, carnival-stained T-shirt. Keeping my arms aloft, I turned around and around, slowly embracing the glowing moon, the shimmering stars, the rugged mountains, the dark green hills, the uneven grassy pastureland pockmarked with rocks and weeds, the fertile bottomland with growing crops, and the rippling, babbling, singing river.

"It's good to be home," I said in a whisper. There was a splash from the river, then the soft settling of its currents.

Likely a muskrat or a beaver, I thought to myself.

I reached down and picked up Pudge's toy bear. Holding the soft plush bear against my chest, I walked toward the old farmhouse, which made up only a tiny fraction of the expansive residence I now considered my home. I lingered on the porch, savoring the rambling, sprawling, spread-out dwelling place Grandpa Charlie had given me. Coming from the stand of thick pine trees comprising most of the forested land behind the house, I heard the hoo hoo hooing of a Great Horned Owl, a welcome visitor and as good a mouser as any cat. Already he was making himself at home in my new guest bedroom.

After I thank Grandpa Charlie, I'll tell him that my guest bedroom is the forty acres of timberland behind the Grayson farm house. That'll tickle him, I thought. *I'll tell him that Three Top Mountain makes the trio of gables on my house's roof. I'll tell him the New River is my bathtub and the Blue Ridge Parkway is my footpath. Then he'll know I understand and appreciate his gift.*

I stood on the porch just outside the screen door, facing the shimmering, moonlit river, and set Pudge's bear in a rocking chair. I pushed the back of the chair and the bear rocked back and forth, soberly regarding the river with his black button eyes. Wind ruffled the still water near the river's bank. From that bank, Pudge, throwing side arm, could skip a flat rock five times before the missile either reached the other bank or submerged in the deep water. Serene now, with water warm enough to swim in, the rolling currents of the river were ever-changing, forever altering its banks.

In times of drought, the river water sank low, uncovering more of the big gray rocks located midstream in front of the Grayson farmhouse. During one extremely dry summer, the water levels dropped precipitously and the shorelines expanded until the broad New River resembled a big creek. I discovered I could wade all the way across the river without getting my knees wet. The low-water had circumvented any thought of swimming, but heavy rains had come in late July, restoring the river to its normal summer depths.

The flowing water froze so firmly in a harsh winter's bitter, below zero cold that even Tank could walk safely across the thick, solid ice. As the dense ice thawed, the volume of the crackling ice floes, while they piled one upon another, was loud enough to wake a weary farmer from a deep, peaceful slumber. The percussions were ominous on a dark, cloudy night; however, the icy drumming was an early harbinger of spring.

Often in springtime the New River flooded, creating new islands while washing old ones away. The newly formed islands, after a few years of advantageous flooding, sometimes grew large enough to support low-growing foliage and even small trees.

Two summers ago, a Great Blue Heron had chosen one of the islands as his favorite hunting spot. The feathered stalker waded in a circuitous route around the island, spearing small fish and amphibians along the way. After dining on the river's bounty and bathing in its tepid waters, the large bird, with its wet wings spread, sunned itself on a branch of the newly formed island's single small but sturdy tree.

While visiting me on one pleasant Sunday afternoon, Gene had waded out into the river's shallows and had taken a shot at the heron with my bow and arrow. Unaware of Gene's intentions, I sat on the riverbank, stuffing extra padding into my baseball glove in preparation for a game of catch. Looking up from my first baseman's mitt, I noticed Gene placing the arrow in the bow. Standing ankle-deep in river water, the skinny guy took careful aim at the sunning bird and released the arrow. The shaft whizzed a few feet above the water before it skimmed the surface and then sank into the river's shoals. Startled, the great river bird rose in the air and gracefully flapped away. Gene and I spent the better part of the afternoon looking for the stray shaft. We spotted the arrow in the clear, knee-deep water near the Great Blue Heron's adopted island. I retrieved the arrow, but put it and the bow away inside the house. I explained to Gene that I had taken a liking to the wading water bird and wanted no harm to come to it.

"Tarnation, Hal! Do you think I'm William Tell, Green Arrow, or Robin Hood? Well, I ain't no archer. Today is the first time I ever shot a bow and arrow," Gene had snapped. "It would take me twenty years of practicin' before I could even come close to stickin' a sharp arrow into that big ole bird!"

Jingles whined and stretched his stiff hind legs. My memory of Gene and the Great Blue Heron evaporated as I regarded the old dog resting on the time-worn, ragged rug. Rising painfully from his tattered doormat, Jingles hobbled toward me, growled at the teddy-bear stranger in the rocking chair, sat down with a whimper, and nuzzled my hand. He was reminding me it was past my bedtime. Also, the arthritic dog was seeking more comfortable quarters.

"All right, old pal, we'll go inside." Jingles thumped his tail on the porch's plank floor. He rose and followed me through the screen door. The dog lay down on a brown padded mat near the fireplace. He raised his head and watched me carefully. I went back outside to collect the bear.

Pudge's teddy bear was still resting in Grandpa Grayson's rocking chair with his button eyes fixed on the New River. He looked comfortable enough, so I decided to leave him outside overnight. Jingles whined, softly calling me back indoors.

Before closing the door, I stood in the doorway and looked down at the river once more, all speckled with moonlight and garnished with a few fallen leaves drifting in its current.

I remembered teaching a younger, more vigorous Jingles to fetch sticks from the river when I was ten years old. The energetic, middle-aged dog, possessor of plenty of canine intelligence and more than his share of doggy stubbornness, had pranced and splashed around so proudly with a gray stick, twice his length, clenched between his grinning white teeth. Jingles brought his wooden treasure, a broken branch of gray driftwood, tantalizingly close to me and then scampered away with it, his tail tucked so that I couldn't grab him. He played his favorite game: keep away. When he finally dropped the stick at my feet, I picked it up and tried to fling it at least halfway across the wide river to give the lively pooch a good swim. Jingles dashed into the water, swam feverishly toward the bobbing stick, mouthed it, and then turned toward the bank, dogpaddling with all his might. On the sandy embankment, he threw the stick down in front of my tennis shoes and barked happily.

"Good dog, Jingles! Good boy!" I praised him until he wriggled with doggy delight.

I recalled catching my first fish from the river's bank and Grandpa Grayson making me throw it back because it was too small. I had cried and angrily stamped my seven-year-old foot. I also remembered being baptized in the river's clear waters after turning away from my life of egregious sin. I was barely twelve years old.

I remembered learning to swim in the waist-deep river after coughing up quarts of water during my previous futile efforts. Pudge and I had mastered swimming on the same day, and we had celebrated with Milky Way candy bars and Coca-Colas purchased with nickels and dimes at the Riverbend Store.

I thought of Tank cannonballing from a high bank into deep river water. I remembered how high the water had splashed and how loud he had laughed afterward.

"Come on in, guys; the water's fine," he shouted, slapping the river's smooth surface with his hands, "except for the water moccasins, the snapping turtles, the alligators, and the Loch Ness monster!"

I wondered how many boys in the past—white boys, brown-skinned boys, and black boys—had grown up near the New River like me, Tank, and Pudge. And how many girls like Ruthie and Sophia had picked blossoms for bouquets as they strolled along its paths and shorelines? I wondered how many young people in the future would fish from its flowered banks, splash in its warm waters, and ride its lazy currents downstream.

A wave of fatigue, dulling my senses and half-closing my eyes, washed slowly through my body. Like a tired hobo, hopping off a train and seeking a night's full serving of solace under a broad-leafed tree, my spirit called out for a peaceful, quiet respite. My trip to the Stephens Brothers Carnival had left me exhausted and bruised. I needed rest. My body needed healing. Surely Sophia,

Ruthie, Tank, Pudge, and Gene were already asleep, dreaming their teenage dreams, worthy or wicked—or somewhere in between. Involuntarily I stretched, gaped, and yawned.

The night grew still, so still that I could hear my heart beat. Then a mild breeze rustled through nearby trees, releasing several leaves that glided down into the broad river. From the restless, ancient waterway, a silvery fish, seeking hovering insects from the world of air, leapt toward the moon, snapped in vain at a fluttering white moth, and then splashed down into the depths of the wide stream.

The soft rippling waters, bubbling over and between immovable river rocks, made the tender sound of laughing children. Over the years, I had learned a few of the river's many voices: under crackling thick ice and after days of biting cold, the river, struggling to push forward and escape the ice prison, groaned and moaned like a feverish old man; with rising floodwaters, flung forward by driving rains and gale-force winds, the river emitted the sustained, deep-throated hiss of a giant snake; and with the coming of early summer, the crystal, looking-glass river, calm and serene, whispered its well-kept secrets as it trickled through the large, mute boulders warming their shoulders in the sun.

"Good night, old friend," I said as I gently closed the door and withdrew into the confines of the old frame house. Jingles cocked his graying head, lifted his over-sized ears, and thumped his tail on the thick mat by the fireplace, but I wasn't talking to him.

THE FISTICUFFS

His bony knuckles landed on the side of my face, just behind my left eye. My brain shifted inside my skull. Most of the flesh on the left side of my face transferred abruptly to the right. Spittle flew from my open mouth. My right arm and shoulder involuntarily thrust forward, ramming my fist toward Wilbur's face. The fact that I had counterpunched amazed me. Then things got hazy. I staggered drunkenly. My eyes were out-of-focus. Wilbur became a blur, and yet I saw colorful planets orbiting and revolving through sparkling, multicolored shooting stars. They were so beautiful. The heavenly bodies began to melt together blending their striking colors. I wanted to reach up and touch the kaleidoscope of spreading shapes and colors. This dazzling light show was followed by a rainbow of exploding Fourth of July rockets decorating the dark sky inside my cranium.

"Sophia, the fight was over you," declared Pudge, frankly and succinctly. Sophia's green eyes widened. Her face blanched. Her pink, glossy lips opened in surprise.

"Over me?" she gasped. Sophia's hand reached for the back of a cafeteria chair, and she clutched it for support. "Did you say Hal and Wilbur fought over me?"

Sophia flashed a glance toward me. I nodded. An expression of dismay that I had never seen before crossed her face. Sophia turned to Pudge who had more to say.

"Hal just didn't want to tell you the reason for the fight, but facts are facts," Pudge continued. "Sophia, you were the motive behind the fight. Wilbur Bledsoe got a crazy notion in his head. Wilbur thought that if he whipped Hal in a fight, you would want to go out with him. It's sort of a caveman attitude that some guys have. Wilbur challenged Hal in front of his friends. Hal tried to get out of the fight, he really did; but under the circumstances, he couldn't back down. I was there. I saw and heard it all."

"I was there, too," said Tank, stepping forward. He took Sophia's slender hand. "What Pudge says is true. From Hal's perspective, the fight was unavoidable. There was no way around it. I can tell you, Sophia, he tried to get out of the fight."

For a few minutes outside in her church's parking lot, standing between the parked cars, Sophia and I—a freshman girl and a junior boy—under the sway of a bright moon, drifted into a play of our very own. As she snuggled against my chest, we proved that indeed all the world really is a stage.

"Sir, I believe you asked for just one goodbye kiss and you have stolen two. I should not say "stolen" for the two kisses were freely given to you. You are no thief; I admit my weakness when I'm in your arms with the moon above. Now I'm tempted to give you a third kiss because I find you a worthy suitor, but there must be no more goodbye kisses, or we shall be here all night. My parents wait for me inside my church's doors. I can stay with you no longer. Surely we can find a better place, a better time," she said with her voice as soft as melting butter. Sophia looked up at me with the sad eyes of a Basset hound puppy as she fiddled with my tie. Then her eyes lit up and she smiled impishly.

Moving her white gloves, which she was holding in her left hand, to her right hand, she lightly slapped my face. Sophia said, "Sir Hal, I hereby challenge you to a duel."

www.ingramcontent.com/pod-product-compliance
Lightning Source LLC
Chambersburg PA
CBHW030644260626
47157CB00007B/2484